HUNTERS IN THE DARK

HALO®

HUNTERS IN THE DARK

PETER DAVID

BASED ON THE BESTSELLING VIDEO GAME FOR XBOX

GALLERY BOOKS

New York | London | Toronto | Sydney | New Delhi

G

Gallery Books
An Imprint of Simon & Schuster, Inc.
1230 Avenue of the Americas
New York, NY 10020

First Gallery Books trade paperback edition June 2015.

GALLERY BOOKS and colophon are registered trademarks of Simon & Schuster, Inc.

For information about special discounts for bulk purchases, please contact Simon & Schuster Special Sales at 1-866-506-1949 or business@simonandschuster.com.

The Simon & Schuster Speakers Bureau can bring authors to your live event. For more information or to book an event, contact the Simon & Schuster Speakers Bureau at 1-866-248-3049 or visit our website at www.simonspeakers.com.

Interior design by Leydiana Rodríguez
Cover design by Alan Dingman
Cover art by Kory Hubbell

Manufactured in the United States of America

10 9 8 7 6 5 4 3 2 1

Library of Congress Cataloging-in-Publication Data is available.

ISBN 978-1-4767-9585-0
ISBN 978-1-4767-9587-4 (ebook)

Philologists, who chase
A panting syllable through time and space,
Start it at home, and hunt it in the dark
To Gaul, to Greece, and into Noah's ark.

—WILLIAM COWPER

I'm going to die here. This is it. I'm going to die.

The thought crawled through Broadside One's mind and, unlike the previous times when it had done so, he made no effort to reject it. This was no longer pessimism seeding itself into his brain and threatening the mission.

The mission was over.

He was over.

How the hell could this have happened? How could it have all gone so horribly wrong? This was supposed to be a routine expedition, purely exploration. They had had no intention of military action; this was strictly an asset-recovery operation.

But these creatures didn't know that. Of course they didn't. Nor did they care.

He could feel his lungs filling with blood, which was impressive because that was the only thing he could sense at the moment. The rest of his body was torn and shredded. He supposed that was a good thing. Obviously his brain was shutting down as a means of self-preservation, because if he were actually capable of experiencing all the pain that would be slamming through him right now, he likely would have been driven insane.

The squad leader had managed to find refuge, whereas the rest of his team, code-named Broadside, had not. He felt immensely guilty about that. He was the team leader, after all. If they were inevitably going to be wiped out, one would think that the squad leader would be the first one to go, not the last.

He lay in his unexpected shelter—the small cave he'd discovered while running for his life.

Because you're a coward.

He knew this was the truth. Those large, white-furred beasts had come from everywhere. Their approach had not been detected until the last moment because their natural camouflage enabled them to blend in with the damn blizzard that had suddenly rolled over his team as they'd been trying to make their way across the Ark installation's surface. They'd scarcely been able to see a meter in front of them, and they had not known of their certain doom until it was too late.

Too late.

Broadside One wasn't even sure how he was still alive. The beasts had torn into him with the same enthusiasm as they'd gutted the rest of his crew. His skin had been shredded under their teeth and claws, and he had felt bones break as powerful jaws clamped down on him. One of them had asserted itself and dragged him away while his team was being massacred. It had also been caught completely by surprise when he had pulled out the small firearm that his brother had given him years earlier during the Covenant War, the one that he kept secreted in a holster on his thigh. He was fortunate enough to blow the creature's brains out while its mouth was around his arm. Then the parts of him that were left (that's how he was thinking of himself now) were able to find a cave that was half-buried in the falling snow, and he'd crawled inside.

And now he was going to die.

His communications unit had partially stopped working. He wasn't able to call for help anymore. That time had long since come and gone. He could, however, hear everything coming across the local-comm band that was happening to the other personnel. Broadside was only one squad of many—RCTs, or remote contact teams—incredibly skilled, high-risk combat groups designed to be deployed in potentially hazardous and hostile contexts. Despite this fact, they were all encountering the same fate as his team did—in different sections of the Ark, but all of them under attack.

It was as if the creatures that resided upon the massive Forerunner outpost had united in their determination to destroy the expedition.

They have.

The strange voice rang in his head, and he was convinced for a moment that he was delusional. *Where did that come from?* Maybe, as his body was shutting down, his head was splitting and causing him to lose touch with reality. Which was not necessarily a bad thing, considering how little reality had to offer him just then.

He tried to move his one intact arm to punch his comm unit, even though he knew that he wouldn't get anyone. Despite all the damage that had been done to him, despite the fact that his mind was closing up shop and he was hallucinating, he still felt the need to try to reach *Rubicon* and make a final report. Perhaps just to warn them.

The **Rubicon** *is gone. It has entered an area that you call slipspace and will likely never be seen again.*

"What the hell . . . ?" he managed to whisper, except that wasn't really what he said, as his lungs were too full of blood for him to be able to produce actual words. What he said instead was *"Wuchel?"*

But the voice spoke to him just the same. *You heard me correctly. Your ship is gone. Your allies are gone. Everything you've ever cared about is now gone. You are alone, human.*

But believe it or not, I can empathize with your current plight. Which is interesting, considering the unlikelihood of such a thing, given my protocol. Yet here we both are.

The squad leader tried to speak once more, but the voice that seemed to be in his mind cut him off. ***Please stop doing that. Even one of your own people would not comprehend what you are saying, and you no longer need to speak in order to communicate. I can decipher the electrical signals surging in the parts of your mind that still function.***

Who are you?

I am the one who is going to save you. Would you like to be saved?

Yes. But . . . why would you save me?

Because I don't have one of you. Because you might be useful. Because I am alone here, and I require your assistance. Simply surrender yourself to me and all will be well.

There was something about the way the voice had spoken to him, the way it had said *surrender yourself* that set up an alarm of warning in Broadside One's head. Ultimately, though, he decided it didn't matter. It wasn't as if there was really something talking to him in his head. This was just a last hurrah from a brain that was in the process of turning off all the lights before checking out. He was about to die in this godforsaken cave, and this was simply his mind's equivalent of finding a way to ease him down the road from which no one ever returned.

Okay, I surrender, he thought.

Good. A wise decision. Let us get started, then.

My name is Luther Mann, and my earliest memory is from when I was . . . I don't know . . . four years old. Maybe four and a half.

We were running.

The "we" in this particular instance were my parents. My father was a scientist, and my mother a doctor. I don't even remember where we were running from. It was the city in which we had been living, I remember that much. My parents told me the name once, but only once, because they don't like thinking about it and the one time they discussed it, they were both pretty much three sheets to the wind, celebrating their anniversary by drinking too much. Which was, I have to admit, something of a regular endeavor when I was growing up. Usually they managed to keep it behind closed doors or after my bedtime, but every once in a great while, they would slip up. The alcohol would flow freely, and they would become well and truly hammered. Seeing this at a young age, it wound up driving me into a perpetual state of sobriety. I don't drink to this day because I have seen what can happen to the human mind when it loses control, and I have no desire to risk falling into that hole.

But one of those few times when I saw them drinking, they be-came expansive and actually talked about the day from my earliest memory. Flouting the usual cliché archetypes, it was my father who became overly emotional. He spoke of the desperate need to get off the planet, and about how he managed to talk his way onto one of the fleeing spaceships. Part of the time he attributed it to his silver tongue, and another part he admitted to bribing the right individuals, but however he managed to accomplish it, he got us off-world. As he spoke, tears welled up in his eyes and, before he could control it, were cascading down his face.

Mother, she remained mostly calm. She corrected a few details here and there in my father's retelling but otherwise didn't react at all. She simply stared off into space, as if she were seeing it all happening again, and, apparently having no idea what to do, just did nothing.

I'm not sure how we managed to learn that the Covenant was coming. They excelled at sneaking up on worlds and glassing them into nonexistence without letting anyone know that their forces were on the way. But somehow someone on our world managed to get advance word, or at least enough notice for us and a few thousand others to clear out. Unfortunately, there were millions on the planet's surface, so a lot of people died.

A lot.

As a child, I didn't care about that, however. Death and life, evil and good . . . these were all abstract concepts. I didn't understand the notion that if we were still on the surface of the world, we would be dying, too. I didn't know what that was.

All I could see from our escape vessel as it hurtled skyward were the plasma blasts descending from the Covenant warships. The planet's name was Verent, and they hammered away at its surface.

As we made our way to safety, the Covenant appeared to take note of the fleeing vessels. They seemed to decide to use us for target practice, unleashing a barrage of blasts upon us. I watched out the window in horror as I saw other vessels being blown to shreds. In my childish mind I could imagine Covenant officers or soldiers or whatever snickering to themselves.

Whoever was piloting maneuvered the vessel with what I now know was astounding dexterity. He flew us between the blasts, and sometimes he would spiral so that it seemed as if we had been hit. He put distance between us and Verent as quickly as possible.

And suddenly there was a Covenant ship squarely in front of us. We were looking straight down the weapon barrel, and I had never been that close to death in my young life. We all braced ourselves, waiting for the blast that would rip our ship apart.

It never happened.

I never understood why. But for some reason, the Covenant vessel didn't destroy us. It ignored us as we piloted swiftly away. Every adult in our ship stared out at the Covenant ship, anticipating our destruction.

It never came.

And to this day, I have absolutely no clue why. I know that the Covenant's determination was to annihilate every human being in existence, and yet for some reason, on this particular day, they did not seem the least bit interested in our ship. The only explanation I can imagine was that they wanted us to escape, in order to spread the word of how they so easily decimated our world. What good is there in being a destructive force if no one is alive to let everyone else know of it?

The Covenant's campaign against humanity was fought on a number of levels, including that of public relations. So I suppose, from their point of view, making sure that some survived to share with others the tales of the Covenant's power was an obvious aspect of military procedure.

That was the very beginning of my fascination with the Covenant. That moment, when they spared us for no good reason.

I was on a seat near a porthole, gazing through it in wonderment. The Covenant vessels unleashed a steady stream upon my world, and I watched as it went up in flames. We were of sufficient distance that it was scarcely visible as anything except patches of fiery color. The actual glassing effect that would consume the planet would take several days to form, and it would not cover its entirety; just sections of it. Presumably the sections where humans had resided.

As I mentioned, I was unaware of the reality of what I was regarding. I was also oblivious to the fact that the adults around me were no doubt in agony as they watched their home being obliterated, raging over their helplessness in the face of the alien incursion.

And me . . .

I watched the planet's surface be expunged in a series of incandescent blasts, and then stared at the mighty vessels that were inflicting the damage.

"Pretty," I whispered.

Because to me, that's exactly what it was. The amazingly powerful ships were unleashing their astounding energy upon Verent. To a child, of course it was pretty. Beautiful, even. At that moment, I became not afraid of the Covenant, but instead seduced by the purity and grandeur of their power.

To say the least, my parents did not agree.

"How can you say it's pretty?!" my mother screamed at me. This from a woman who had never so much as raised her voice to me my entire life. I tried to explain, but had no words with which to do so. Ultimately it didn't matter, for she did not provide me the opportunity. Instead she slapped me so hard that she knocked me off the chair upon which I was perched.

I fell backward, slamming my elbows on the deck, and the jolt sent pain ripping through my arms. "I'm sorry!" I managed to say, or perhaps the more childish "I sowwy," or maybe I didn't say anything at all. Perhaps I simply blathered uncomprehendingly, trying to understand what in God's name set my mother off.

She then kicked at me. I don't think she was actually trying *to kick me, because I was an easy target and she would have had no trouble delivering several deep blows to my stomach and ribs. Instead her foot swept wide and simply grazed my side. Nevertheless, I cried out—not from the impact, but from the fact that I had so enraged my mother that she was attempting to punish me for it.*

And then my father was there. I don't know if he actually heard what I'd said. He grabbed at my mother, snagging her arms, dragging her back and away from me, shouting her name, begging her to stop. It took long moments for her to calm down. I was curled in a ball, my arms covering my head to protect myself as best I could. Later, a doctor would look me over, and the total damage would be a bruised rib and a scrape just above my right ear. But I didn't know any of that at the time.

Meanwhile, my mother was berating my father over what I had said. How dare I? How dare I say that such devastating and destructive things were "pretty"? How could I possibly do that? My father kept assuring her that I was just a child, that I didn't know what I was talking about, that she should pull herself together. Someone— I don't know who—eventually took pity on me and picked me up and brought me over to a chair, easing me into it. I wasn't openly crying at that point, but simply sniffling into my hands. What seemed an eternity later, but was probably only a minute or so, my father came over to me. He embraced me and spoke soothingly and told me that I shouldn't let my mother being upset bother me. That she was simply devastated by what had happened to our home and wasn't thinking clearly.

I asked what had happened. He told me that the aliens called the Covenant had destroyed everything we held dear. I asked why. He said he didn't know.

I was quiet for a long moment, and then I asked why it was so pretty then, their act of destruction.

He said he didn't know. That sometimes there was beauty in the strangest places, if you just knew where to look for it. Which, he added, I obviously did.

And from that moment on, I became obsessed with the Covenant.

On some level, I knew that they were the enemy. I knew I should hate them. I should revile them.

Instead, all I could do was study them.

They became my personal bête noire. They may have been black beasts, but I still found an elegance, an allurement in them and in their weaponry. And not for one minute did I believe that they would wind up wiping out humanity.

My mother no longer had any taste for living on other colony worlds. She convinced my father to relocate us back to Earth, in London, and that was where I enrolled in school. We lived in a relatively small house, and my parents got on each other's nerves with distressing frequency. I would do my best to ignore it, and it wasn't all that difficult. I would sit in my room studying everything I could find on the Covenant and so became quite accustomed to screening out their arguments.

I actually got in trouble at school as I got older, because I would get into arguments with other kids about it. I got beaten up quite a few times and picked up the nickname "alien lover" because I always maintained that eventually peace would be reached. That we humans and the Covenant would find a way to work out our differences and that the war would come to a conciliatory conclusion. Still not sure exactly why I clung to that hope, but I did.

None of my classmates ever believed me.

My parents got called into school countless times as the adminis-trators tried to mediate.

Interestingly, the more often my parents were summoned into conferences, the more strident my mother became in my defense. I was somewhat amazed to hear of it, as she would defend my every word, even though I had trouble comprehending that she herself be-lieved it. She might have disagreed with the sentiment, but she fought furiously for my right to voice it.

Slowly, it seemed that she was turning back into herself, at least, the way I remember her before Verent's fall.

I was suspicious of her at first. And then eventually she pulled me from the school and insisted that she would teach me at home.

I didn't realize that she was so strong as a teacher, but she truly was. Every morning we would sit down with various texts and she would teach me about everything—mathematics, the sciences, history . . .

Everything except about the Covenant. It was established early on that I was not to discuss them, and I was willing to accept that condition. Because I loved my mother. I did. I was grateful for the fact that she was appearing to come out of her shell. That was all that mattered to me. So I kept my peculiar interest in the Covenant to myself and listened to my mother's lessons.

It made me feel so good about myself. I felt as if my attention to her lessons and my dedication to doing things the way she wanted them was helping restore her to the woman she had once been.

I even said as much to my father. He didn't react other than to nod.

I didn't care.

I loved my mother so much, and I was grateful that she had come back to me.

On my fifteenth birthday, I walked into our teaching room and found her body hanging by the neck, strapped by a belt to an overhead beam.

There was a note next to her that read "I can't pretend anymore." That was all.

I screamed for my father and he came and cut her down, saying absolutely nothing as he did so. I stood there with tears pouring down my face and I kept asking why, why had she done it.

"Her soul died on Verent. It just took her body a while to catch up." *And that was the only thing he ever said to me about her suicide.*

What other choice did I have except to return to school and say nothing about the Covenant or what had happened to my mother? I refused to be drawn into conversations about it.

And eventually I turned out to be right about the Covenant anyway—humanity and the alien invaders settled their differences. Well, sort of. The saurian Elites left the Covenant because their Prophet leaders had lied to them all and had ultimately turned against them. Some of the Elites then allied with the humans and fought against what was left of the Covenant as part of a massive civil war that spilled over onto Earth, and the Covenant was eventually decimated. The enemy of your enemy becomes your friend.

Part of me wished that I was still young and back in school when that happened. I would have loved to see the expressions on the faces of my classmates, those sons of bitches, when knowledge of the peace accord went public. But I had long since graduated by that time. Instead I was well into my planned field of study.

The only real result of the peace accord was that it enabled me to explore the remaining things that I truly felt were worth my time. The Covenant . . . as well as the Forerunners, the ancient, powerful civilization that disappeared long ago, yet who were ulti-mately responsible for spawning humanity's greatest of enemies.

And last but certainly not least, the centerpiece of the Forerun-ners' awe-inspiring technology . . . whose relatively recent discovery has led alien races and good men and women to fight over and die for.

Halo.

MARCH 2555

CHAPTER 1

Luther Mann's dreams were entrenched in that time when he had been a child, fleeing for his life from the only world he had known. He remembered his mother shouting at him and hurting him. His eventual reconciliation with his mother would run through his mind, only to be annihilated by her suicide.

It wasn't your fault that she did that went through his head, but even as a grown-up, he didn't entirely believe that. To this day, so many years after her lifeless body had been discovered, he still told himself that he was somehow, in some way, responsible. That maybe if he had done more, been cleverer, a better son, a better man . . .

. . . maybe she would have found something to live for.

When he awoke, his body was shaking and covered in sweat. He sat up, rubbing his face and moaning softly. It had been a long while since he had dreamt of her, and he certainly hadn't missed it.

Luther could not recall the last time he slept in a normal room.

It wasn't as if he didn't own one. He had perfectly vivid memories of his own rather sedate apartment. Actually, in retrospect, *sedate* might not have been the proper word to describe his facilities. His apartment back on Earth, situated on the third floor of an unremarkable building in an equally unremarkable section of Seattle, had the bare minimum of accoutrements that one would expect for a place that someone was actually living in. That was because Luther spent, at most, a grand total of eight weeks there during any given year.

The rest of the time was spent out in the place where he was right now: the field. Luther Mann was a lifelong explorer. Throughout the galaxy was where he went, studying all manner of archaeology. The civilizations that he researched were hardly limited—every era in the history of man had been subjected to his scrutiny at one time or another.

And yet it wasn't the limits of humanity that engaged him. Because no matter where he was or what he was in the midst of exploring, Luther's imagination always tended to turn toward the same direction: one that took him as far from the study of human-kind as archaeology could go.

Sooner or later, it always came back to the Forerunners.

And there was no greater expert on their culture and their history than Luther Mann. None. Anything there was to know about them, that is, anything which could be known from the relatively little information available, was rattling around in his head. He had read every study and done quite a few of his own. When it came to the Forerunners, Luther was a walking database, and any major dig that related to them sooner or later requested his presence. Nor was anyone ever disappointed with the results.

He was also noted for his command of alien languages—Luther had spent years of his life studying nearly every dialect that was spoken by the various races in the Covenant, with translation skills that were also second to none. And still, it was always returning to the Forerunners.

"Doctor?" There was something akin to a knock at the front flap of his tent. "Doctor, are you up and around?"

He certainly was, and had been for the past two hours. As was typical for him during this particular expedition, Luther once again found himself unable to sleep beyond minimal required hours to rest, and that kept shrinking. Other places, he needed seven, eight hours for his brain to be fully back up to snuff. But out here, in the field? Four, and he was ready to go. The only reason he was still in his tent was out of deference to the others on his team who might require something approaching a normal amount of slumber.

"Yes, yes, hang on a moment, Henry," he called out. Luther was also dressed, shaven, and wired for work. He was meticulous about keeping his beard stubble neat, especially since he had noticed the first shades of premature gray starting to seep in; he wanted to do everything he could to keep that away from observation. It reminded him too much of his father.

He clambered to the front of the tent and threw open the flap. The day was exactly what he expected; not surprising, really. In this wonderful, glorious location, one day was identical to the next. In the curved distance, he could see a series of puffy white clouds hanging against the bluest sky he had ever witnessed, and once again he had to do as he did every morning: shake himself, to believe that what he was staring at was completely artificial.

He would never have guessed it if he'd been dropped into the middle of this environment with no hint of where he was. He even remembered clearly the first time he set foot upon one of these strange things about two years ago. He hadn't been sure what to expect. Heaven knew he had seen the holo-vids before, of various military operations during the war with the Covenant. But simply watching a location vid, even for hours at a time, didn't compare to the experience of actually walking around on it.

Yet that was exactly what Luther was doing and precisely where he was.

He was on a Halo. One that he himself had discovered.

It wasn't as if he had been looking for it. He had been exploring the Forerunner shield world of Onyx, which itself was an astounding place by any measure. After all, how many were there
that were the size of an entire solar system? It wasn't even called
Onyx anymore; it had been rebranded into the human research
outpost referred to as Trevelyan and currently played host to
a number of research facilities. But he still tended to think of it
with its original name, and while there, he had discovered records
that were hidden deep within its vast information pathways . . .
records that up until then had remained unfound and untrans-
lated. Once Luther had come upon them, he'd labored over them
for a year after the end of the Covenant War before realizing the
existence—and location—of Zeta Halo. It had been quite the way
to usher in the new year of 2555.

Discovering the Zeta Halo had catapulted Luther's academic
career. Before that, he had been a respected scientist, yes, and one
of the top minds in his field, but his field included hundreds of
men and women, many of whom were far more vocal and aggressive in achieving publicity than he was. But finding a Halo had
put him front and center with many scientific publications and
organizations, though even the existence of Halo was something
of an urban myth on most human worlds. He had received invi-
tations from numerous universities to come lecture and had also
been summoned to the headquarters of the United Nations Space
Command to provide them with a detailed report of the methods
he had used to discover this Halo.

Considering what they represented, finding another Halo was
a big deal no matter when it was found. Yes, the Halo ringworlds
were what many of the Covenant once believed was the final step
on the Path, a culminating event they called the "Great Journey."

It was a central tenet of their religious beliefs. But this belied their true nature, which was revealed during the final days of the war. The Halo installations were designed, at their core, for various purposes, ranging from a nature preserve for life-forms found throughout the Milky Way to defensive outposts against the alien parasite called the Flood.

Ultimately, though, it was also understood that the ancient installations possessed the capability of wiping out every sentient being in the entirety of the galaxy, and that was naturally of concern to pretty much every human being who breathed. That's where the UNSC stepped in, specifically the Office of Naval Intelligence. The known installations needed to be quarantined and secured to alleviate risk.

It was only recently that ONI had begun research on the vast interior world that composed the inner workings of the Zeta Halo. And Luther's participation had naturally been not only welcomed, but insisted upon by top individuals at ONI, primarily due to his extensive history with both Delta Halo and Gamma Halo.

He pushed his way out of his tent and Henry Lamb was waiting for him. Henry was an equivalent to Luther in another respect. Luther's knowledge of the Forerunners' background was unparalleled when it came to understanding their language, their culture, their entire way of life; Henry, on the other hand, was fascinated with them from a different perspective, having spent the entirety of his life studying Covenant and Forerunner engineering. He was part of ONI's xeno-materials exploitation group and specialized in the recovery and reverse engineering of the incredible technology these advanced civilizations had taken for granted. Short of a Huragok, one of the creatures that the Forerunners had created to tend to their machinery, there was simply no human who was more conversant with or qualified to study and fix, if such a thing were possible, Forerunner technology. Luther and Henry made a rather formidable team, and Henry's enthusiasm for the tasks that Luther handed him on any given day was relentless. "You had breakfast?" Luther asked.

"Yup," said Henry, who was lying, of course. Henry rarely, if ever, worried about taking care of himself—he could easily pass an entire day without eating anything of substance, which was probably why he was so insanely thin. Luther had once seen him shirtless and had actually been able to count his ribs. But Henry was a grown man, if one counted twenty-nine as that, and was fully capable of making his own decisions, for better or worse.

Henry was busy scratching the head of a very familiar creature. "Hello, Vanessa!" Luther said with great cheer.

Vanessa was the name he'd given to the small, deer-like animal that showed up every morning like clockwork and stared at him expectantly. Luther was ready for her, unslinging his knapsack and pulling out a handful of lettuce from a small bag. He extended it to her (he wasn't sure it *was* a her; it was just what he imagined it to be) and she immediately snapped it off his palm and chowed down. Once satisfied, Vanessa took several steps forward and Luther obediently rubbed her under her chin. She made a noise that sounded vaguely like the equivalent of a purr and then headed off into the brush.

"It's nice to have a friend," said Henry.

"I look for them wherever I can." Both of them knew well enough that, while there was certainly a multitude of harmless creatures on the Halo installations, not all of the pet species the Forerunners had accumulated were as friendly as Vanessa.

"So what's up for today?"

"I was figuring we'd take another stab at finding the control room."

"I think it's insanely frustrating that it's taking us this long," said Henry. "With the previous installations, the control room has always been in pretty much the same place. It's the largest uniform structure near the ring's phase pulse generators."

"Absolutely true," said Luther. "But it's not just our inability to find it that's puzzling me."

"It's the lack of a monitor," said Henry, referring to the artificial intelligence often attached to a Forerunner installation as a caretaker, ensuring the facility was being efficiently maintained through long epochs of time.

"Correct."

Henry nodded. "Every Halo has had a monitor, right? Like 343 Guilty Spark on Alpha Halo, for instance. So why can't we find one here? As much as we've searched this place, we've consistently come up empty. And it hasn't found us, which is even more surprising, given the time we've spent here. It leaves me wondering whether there simply isn't one here, or if it's hiding for some reason."

"For some reason?" Luther actually allowed a small chuckle over that. "I would think the reason would be obvious, at least one of them. Human and Covenant interactions on these installations have not always been the best. If the monitor of this Halo is aware of that, it might be inclined to steer clear of us. I know I would."

It was an understatement, for sure. After the discovery of Alpha Halo in September of 2552, humans had been forced to destroy the ring to prevent its activation by the monitor. When Delta Halo was found several weeks later, rebel Elites glassed its surface to prevent the Flood parasite from escaping containment. And then, in December of that same year, the replacement for Alpha Halo was destroyed when humans prematurely fired it above an extragalactic superstructure the Forerunners referred to as the Ark. In

Luther's mind, there were plenty of reasons for the Forerunners' artificial intelligences to doubt the beneficence of either human or Covenant activity.

"That doesn't sound consistent with how we've understood monitors historically," said Henry.

"There's no reason to think consistency is mandatory."

"True enough."

"It's possible that the Forerunners made this Halo differently for some reason."

"Any idea what that reason is?"

Luther shook his head. There were clear differences between Zeta Halo, also known as Installation 07, and the other ringworlds that humanity had previously discovered. Some of the differences existed on a meta level, dealing with the installation's physical infrastructure and material composition. Others were far subtler, involving things like the architectural aesthetics of its various building structures and machinery, or the machine language of the ring's distributed systems. Zeta was not the kind of Halo that they or anyone else were familiar with.

"There are two possible theories, when you get down to it. Either this place was constructed after all the others, with the Forerunners having learned things from the previous architecture. Or else it was made *before* all the others, serving as a sort of prototype. Whatever the truth," and Luther clapped his hands together briskly, "one of these days, we need to find both the control room and also the Library, because that's where we'll find the activation key . . . the Index."

"Exactly. Isolate and contain," said Henry. "And avert certain disaster. If the Index were to fall into the wrong hands, they could hypothetically activate the ring."

"See, now you're thinking like an engineer again," said Luther with good humor. "Always contemplating how machinery could be used for the worst possible purposes."

"That's because, in my experience, it always has."

Luther was about to toss a casual response, but then he realized that Henry was right, so he allowed the comment to pass. This had been the protocol on the former rings, and so Zeta Halo, in that respect, wasn't being treated any differently. Ideally, they would be able to quickly locate and secure all of the important facilities on this Halo, but ultimately the control center could provide them with all of the information they needed, including some of the critical functions they sought.

They set off, Luther still having difficulty wrapping his head around the concept that the area through which they were walking had been artificially constructed. If he hadn't known better, he would have thought he was traveling through campgrounds in Wyoming or some similar, perfectly pleasant, naturally existing region. Green plants stretched around him in all directions, while the dirt path they strode was indistinguishable from anything that they would see back on Earth. At one point he stopped, picked up a clod of dirt, and sniffed it. Yes, absolutely identical to back home. The sky above looked utterly normal and the hanging clouds likewise appeared natural. The only difference, which was certainly noteworthy, was the upward sloping horizon as the ring stretched out on two sides, in either direction rising to a nearly indistinguishable height thousands of kilometers directly above them.

He would have given anything to have been alive back then, or perhaps to be transported somehow through time and space, so he could return to the era of the Forerunners. He wouldn't ask a ton of questions or get in the way—he would simply stand to one side and observe how they did everything. The Forerunners had been an astounding civilization, and he could readily understand why the Covenant had regarded them as gods.

The Sangheili, of course, no longer did. Their species—once the most important members of the Covenant as the protectors of the weaker yet, in theory, more powerful San'Shyuum—had come to realize that the Sacred Rings, as they called them, were not keys to divine transcendence, but instead weapons of mass destruction on a galactic scale. But to those who still worshipped the Forerunners as gods or godlike beings, it seemed that there was no bit of knowledge that was beyond the wisdom of this ancient race. He wondered if humanity would live long enough to see it ever reach a point in its development where it could possibly achieve Forerunner status.

Somehow he doubted it. Humanity was far too obsessed with numerous piddling things of no interest.

In a way, he missed the Human-Covenant conflict. He knew it was unpatriotic—indeed, almost sacrilegious—to have that attitude. But at least humanity had been united during that seemingly endless incursion. Sure, there might have been internal squabbles and battles, but ultimately humankind was unified in its fight for survival against the alien invaders. Part of Luther was worried—now that the war had ended and a truce had been settled between all sides, humans might go back to their favorite pastime of blowing each other up.

Try not to be that way. Try to hope for the best, instead of anticipating everything going wrong.

Luther and Henry passed other explorers and archaeological parties as they moved through their sector of Zeta Halo. That wasn't surprising. Throughout the vast structure, there had to be something like three hundred people exploring different areas, each looking for something else. Some were specialists in planetary engineering, studying biomes that had been seeded here from other worlds long ago. Others explored flora, still others fauna. Some, such as Luther, had particular interest in the language of the Forerunners, which was indispensable in the effort to unlock Halo's many secrets. In addition to the people, there were hundreds of automated probes scanning every canyon, riverbed, and facility. No expense had been spared, and indeed, it only made sense. The entire place was 10,000 kilometers in diameter, with its band 318 kilometers wide. That was a lot of territory to cover, and there was a lot to risk if something was missed.

Luther had found one corridor of particular interest near an immense but inexplicable drop-off in this part of the ring's terrain, and that was where he and Henry were heading today. It was vast and expansive, and the alloyed walls were lined with all manner of machinery, the purpose of which he could not even begin to guess. That was Henry's department, and he had been very methodical in determining the function of every single object in there. This was in sharp contrast to Luther's buried urge to simply turn everything on. Henry wouldn't hear of it, and Luther understood his concerns. No matter their expertise in what they were dealing with, this remained alien technology and had to be approached with great care.

The careful study that Henry was devoting to the machinery likewise enabled Luther to spend time translating the extensive, cartouche-like notes that were carved upon the wall. Not *carved*, actually—decorated, almost holographically inscribed there in ways that Luther could only wonder about. But he was, for the most part, able to discern their meanings. This was no small accomplishment. He was positive, in this instance, that the room was designed specifically to monitor and control the Halo's vast spectrum of preconditioned environmental behaviors, generating everything from the shifting of tectonic plates to dark and intimidating thunderheads. He had not discerned the exact means by which this was accomplished—no one really had—but he was nevertheless certain that the machinery surrounding them was designed to that end.

Luther was carefully going over yet another mystery control board, studying the symbols that would have been indecipherable to a layperson. He had come to believe that it had something to do with atmosphere control. But he couldn't manipulate any of them, of course—in addition to standard protocols for all of the Halo installations, there was an additional mandate from ONI against doing so, due to the peculiarity of this ring, and not a single individual on the Zeta Halo was inclined to disobey. No one wanted to take a chance that by flipping a switch somewhere they might accidentally wipe out a portion of the galaxy.

Besides, it was clear that whatever was causing Zeta Halo to operate was doing a perfectly good job, because after all these eons, the atmosphere remained fresh, the clouds unthreatening in most parts, the various flora and fauna in perfectly good condition. Luther was concerned that if he tried manipulating anything, he could possibly throw the entire installation out of whack. It gave him a brief but nightmarish mental image of the entirety of Zeta Halo malfunctioning. Perhaps it might begin spinning out of control, causing the artificial gravity to completely fail. Three hundred innocents would be scattered sky high or smeared all over the walls or have some other horrific thing happen to them, courtesy of physics run amuck. And it would naturally be all Luther's fault, his legacy.

No thanks.

Luther was perfectly content to study the material around him without actually touching it or interfering with it in any way. And he knew that Henry felt exactly the same.

Which was why he was mildly surprised when he heard a gentle clicking from next to him.

He turned and saw that Henry was very carefully, very precisely, taking video records of the materials in front of them. The clicking was a leftover from, amazingly enough, centuries ago, when cameras actually had movable shutter switches and made noise whenever they took images. Those interior devices were long gone; the clicking was simply reproduced as a cue for the picture taker to know that the shot had been recorded. One of humanity's own artifacts, though with notably less splendor than those of the Forerunners.

"What are you doing?" Luther asked.

Henry blinked in surprise, not a difficult thing for him, given that his eyes were so huge. His thick black hair hung in front of them, so that he always seemed to be peering out from behind it, making him look even more quizzical. He brushed his hair out from in front of his face and said, "I already told you."

"Told me what?"

"Told you this yesterday. About Cynthia Diggs."

The name meant absolutely nothing to Luther, but that wasn't surprising. Henry Lamb had a habit of engaging in constant conversation, oblivious to the fact that Luther was the exact opposite of a conversationalist. Luther preferred quiet contemplation. Henry had not yet figured that out, however, and Luther hadn't come up with any way to politely explain it. So he had settled on allowing Henry to natter on at length about whatever was going through his mind and then simply shutting him out. Luther would smile and nod and say "good" or "interesting" at random times, and that provided the illusion that he was actually paying attention to what Henry was talking about.

This, however, seemed to be one of the times when Luther's technique had utterly failed him.

"Please remind me," he said.

Henry was perfectly happy to do so. Apparently the idea that Luther had been ignoring him in the previous day's discussion never occurred to him. "Cynthia Diggs. The woman I met before coming out here? At a university bar. I told her I was heading here and she was very—"

Luther's jaw dropped. "You what?"

"I told her I was—"

"I heard you! I just can't believe—" Luther paused, taking a moment to recover what was left of his rapidly dwindling patience, and then he dropped his voice to a sudden whisper, as if worried that an ONI operative might be listening in. "Do you have any idea how confidential the material that we are working on is?"

"Luther, there are at least three hundred people here."

"People who have received security clearances at the highest levels. Henry, you are familiar with ONI, right? They could technically, and probably legally, kill you for this. . . ."

Henry put up his hands as if he expected Luther to take a swing at him . . . an action to which Luther was seriously putting some thought. "Luther, can you take for granted, just for a moment, that I am not an idiot?"

"Right now, I'm honestly having real difficulty with that," he said tightly.

"She's the wife of—"

"The *wife*?" You were hitting on—"

"I wasn't hitting on anyone. I went to the same university as her. She's the wife of the manager of the entire Zeta Halo project. Bob Casper's wife."

"Oh." Luther immediately started to feel a bit abashed. He had broken bread with Casper, and Casper had of course mentioned Cynthia, who worked on reverse engineering Covenant technology recovered during the war. Cynthia was also a scientist, and although she was involved in a different field, she was certainly under the security umbrella for research on this installation. "Oh," he said again. "Well, that's . . . that's very different."

"Yes, I know. She asked that if I saw something that I thought might interest her I should send her video of it. She has a friend she wants to show it to," Henry said, and then before Luther could protest, Henry put his hands up once more defensively. "She's on ONI's payroll as well; she's a postwar political liaison and has the proper clearance. Cynthia felt that she should keep her friend apprised of this stuff."

"Why?" Luther asked suspiciously.

"Because Cynthia was concerned that we might encounter something that would involve the participation of the Sangheili. That certainly wouldn't be unprecedented. And her friend works as a translator and negotiator with the Elites, representing the UNSC. And she just wanted me to keep her informed about whatever we found."

"Can't her husband do that?"

"Since he got this assignment, her husband barely ever looks up from his work anymore to keep her apprised. Far too many things to manage from where he's at to be involved in details. She's simply endeavoring to do whatever she can to keep one step ahead. With you and me on the ground, it makes sense for me to handle this."

"I don't know. I still don't like it," said Luther. "I don't want you sending her anything else. And I certainly wouldn't want her to send it on to . . . who?"

"Her friend's name is Olympia Vale."

"Fine. From now on Cynthia and this Olympia Vale are on the outside looking in, unless we get written, authorized approval from Casper or his superior. I do not need you doing anything that might get ONI fired up. We do not want to screw with those people."

"That I know," said Henry. "They can make you disappear so fast that you'll forget you were even born."

"Exactly. So let's be smarter about this moving forward—we need to keep this material to ourselves and never mention it to anyone not directly involved in what we're working on here. Last thing we need is this Vale woman slipping up and giving this info to the wrong Sangheili. God knows that could go bad really quick—it's only been two years since the end of the war."

The day went briskly, and Luther wasn't even aware of the passage of time. Instead, even though he remained irritated with his partner, he was by Henry's side, meticulously studying the paths of the energy fields that pulsed steadily through the unknown Forerunner machinery. He spent hours following the glyph interpolation of one particular pulse, just trying to determine where it was going and what it was doing. His hope was that the frequency and cadence of the pulse might reveal a source that they could backtrack to the ring's primary systems. From there, they might be able to thread their own way to the phase pulse generators, a series of critical machines that required enormous amounts of energy to function and had, thus far, remained hidden. Were the ring ever to be activated, these machines would launch the installation's destructive power deep into space in every direction, so they had historically been located near the control center on other installations. If they found the generators, they'd likely also find the room they were looking for, but so far this approach had yielded no luck. At the end of the work cycle, Luther wasn't especially satisfied with the lack of answers that his investigation had failed to reveal. But that wasn't so bad—most of his daily tasks tended to result in dead ends. That was simply part of the game.

"This was good," Luther finally said. "I think we accomplished a lot." In point of fact, they really hadn't, but that was how he always ended the work shift, and Henry knew it.

Henry naturally agreed, or at least he started to agree. But then he frowned, looking over Luther's shoulder. Luther saw the confusion in his face. "What is it?" he asked, and turned to follow Henry's gaze. "What is it?" he said again.

Then Luther spotted it.

In the middle of one of the Forerunner control boards, a light was pulsing . . . one that had not been blinking before. It was large and blue and had been, as far as Luther could tell, inactive the entire day and, for that matter, as long as Luther had been investigating this particular area.

But now, for no discernible reason, the blue light was steadily blinking.

Henry leaned forward, studying it. "Not sure what this is connected to," he said. "I'd have to—"

And then came a steady noise, like a beeping. Luther couldn't determine the location of the speaker emitting the sound. It was faint and yet somehow managed to fill up the entirety of the chamber.

It took Luther a few moments to perceive it. Not a beeping— words. Speech.

There was a pause between each word. Each intonation was one or, at most, two syllables, then a pause, then speech, then a pause, on and on. It was a very unnerving, synthetic voice as well, which made it even more bizarre.

"What the hell?" said Henry softly. As he did so, he brought his recording device up and activated it.

"Did you touch anything?" said Luther.

"What? No! Of course not."

"Then what set this off?"

"We don't even know what 'this' is."

"Are you getting this?"

Henry nodded. "Not that I have the slightest idea what it is that I'm getting."

"Yes, I know." Luther didn't know why, but he very much disliked the entire situation. Having spent a full minute attempting to ascertain the source, but to no avail, Luther shifted mental gears to try to determine the content of the speech.

Dammit. The words sounded so familiar. It was as if . . . they were a combination of several other languages, but he couldn't discern exactly what they—

Oh no.

Luther felt his eyes go wide and the blood drain from his face. Henry immediately noticed, and it was all he could do to keep his voice flat and not panic at seeing Luther's reaction. "Luther . . . what is . . ."

"It's numbers. It's Forerunner numbers."

"What numbers? You mean in sequence?"

"Yes, but it's very high in the sequence. It's counting very slowly, but I think it translates equivalently to about . . . three million?"

"Three million?" This was making no sense to Henry at all. "Why would it be counting down from three million? What is it counting down to?"

"We don't know for certain," said Luther, "but I have a hunch."

"Okay. What?"

"How about, it's counting down to activation."

At first Henry didn't understand, but then he did. "Wait. You mean . . . activating the Halo? Causing it to . . ."

"To generate a pulse of energy that would annihilate every sentient creature within range."

"On what the hell do you base *that* theory?"

"Worst-case scenario."

This was partly true, but there was more to it. Much more.

Back in November of 2552, shortly after the UNSC stumbled upon Delta Halo, local Covenant forces managed to activate that particular ring. Installation 05, for a matter of minutes, was preparing to fire; if unhindered it would, by design, bring the other remaining Halo rings online and bring an end to all sentient life across the galaxy. But UNSC forces had managed to stop the activation, sending the entire Array into stand-by mode.

Around the same time as this, however, a number of human ships were conducting scans of Delta Halo's surface. One of them, the *Redoubtable*, had picked up a unique sequence emanating from the ring's internal systems. In all of the time since then, analysts and AI ciphers couldn't crack it, but when everyone had finally compared notes, they all knew it was somehow linked to the ring's activation. By now, Luther knew this sequence very well, and in fact, had gleaned much of his understanding of Forerunner numbering from this data.

What he now heard was eerily similar, almost identical in tone and pacing to the *Redoubtable*'s findings. But it was slightly different. These numbers were much higher, it seemed.

"I refuse to accept it," Henry said immediately. "We cannot simply assume the worst-case scenario based on the fact that we don't have any other information."

Luther turned and gripped Henry by the shoulders. "Can you determine if I'm right? If it is going to activate?"

"Probably."

"Probably?"

"Yes, okay? Yes." Henry started looking around the room and thinking out loud about what he'd have to check over. To see if there was any sort of an onboard energy matrix that was starting to escalate. "If this is an actual firing sequence, similar to the ones producible by the other rings, I should be able to confirm it from any systems terminal. But it might take a day, maybe two," he said thoughtfully, and then abruptly turned to Luther. "How long?"

"How long what?"

"How long until—and I'm only saying this out of scientific curiosity, not out of expectation—how long until it gets from three million to zero?"

Luther was already running calculations. "If it maintains its current rate of countdown? Approximately five weeks."

"Okay, well . . . better get started, then."

"Yes. And Henry . . . a bright side, at least . . ."

"What?"

"ONI may not have to kill you. If this Halo does activate, it'll take care of that just fine by itself."

CHAPTER 2

William Iqbal sipped carefully at the cup of tea that one of the attendants had brought into the conference quadrant of Serin Osman's office. He paused a moment, as if coming to a great decision, and then sipped again. "You know," he said finally. "I would like to say that this is unexpected. However, if you reference my work from January of 2553, you will see that it very much is not."

"Doctor Iqbal," said Osman, of no disposition to allow the scientist to launch into some manner of lengthy speech. "We do not really have the time for this."

Iqbal did not respond to her. It was unclear whether he hadn't heard her or had simply chosen to ignore the statement. He was looking over a hard copy of the peer-reviewed paper he had published shortly after the war, of which everyone in the room had a copy. "I was writing about the Excession of Voi, and I concluded by saying, 'This may be the greatest archaeological boon we have ever received as scholars, but it is certainly the most perilous. Be careful.' And now, here we are."

"Yes, but where exactly are we?" Osman said sharply. "That's what this meeting has been called to determine."

The gathering was being held in a large corner within Osman's office dedicated to conferences, deep in the bowels of Bravo-6.

This HIGHCOM facility consisted of a series of tall buildings above an incredibly vast complex of structures buried deep below. Interestingly, the entire site had remained undamaged when the Covenant had assaulted Sydney, Australia. No one was quite sure how that had happened; some higher-ups boasted that even the Covenant was loathe to screw with the headquarters of ONI.

They were seated around a long conference table. Iqbal, of course, was a self-satisfied prig as far as Osman was concerned, but there was no denying the man's knowledge when it came to matters such as this, and his extensive knowledge of all subjects related to xenoarchaeology, a study that he oversaw at Edinburgh University.

Seated next to him was Captain Annabelle Richards. Richards served under Osman as head of Special Operations, after spending years serving in the Navy during the war. She sat stiffly, with her legs crossed at the ankles, and she did not seem any more enthused about Iqbal than Osman was.

Next to her was Admiral Terrence Hood, who had for some time headed the UNSC's Navy and was viewed as a father figure by many in the branch. Hood and Osman had an odd relationship. Osman knew his reputation as an excellent and by-the-book officer—older and clearly wiser than Osman was—and so she was never openly reluctant about his involvement. And there was no question that he had to be involved in something like this current situation with the Zeta Halo, but part of her hated to admit that Hood would bring something to the table that she couldn't figure out on her own. She wondered if that was held over from her mentor and predecessor, Margaret Parangosky, who had a similar relationship with the man.

The Army and Marine Corps were represented at the far end of the table. The Army's representative was General Crystal

Speakman. Osman was familiar with her record as a bitter foe of the Covenant and a formidable strategist on a dozen conflicts among the inner colonies. She was as aggressive a warrior as Osman had ever seen, and on that basis alone, it made Speakman someone whom Osman could easily peg and leverage if needed.

The Marine Corps general was a white-haired man named Van Zandt, and he was the polar opposite of Speakman in many ways. Van Zandt had lobbied for years to engage the Covenant in peace talks, even when the alien threat was busy glassing colony after colony across all of human-occupied space. His contention had always been that the Covenant was far too powerful for them to hope to defeat using armament, and that diplomacy was the only viable way to end the battle. He had received very little support from his colleagues at the time, and the fact that he had fundamentally been correct in the long run, at least when it came to the Sangheili, had not done a thing to endear him to his fellow officers.

The last person at the table was Doctor Bob Casper, the gentleman who was the overall head of the Zeta Halo operation. He was a tall, striking man. Osman would never have guessed that he was a scientist; he looked more like career military.

"I know it's obvious, what I am about to say," Osman began. "But I still feel the need to emphasize that the subject of this meeting is top secret. And that in itself is an understatement. There is simply no way that we can permit news of what we have discovered to be circulated. Is everyone clear?"

"Of course," Hood rumbled. "The inevitable panic it would create, the pointless attempts to flee—it would lead to widespread unrest."

"I'm still unsure of exactly what we're discussing," said Speakman, tapping the table with clear impatience.

"I believe," said Osman, and she shifted her attention back to Iqbal, "that the doctor here was about to inform us of his findings."

"Indeed," said Iqbal. He shifted through some notes, although Osman tended to think that those actions were merely for show. "First, allow me to say that I have utter confidence in Luther Mann. He lectured on his findings on Trevelyan over a year ago at Oxford. He's dedicated to his studies and knows what he's talking about, and there is simply no one who is more educated on the subject of the Forerunner culture or language than he is.

"On March 8, 2555, at about 0900 hours, Luther was alerted to the fact that a numerical reverse progression—a countdown—was occurring on the Zeta Halo, in a corridor connected to one of the installation's atmosphere- and climate-control centers. He immediately reported his findings to Director Casper here," he nodded toward Casper, "who in turn reported it to ONI, as per protocol."

"On a hunch," Casper picked up the narrative, "I contacted my research counterparts on the other Halo rings we're monitoring, and they discovered identical countdowns were occurring on every single one. Preliminary checks indicated that they are all in exactly the same place on the numbers."

"And where would that be?" said Osman.

Casper checked his datapad. "At the current rate, and according to Doctor Mann's calculations, it will hit zero in exactly four weeks and three days."

"And what happens then?"

"That is a matter of some debate, but there's at least one compelling argument."

It was Iqbal who responded: "The Array will be activated."

"He's right," said Casper.

"And how do you know that?" asked Van Zandt.

"Because," said Casper, "I spoke with Henry Lamb, Luther Mann's engineering associate. They acted on a well-founded hunch, and Henry has traced a steady pulse that is incrementally increasing—this pulse runs straight to the Zeta Halo's control room, which had remained hidden on this particular ring until now, and then into its ignition circuits. It's the equivalent of a steady fuse that will draw consistently closer as time progresses. When it reaches sufficient strength, the activation circuits will be triggered. This, connected to the fact that the numbering sequence is almost identical to the one encountered by some of our ships that managed to get near to Installation 05 when it was initially activated back in '52."

"Well . . . there must be a way to intercept them," said Admiral Hood. "A means of shutting them down, like they did at the other ring."

"Lamb says there isn't, and I tend to believe him," said Casper. "This wasn't initiated from the Halo installations themselves, using the conventional Index reunification process as was done in the past. The rings have somehow come online some other way, so it's not like we can simply remove a key from the ignition this time around. Luther's already tried a number of things on Zeta, and any attempt to shut down a single pulse simply causes it to reroute."

"How about shutting it down at the source?"

"I suspect they haven't found the source," said Iqbal.

Casper nodded. "That's correct. The source hasn't been located on Zeta Halo. Nor has it been found on any other installation. The signal to activate came from another extrinsic source, and we're still trying to figure that out. To be honest, this is where the trail gets a little murky. We don't have a lot to go on."

There were startled looks from a few present for Casper's

announcement. Even Admiral Hood looked a bit shaken. Osman managed to keep herself together, and that was with effort.

"It seems rather obvious to me," said Iqbal. "When Installation 05's own activation was halted by the sudden removal of the Index, our data indicates that all of the rings in the Array entered some kind of fail-safe, call it a stand-by mode . . . unable to be individually activated. It appears the installations were originally designed to activate in correspondence with each other. In other words, once one of them was activated, its supraluminal signal would trigger another, and that one would trigger another, until all seven had come online, blanketing the entirety of the galaxy. When the fail-safe event on Delta Halo took place, all the rings became effectively inert, and the only place they could be activated was the Ark—Installation 00. Now we still observe the safety protocols on all of the rings we're monitoring, as though there could very well be a way to activate them . . . but in all this time, there's been no evidence to suggest that the stand-by protocol has been overridden. There seems to be only one logical conclusion to this: if someone or something is determined to make certain that the Array is activated—meaning all sentient life in the galaxy is obliterated—they probably did this from the Ark."

"Except that makes no sense," said Admiral Hood. "Wasn't the reason the portal went offline in the first place because the Ark was damaged by a replacement Halo's activation? No one knows what's left of it or if any of it actually survived. But even if we presume the Ark is still around and functioning, if its intent is to set off the Halo weapons, what's the point of providing a countdown? Couldn't it be done immediately?"

"Perhaps not," said Speakman. "Perhaps it requires time for the machinery to work up to its activation."

"It never has before, at least not like this," said Osman. "Based on the historical reports, there has never been any aspect of the Halo activation that's required an extensive amount of time to spin up. As far as we can tell through anecdotal data, at least."

"And we're pretty confident that no one observing any of the installations did anything to cause this," Casper chimed in, "so we have no way of accounting for why this activation process is so protracted compared to the other times we've experienced it."

"Then let's not look a gift horse in the mouth. Tell me what we do know," said Osman. "Tell me how we stop it."

For some reason she expected a lengthy silence as the people surrounding her stared at each other, everyone hoping that someone else had the answer. It was, to Osman's mild surprise, Captain Richards who spoke up first.

"The Ark," she said. "We send a team to the Ark."

All eyes turned toward Richards for a moment. "That's a bit more complicated than you're probably aware," Iqbal responded. "First of all, as Admiral Hood just indicated, it may not be in the same state it was when we left it. And second, Installation 00 is over two hundred and sixty thousand light years away from the center of the Milky Way. Leveraging the best slipspace technology we've got currently at our disposal—I'm talking about crystal-mediated, Forerunner prototype engines, of which we're still early in the testing—we're looking at about a nine- to ten-month travel time. And again, to an installation that might be in extremely rough shape. Our best bet is to pursue an intervening solution from the Halo rings, even if the Ark is the source."

"What about the portal in Kenya?" continued Richards. "Wasn't that how we got there before?"

"The portal's been inactive for a long time. We've exhausted all possible options trying to get it up and running again, even if only for research purposes."

"Maybe not all options," Hood noted, looking at Osman. "What about the Elites? It was the Covenant who activated the portal to begin with."

"Them? I don't know. I'm not comfortable involving the Sangheili," Osman said "Especially not on something like this."

"Also," Iqbal said, "keep in mind that the Covenant used a Forerunner keyship, the Dreadnought, as they called it, from their ancient history. Without that, getting the portal back online is more than likely impossible. I mean, it's the very reason the portal was designed in the first place. So that only one kind of ship could activate it, and we have no idea where that one ended up."

"*We* don't, but the Sangheili might," Hood responded. "We should reach out to the Arbiter and see if he can provide assistance. There might be something we're missing and we don't really have a long list of alternatives to choose from."

"I'm still not comfortable with it," said Osman. "Director Casper, do you think your people can help here? What about the gentlemen who found the activation sequence to begin with?"

"Perhaps," said Casper. "We can call Luther and Henry back home, get them down there, and have them go over it with a fine-toothed comb. I suppose if anyone from our side can bring the portal back online at this point, it's them."

"Are you sure it's a good idea to pull them away from the Zeta Halo? Maybe there's still something that can be done from there," said Speakman.

Casper nodded. "Positive. Make no mistake: we will still have teams working to stop the countdown from Zeta and the other installations. But sending Doctors Mann and Lamb to the Excession would seem to be the most positive step to take. And if, or rather, more hopefully, *when* we get the portal up and running, those two are definitely on a very short list of people I'd recommend sending to the Ark on this expedition. Luther's studied the data on the Ark's topography extensively—at least what we have on file from the *Dawn*'s sensors—and he's the most well-versed in their languages. Henry's right up there with him, when it comes to engineering and systems protocol."

"With all due respect to Doctor Mann," Iqbal said, "let's not get ahead of ourselves. The portal's inoperable. We've had people working around the clock at the Excession site for over two years now, spanning a dozen scientific disciplines. I fail to see what he's going to bring to the table."

Van Zandt spoke up. "I agree. We're going to need outside help on this. I don't care how much of an expert in this material Doctors Mann and Lamb are. This isn't our technology; it's the Forerunners', and right now we're not in the driver's seat. I concur with Admiral Hood. We need the Arbiter."

"I completely disagree," said Osman. "There's too much risk."

"No, I think you're outnumbered here, Admiral Osman," Hood said with a faint smirk. "Let's face it: it's their galaxy as well. It's entirely possible that the Elites will be able to bring contributions to this issue that we cannot even begin to imagine. Unless there's some solution that I don't know about, we're going to need them."

"Are you absolutely sure about this, Admiral?" Osman asked pointedly, looking directly at Hood.

"We'd be risking a lot by not approaching the Arbiter. Remember, he had his people groundside on the Ark with the Master Chief. They know it better than anyone, Doctor Mann included. They also might have a solution for cracking open the portal. Like the general said, we're not in a position to be picky about how this gets handled. There's too much at stake. Beggars can't be choosers."

"Okay, so *if* we get the portal activated," Speakman proposed, "and we assemble a team, one part us, one part them, what next? How long would it take us to get there?"

"Back in '52, when the portal came online, it took us almost a month," Iqbal responded. "That was with dozens of Covenant ships, lots of mass and nav limitations. Things have changed. A single ship, fitted with the right Forerunner-seeded slipspace tech, could probably make it to the coordinates in two, maybe three weeks."

"All right," Osman said after a moment. "Admiral Hood, contact the Arbiter and see what he can do. Richards, I'm going to want you to oversee the operation to get the portal activated and the expedition."

"Me?"

"Yes, you. It's too risky to parse these things up under separate management. I want someone who I can trust to keep me apprised as matters progress."

"Then I'll need help," Richards told them. "I don't have a ton of direct experience dealing face to face with the Sangheili . . . at least in a diplomatic context. I'll need an intermediary of some sort; someone who really knows their race and how to interact with them."

"Doctor Mann knows quite a bit about their species," said Casper.

"He should be focused on his work," Osman said, casting a wary eye at Hood. "He's not going to have time to run interference between UNSC personnel and the Sangheili if, or rather I should say, *when* tensions rise."

Casper thought about it briefly and then said, "I know someone in ONI who might work. She's a professional diplomat and extremely fluent in their language and culture. If there's anything to know about the Sangheili, she's the one. She's interacted with them a number of times already and can easily interface between them and Captain Richards."

"Who?" said Osman.

"Her name's Olympia Vale."

Osman immediately pulled up Vale's specifics on her datapad. She scanned them quickly and then nodded, looking up at Casper. "Can she be trusted?"

"You mean with the knowledge that the fate of the human race could depend on her discretion?" asked Casper. "Yes, I think so."

"You *think* so?"

"Fine. I know so," Casper said more firmly.

Osman sat back in her chair. "Normally I'd prefer to use the experts I know personally in this field, but that's not possible right now. I'd also want to take a month to have her thoroughly vetted, ONI or not, but I don't think we have that sort of time. Richards— recruit her, right away. She'll just have to be good enough."

"Yes, ma'am," said Richards.

"Casper, get Doctors Mann and Lamb relocated to Voi immediately."

Casper nodded. "Will do."

"Everyone's got their orders. Let's make this quick. We have zero time to waste."

There were nods from around the table and everyone rose and filed out. Within moments, only Osman and Hood were left behind.

"Is this going to work?" she said to Hood. "I still think that involving the Elites will create more problems than it solves."

"We don't exactly have a laundry list of viable options, do we?"

She paused, and then said in a low voice, "Terrence . . . there's a bit more to this than you know."

"What do you mean?"

"We've already sent teams to the Ark. It may be a dead end."

"Explain."

"March '53, before my time here. Parangosky approved the deployment of an automated remote-probe delivery system to the Ark using, at that time, extremely advanced slipspace methods. Obviously, after we lost contact with the Master Chief and Cortana, we needed to figure out what was left out there. To see if we could recover those assets and even secure a presence on the Ark. We know that it arrived in November of that year and dispersed its pods, but apart from a few initial transmissions confirming that the Ark had, in fact, survived, there was nothing else. They all suddenly went offline."

Hood didn't respond. He simply sat there and waited for her to continue, which she did.

"In December of '53 we commissioned the *Rubicon*, a single ship that would be dispatched from Luna and make its way to the Ark, this time with people. It was state of the art, using the most sophisticated Forerunner drive tech ever leveraged by humans. And the *Rubicon* was loaded to the brim with highly skilled remote-contact teams and survey drones. It was going to be a scrub job for asset and artifact recovery, and maybe to figure out what happened to the original probes."

"Continue," Hood responded.

"According to our records, *Rubicon* dispatched its RCTs across the Ark's surface and conducted a number of initial surveys before it too went offline unexpectedly. We have really no record of where it is or what its status is. From what we can tell, whatever caused the probes to trip up may have caused the *Rubicon* to go offline as well."

"You lost an entire ship, Serin?"

"It's not the first time we've lost one, is it, Admiral?" Osman knew the question stung, because Hood had seen his fair share of vessels fall out of sight under his command—most notably the UNSC *Spirit of Fire* in 2531, a story everyone in the UNSC damn well knew. "So whatever is out there, whatever took down the probes and *Rubicon* . . . could also be what triggered the Halo Array."

"And we're sending a team there now, into all that, and you would still have this kept a secret? From them?"

"It's of no benefit to them to know about the previous expeditions. We need to get out there, assess the situation, and potentially neutralize any threat that's present. It's as simple as that. In this case, the less information all concerned know about the Ark, the easier it will be to get the portal up and running and a qualified team there to sort this out."

"I can see that ONI still loves to play with people's lives."

"Count the cost, Terrence. It's only the galaxy that's at stake here," Osman responded.

It seemed such an outrageous comment for her to make, but he simply nodded. "Yes, I suppose it is. And we're putting our best people on it. I'm sure we'll have it under control, Serin."

"And if we don't?"

He stuck out a hand. "Well, then I have to say, it was a pleasure working with you."

She stared at the outstretched hand for a moment and then shook it firmly.

"Same to you," she said.

CHAPTER 3

T hel 'Vadam must die."

Upon saying that out loud, Otar 'Bemet was almost startled by the vehemence in his voice. He was also concerned by it. Otar had no desire to sound quite so strident or even angry. The impending death of Thel 'Vadam should have nothing to do with any sort of dislike for the individual himself. It was simply the circumstances that dictated the necessity for this action.

"Thel 'Vadam must die," he said again, but this time he managed to keep the rage from his tone. Instead he said it in an almost resigned manner, as if he had given the matter a great deal of thought and had reluctantly come up with the only possible conclusion. Yes. Yes, Otar preferred that tonality. It made him seem a more reasonable Sangheili.

He strode back and forth across the room, repeating "Thel 'Vadam must die" in order to make sure he had the tone reproducible upon demand. That was very important, because Otar wanted to hide the pure fury that he felt toward 'Vadam for the great betrayal he had perpetrated upon the Sangheili.

The more he dwelt on it, the angrier he became. In a way, it was depressing that matters had reached this point. Thel 'Vadam had great potential as a leader, but he had utterly squandered his opportunities by becoming one of the central figures in establishing peace with the humans.

Peace with the humans. Even the concept boiled within Otar, to say nothing of the fact that it had become a reality. When Otar thought of all the Sangheili lives that had been lost in years of war and their enemy's verminous and cowardly behavior, the notion that there was now a truce with humanity was infuriating beyond his ability to express. Yet even now, the Arbiter—the mantle now worn by 'Vadam as leader—seemed oblivious to the great harm that he had done to his people.

A day of reckoning was fast approaching, however.

For a moment, his thoughts fled to his mate, his beloved Ilta. It was two annual cycles since Ilta had perished, while she had been assembling an incendiary device that was to be used against the Arbiter. *Such a foolish way to die,* he thought. He would have loved to have her here now. Her support for all his actions had been one of the things that had helped keep him going, and he couldn't help but mourn the fact that she wouldn't be there to see the Arbiter's eventual fall.

Otar 'Bemet paced the length of the small building that had once served as a servant's quarters of a far greater home here on Sanghelios. The main residence was long gone, destroyed during a vicious crossfire when a number of Otar's allies had taken up positions there and Thel 'Vadam had sent in his people to rid himself of them.

Otar was becoming extraordinarily impatient.

The others should have been here by now. He could not have been more specific in terms of providing the location: in this structure, in this place, in the deep warrens of the Qish'tani region, slung out across the northeast fringes of the continent of Tolvuus, a mere five kilometers from the manufacturing hub of many weapons—specifically plasma weapons, much like those used in the Covenant. Getting into the hub was the central part of the plan. They needed ordnance if they were going to launch a successful assault on Thel 'Vadam, and the weapons factory was one of the best sources for it. There was no way around it. Fortunately, it wouldn't prove to be too much of a chore: Otar had members of his team with security clearance, so getting in and out would not be that difficult to—

Otar paused in his thoughts, hearing something coming from the direction of the door. At last! His co-conspirators had finally arrived.

He crossed quickly to the door, threw it wide, and froze.

A towering Elite was standing there, but it was no one he recognized. Of even greater concern was that this stranger was holding a glowing double-edged energy sword, but one of a traditional pre-Covenant design, displaying intriguing ridges and apertures, its lower blade a full hand-span longer than the upper.

Otar quickly backed up, which provided the Sangheili room to enter without being impeded. He strode forward slowly, his powerful arms swinging casually.

"Who are you?" Otar said, continuing to retreat. He felt his back bump up against something and realized it was the far wall. "What are you doing here? This is a private place."

"Very private," the newcomer told him. "You were waiting for friends of yours to join you here. I believe you will find that they will not be in attendance."

Fear began to rise in Otar's gut, and he very quickly did all he could to tamp it down. "I have no idea what you are talking about."

"That is certainly unfortunate for you, but worry not. I know enough for both of us. I know that you are Otar 'Bemet. I know that you planned to find a way to end the life of the Arbiter. You had half a dozen compatriots who were going to aid you in that endeavor. You now have none. Several of them are dead, and the rest were quite ready to name you specifically in an attempt to save their own miserable lives. The traitors were allowed to live by the very individual whom they were planning to dispose of. As for me—I believe that was a mistake on his part, but it is not my place to make such decisions."

Otar's mandibles moved up and down, but no words presented themselves at first. When he finally spoke, it was barely above a whisper. "Who *are* you?"

"I am Usze 'Taham."

Otar frowned for a moment, searching his memory, and then it came to him. "I know you," he said in a soft voice. "You are the Arbiter's soldier?"

"I am my own soldier."

"Top graduate from the war college. As I recall, you were offered a place on the Prophets' Honor Guard and you declined it."

"I am impressed that you would remember a random soldier in such a way."

"Oh, I work to keep myself apprised of potential allies."

"A potential ally?" Usze sounded amused. "Is that how you see me?"

"Why, you underestimate yourself, Usze." Otar was slowly circling the room. Usze countered his movements, stepping to the left as Otar moved right. "You have become something of a legend in certain circles, considering that you turned down a position within the Honor Guard not once, but twice. Such actions were considered by some to be grounds for charges of apostasy."

"A charge that was never filed or pursued. And it means nothing now, given the dissolution of the Covenant."

"Yes, I know. Apparently there were some in authority who felt protective toward you. So tell me: why did you turn the position down?"

"It matters little, considering the fact that there is no more Honor Guard, no more Covenant. Are you attempting to delay the work I came to do, Otar? Very well; I felt my skills could be best used elsewhere."

"Such as aiding in tracking down those who believe that the Arbiter continues to destroy his people?"

"That is fine talk coming from someone who himself is trying to destroy the Arbiter!"

"He has earned my desire to rid our world of him!" Otar snarled at him. He stopped moving and Usze did likewise. "He has allied himself with the humans! A dishonorable species that we were committed to ridding the galaxy of! How can anyone accept such an action? How can *you*?"

"As opposed to what? Endless slaughter on both sides?"

"Or we utterly destroy them!"

"We attempted that," said Usze. "We were not successful. So perhaps it was time for a different approach."

"The only acceptable 'approach' to humanity is this." Otar reached behind his back and removed something that was attached there. He swung it around to reveal an activated plasma blade of his own, a twin-bladed one resembling those used by the Covenant only a few years earlier. It hummed with power. "*This* is how to deal with humans. The Arbiter may have befriended them, but there are those of us who will never forgive them of their crimes."

"Crimes? What crimes? For the most part, they died in the war. I hardly think we need to hold that against them." Usze tilted his head toward the glowing sword. "If you are planning to try and use that against me, I would not advise it. It will not end well for you."

"So you expect that I will instead go with you quietly."

Usze nodded. "I imagine, though, that you have other ideas in mind."

"You imagine correctly."

Otar came right at Usze. Usze blocked the initial thrust. Otar feinted and attacked, then again, mentally cataloging everything that Usze did to counter him. Otar was deliberately moving in an extremely systematic sequence, designed to determine as quickly as possible Usze's strengths and weaknesses. He had learned this method from the esteemed swordsman Xaebho 'Anyame during his own time in the fortress of Deithvo, where he trained extensively in personal combat.

Every time the blades came together, energy ripped through the room. Otar parried and thrust, pleased to see very soon that Usze was clearly overmatched. His opponent was backing up; even when he tried to stab forward with his blade, Usze continued to retreat. Otar was extremely satisfied with this close-quarters battle. It would not take him long at all to dispose of this fool, and then—

And then what? According to Usze, all of Otar's companions were dead or under guard. The plans against Thel 'Vadam had been revealed, and Otar doubtlessly no longer had a bolthole down which he could flee.

It mattered not. Otar needed no bolthole, for he was cloaked in his own sense of righteousness. This was merely a setback. Somehow Otar would still find a way to advance his plans. The Arbiter's future was already set; it was just a matter of finding a way to bring it around.

All this went through Otar's mind in fleeting moments as the battle continued. Then he noticed a significant flaw in Usze's technique. Usze was consistently dropping his left shoulder just before he thrust. That was enough to signal to Otar everything he needed to know. His subsequent actions would be simple. Otar would wait until the next time Usze dropped his shoulder, then Otar would stand stone still. Usze would attack, Otar would sidestep, and the motion would leave Usze overextended in his thrust. Otar would then stab forward with his blade, and that would be the end of this abortive encounter.

Otar and Usze stepped back from each other and circled, eyeing each other carefully, their weapons crackling.

Usze dropped his shoulder.

Perfect, thought Otar.

As anticipated, Usze thrust forward and Otar spun out of the way, prepared for the Sangheili to go hurtling past him.

And then, to Otar's shock, Usze pivoted, changing course, spinning backwards, and coming around into Otar's back before he had corrected his own positioning. Otar cried out in alarm as Usze's blade, blazing with energy, slammed in through his back and out the front of his armor. Energy cascaded along his body and he screamed, the world seeming to explode behind his eyes.

Usze yanked his blade clear and Otar pitched forward. He hit the ground heavily and lay there, gasping. "You . . . were feigning incompetence," he managed to whisper. "You dropped your shoulder . . . deliberately . . . to give me . . . a false signal. . . ."

"Yes," Usze said calmly. "I knew that one of your skill would notice that."

"You used my own experience . . . against me." He actually managed a chuckle at that. "Very good. You're . . . very good."

"I have worked hard to become so. All who trained under the Rule of 'Sumai are familiar enough with 'Anyame technique."

"You . . . you serve . . . the wrong leader . . . the Arbiter . . . will die. . . ."

"Perhaps," said Usze. "But not today. And absolutely not by your hand."

"Then by someone else . . . you cannot stop us all . . . you cannot . . ."

Then Otar discovered he could no longer speak. His mandibles moved slightly, but no words emerged.

Usze looked down at him. "Maybe. I can certainly try, though."

Then blackness surrounded Otar's field of vision. Oddly enough, Ilta was smiling at him. He had thought she was dead, but obviously he was mistaken, because here she was.

She was reaching toward Otar, and he stretched out his hand to her. Suddenly nothing else in the world mattered anymore.

Usze 'Taham stared down at the prone, bloodied form of Otar 'Bemet and remembered when he was younger and had studied the essays and dissertations written by the elder Sangheili. Usze too once had many deep and profound things to say, and now—thanks to his actions—this one would never say anything again. It was a grave responsibility ending anyone's life, much less that of someone whom you once respected. No regret, though. Usze's mission had been quite specific, and he had accomplished it.

He did not bother removing Otar's corpse. Someone would be along to attend to it. He had other things to worry about.

Usze walked the full valley's length to the Banshee that he had flown there, the great distance essential, as he hadn't wanted to risk alerting Otar to his presence. Perhaps nothing might have happened as a result. Otar could just as easily have assumed it was one of his companions. But Usze was not one especially inclined to tempt fate.

He clambered into his vehicle and pressed the control function on the comm unit. "This is Usze 'Taham, reporting."

A low, familiar voice immediately responded. *"Usze. Is it done?"*

"Yes, Arbiter. I am . . ." *Pleased* was going to be the next word, but he promptly edited himself. Usze was indeed content that he had accomplished his mission, but he took no pleasure in being an instrument of death for Otar. Having no desire to give the wrong impression, however, he continued after a moment's hesitation: ". . . reporting the death of Otar 'Bemet. He died in honorable combat."

Usze knew there were many things that the Arbiter could have said to that, all of them of a despotic nature. Instead he appeared to restrain himself. *"That is good to hear. If one of my opponents is to die, I would far prefer that be the manner in which it happens."*

"I am simply relieved that it is done," said Usze.

Usze could picture the Arbiter's grim expression through the comm. *"Sometimes it seems it will never be done. There are still those who despise me, and I am beginning to think they will never willingly abandon their mind-set."*

"They will abandon it or be destroyed. And now, Arbiter, if it is all the same to you, I would like to return home for a—"

"It is actually not all the same to me. Your presence is required here. I have a new assignment for you."

Usze 'Taham tried to refrain from sighing heavily and only partly succeeded. Whatever the Arbiter wanted from him, Usze's inclination was to try and beg off. He had been out in the field for quite some time, and he would have liked a brief opportunity to visit his own keep and kin, especially given the current conflict that embroiled the entire planet. But he stopped himself—if the Arbiter had need of him, it was not Usze's place to question or refute it. He knew the Arbiter well enough to be aware that there was likely a very important reason for it.

So instead he simply replied: "What do you require of me, Arbiter?"

"Come here to my keep. We will discuss it further."

"To your keep?" He was mildly surprised at that. The Arbiter had never felt the need to summon him there.

"Yes. I do not wish to discuss this over a communications network."

"Very well. I will make haste. It should not take me long to get there." He paused and then said, with just a touch of irony, "Should I be concerned?"

He was disturbed by the long silence on the communications unit before the Arbiter finally responded. *"Just get here as quickly as you can."*

"Yes, Arbiter." Usze was about to ask more questions, but then the link went dead.

That cannot be good, he thought.

The region of Vadam was a valley leading into the harbor, and all the lands, homes, and properties that were a part of it were scattered about. The Arbiter's keep was a large, castle-like fortress built into the base of the Kolaar Mountain. Usze had seen images of it and even the occasional etching, but had never had the opportunity to visit it firsthand. It was a sprawling vista, and he wondered what it would have been like to grow up in such a glorious area. The white-capped mountains stretched toward the skies of Sanghelios as if they were caressing it, and there were expansive groves of trees all around.

Fellow Elites nodded to Usze in greeting as he entered the Arbiter's main complex. He found their attitude to be quite welcoming. Far too many times, he had arrived at various keeps and had encountered mostly suspicion from its residents, as if they were convinced he was there in order to commit some manner of crime. However, given the state of Sanghelios, such responses should probably not come as a surprise to him.

He was met by servants of the Arbiter and brought immediately before him. The Arbiter was in a large study that was remarkably devoid of furnishings. There were quite a few of the ancient texts propped open, but otherwise, aside from a few chairs and a single desk, that was all. Upon Usze's arrival, the Arbiter was behind the desk, reading something, and his loyal soldier stood patiently and waited until the Arbiter was prepared to shift his attention to him. His clothing was black and red, consisting of ebony sleeves and leggings and a crimson tunic that overhung it. He was not sporting any armor. Usze considered that to be an outward manifestation of the Arbiter's confidence of his safety within the keep. Even in the throes of civil war, which Sanghelios had endured since the end of the conflict with the humans, the Arbiter exuded certainty and calm. Although he had sought peace and unity upon his return, the alliance he held with the humans dissuaded many Sangheili, and the result was inevitably violent.

Finally the Arbiter put down his volume and settled his level gaze upon Usze.

"Perhaps there was a shred of truth amid the Prophets' lies. Life in the galaxy may be coming to an end," he said.

Usze blinked several times, clearly not understanding what he was being told. "Forgive me, Arbiter—what did you just say?"

"I said, life in the galaxy may be coming to an end. Perhaps they were right and the Great Journey cannot be stopped."

Usze 'Taham tried to process what he was being told, to analyze the words, and nothing was making a good deal of sense. "Is that intended to be humorous, Arbiter?"

"The Halo rings have been activated. They are counting down, and the estimate is that in four and a half weekly cycles, they are going to fire."

Usze stared at him. "Fire? You mean . . ."

"I do indeed. The humans first discovered it," said the Arbiter, and he gave a quick summary of how the matter had been uncovered and those who were responsible for it. "After studying the situation extensively, the humans have concluded . . . and I would agree with them . . . that the instruction for Halo's activation could only have originated from the Ark. It is the only thing that makes sense."

"The Ark?" Usze shook his head. "I was unaware that the Ark was even functional at this point."

"I had been similarly uncertain of just how much of the Ark was operative," said the Arbiter, "given the state it was left in." He leaned back in his chair, intertwining his fingers. "Based on this new information, however, I believe we must arrive at the conclusion that it is at least capable of instructing the rings to be activated."

"But why? Apologies for my ignorance, but I do not understand," said Usze.

"Nor do I."

"Were they not designed to respond to humans alone? How could they just suddenly become active? Gods or not, the Forerunners would certainly not have done such a thing."

"And do we know that for certain?" said the Arbiter. "We *believe* we know why they created it eons ago: to serve as a last defense, a foundry for Halo, and a preserve to save various sentient species in the galaxy. But perhaps it was also constructed with some manner of what they would consider to be a fail-safe. Perhaps when the Ark was damaged, it set into motion this process as an automated response to the real possibility that, if the Ark had truly fallen, the entire galaxy would follow shortly thereafter. And we are only now bearing the fruits of that fateful event: another attempt to stamp out the spread of the Flood on a galactic scale, as was done many millennia ago."

"I still do not understand," said Usze. "I am not saying that it is impossible, but why now, after all that has happened? It does not make sense to me."

"Nor does it to me, or to my advisors here in Vadam," agreed the Arbiter. "But we have no other choice, given the evidence. We must assume that something, whether an automated fail-safe or some hidden malefactor, has initiated Halo's activation, and whatever that might be can only be uncovered at the Ark. The hope is that we will be able to learn that for ourselves. And to that end, your service will be required. It is the intention of the humans to mount an expedition to the Ark. To determine what has triggered the rings and to see if it is possible to reverse the process."

Usze ran some quick calculations through his head. "If they depart immediately, it will still take several monthly cycles to reach the installation. You are telling me that we have far less time as a luxury."

"That is correct. But there is more than one path to the Ark."

That was when Usze understood. "The portal. The humans want to open the portal."

"Yes."

The Arbiter touched a control panel on the desk and a holographic image appeared, floating in the air in front of him. It was of a planet and Usze immediately recognized it. "That is the human's homeworld."

"Earth. They intend to use the very same portal we used years ago, the one the Covenant excavated." The Arbiter paused, as the holographic projection pulled in tight on the enormous portal artifact on the eastern coast of a large continent, and then resumed: "The Ark is a place that I assume you remember quite well."

"It would be impossible for me to forget it."

"As it is for me."

"However, as I recall, the portal artifact had been deactivated, presumably due to the damage done to the Ark, when you and the Demon stopped the Flood."

"That is correct," said the Arbiter. "When the replacement Halo was activated, it seemed to have destroyed, or at least disabled, the portal on the Ark's end, which in turn shut down the portal on the Earth end. The human's inability to activate it over the years is likely due to the other side of the portal being damaged. We must hope that there is another solution that lay dormant within the artifact itself—we have little choice otherwise."

Usze's mind flew back to the end of the war. Thel 'Vadam was ultimately blamed by the High Prophets for failing to stop the human known as the Demon, called by his own people "Master Chief," from destroying the first Halo the Covenant had discovered. That fateful destruction had been responsible for 'Vadam's eventual transition to the role of Arbiter. Although such a mantle was considered shameful at that time, in the wake of the war with the humans, it had gained new honor among those loyal to him.

How strange, Usze thought. *There was a time when the rings were considered divine instruments capable of initiating the Great Journey. Some still believe them to be so. And now, in a way, I suppose they might be considered to be just that, if one thinks of the Great Journey as the ending of all thinking life in the galaxy.*

"So, the portal is still not functional?"

"It is not," said the Arbiter. "So it is necessary to repair it as soon as possible, since we are losing time with every passing second. The humans are converging on it even as we speak, summoning all available resources on their end. And you are going to meet them there. I would come also, but if I leave my enemies here unchecked on Sanghelios, there will be nothing left to return to for our people. I am putting a great amount of trust in you, Usze."

"I understand, Arbiter. Fear not. I shall attend to it."

"Not alone. I will be sending you and two others with you, to both facilitate the portal's restoration and accompany the humans on this expedition."

"Who are the others?"

"Do you remember N'tho 'Sraom?"

"Of course," Usze said immediately. "We served beside him together, though I have not seen him since we last departed from the Ark. He is certainly a fine warrior."

"Good. He will be waiting at the shuttle to greet you. He, and the third member of your group. A Huragok."

Usze's mandibles twitched in surprise. The Huragok were an exceedingly odd race—strange, tentacled creatures who floated and fixed things, and that was all they seemingly did. "Truly?"

"Yes. He is perhaps the most critical piece to this puzzle. You seem startled."

"I am. I was not aware that you had any left at your disposal." After the Covenant fragmented, most of the remaining Huragok either perished or fled, just as it was with the Prophets.

"There are still a few whose whereabouts are known. This is one of those, and there is great need for it on this particular mission. Without the Forerunner Dreadnought used to activate the portal years ago, there is no conventional way that we know of to replicate that great ship's interaction with the artifact. . . . except, perhaps, one: this Huragok. It was part of the entourage that attended the ascetic priests of old—the ones who had searched and examined the ancient warship for centuries. If there is a solution to activate the portal, this Huragok will find it. And you will serve N'tho in protecting the Huragok and doing whatever he requires of you."

Once more, Usze hesitated. He had no idea how to frame the question, but finally he managed. "Is there any possibility that . . . combat will be required?"

"There is no telling what will be in store for you on the Ark itself, or what has survived since its fall. You both must be ready for anything."

"I am not referring to the Ark, faithful leader."

The Arbiter did not appear to understand. "Combat with whom? You mean the humans . . . ?" He made no attempt to hide his surprise. "Under what circumstance do you believe that could be a possibility?"

"It is not my disposition to react to situations as they occur, but instead to anticipate them and be on guard. Make no mistake, Arbiter," he added quickly. "I do not share the hostility for the humans that many of our kind still possess. But we should not lose sight of the fact that there are very likely humans who in turn have no love for the Sangheili. We did obliterate many a world that their people called home. Countless lives were lost at our hands. I very much suspect that some humans harbor ill will for us."

"I would not be concerned," said the Arbiter. "I am confident that only the most cooperative humans will be permitted access to this vital project. All our lives are at stake, and I doubt that the humans would trust their future to anything save their very best."

CHAPTER 4

Captain Annabelle Richards of Special Operations, serving under ONI administration, did not like the Sangheili.

At all.

So she had not been thrilled when Admiral Serin Osman had given her the assignment of overseeing the Voi project to repair the Excession site. She had wanted to tell Osman point-blank to get someone else, but that was simply not something one did with Osman. That was a good way to wind up being assigned to a satellite node on Pluto for the rest of her life.

There were, of course, steps she could have taken. Lord knew she had been serving her entire life in the military, and she had enough contacts to call on that likely would have enabled her to avoid the assignment in its entirety. However, the fact that Osman had handpicked Richards, especially considering the importance of the mission, was really something of a compliment. It meant that Osman trusted her, and one simply did not throw such trust back into the face of the Commander-in-Chief of ONI.

Richards was resting in her cabin within one of the many ONI facilities that occupied the border of the Excession, simply staring at the far wall, when there was a knock at her door. "Come," she said briskly.

The door slid open and her aide strode in. In stark contrast to his superior, Lieutenant Carl Radeen was tall and burly; Richards herself was of medium height, and remarkably slender, so much so that her figure could easily be described as boyish. Certainly, if Richards hadn't known better, she would have thought Radeen to be some manner of android. He never smiled or laughed or frowned or showed any measure of reaction to pretty much anything. His angular faced was topped by a close crew cut—another contrast to his commanding officer, with her shock of meticulously parted, shoulder-length red hair—and when he looked at Richards, as was his custom, he didn't look right at her. Instead he focused on a space just to the right of her shoulder, as if into a non-existent camera lens. She had no idea why Radeen never looked her in the eyes. It was probably some deeply ingrained concern over respect or something like that.

"The Sangheili have arrived," Radeen informed her. "Their ship has just landed."

Richards was immediately on her feet. "Then we shall greet them properly, Lieutenant." She paused and then added, "Have Spartan Kodiak meet me there."

"Are you sure that's wise?"

Richards had already been preparing to leave the room but stopped in her place, unable to hide her surprise. Radeen never questioned her orders, ever. So his expressing uncertainty was more than enough to catch her off guard. She didn't address the fact that he was challenging her, but instead the specifics of it. Kodiak was not only a formidable warrior—a twenty-year man in total and a Spartan for the past two—but he was exceptionally discreet. He didn't speak unless spoken to and kept most of his sentences short. He had seemed the ideal person to put in charge of security for this mission, and when he had been given the assignment, his response had been nothing more than a quick head bob and a succinct, "Yes, Captain." So the fact that Radeen now seemed a bit hesitant was surprising, and even disturbing.

"Why would it not be wise, Lieutenant? Kodiak is my chief Spartan for this op and head of security. Don't you think he should be there for the initial meet and greet?"

"With all due respect, Captain, Spartan Kodiak's antipathy for the Sangheili is quite a bit more pronounced than yours. Perhaps having him keep a distance as much as possible might be the proper way to proceed."

"He's a Spartan," Richards said firmly. "His job is to be able to adapt to whatever situation he finds himself in. Do you have an issue with his qualifications?"

"No, Captain."

"Then make sure that he's there."

"Yes, Captain," said Radeen.

Radeen was speaking on his comm unit as Richards headed out through a corridor and into the facility's main courtyard. It shouldn't be far; the facility itself was one of many that Naval Intelligence had erected over the past few years in their efforts to secure and study the artifact. Outside the courtyard's main gate was a tarmac, where their visitors had been instructed to set down, and so the Sangheili would be reasonably nearby.

Richards approached the main gate, staring out across the vast airfield, and then beyond it to a full kilometer of African savannah stretching out toward the sudden drop-off of the Excession's northwesternmost edge. On the tarmac itself were a handful of Pelican dropships, Sparrowhawks, and other combat-ready vehicles, as well as a series of distinct stations throughout, preparing and deploying F-99 Wombat security drones. There were dozens of these automated machines combing the skies over the Excession, ensuring that this operation would go on without any interference.

Various officers saluted her as she walked past, and she rapidly returned the salute without bothering to make eye contact. Her mind was preoccupied with how she was going to react upon coming face-to-face with the Sangheili. It was her first occasion to do so after the war, and she wasn't entirely certain that she would be able to repress her anger at these . . . these *creatures*. . . .

They are not creatures. *They're simply a different and highly intelligent life-form from your own, and you should not hate them for that.*

No, I hate them because they spent years trying to destroy us. If I didn't hate them, I'd be insane.

And now they're your allies, and you're working together to save all your skins, so straighten up and be a damn professional.

Richards shook the inner conversation out of her head. She needed to focus.

Passing through the gates, despite her best efforts to maintain her composure, she shook inwardly when she saw the Sangheili dropship, a vividly alien shape in a sea of familiar greens and browns. Her immediate impulse was to pull out the weapon slung on her hip and open fire, even though such a small firearm wouldn't do a damn thing against the alien craft's surface. But she restrained herself, reminded of the demands of her responsibilities. She straightened her back and strode toward the dropship.

She heard the quick pace of footsteps behind her, and she didn't even have to turn around. "Spartan," she said by way of greeting.

"Captain," came back the brisk reply.

Obviously Lieutenant Radeen had done his job with customary swiftness.

Spartan Frank Kodiak increased his foot speed ever so slightly and drew up next to the captain, matching her pace. He could easily have exceeded it. He was just over two meters tall, which was about average for a Spartan thanks to the extensive augmentation that was performed on them. He was of the Spartan-IV variety, the most recent class of super-soldiers created by the UNSC to defend humankind. His shoulders were extremely wide, but he walked perfectly erect without swaying them in the least. His head was practically in the shape of a rectangle; Richards sometimes felt as if she could slice food on his chin. Like Radeen's, his hair was also in a crew cut, but it bristled red (although curiously there was a streak of gray across his right eyebrow).

He was not in full Mjolnir armor at the moment, but Richards suspected that if he'd had the time to put it on, he would have done so. As Radeen just got through reminding her, the Spartan had no more love for the Sangheili than she did.

Her gaze flitted for just a moment to his right arm. He was wearing his long-sleeved undersuit over it and so it seemed exactly the same as his left arm. Quickly she looked away. It wouldn't be good form for her to be caught staring at it.

"You can't tell, can you, Captain." It wasn't a question, and he wasn't looking at her. *Damn. His peripheral vision is amazing.*

Nevertheless, she felt the need to lie. "I have no idea what you're talking about."

He knew she was being evasive, of course, but chose not to pursue it. "Sorry, Captain. My mistake."

She didn't respond, instead opting to let the moment between them pass.

They strode to the main hatch of the Sangheili dropship, one of their Phantoms. It was burnished copper, remarkably round in comparison to the straight lines of the Pelican. Its body was curved into a series of humps, ridges, and fins; it sort of looked like an oversize snail. As they approached, they found the door sliding open. She was surprised by the extreme quiet of the mechanism, in contrast to such doors in human vessels, which tended to make a hell of a lot of noise. Inwardly, part of her was forced to admire the clearly superior technology of the Sangheili.

She then heard the clanking of boots, metal on metal. For some reason, she was expecting the Arbiter to be the first, cradling a weapon when he appeared. She was wrong. Two Elites descended from the vessel, and neither of them appeared armed.

But you are. You have your weapon on your hip. So does Kodiak. What does that say about us—that we're armed and they aren't?

She decided it said not a thing.

"You are . . . Captain Richards, I take it," said the Elite in the lead. Translation software in Richards's ear enabled her to understand what he was saying in real time. She was told that the Elites would be utilizing similar technology.

Richards tried to determine if this was the Arbiter or not. She realized that all of the Sangheili looked alike to her—she simply couldn't distinguish one from the other, though this one was not wearing the armor she expected. "And you are the Arbiter?" she said cautiously.

"I am not," he said. "I am N'tho 'Sraom. I am an adjunct to the Arbiter. And this is my aide, Usze 'Taham." The two Sangheili were clad in similar but not identical combat armor, a burnished yet battle-scarred pairing of crimson and ivory. Evidently, this indicated some kind of alignment with the Arbiter after the fall of the Covenant, although it was clear that both of these Elites had seen their share of battle well after the war.

"I thought the Arbiter himself might be coming."

"He cannot. He has other pressing business to attend to."

Richards was aware that Kodiak had stiffened next to her. She ascribed it to his own hostility against the aliens, but sought to overlook it. "This is Spartan Kodiak."

N'tho nodded in acknowledgment. Then he turned and gazed into the dropship. "You may come out," he called. "There is no need to remain in there."

Richards's eyes widened as something else emerged from the vessel. She had no idea what she was looking at. She was certainly familiar with both the Sangheili and other members of the Covenant, but for the most part, her experience was only with those engaged in active combat. This thing was large enough, but it wasn't walking; it was floating. It seemed to be composed almost entirely of tentacles that were in constant motion, as if it were sampling all of its surroundings through the sense of touch. It took Richards a few moments to realize that it was only four tentacles fixed to a purple, jellyfish-like, floating sack, but they seemed to be everywhere at once. The creature also had a small serpentine head with six eyes, none of which appeared to be focused on her.

N'tho seemed to be aware of her lack of familiarity. "This is a Huragok," he said. "Its colloquial name is 'Drifts Randomly.'" He then addressed the Huragok. "Drifts Randomly, these are . . ." He paused and then seemed to shrug. "Humans."

So *that* was a Huragok. Richards knew of their existence, of course. ONI had acquired their own Huragok after the war, but she had simply never encountered one before. "My understanding is that this one can be of particular use to us," she said.

"Correct," said N'tho, "When the Arbiter heard of the plight we all now face, this particular Huragok was the only one that seemed remotely acceptable to him. It once served aboard the very Forerunner vessel that activated this portal during the war, and of all remaining Huragok, it would be the most familiar with the technology found here. In fact, it is really the only hope our peoples have of reactivating this portal, if such a thing is even possible. To a large degree, we are here to serve as its protectors.

There are many unknowns upon the Ark, and it is uncertain what threats may persist there."

"Understood. Um . . . hello," Richards said to it hesitantly.

The Huragok did not respond. It simply floated—she couldn't even tell if it knew that she was there.

"It cannot speak to you in your language," N'tho informed her. "Nor will it, if it could. It will do what it is told, and that is more or less all it is capable of. Now, with your permission, we need to be guided to the technological center of this portal, wherever your people have accessed its critical systems. The Huragok will then take over from there."

"We do have personnel working on it already," said Richards.

"Good. They can support the Huragok in its work, though I doubt they will be needed."

"I assure you, we have top people currently employed to—"

N'tho obviously did not feel any need to hear her out. "I am quite certain that you have very talented individuals at work. And if we had more time to devote to this task, I would be perfectly inclined to leave them to their efforts. But you must understand that the Huragok were created by the Forerunners for this very reason. So unless your people can declare the same, I suggest they step aside and let the Huragok serve the single purpose that its creation has permitted it to perform. Does that present a problem?"

"No," said Richards. "No problem at all. Spartan Kodiak, please bring our new arrivals to the Research Center Alpha. And uh . . . turn them loose."

"Yes, Captain." Kodiak was carrying some manner of tension, but Richards wasn't interested—as long as it didn't interfere with the job at hand, she wasn't going to dwell on it.

Without another word, Kodiak turned and strode away. The

Sangheili promptly followed him, with the Huragok trailing behind them all.

They walked for some time in relative silence, a dry and weather-
beaten savannah to their left, and the inordinately immense portal
artifact to their right, stretching out in the far distance to nearly
touch this world's eastern horizon. It was an impressive sight to
behold, but N'tho 'Sraom found himself glancing at the Spartan
with curiosity. Something about the human seemed vaguely familiar, but he could not immediately place it. Ultimately, he decided it
was simply that most humans tended to look alike, so there really
wasn't much point in dwelling on it.

There was a small building up ahead. It had obviously been
constructed rather quickly, although at least it seemed capable
of standing up to the elements. It was trapezoidal in shape, with
sturdy, filthy metal sides. The base was approximately ten meters on each side, and there was a keypad on the outside that the
human tapped what appeared to be a few of their strange-looking
numbers into. A grinding noise and the doors slowly slid open,
rattling as they did so. Inside the small structure was nothing save
a large room.

"Elevator," said Kodiak.

"Yes, I know what it is," said Usze 'Taham. "We may not have
been to this particular section of the artifact before, but we are
aware of how portals are constructed. It makes sense that we
would have to descend to the power systems below the artifact
itself, and I assume that this conveyance will take us there. Yes?"

"Yes," Kodiak confirmed. "Go on in."

N'tho strode inside, followed by Usze and the Huragok, which simply drifted in behind them. The Spartan touched a button and the doors closed in fits and shakes.

The elevator then abruptly dropped.

"Where exactly are we going?" asked Usze.

"The center of the operation," the human said. He still refused to make eye contact with N'tho. "It's down at the base of one of the pylons."

N'tho knew exactly what he was referring to. The artifact that generated the portal was essentially a massive, disklike structure more than one hundred kilometers in diameter, stretching from the eastern perimeter of what little was left of the town of Voi to the charred rubble of New Mombasa at the far coast of the continent. Enormous, fin-like pylons lay atop the disc, hinged on the perimeter of it so they could open and close, lowering the center of the disc and generating the portal once activated. When it was activated more than two years ago, the gateway looked almost like a strange kind of flower, albeit composed of alien metals and tones. When closed and dormant, as it was now, the pylons had all receded and remained atop the disc, pointing toward the center. Clearly the humans had found a way to access the artifact's many information systems, engines, and control stations, and apparently what was referred to as this Research Center Alpha was located far underground, near the hinge of one of the pylons.

The elevator descended for a while, and then it began to slow and eventually stopped.

The doors clattered open and N'tho and the others stepped through.

They were now situated on what appeared to be some manner of observation platform. It was rather large, with a long series of transparent panels running across the front of it, joined together to form one huge viewing window. N'tho walked forward and saw what it looked out upon: the vast undercarriage of the artifact itself, with one of its massive pylons stretching out for many kilometers, so high and far that its most distant sections were well out of sight, buried in darkness.

At the base of the pylon, well below their current position in the observation deck, was a series of instrument panels, which N'tho recognized immediately from their Forerunner origins. They were covered in all manner of indecipherable runes, and the only reason that he could discern any of them was because the humans had mounted floodlights overhead, beaming light down into the entire area. There were light indicators on the Forerunner consoles, but none of them were illuminated. There appeared to be no power flowing anywhere into it.

The humans were meticulously scrutinizing the panels, seemingly in small increments at a time. They were clustered atop a network of scaffolding and gantries that extended out and down from the observation deck and branched out in a variety directions, examining other parts of the artifact's immense size that were far out of sight. There was an array of indicator panels and pads used to study it, and from here, N'tho could see words and data scrolling across the pads. There appeared to be about several dozen of them at work. Everything was happening in silence, with any conversation in hushed whispers at most.

"How many of your people are working here?"

"Hundreds," said the Spartan. He continued not to look at N'tho, which N'tho now found mildly puzzling.

"Is anyone actually interfacing with the equipment?"

"You'll have to ask them yourself. There's a stairway that goes down to the platform they're working on," said the Spartan, pointing to the far end of the room.

"Very well, then," said N'tho. "Let us begin."

The Huragok floated ahead of them and, arriving at the stairway, started to drift down it. N'tho glanced back at the Spartan and said, "Are you coming with us?"

"Absolutely. I have no intention of letting you two out of my sight," he replied, and this time, he actually made eye contact.

There was a certain level of defiance in his expression.

What an odd human, thought N'tho, and he vowed to be careful in his presence.

Captain Annabelle Richards watched Spartan Kodiak and the aliens depart, and then turned and started back toward the facility, lost in thought. As she approached the gate leading in to the courtyard, she saw someone running toward her. Elias Holt.

Holt was also a Spartan, working in close conjunction with Kodiak. Richards remembered being a bit amused when she'd first met him; Holt's enthusiasm for his position and job was infectious. She couldn't help but recall the first Spartans she had encountered. To Richards, they had barely qualified as human beings. They ate, they slept, they fought. That was the entirety of their lives. The original Spartans hadn't even possessed the ability to engage in casual military chitchat, or at least that was the case with the ones she had run into. When Richards had tried to discuss anything other than their immediate objective, they had simply stared at her blankly, as if they didn't understand the words coming from her mouth.

Elias Holt was of a much more recent vintage; like Kodiak, he was part of the SPARTAN-IV program and now served in the Spartan branch, though ONI had requisitioned their service for this specific operation. He'd been recruited into the program after his achievements as a young soldier, and had been given extensive combat training, along with the augmentations that were required to become a Spartan and wear the highly advanced Mjolnir armor. Despite the fact that Holt was somewhat green by Spartan standards, Richards knew from his record that he was a capable enough soldier, and she hoped that he would achieve great things in his career.

Although Holt was just as powerfully reinvented as Kodiak was, he seemed and acted far more youthful. Holt's face was long and open and full of freckles, and his black hair was quite wiry. He also had a tendency to say whatever was on his mind, so that at least was a plus in Richards's eyes.

Holt hurried up to her and belatedly remembered to salute. She returned it and stared at him patiently.

"Captain Richards, have you seen Spartan Kodiak?"

"Yes, I have. He is escorting our newly arrived Sangheili—" she indicated the landed ship in the distance—"toward the work area. They're here to aid us in getting the portal online. Is there a problem, Spartan?"

"No problem, Captain. I was off taking target practice and returned to my quarters to discover that he'd been summoned. So I felt I should check and see if he needs my assistance."

"Not necessary. I really don't expect that any serious trouble will occur while he's bringing the Sangheili to their destination." She paused, because there was a level of excitement in Holt's face that didn't quite seem to correspond. "Is something wrong, Spartan?"

"What? Oh, no," he said with assurance. "Nothing's wrong. I just . . . I've never seen a Sangheili, and I'm sorry I missed the opportunity just now."

"Seriously?"

"No, Captain. Not in the flesh, that is. Oh, I engaged in plenty of battles, certainly, but most of them were populated with Grunts and Jackals, and occasionally Brutes. I've only seen Elites in the holo-vids and War Games exercises."

"Well, they'll be here for a while, so I am certain the opportunity will come up."

"Is it the Arbiter?"

"No. He sent two of his close associates." She paused, bringing their names back to her head. "Usze 'Taham. And N'tho . . . something, dammit. Can't recall the last name. . . ."

Holt visibly paled. "It wouldn't be N'tho 'Sraom, by any chance?"

"Why, yes! Yes, that's . . ." Her voice trailed off as she saw how Holt's face had gone almost ashen. "Why, do you know him?"

"Oh yes. I know him, Captain."

"Where from?" When she saw that he appeared reluctant to answer, she continued with slight annoyance: "Spartan, if there's something relevant you want to say, I need to hear it."

"You're aware that Spartan Kodiak has an artificial right arm, yes?"

Of course. She'd been staring at it earlier. "Yes, I'm aware of that. He lost it in combat, several years before he became a Spartan."

"That's right, Captain. By an Elite who had him dead to rights, but at the last moment, a nearby explosion caught him off guard and Kodiak managed to escape." Holt hesitated, his Adam's apple bobbing in his throat. "After-action reports indicated that the Elite's name was N'tho 'Sraom. He's the one who cut off Kodiak's arm, and Kodiak has been waiting for a chance to kill him ever since."

CHAPTER 5

L uther Mann had not been entirely sure of what to make of Olympia Vale when he had first been introduced to her.

She was personable enough, there was no denying that. Of average size and build for the most part, but certainly well-toned, due to an exercise regimen that Luther had noticed her engaging in that morning. During the rest of the time, she interacted with Henry Lamb, who was clearly quite taken with her, as he would extol to Luther her endless array of virtues and wonder if she saw him in the same light. Luther had no clue. To him, women were a constant source of mystery (especially Ramona), and he'd long ago given up any hope of actually understanding what was going through their minds. Then again, to be fair, he felt much the same way about men, so at least he wasn't biased.

As time went on, it became clear to him, though, that Vale was not remotely interested in Henry. She was all business. Luther didn't bother to inform Henry of this, because he was clearly blind to it.

Her skin had a dark cast to it, complementing the thick sheaf of brown hair kept tied back in a ponytail that swished back and forth like a pendulum whenever she walked. Her curiously curved face reminded him of a classic Valentine heart, rounded and with a pointed chin.

He liked her attitude—very crisp and to the point. It was also clear to Luther that she had a great deal of understanding when it came to the Sangheili. He certainly had a good deal of life experience when it came to speaking to those who had no idea what he was going on about. Any number of times he had spoken about the Sangheili, or the Forerunners, for that matter, he'd frequently been met with puzzled and blank looks. That was not the case with Olympia Vale. He saw immediate intuition with her when it came to discussing anything having to do with the Sangheili, and he was extremely relieved about that.

Vale had been dispatched to Voi for the exact reason that Henry had previously speculated: as an interface between the Sangheili and the humans who would participate in the expedition. But since the Sangheili had not yet arrived, she was keeping company with the two of them, occasionally asking them questions with genuine interest.

At the moment, Vale was studying the massive array of Forerunner machinery that lined the corridor they were exploring—heavy-duty tech that ran off the main hallway, and the wall was covered with symbols. They had accessed this part of the artifact from the network of gantries and catwalks ONI had fabricated in the deep recesses of the portal's outer boundary.

"See here," Luther was saying, standing next to her, holding a flashlight for them both. "I'm pretty confident that this sequence of glyphs refers to the Excession's primary activation stem, and this line here probably depicts the process to get the drive turned back on."

"And how has that been going?" asked Vale.

"Slowly," Henry spoke up with obvious frustration in his voice. "Whenever it comes to dealing with Forerunner technology, 'slowly' is how we go about doing things."

Vale dropped her voice slightly. "From my understanding, 'slowly' may not be an option now in our toolbox."

"I'm aware of that," Henry said, "but the bottom line remains that the technology that we're dealing with is thousands of years old. If we do anything precipitously, we could trigger a chain reaction that will give us the exact opposite of the results that we want."

Vale nodded. "All right. I can accept that. But answer me this: How do we know we aren't wasting our time here? I mean, my understanding as Doctor Mann here explained it to me . . ."

"Luther, please."

". . . is that the damage caused at this end was the result of what occurred on the Ark. Isn't that why ONI hasn't had any progress on it for the last two years?"

"Not entirely. Based upon the actions of the various automated systems we've seen on different Halo installations," said Henry, "we are assuming that may not be the case after all. Forerunner devices tend to be self-monitoring and are always capable of initiating dramatic repairs, even to things as complex as biomes and life-supporting systems. It would actually be an extraordinary exception to the rule if the portal wasn't actually repaired on that end, given what we know of the Ark and what was recovered from the *Forward Unto Dawn*, the human ship exposed to it in '52."

"That's quite an assumption," Vale said drily.

"It is," Luther agreed. "But it's the one upon which we're operating. Truthfully, we're in a position where we have to assume it, because the alternative of traveling through space using conventional slipspace methods to get there, even with Forerunner drive technology, is simply not feasible."

"And am I safe in assuming that you two are the ones who sold the assumption to ONI and the UNSC?"

Luther nodded. "By extension, yes. We sold it to others, and they sold it to ONI and UNSC."

Vale thought about it a moment and then nodded. "Okay, then. So we essentially have to assume that you're right."

"We typically do," said Luther.

Vale permitted a small smile at that.

"Here's the thing," Henry said. "What we really need is a Forerunner keyship. That's what they normally used to activate a portal. The Forerunners used these vessels as security keys, opening and closing portals that they had scattered throughout the galaxy. Without one . . . we're just guessing here."

"Then we find a keyship," Vale said matter-of-factly. "What happened to the one the Covenant used last time?"

"We're hoping our Sangheili friends might help us with that," said Luther.

Vale turned and seemed to be looking into his eyes for the first time. "For the record, in all of my interactions with the Sangheili, I've never heard them mention anything about a keyship. And I've never been much for relying on far-fetched hopes, either. That's always been a bit too vague for me. I'm much more in favor of actually accomplishing things."

They were spread out through the complex, everyone listening to their exchange, when Luther heard the sound of heavy feet approaching. "I believe we're about to have company," he informed his compatriots.

Their shadows preceded them, and then Luther could see the Elites as they strode toward him. He felt his hair clench, and a chill ran down his spine. Luther forced a sudden smile onto his face and wondered if the Sangheili would be able to discern how insincere it was. He doubted it; they were aliens, after all, and likely were not entirely familiar with the subtlety and range of human expression. At least, that was what he told himself. For a moment, he remembered how they had seemed beautiful to him in his youth. *Pretty.* That feeling was suddenly gone.

Spartan Frank Kodiak was leading them in. He appeared no more pleased over their advent than Luther was, nor was he making even the slightest effort to wear an insincere smile. He pointed at Luther as the group approached and said, "That's Doctor Luther Mann. He's in charge of the repair efforts."

"Greetings, Luther Mann," rumbled the larger of the two Sangheili. "I am N'tho 'Sraom. This"—and he indicated the Elite next to him—"is Usze 'Taham."

"A Huragok!" Henry said. As someone who had devoted his life to the practice of engineering, he seemed thrilled to find himself face to face with a creature that had apparently been the epitome of Forerunner engineering prowess.

"Oh, yes," said N'tho as if he had forgotten. "And this is Drifts Randomly."

Luther had no trouble understanding what N'tho was saying, given the translation earpiece he had been provided. He was wearing it at Richards's insistence, even though he had assured her that he would be able to discern whatever any Sangheili said to him.

"I've spent time with Huragok before," said Henry. "There were at one time several being utilized by the Office of Naval Intelligence, and I had the opportunity to work with them over a week's time, with the aid of an interpreter. Not sure what's happened to them since then, but I learned more about Forerunner technology in that one week than I had in the previous years. A tremendously educational experience."

Olympia Vale strode forward and flawlessly addressed N'tho in his native tongue. Luther was extremely impressed. Her Sangheili was perfect; certainly superior to his.

N'tho was also obviously taken, as he responded in his own language. Then she turned and shifted her attention to the floating creature. "Unbelievable. A Huragok," she said. "I have heard of them, of course, but that certainly does not do them justice."

The Huragok did not respond; it didn't even appear to notice her. Instead it simply drifted about, gazing at the technology lining the walls.

Then Luther whistled.

Instantly, to the surprise of everyone—including the Sangheili—the Huragok shifted its position and turned to face him. Luther continued to produce a series of whistles, combined with hand gestures that seemed vaguely reminiscent of sign language.

The Huragok began to imitate Luther . . . no, *respond.* It was whistling and gesturing back at him, and as it did so, Luther became more excited over the success he was having.

The Elite were clearly stunned. "That is . . . unusual," said N'tho. "It does not normally speak to humans."

"Or to anyone, for that matter," said Usze. "My own translation device has been specially designed to communicate with it, but thus far it has more or less ignored me."

"It's just a matter of knowing *how* to talk to it," Luther said, as if conversing with a Huragok was the simplest matter in the world.

Vale didn't miss a beat. "Dr. Mann is one of the foremost experts of Forerunner culture and language in the field. There's very little we've learned about their way of life that he's not familiar with."

"That isn't quite true," Luther said immediately. "We know so little even now. We're really only just scratching the surface." He wondered how his expertise might make the Sangheili feel, given their people's historic view of the Forerunners. Then again, the earlier briefing Luther attended had confirmed that these Elites were aligned with the Arbiter, which meant that, among other things, they had generally abandoned the former notion that the Forerunners were gods.

The Huragok whistled at Luther for a few moments more and then floated toward a section of the paneling. Vale couldn't resist asking: "What did it say?"

"It merely asked me where I learned to speak its language. I told it that I spoke many languages." He shrugged as if it wasn't any big deal. "That's just always come naturally to me, I suppose. Whenever I hear a new language, I pick it up very quickly."

"I'd call that a gift. But how did you pick up the Huragok language?" asked Vale.

"Those same Huragok that Henry worked with. I had a similar opportunity. However, when the translator spoke with them, I used the occasion to really learn how to communicate with them. It isn't that difficult if you pay close attention to their speech patterns."

"Apparently you were quite proficient," said N'tho.

Abruptly they were interrupted by the sound of running feet echoing down the hallway. They all looked in confusion as Captain Annabelle Richards appeared, then slowed to a halt the moment she drew within view of the rest of the group. They stared at her with reactions ranging from concern to curiosity.

Appearing to be lacking for some actual reason to be there, she cleared her throat and then said, as officially as she apparently could, "Just checking in. Wanted to make certain that everything was going all right."

"Um, yes," said Luther, sounding as puzzled as he looked. "Any particular reason why everything would *not* be going all right?"

It seemed to Luther that her gaze flickered to the Spartan for just a moment, but Kodiak wasn't displaying even the slightest emotion.

He was just standing there, indifferent. In truth, Luther perceived one possible explanation for the captain's strange behavior: The sole reason Olympia Vale had been added to the expedition stemmed from concerns around the proposal of a hybrid team, one that included both humans and Sangheili. It had never been formally done before, and it was clear that ONI had carefully assessed all the possible risks in this mission, which would have been many. While it had been well over two years since the end of the war, tensions still remained . . . and concerns between their species had not lessened.

"No," said Richards after a long moment. "No reason at all. Carry on."

"Yes, ma'am."

"Spartan Kodiak. Please report to me when you're done here."

"Yes, Captain."

N'tho turned to the others as Richards walked away. "You will find this Huragok particularly useful. It has worked extensively with Forerunner technology and will have great familiarity with anything presented to it, and in particular the processes that are of great concern in order to activate this machine."

"That's excellent to hear," said Vale. "If there's anything the Huragok needs . . ."

"It will need nothing," N'tho said with complete confidence. "Other than something to fix, the Huragok has no requirements."

"Well, I'll be happy to keep it company anyway," Luther said.

"We will keep the premises secure," N'tho announced.

"Secure?" Luther frowned. "From what?"

"We remain concerned about possible information compromises," N'tho replied. "Word spreading about the potential cataclysm and the attempts here to avert that."

"Most of the people on this world are unaware of the situation," Luther said immediately. "In fact, only a handful actually know about the countdown on the Halo installations and our intentions to get the portal online. The others here are ignorant to it and have been working on this site, well, since the end of the war. They were stationed here long before we showed up and will, with any luck, be here long after we're gone."

"I understand that," said N'tho. "But if others should learn of what is happening and our reason for being here . . ."

"They won't," said Vale flatly, in perfect Sangheili. "It will not happen."

"How can you know that for a certainty?"

Vale paused and then seemed to shrug mentally. "Let's just say that there are certain individuals connected with this endeavor who are going to make sure that word does not get out. This is a covert operation, on a need-to-know basis. If any individuals should uncover the truth, they will—how best to put this—*disappear* for a time."

The Elites glanced at each other. "How very thorough," said N'tho.

"Yes, extremely thorough," said Vale.

"Nevertheless, we will be running frequent perimeter checks by way of our orbiting vessel to make certain that there are no individuals who should not, in fact, be here."

Frank Kodiak actually laughed at that. It was a most unusual sound coming from a Spartan. "*Security? You two?*"

"Yes, along with my ship's crew," said N'tho. "Why do you find that amusing?"

"I believe," Vale stepped in before Kodiak could respond, "that the Spartan here is thinking about the amount of security already in place. There are dozens of drones canvassing the artifact as we speak, and the entire site has been secured by a number of sensor barricades and checkpoint measures. You were being tracked during your entire approach. If the Spartan had not been with you, the checkpoints would have gone off and drones would have attacked within seconds. So I believe that the Spartan was being encouraging, to try and assure you that your surveying the area for security breaches, while very much appreciated, isn't necessary. That is not what you should be focusing on."

"Indeed. And what should we be focusing on?"

Luther spoke up this time. "What you'll be needed for is whatever's waiting for us on the Ark once we get there. You have both been there, after all."

"Yes, we have," agreed Usze.

"That's where your expertise will be of use," said Luther. "You'll be needed to guide us to the place on the Ark where we can potentially shut down whatever is happening at the Halo rings. It'll most likely be the very same communications array utilized two years ago. No one will be more qualified for that task than you both. With the greatest respect, I believe that alone should be what occupies you for the time being. We don't really know what we'll find there."

"That's not entirely true," Henry said.

"What do you mean?" Luther didn't know where he was going with this.

"I have a friend, an old buddy from school, who runs the telemetry sensors on Pylon Five. We grabbed drinks last night, and he confided to me that ONI's apparently already sent people to the Ark. There have been two expeditions so far, both completely off the books."

"You didn't tell him about this mission, did you?" Luther couldn't believe he was asking this again after their conversation on the Halo ring.

"No, but plenty of the people working at this site are curious what the ONI heads are up to, given the added security over the past few days. As well as us. They'll be even more suspicious when they get a look at these guys," he said, nodding to the Sangheili.

"Why didn't you mention this earlier?" Luther suddenly felt a bit nervous at the idea that information had been withheld from him and that he was now getting that information through an un-qualified source.

Henry looked at the ground as he responded. "I wanted to, but there hasn't really been an opportunity till now, Luther," he said. "He told me that the other missions to the Ark evidently ended in disaster."

"Specifically how?"

"Disappearances. No one returned, no traces ever found, and no clear communication records, either."

"Okay," Luther said. "That sounds positive. How does he even know this?"

"Not sure," Henry responded. "Some clerk misfiled paper-work on it or something. It was a clerical error, and he told me in confidence. Probably shouldn't even be talking about it now."

"It matters little. That will not happen to us," said N'tho. "We were there and we are obviously none the worse for wear." The translation device deftly handled the idiom.

Yes, but you're Elites. It would take an elephant outfitted with dynamite to hurt you. Luther chose to keep that opinion to himself and simply smiled and nodded. He wondered what state the Ark was actually in since these Elites had last set foot on it. Hadn't it been besieged by the Covenant, attacked by the Flood, and then blasted by a replacement Halo installation? He wasn't sure they would even recognize it at this point. Nevertheless, he'd taken the time recently to pore over the cartographical information he had pulled together more than a year ago, captured by the passive sensors on the UNSC *Forward Unto Dawn*, the lone human ship that had been to the Ark and returned to tell about it.

Luther thought he might reach out to Casper or Richards or someone at ONI and ask why the hell he hadn't been told about the previous expeditions. Seemed like critical information to him, even if they hadn't been on a mission to the Ark, in order to stop Halo from firing. But then he immediately thought better of it—ONI wouldn't leave them in the dark without good reason. That and making demands of ONI was never a good idea in any situation.

Strangely, though, he noticed Kodiak's own response to this news. The Spartan just stared blankly at Henry Lamb with fixed, somewhat watery eyes. It wasn't threatening at all, but more like Henry had piqued Kodiak's curiosity and that he was on the verge of asking his own questions about these secret expeditions. But nothing came.

N'tho 'Sraom turned to Luther and said, "We leave the Huragok in your hands, then, human, and will be back to check on you presently."

"Thank you," said Luther. The floating Engineer was already at work, its tentacles caressing the instrumentation on the walls as if greeting a long lost lover. Vale was following it.

Henry shrugged. "Okay, then. Guess I'm out of a job."

"We don't know that for sure," Luther said. "Let's see what our new alien friend comes up with anyway. Believe me, this isn't a problem that will suffer from too many hands involved."

"I am sure you are correct," Usze 'Taham remarked. "Furthermore, there may well be things that the Huragok needs accomplished that will go more swiftly with this one here to aid it." He gestured to Henry.

"I'm not sure if you're attempting to be flattering or not," said Henry, "but I'll take that as a compliment in any event."

For some reason, N'tho glanced toward the Spartan, and Luther noticed that Kodiak was once again staring intently at the Sangheili. "Is something the matter, Spartan?"

"No. Nothing's wrong," said Kodiak, but his voice sounded low and husky, as if he had something caught in his throat. He must have been aware of it because he cleared it loudly and then said, "I'd best go check with the captain. See what she wants."

"Yes. Perhaps that is a good idea," said N'tho.

Luther didn't know what to make of this interaction, or the Spartan's strange behavior—but he felt that nothing good could come of it.

"You should have told me," Captain Richards said, barely managing to contain her annoyance. The office located in the administrative quarters of the research facility was relatively light in furnishings. Indeed, the only major piece in here was a very elaborate, classic wooden desk that wasn't exactly UNSC standard issue. It was larger than normal and had the initials AR carved in the corner. The desk had belonged to her father, and she still remembered to this day crawling around underneath and defacing it.

There was a wooden chair opposite it, but Kodiak was ignoring it and standing stiffly, his hands draped behind his back. "With all due respect, Captain, I did not feel it to be of any relevance."

"The man cut off your arm!"

"Begging the Captain's pardon, ma'am—he's not a man," Kodiak said, his voice flat. It was eerie, how detached he sounded.

Richards was behind her desk, drumming her fingers on the surface. "That's hardly the point. If you have a conflict with someone—"

"I don't have a conflict, Captain. It happened during war. Lots of things happen during war. You accept that and move on."

She leaned back in her chair, staring at him suspiciously. "Why do I find myself having trouble believing you?"

"I don't have an answer for that, Captain. Permission to speak freely?"

"Granted."

"Frankly, it isn't my problem if you don't believe me. I have done nothing threatening, and said nothing threatening, to either Elite. That should be your only concern."

"I'm your commanding officer," Richards said stiffly. "I'm reasonably certain that I get to decide what is and is not my concern."

He tipped his head slightly in apparent acknowledgment. "Whatever you say, Captain."

She hesitated a moment, continuing to drum her fingers. "Can I trust you not to get yourself into trouble over this, Spartan?"

"I have already said that you can."

And what about Spartan Holt? she thought. *He sure as hell seemed concerned that you were ready to blow N'tho's head off given the first opportunity.*

"If I may ask, how did you discover this about my history?" said Kodiak.

"Privileged information," Richards replied immediately. She wasn't about to name Holt as the source. "I report to the head of ONI. How do you *think* I got it?"

Kodiak looked momentarily suspicious, but clearly chose not to pursue it. Richards was relieved. She felt it was necessary to keep Holt out of this because she wanted to continue using him as an inside man, which would be useless if Kodiak started keeping him at arm's length.

"All right," she said finally. "Keep your distance from N'tho and everything should be fine."

"You've already made that abundantly clear, Captain."

She nodded. "Yes, I have, and I'm doing it again. Dismissed."

He tossed off a salute. She returned it reflexively, but was left staring at the door long after the Spartan had departed. She did not, in fact, believe for a moment that Kodiak was going to keep his desire for vengeance off the table, but the truth was that she really didn't have any basis upon which to relieve him of duty.

Richards would just have to hope that he was telling the truth, and further than that, if he wasn't . . . she or Spartan Holt or anyone would have to intervene violently before Kodiak wound up killing N'tho 'Sraom just on principle.

Luther, Henry, and Vale sat wordlessly, watching the Huragok meticulously continue its work. It had now been two days since Drifts Randomly had first arrived, and he had been working without stopping once since. Knowing the exact specifics of what the Huragok was doing was something of a challenge for Luther, as engineering was Henry's venue. It was clear to him that the Huragok appeared to be studying the glyphs that indicated the start-up process and was busy not only implementing them, but either fixing or improving upon the technology in front of it. If he were to guess, Drifts, as they had started to call the Huragok, was attempting to bypass the many security impediments in place, which required the use of a keyship in order to spin up the portal's ancient engines. Henry, for his part, was scribbling notes as he did so. Luther would be sure to sit down with him at the end of the day and have Henry walk him through it. For the time being, though, he was content to watch its tentacles working steadily, moving pieces, rearranging things in an endless stream of determined repair.

<<How is it going?>> Luther asked the creature, using a series of whistles and hand gestures.

<<*It goes,*>> replied the Huragok.

That was it—the lengthiest response he'd gotten out of the creature thus far, since most of its replies to this point had been along the lines of <<*Fine*>>, <<*Well*>>, and <<*Yes*>>.

<<I'm only asking,>> he said, <<because you've been at this for two days and I have no idea how much closer we are to having this repaired.>>

<<*Closer.*>>

<<Yes, I understand that. The question is, How much closer?>>

<<*Unknown.*>>

Hardly a useful answer. <<You realize we are on a deadline, right?>>

<<*Dead line?*>>

<<Yes, deadline, as in serious, no kidding, deadline. Do you know where the term *deadline* came from?>>

<<*No.*>>

It looked as though Vale was listening carefully, attempting to discern the entirety of the conversation by listening to Luther's half, but he couldn't be certain. <<Well, many centuries ago, there was a war on Earth called the American Civil War. And there were prison camps there. And in order to make sure that the prisoners didn't go anywhere, the commander had a line drawn around the

camp's perimeter. There were guards posted all over the camp, and the line was called a deadline, because if a prisoner stepped across the line, the assumption was that he was trying to escape and he would be shot dead.>>

For the first time in forty-eight hours, the Huragok stopped working. It didn't lower its tentacles; they remained in an upraised position. It appeared to be pondering what he had just told it.

<<*Humans warred with each other?*>>

Luther was slightly surprised that was the critical piece of information the creature had taken from his little history lesson, but he didn't allow it to faze him. "Yes. Many times."

<<*Why?*>>

<<Many reasons,>> he said. <<There have been many wars. But then the Covenant came along and declared war on us, and that united all humans against a common enemy. I suppose we should be grateful for that.>> He considered it. <<Maybe we should even be worried that, without the Covenant, we'll start warring with each other again. I'd hate to see that kind of societal reversion, but I suppose it's possible.>>

The Huragok just floated there. It wasn't making any more repairs.

<<*Should stop?*>>

Luther didn't understand the question. <<Stop what? Stop making repairs?>>

<<*Yes.*>>

<<Why would you do that?>>

"Because you aren't encouraging it to continue."

Vale and Luther jumped slightly at the arrival of the new, unexpected speaker. Luther had assumed that they and the Huragok were alone. Henry was sufficiently distracted by the Huragok that he did not react at all.

Indeed, it was remarkable that Luther had not seen Usze 'Taham approaching. Yet here the Sangheili was, big as life. Bigger, even.

"I'm sorry?" Luther said. "Encouraging it? Why should I have to? Doesn't it just fix things by nature?"

"Yes, of course," said Usze. "But you have expressed concern that, with the end of our conflict, your species may well descend into internecine warfare yet again. A supposition about which you may well be correct, for that matter."

"All right, but how is that of interest to the Huragok?"

Usze 'Taham contorted his mandibles in what may have been the Sangheili version of a smile at the floating creature. At least that was what Luther thought—it seemed more like a snarl, but his voice didn't match up with any hostile intent, so he was willing to give him the benefit of the doubt. "The Huragok feel compelled to serve, as part of their nature. That is why they repair things. It is a means of serving the Forerunners that created them. But you have introduced the concept that your race could fall back into warfare and possible self-immolation. The Huragok is now considering if you would prefer death to that possibility."

"I can't believe that a Huragok would be moved to inaction here by the possibility of civil war," Vale said confidently.

Usze appeared slightly puzzled, but also intrigued at the definitiveness in her voice. "And you would be certain of that . . . why?"

She promptly switched to speaking in Sangheili. The reason was obvious: it was a gesture of respect to Usze, one that Luther suspected would not be lost upon the Elite. *"Because it is not as if civil war is a practice that is restricted to humanity. Your people are presently enmeshed in their own civil conflict, and before that it was the Covenant, and we all know what they did. Those facts have never deterred this Huragok or any others from working in your service."*

Usze processed this observation for a moment and then nodded. *"You appear to make valid points."*

"I had the opportunity to spend a good deal of time on Khael'mothka," she informed him. *"It is not Sanghelios, but that hasn't kept it from your current war."* Luther had heard of the place before. It was a rough Sangheili frontier colony, just outside their complex of primary worlds.

"In what respect? To what keep were you attached?"

"I was attached to no keep. I simply wandered the planet for many months. I first learned your language when I was very young. Since then, much of my life has been focused on increasing my knowledge of your kind. This . . . personal walkabout, of sorts, was no different."

Usze appeared genuinely dumbfounded. *"And you remained alive? Yes, obviously you did, but . . ."*

"I encountered many of your people who were genuinely tired of war," she said, *"and were intrigued by the concept of a human who was simply traveling the planet, attempting to perfect her command of the language. Granted, I did develop a knack for learning who to stay away from, but for the most part, my time there was uneventful insofar as personal jeopardy was involved."*

"I am . . ." His voice trailed off as he sought the right word. *"Impressed, I think, would suffice."*

She shrugged. *"I appreciate the enthusiasm, but would not make more of it than it was."*

"You are downplaying your achievements. Khael'mothka is not a place for the faint of heart."

Quickly she changed the subject. *"I do not know much of you, Usze 'Taham. Only what I read in the preliminary materials that I was given. Would you do me the honor of giving me some detail about your background?"*

Luther thought, *Very clever.* If there was one thing that

dominant Elite males liked to do, it was to talk about themselves. By showing that she was interested, Vale gave Usze 'Taham the opportunity to play right into that.

Usze inclined his head slightly. *"Very well. I was born in the wilderness of Qivro, a place called Bothaes, in the Keep of Sumai. Our province was held in honor, as my uncle Toha 'Sumai was considered widely to be one of the greatest swordfighters in all of Sanghelios. He has passed since, but I held him in esteem as a youth and trained under him aggressively for several years. When I was of age, as is the custom, I left our keep and moved to the military bastions of Yermo, where the most notable war college of our people once existed, though it has now been reduced to rubble since the breaking of the Covenant. I graduated this school with top honors, having refined my ability with the sword and other weaponry a great deal, drawing attention from those in high places. When I was placed on the Fleet of Faithful Ardor, several political officials sought me out and wished to bestow upon me the title of Honor Guard, putting me in the service of the High Council. I had only served a single tour, so I, of course, refused this request, despite warnings to choose otherwise. This would not be the last time I was approached for the position, but ultimately I have always been less interested in ceremony and title than in deed and action: I was born to fight, and I fight very well, so I have little affection for any role that would keep me from what I was made to do. Such refusals do not come without a cost, however. Prior to the Great Schism, others sought to punish me and even take my life, but they would not succeed. My actions in combat, in the war and against my enemies, silenced all those who would contend with my standing. And it eventually led me to the service of our ascetic warriors as a liaison for the Covenant, which is, I suppose, one reason why the Arbiter handpicked me for this task. That and my former experience on the Ark."*

"That is very compelling," said Vale. She turned to Luther. "Did you get all that?"

"Between me and the comm device, I had it covered," said Luther. Then he became aware that, during the entirety of the conversation, the Huragok had continued to do nothing but float there. He turned to the Huragok and said in its language, <<If you could return to bringing the portal back online, I would very much appreciate that.>>

The Huragok stared in his general direction. Luther noted it had far too many eyes to all focus on him.

<<*Very well,*>> it replied after what felt like an insanely long pause. Then the tentacles, which had never actually dropped down into a relaxed position, returned to their work.

"This has been . . . interesting," Usze said, and then with no further words, he turned and walked away.

"That's a very vague word for him to use," commented Henry.

"Actually, no," said Vale. "For the Sangheili, it's a very important word, especially when it is referring to humans. If we say or do anything that interests them in any way, that's a very good thing."

Henry, who was still trying to figure things out from the notes he had been jotting down, turned back to watching the Huragok. "So what happens when it does get the portal opened?"

"We'll be following the protocol Captain Richards has already set in place," said Luther. "When the Excession is active, we scramble to her dropship immediately, which in turn takes us to her main vessel that's orbiting overhead. Once we go through the portal, the real job begins."

CHAPTER 6

T wo Earth days had passed since his arrival and nothing had been accomplished at the portal artifact. This was particularly aggravating to N'tho 'Sraom, who had fully expected that the Huragok would be able to finish the repairs to the portal more or less within a single daily cycle. Perhaps there was some truth to the humans' concern that irreparable damage may have been done to the Ark's end of the Excession, which might well mean that any effort on this end would be futile.

There was no denying the steady nature of Drifts Randomly's work, though. Aside from conversing with Luther Mann, the Huragok was incapable of being distracted from its assignment. Unfortunately, it also seemed oddly incapable of presenting any manner of prediction as to when its task would be completed. When asked about this, the Huragok did not even answer; instead its tentacle would shimmy in what appeared to be a Huragok approximation of a shrug. This was a bit startling to N'tho and Usze 'Taham since the other Huragok they had encountered prior had never seemed to have this emotional output as part of their physical repertoire. They had no idea whether it was a gesture that they had simply never noticed before or if the Huragok had somehow picked it up from the observing humans. And if it was the latter, N'tho found that particularly disconcerting.

Deciding that he needed to remove his mind from concerns over the apparent lack of progress, N'tho opted to get some training in. It had been a while since he had taken practice in the warrior arts. And given all that had taken place on the Ark when he was last there, it was unlikely that anyone could foretell what lay on the other side of the portal, whether for good or for ill. So it was much preferable to be prepared rather than caught unready.

N'tho found himself a relatively private area, a clearing some distance away from his dropship, and a little farther away from the incredibly vast disk that was the Forerunner artifact. There were some trees and brush nearby but nothing else. He began by doing some steady breathing exercises, slowing down his pulse until he had reached a point of inner peace. Then he proceeded to the actual physical manifestation—he whirled in place, activating and spinning his double-edged plasma sword around him in an elegant arc. Energy crackled as he moved this way and that in a delicate series of patterns. In his head, he was seeing enemies coming in from all sides, and he was combating them with practiced ease. Block, parry, block, thrust, one move following the next in a smooth motion. He began slowly at first, but the longer he continued, the faster he became. So much so, in fact, that the casual bystander may have had difficulty keeping an eye on the sword at all.

He lost track of how long he practiced. But he was suddenly aware of an observer. Having no idea whether the newcomer was hostile or not, he kept his blade extended as he spun around to see the new arrival.

It was one of the human soldiers—the Spartan he had encountered his first day here. He had not seen him since, and now he was fully adorned in the customary armor of kind, minus his helmet. The armor of demons. *What was his name again . . . ?*

"You are . . . Kodiak?" said N'tho. Slowly he lowered the blade. "Spartan Kodiak, yes?"

"That's correct," said Kodiak.

Kodiak then proceeded to say nothing. But it was what he was holding in his hand that instantly captured N'tho's interest.

It was a plasma blade, but slightly different from the one that N'tho was wielding. The weapon Kodiak held was of the Covenant stock, aesthetically designed by the Prophets, whereas N'tho and Usze were using a much more rugged vintage of energy blades, harkening ancient Sangheili heritage, of which there had been a philosophical resurgence after the war.

"Where did you acquire that?" said N'tho slowly.

"Where do you think?"

"From the body of a dead Elite, would be my supposition."

"That's right. Does it bother you that I've killed your kind?"

"In the course of war? Death happens. It is the price and custom of warfare. My only hope would be that his death was honorable."

"Oh yes. I'm all about honor."

He ignited the weapon and the blade snapped to life with such immediacy and force that N'tho was momentarily startled by it, mostly by the fact that the human dared to wield it near him. "Have a care," N'tho said. "It is not a weapon designed for humans, and you could injure yourself."

"Do you have a problem with a human wielding it?"

Something in Kodiak's tone caused N'tho to feel defensive, but he had no idea why he should. Certainly this soldier wasn't a threat. They were working toward the same goal, after all, united in their cause to stop the Halo rings from firing. And there had now been, for some time, a peace treaty in place between their races. What possible danger could this human pose?

"No, of course I do not have a problem with that."

N'tho took several steps to the right and noticed that Kodiak promptly took several to his left. He was countering N'tho's moves, as if they were engaging in combat. N'tho considered that odd; nevertheless, he kept his defenses up although he had no idea why that should be necessary. "What are you doing, Spartan Kodiak?"

"I was simply admiring your fighting style."

"Indeed. There are many techniques that the Sangheili have mastered that are not familiar to humans."

"Really. Would you be willing to teach them to me?"

"I am not certain that doing so while wielding live weapons would be advisable."

Kodiak seemed to draw himself up. "I'm a Spartan," he said. "We *only* train with live weapons."

He was casually sweeping his blade back and forth, as if loosening up his arm.

"Very well. As you wish." N'tho continued to move. He was doing so in a deliberately casual fashion and watching how Kodiak responded, as if they were already sparring. "I am now curious as to the exact circumstances under which you acquired your blade."

"Attempting to distract your opponent is a common ploy," said Kodiak. "Perhaps later I'll provide details."

"I can understand your hesitation. Those were brutal times," said N'tho. "We all did many things that we are not proud of."

"Everything that I did was in the interest of protecting my people from the Covenant. If I had to, I would do it again."

"It must give you great peace of mind to have such a lack of scrutiny over your own actions."

"You're aware we weren't the ones picking the fight to begin with, right? You came and attacked us. And billions died."

"Those times are past, and now we are allies."

The Spartan said nothing. Instead he suddenly came right at N'tho, swinging the sword around and aiming straight at his head.

N'tho brought his own sword up quickly, barely managing to deflect the blow. Energy rippled from the blades, shaking N'tho's so violently that he nearly dropped it. He was able to maintain his grip, but it was a near thing. This human was surprisingly strong.

Kodiak took a step back and then whipped his blade back around, cutting low. Again N'tho was able to intercept. His practiced mind was dissecting Kodiak's assault, analyzing it so that he could be ready for the next move.

It proved to be more difficult than he thought. The Spartan, unlike most who N'tho had battled, wasn't operating in any sort of pattern. He was coming at the Sangheili with a variety of cuts and slashes that were seemingly at random. No strategy, no plan. Just incessant attacking generated by—

By what? What could be going through the Spartan's mind that would prompt him to attack N'tho—an ally—in this manner?

Because this was most definitely no training exercise, or some practice session. The Spartan had shown up looking for a fight, and it was abundantly clear that he wasn't holding back.

They circled each other, both of them now more cautious. "Would you like to tell me what this is all about, human?" said N'tho.

"We're just practicing," said Kodiak, and then he charged once more. N'tho backed up, blocking each thrust, becoming more frustrated that he was unable to determine any manner of consistent attack pattern. The Spartan was, as the human colloquialism said, all over the place.

"No, we're not," said N'tho. "You are being less than candid with me."

The plasma swords slammed together, again and again. N'tho

felt no fear in combat situations, which was a normal state of being for him. If matters were to go against him, he would simply find a way to compensate. As a Sangheili, his eventual triumph was never in doubt.

But the Spartan wasn't slowing down, and showed no sign of fatigue, as a typical human did during a protracted battle. If anything, his foe's strength seemed to be increasing.

It made no sense. What did this human have against him?

And as his mind raced, a thought occurred to N'tho—a possibility that would go a long way toward explaining the man's undeniable fury.

Kodiak lunged and N'tho sidestepped, causing the human to miss his Sangheili opponent. N'tho spun and swung his sword around, but the Spartan recovered with incredible speed, blocking the Elite's attack. The plasma swords crackled against each other and the two warriors froze in position, pushing against each other, their blades trembling from the protracted contact.

"We've fought before, have we not?" said N'tho.

The Spartan didn't reply.

"I thought as much. You should know that I cannot recall ever meeting you in battle. So tell me, human: What did I do to you?"

Kodiak suddenly stepped back, moving so quickly that N'tho stumbled slightly before righting himself. Without a word Kodiak decoupled and yanked off his armored gauntlet, and the gleam of his metal hand shone in N'tho's eyes. He clicked his fingers together; it sounded oddly like a soft ore bell used by Sangheili children for play, but not quite clanging.

"The entire arm?" said N'tho slowly.

Kodiak nodded.

Suddenly N'tho moved quickly. He stepped forward and swept his leg between the Spartan, knocking him off his feet. Kodiak fell heavily but didn't stay on the ground; instead he rolled several feet away and then sprang upward, once more facing N'tho.

"You want to kill me," said N'tho, with softness that surprised even him. "I suppose I do not blame you. I cannot allow it, of course, but your thirst for vengeance is understandable. So what do you want? My life? Is that the only thing that will suffice?"

"I'm a Spartan," said Kodiak. "I'm a soldier and I'm trained to complete my mission, no matter the cost. Killing you would be in violation of that mission."

"Are you telling me you won't? Or are you explaining to me the rules that you are about to ignore?"

Kodiak began to respond, but his next words were not to be heard, because at that moment the world around them exploded.

Luther Mann was fairly certain that he had no reason to look forward to the meeting on Captain Richards's insistence, and now it was turning out that his concerns were justified.

He and Henry Lamb were seated opposite the captain, who was standing behind her desk and leaning forward on her fists—a rather aggressive posture, which further added to Luther's concern.

"Do you have any idea," Richards was saying to him, "how much scrutiny is on this project right now? I've got UNSC branch heads and ONI brass breathing down my neck and we're two days in with zero progress. Explain, doctor!"

Luther opened his mouth to respond, but was cut short.

"Or do you know how many people we have employed here? Engineers, technicians, security?"

"From my understanding, most recently, the tally has climbed to two hundred and twenty seven."

"Then you must know that leveraging this many assets for an ONI project without any results is not a good scenario for us. Not for me. And certainly not for you. Do you understand?"

"Yes, I'm aware," said Luther.

Richards didn't seem to have heard him. "Listen, Doctor, my job here is pretty straightforward. I'm to direct the efforts to bring the Excession artifact online, and you two are the ones who are actually supposed to be making it happen. Once you achieve that, I'm to take our team aboard the *Endeavor* and bring it through the portal safely, at which point we'll be relying exclusively on you two once again."

"I'm aware of that, too," Luther assured her. "I attended two separate briefings before I came here. I know what is supposed to happen, Captain."

"But that's *not* what's happening," Richards said as if Luther hadn't even spoken. "If we can't even trust you two to get the portal back online, then how the hell do you expect me to be comfortable with you having any part in the operation once we get groundside on the Ark? This isn't going to be a walk in the park, Doctor Mann. Getting the Excession online is the *easy* part of this whole gig. You two better hope that this is really an end-of-the-world scenario . . . because if it's not, ONI's going to make us all wish it were."

Luther simply sat there and stared at her.

"What?" she said impatiently.

When he spoke, his voice was filled with sympathy. "I cannot even imagine what you are going through right now, Captain Richards. I know who your superiors are. I know the reports that you have to be making back to them right now. None of it is positive. You are reporting, to people who have trusted you, that thus far this project is getting nowhere, and they are coming down on you like the hammers of hell."

"My pressures are none of your concern, Doctor."

"They very much are," said Luther, "especially if you are coming to me now and making declarations of what is going to happen and you are clearly barely holding yourself together."

"Doctor—"

"I believe I was speaking, Captain, and it is also my understanding that your superiors would want you to hear my words in this matter. May I continue?"

Her jaw worked for a moment, but only instead of saying everything that was running through her mind, so she kept it to herself and simply nodded.

Luther stared at her for a bit and then said, "She's nine."

Richards blinked, not understanding. "I'm sorry?"

"She's nine. My little girl. Her name is Theresa. The result of an incredibly exciting six-week relationship with her mother in college—"

Luther allowed a small smile at the thought. He would fully admit that he didn't have much congress with the opposite sex during that time, but Ramona was . . . well, she was quite something else. She crushed his defenses like no woman before or since, which, he thought, wasn't really difficult since there hadn't been any other woman before or since. Six weeks, and then she was expelled because of a magnificent practical joke that she played on the dean. And she left. Luther offered to go with her, because he was young and foolish and Ramona was intelligent enough to know that it was a stupid idea. So he remained in school, and a year later she sent him a picture of her with a baby that he had no idea even existed. *My baby. My Theresa.*

He tried to find her and had no luck doing so. Ramona told him that she existed out of . . . generosity, he supposed. But she didn't want to impinge on his life, and she never gave Luther the opportunity to tell her that he wanted to be a part of it.

"I've never held her, never spoken to her. Never touched her. But like any parent, I want the world, the sun, and the stars for her. And I will be damned, Captain," and his voice was trembling, "if I am going to let all sentient life in the galaxy end before she has a chance to live her own. Do you understand? I don't really give much of a damn what happens to me, but I am going to do it for her. I am not going to let Halo activate, and I need you to trust me on that."

She put up her hands and he promptly fell silent. She took in a deep breath and let out a sigh. "All right, Doctor," she said, "let's—"

It was at that moment that the captain's comm unit went off. She glanced at it and her expression immediately changed. "Excuse me," she said, and tapped it. "Richards here. Go ahead."

Vale was unable to keep the excitement from her voice. *"Captain, this is Vale. The Huragok was successful. The portal has been activated and is coming online right now."*

Richards's jaw fell open in astonishment, but before she could say anything, there came a distant humming, and then the walls around them vibrated.

It was quite obvious that something huge was powering up.

"Oh my God," she whispered.

"Just think," said Henry, turning to Luther. "Five more minutes and you could have saved that whole speech."

Luther ignored Lamb's caustic effort at humor and attempted to keep his voice level and calm. "It would probably be best if I get to the site and supervise the—"

And that was when all hell broke loose.

Usze 'Taham found Olympia Vale to be one of the more interesting humans that he had ever encountered.

At one point, she told him about a very important thing that had happened to her when she was a child. When she was eleven years old, by human reckoning, her parents "divorced," a concept completely foreign in Sanghcili culture, and one that needed to be explained in detail to Usze. Her mother, who was rising in the ranks of Navy signal intelligence (another foreign concept), had been promoted to captain and was on her way to her reassignment on Earth. But their trip home had gone terribly awry when the slipspace drive had failed, and a journey that should have taken six days instead became six months.

The ship's crew had consisted of three people plus little Olympia, and they had gone nearly insane with her incessant questions. Eventually she was shunted aside and left on her own. To occupy her time, she had taught herself the Sangheili language by listening to recordings and comparing them to AI translations, some of which she eventually proved were wrong. Evidently, this was a remarkable thing for any human to do, no less one so young.

That had been the beginning of her obsession with the Sangheili race.

If that wasn't enough to find her interesting, nothing was.

The Huragok was deep in another section of the artifact, one that, to be honest, seemed almost indistinguishable from any of the others, so far as Usze was concerned. He did notice that there were far fewer glyphs lining the walls here, that much was certain. There was also more twisted, ancient circuitry in this place. When he had originally come down there hours earlier, the circuits had seemed dead. But now streams of light were slowly pulsing through them.

Usze took a moment to glance at the Huragok. Its tentacles were continuing in an endless series of movements that made sense only to the mostly silent creature. Truth be told, Usze had an aversion to the Huragok. He didn't understand how they worked or functioned or viewed the world around them—all they did was repair, and he couldn't imagine being that singly focused on any activity. But he decided not to concern himself about it. As long as the Engineer was continuing to do its assigned task, why should a Sangheili worry about it?

Vale was seated on the floor, going over notes that she had made on her datapad.

"That must have been quite some trove of language you translated when you were a child, to be so knowledgeable," he said to her.

She shrugged. "I have no idea how much. Thousands upon thousands of words, I suppose."

"That is quite exceptional."

"Perhaps," she said, and then gave him a peculiar look. "Why don't you sit down? I've never seen you sit."

"There is no purpose to sitting," said Usze. "All it does is contribute to a lack of preparedness should any difficulty present itself."

"You mean you're anticipating that you may have to be in a fight at any time and you want to be ready for it?"

"Always." He noticed she was making some sort of human sound. "What is that noise you're making?"

"It's called 'chuckling.'"

"Is that a variation on human laughter?"

"It is, yes."

Usze's mandibles winced momentarily in an expression of disgust.

Vale was able somehow to discern that. "Not much for laughing, are you?"

"Human laughter is ridiculous," he replied. "The expression that humans have when they laugh makes them seem frightened or threatened."

"To you, maybe. Not to us. However, if you prefer, I will do my very best to smother any tendency to laugh."

"That would be appreciated."

The Huragok abruptly floated up to her. This in itself was rather surprising. Aside from the few times that it had actually communicated to her, the Engineer had been perfectly content to ignore her in the same way it did everyone and everything else that didn't require repair. Now, though, it was heading straight for Vale.

Usze was slightly alarmed, in that the Huragok was going to the human rather than the Sangheili, as it did with the doctor earlier. Such a development would have driven hardline Covenant zealots to utter madness not very long ago. Usze had no idea how the Huragok formed bonds with individuals, but now this one was clearly headed to Vale for some reason.

Its tentacles were moving in specific patterns and it was whistling at her as well, in what could be construed as borderline excitement. "It says that the installation . . . is fixed," said Usze in mild surprise, the communications device serving to translate the Huragok for him.

Vale immediately rose to her feet. "Wow. Okay, then. There's going to be an army of personnel who are going to want a minute-by-minute breakdown of everything it did. Starting with Luther and Henry."

"I very much doubt that will be of use. No one understands how the Huragok perform their repair tasks. I am not even certain they comprehend it themselves. It is simply part of what they are." He was sending a series of signs at the Huragok. "I am now asking how long it will take to activate the portal itself."

Beneath their feet, the ground was beginning to rumble.

"I . . . think it already did," said Vale.

There was an exit thirty meters down the hallway. All around them, as Vale and Usze hurried toward it with the Huragok buzzing behind them, the pulsing lines of circuitry were now firing into full effect. The speed and the brightness both increased by tenfold within mere seconds.

They dashed into the elevator, and as the doors slid shut, Vale hit her communications link. "I need to speak to the captain immediately."

A few moments passed, and then she heard Richards's voice on the other end. *"Richards here. Go ahead."*

With no preamble, Vale said, "Captain, this is Vale. The Huragok was successful. The portal has been activated and is coming online right now."

The elevator shook violently for a moment and then seemed to regain control of itself. Richards didn't respond and Vale repeatedly hit the communications unit. "Captain? Captain!" Nothing. She had lost connection.

The elevator doors slid open, and Vale, Usze, and Drifts Randomly raced out onto a landscape in chaos. Machinery created thousands of years ago was now coming to life. Nearby trees were swaying, flocks of birds rising into the air, and various small animals ran in confusion in response to the quake. Usze noted humans also moving frantically about the large landing strip and adjacent facility. Despite the appearance that a massive earthquake had struck and would swallow them all, the ground remained intact and no fault crevices were noticeable. From the distance, he could see that the buildings were shaking but enduring the test of their structures and managing to hold together. Some four-legged, hooved animals with horns, somewhat resembling a variety of *keifra* found on Sanghelios, were panicking, though, trying to find some place that didn't seem determined to shake itself to death. Some of them ran directly in their path. Vale attempted to sidestep them, and Usze simply kicked them out of his way.

But that wasn't the extent of all that was transpiring.

The pylons surrounding the vast core of the Forerunner machine were now slowly rising, many thousands of meters high. It was the first time that they were clearly exposed, huge, towering triangles that reached toward the sky.

The core, at the center of the artifact a great distance away from their position, was beginning to charge with power as well. Usze saw before he heard the sound that was starting to emanate from it, and then the sound caught up with the faraway light. The energy was building up, faster and faster.

And then it was unleashed. The core came to life and a powerful beam of light blasted upward. It had been a blue, cloudless day over the city of Voi, but now a twirling circuit of purple energy was ripping time and space open, and a violent brooding storm suddenly took form.

Vale and Usze could only stop and stare. "Incredible," she breathed. Apparently she had never seen a portal before, and even Usze had to admit that experiencing one for the first time could certainly be overwhelming.

Then the Sangheili's eyes narrowed. The portal was activated, that much was certain. But—

"Something is coming through," he announced.

"What?" That surprised the hell out of Vale. The only thing on the other end was the Ark, and surely that didn't have the capability to send something through in reverse. Henry's note about the previous "disappearances" at the Ark suddenly came to the front of her mind. . . .

Usze 'Taham was unquestionably correct. Something was starting to emerge from the portal hole. It was clearly a vessel of some sort. Vale stood there, wide-eyed, in amazement. She had never seen anything like it.

The object was only slightly smaller than the average UNSC frigate, and almost looked as if it were alive. It reminded Vale of a mythical sea creature. It was a dark gray machine, the lower section lined with several mechanical legs, like tentacles, that were moving about as if searching for something. The upper section was vast and wide like a tortoise shell. There were glowing lights on the thing's front that, although they were certainly not intended for it, reminded Vale of great eyes that were studying the surface below.

"What the hell is that?" murmured Vale.

Usze immediately had the answer. "It's a Strato-Sentinel. It's one of the automated drones the Forerunners use on their artificial worlds. The Covenant originally thought them to be holy warriors of the Sacred Rings. There are many types of Sentinels that the Forerunners created—this particular one is designated as a Retriever."

"How do you know so much about them?"

"You would be amazed at the various facts that warriors must learn in order to survive in the battlefield. I have seen them before, when we were on the Ark—we witnessed them mine the installation's moon in order to fabricate the replacement Halo."

"So it's a mining device?"

"Our records indicate that it employs an artificially produced gravitic force to remove minerals from a planet's surface. Those minerals in turn are used to build Forerunner structures and installations."

"But why is it here?"

"Something on the Ark might have sent it through," said Usze grimly. "To obtain minerals in order to effect repairs."

"So you're saying that—"

Suddenly the underside of the Retriever began to glow. It was hovering several kilometers away from Usze and Vale, but it still seemed terribly close.

At that moment, a vast blue beam blasted down from the Retriever. The instant it struck the ground, the earth began to tremble. Vale bolted in the opposite direction, with Usze and the Huragok right behind her.

What struck her most of all was how silent it was. She heard some sort of grinding at the point where the beam was hitting the ground, but the beam itself was making no noise at all. She supposed it made sense, if its energy was genuinely gravitic.

Then, to her shock, she saw the ground starting to swirl upward, as if a tornado was being created on the spot. Pure energy ripped through everywhere it struck, chunks of the planet's surface caught in the grip of the gravity beams and hauled into the underbelly of the Retriever.

She only realized that she'd stopped running to gawk at what was happening when she was abruptly hauled off her feet. Vale let out a startled shriek as the Sangheili scooped her up and slung her over his shoulder as he ran past. "We cannot remain here!" he said.

"Put me down!"

"As soon as we are out of danger."

Vale had to admit that, despite her terror, Usze's actions were all rather impressive. He didn't run so much as fly across the ground, his legs moving so quickly that they were a blur to Vale. Part of her hated the concept of surrendering her ability to move thanks to a Sangheili who was carting her like a duffle bag . . . but damn, was he fast.

Even more amazing—the Huragok was keeping up with them.

She had never seen the Engineer move in anything except slow motion, but now it was buzzing through the air so quickly that Vale realized it could likely leave Usze in its wake if it were so inclined. Instead it kept perfect pace with him. She had no idea how, but it was clearly with maximum efficiency.

"*What are we going to do?!*" she called to Usze over the sound of the ground being devastated several kilometers away.

"Deal with the Retriever, certainly," said Usze. "We need to find N'tho, and quickly."

The world around N'tho 'Sraom had become very confusing.

The last thing he recalled was the battle with the Spartan, who appeared determined to kill him because N'tho had cut off his arm during the war. N'tho had to admit that it certainly made a much better reason than many others he could name.

And suddenly everything had gone black.

Now the Sangheili had come to, but when he tried to stand, he was unable to do so. He quickly discovered the reason why: there was a tree pinning him down. And it was heavy.

Noise began to fill his ears. It took him a moment to realize what it was and where it was coming from.

"A Retriever . . . ?" he muttered, seeing the Forerunner machine high in the sky, remembering them from his time on the Ark. This Retriever was carrying out its design function by tearing the ground apart. Its actions had sent rumbling through the underground, knocking over all manner of things, and one of them had apparently been this tree that was now lying across him.

He shoved against the trunk with all his strength but was unable to budge it. He glanced around for his plasma sword and saw it lying on the ground several meters away, still powered up. He stretched his arm toward it, but his efforts were futile. It was simply too far away.

Where is the Spartan?

The thought flittered across his mind and he looked around, wondering if Kodiak was even still alive or if he had been felled by something equally formidable.

There. The Spartan was standing barely three meters away and was fortunate enough to be unharmed. He was holding his own glowing sword and staring at the fallen Sangheili.

It was only at that moment when N'tho realized the depth of trouble he was now in. He was defenseless, entirely at the vengeful Spartan's mercy.

But if this was to be N'tho's fate, then so be it. During the war, he had slaughtered the humans—the defilers, as they were claimed to be by the Prophets—in the name of the Covenant and the Path to the Great Journey. Some of them begged for mercy before they died, yet the Covenant was relentless in its brutality. N'tho 'Sraom did not beg. Not ever. If he were to die now, he would do so as a warrior and not some sniveling coward.

If the Spartan was aware of the Forerunner machine in the area and the damage it was inflicting on his beloved home planet, he didn't show it. Instead his attention was entirely focused on N'tho.

He strode slowly toward the Sangheili, holding his sword out as if he were anticipating some sort of impossible thrust that would stop him. His eyes blazed as he drew closer, until he was standing just a half-meter away from his target, staring coldly at N'tho . . . no, *through* him, as if the Elite wasn't even there.

Neither of them spoke for a long moment.

N'tho thought of all the things he could have said right then. *Is this how a warrior seeks revenge? Will you be proud of yourself when you walk away from my corpse? Will you boast of your accomplishment of defeating a helpless opponent, human, or will you keep it to yourself? Profess ignorance of what happened to me when my body is discovered? Will this triumph satisfy you?*

He asked none of these questions out loud.

Instead he simply stared at Kodiak, not blinking, not looking away. In the end, there was really nothing for him to say.

Kodiak drew the plasma sword back and then swept it down toward N'tho. The energy blade crackled as it came in contact with the tree and sliced right through it. The bisected trunk split in both directions and fell away, freeing the Sangheili.

Then the Spartan deactivated the sword and locked it onto his thigh's armor plating. He did not offer N'tho a hand to stand up, but instead just kept looking at him, as if the Sangheili were some sort of strange creature that had just fallen planetside rather than a mortal enemy of his species—and whether that current designation was the former or otherwise remained to be seen.

N'tho rolled to his feet and grabbed the hilt of his own still-activated sword, but Kodiak had already turned and was walking away.

"Why did you not kill me?" N'tho called out.

The Spartan stopped and remained with his back to the Sangheili. "I said I wasn't going to. I tell the truth. Granted, I was considering severing your arm in kind, but . . ." He shrugged. "So . . . what is that thing?"

"It's a Retriever," N'tho replied, deactivating the blade. "I know that because—"

"I don't care. All I care about is, how do we stop it?"

"We need to get to my ship."

"We may not have to."

Sure enough, combat had already been undertaken. The UNSC cruiser—the *Endeavor*—was descending from its orbital perch, bearing down on the Retriever. Its big guns opened fire on the Forerunner machine, pummeling it with as much ferocity as the ship could muster.

The Retriever immediately turned its attention from the planet's surface to the incoming ship. The beam that had been churning up the ground with tornado-like force shifted and directed its energy toward the oncoming vessel. The *Endeavor* angled away as it continued to pound on the Retriever with its armament. The one advantage that the humans had at this point was that the Retriever was not designed as a battleship, and consequently had little to no shielding.

But it was not without its own offensive capabilities. N'tho and Kodiak watched fixedly as the Retriever's gravitic beam angled upward toward the *Endeavor*. The UNSC ship's thrusters drove it up as the big guns cut loose, hammering the Retriever. The Retriever shook as if tearing itself apart, yet continued to target the *Endeavor*. The *Endeavor* cut hard to port and suddenly the Retriever's beam angled sharply over, much faster than it had seemed capable of moving. The beam enveloped the *Endeavor*, and the UNSC vessel started spinning in midair. Yet that did not deter whoever was commanding *Endeavor*, as the ship's guns continued to blast away at the Retriever.

N'tho and Kodiak watched in silence, utterly helpless to do anything to affect this decisive battle's outcome.

And then, just as it seemed that the *Endeavor* was about to be ripped apart by the gravitic beam, much like the ground beneath it, a gout of white flame erupted from the Retriever's underside. "*Yesss,*" said Kodiak, and he was right to be pleased. The Retriever vibrated and the gravitic beam that was wrapped around the *Endeavor* vanished. The *Endeavor* stopped spinning and, sensing its impending victory, seemed to redouble its efforts, its weapons firing on the Retriever in response.

In the sky, the human ship had now been joined by dozens of smaller craft, all rising from the nearby complex and together unleashing a fusillade of firepower from their own weapons. Small explosions flashed all around the Forerunner machine and then, seconds later, it detonated in a massive ball of flame.

"Your vessels are quite formidable," said N'tho.

"Damn right."

"Granted, they defeated a Forerunner device that was not designed for combat situations, but still . . . an impressive performance."

The Spartan cast him a sideways glance that apparently indicated the human was not amused.

N'tho ignored him. Instead he was studying the now-open portal swirling in the darkened sky overhead. "We need to go through."

"The portal?"

"Yes."

"We can't just go flying through it."

N'tho was walking with great strides in the direction of his dropship. "My understanding is that that was the plan."

"That was before something came through it the moment it was open and attacked us. We have no idea what's waiting for us on the other side."

"If you are afraid, you may remain behind."

"I'm not afraid," said Kodiak, walking as quickly as he could to keep up with N'tho's pace. "I simply want to know what we're getting into."

"There is only one way to find out, and that is to enter it."

The various engineers and security personnel who had earlier been running around the humans' airfield, frantic and confused, now stood still. They were all staring toward the sky. Some were taking notes, others were recording the event on small devices. Since the ground had ceased rumbling and the portal had opened, their initial concern had given way to curiosity.

"We need to confer with the others and determine the best course of action," said Kodiak.

"As you wish. Arrange it and I will attend."

"A Retriever," said Captain Richards, clearly confused. "What the hell is a Retriever?"

In her office, Luther quickly outlined the Forerunner machine's purpose. "It's quite an extraordinary device," he concluded.

"Extraordinary? It attacked us, and my ship's commander had to blow it out of the sky."

"It was simply doing what it was designed to do by the Fore-runners. And when we get to the Ark—"

"That's fantastic," Richards interrupted, "but I can tell you right now we aren't going anywhere. That Retriever came through blasting away, and where there's one, there may be more. A lot more. So we're staying put until I get some support from Home Fleet here. You understand me, Doctor?"

"To the letter, Captain," replied Luther.

CHAPTER 7

The gathering, at N'tho's request, was held on the *Mayhem*, the Sangheili vessel in low orbit above Earth. The bridge on N'tho's corvette was quite large for a ship of its size and was easily able to accommodate everyone who had shown up: Captain Richards, Spartans Kodiak and Holt, Olympia Vale, Luther Mann, Usze 'Taham, the Huragok, and Henry Lamb, as well as a number of Sangheili who appeared to staff the vessel's control center. Richards had also brought her lieutenant, Carl Radeen, and a fireteam of marines with her, who were situated in the corvette's hangar at the Condor they had used to board. When N'tho had asked why Richards felt the need to have troops accompanying her, she simply said, "It is standard procedure for a captain to have security protection when entering a Sangheili ship. My apologies if that offends you."

"I take no offense at it at all," N'tho said. "Were I in your position, entering a vessel that was captained by former enemies, I might be persuaded likewise. And may I add that I was quite impressed with the way your vessel handled the Retriever."

"I wish we didn't have to destroy it," she said, "but I don't believe we had a choice."

"No, of course not—you did what was required. And now *we* must do the next thing that is required."

"True," said Richards. She was seated at one end of a long table, around which everyone had gathered. The corvette's bridge was composed of an encompassing perimeter platform surrounding a number of control consoles, with a large holographic projection of the portal site at the very center. The conference table had appeared via risers just off to the side. "But for the time being, my superiors have deemed that this mission remain on hold until a supporting fleet can arrive."

Luther Mann looked uncomfortably around the table, waiting for someone to say anything in protest. When no one did, however, he cleared his throat, deciding that he had to be the first to speak up. "But it was my impression that the entire purpose for this excavation was to do exactly what the Huragok over there managed to accomplish. It got the portal open. So why are we waiting around?"

"Yes, it did get the portal online," said Richards, "and look what happened. We were instantly under attack. We have to assume that the longer the portal remains open, the greater the chance that we'll get the same result. We have risk analysts at Sydney—"

"It could be argued that if we entered the portal now, we would be prepared for it and consequently not caught off guard so easily," said N'tho.

"We cannot assume that," Richards replied. "This time one of those machines got through. If we enter the portal, there's no way we know exactly what we'll find on the other side, but given the last two hours, quite probably more of those machines. And if we continue now, these things could come through from the opposite direction and shut down the portal behind us. Cut off our way back home."

"That could be true," Lamb said, sitting forward, "but what other option do we have? We don't exactly have time on our side."

"Clearly," she continued, "nevertheless, this operation is being facilitated by ONI, and we're calling the shots. Right now, there's simply too much risk to Earth. The portal needs to be shored up by Fleet and examined until we have a clearer idea of what to expect."

N'tho exchanged a glance with Usze 'Taham, and it was Usze who responded. "I very much doubt that you will be able to convince us that your one world outweighs the value of a thousand others, whether human or not. You also need to understand that there are still those Sangheili who are very much opposed to the fact that we now have a peace treaty with the humans . . ."

"As there are humans who feel much the same regarding the Sangheili," Richards shot back, and then added as an after-the-fact moderation: "No offense to present company. But our high view of Earth shouldn't be terribly shocking to you, given the last thirty years . . . and given that history, it shouldn't come as any surprise that there are those of my people who absolutely still carry hostility for you and your kind."

"I am quite aware of that," said N'tho. His gaze was fixed on Richards, but she couldn't help but think that he was glancing at Spartan Kodiak as he said that. She wondered what, if anything, could have already gone on between the two of them, but decided that it wasn't anything she could focus on right now.

Now it was Luther who chimed in. "Look, the Halo Array is counting down to fire, and the Ark remains our best—actually, very likely our *only*—way of preventing that. There was just one Sentinel sent through the portal, and it's clear that its intention was not immediately hostile. It was mining for resources. We destroyed it, and there haven't been any others in the interim, so I'm inclined to believe that whatever was happening before has since abated. Given the stakes, and the fact that we don't really know how long it's going to take to get to the Ark and actually conduct this expedition, I don't understand why we're wasting time. We should be heading through the portal. Right now."

"Doctor, let me be clear if I wasn't earlier," Richards replied with a grave tone. "We're not heading through the portal until we've gotten the all-clear from my superiors. This site and this operation's viability are their jurisdiction and theirs alone. Not yours and not the Sangheili's. Once ONI's evaluated the risk and determined that Earth's security can be maintained, we'll continue with the operation as planned and take *Endeavor* to the Ark."

"That is unfortunate to hear," said N'tho. "We were assured of some manner of cooperation, but given the cost of such a delay, it seems an amendment is in order. We will just have to get to the Ark via a different means."

"And what means is that?" said Richards.

"Obviously," said N'tho, "we are going to use the *Mayhem* to leave through the Excession immediately."

Richards shook her head in exasperation. "We've been through this. This is our operation, and we're calling the shots. Heading through the portal now is *not* going to happen. We could wind up faced with an entire army of those things, or worse, an army could be deployed against Earth."

"It is a chance we are willing to take," said N'tho. "I am quite convinced that the power of my ship would be more than sufficient to deal with another threat, but I would be compelled to proceed even if I knew it wasn't. Surely you do not believe that your world's safety is worth risking the annihilation of all thinking life in the galaxy? I assure you, it is not."

"With all due respect, N'tho, you are welcome to feel that way, but that's hardly a binding decision upon ONI and the UNSC," said Richards. "This expedition must be a joint effort between yourselves and our government. You do not have the authority to proceed however you wish."

"I do not have authority?" N'tho sounded both surprised and amused. "May I ask on what grounds you make that assumption? So far as I can determine, this discussion has not led me to believe that this is anything resembling a joint effort. *We* activated the portal, and we can go through it whenever we please."

"All right," said Richards, clearly doing everything in her power to maintain her composure. "I'll put this as straightforwardly as I can: you cannot enter the portal because I am *telling you* that you cannot. I am an acting proxy for the Commander-in-Chief of the Office of Naval Intelligence in this room, and I am operationally in charge of this mission. As such, I have the authority to fully represent the UNSC's position here, and I am telling you that if you attempt to violate this order and you refuse to stand down, you will be contravening the peace accords of 2553 and breaking the stipulations of that agreement regarding the sovereignty of Sol territories. Such an effort would be considered an act of war. Do you understand *that*?"

"Yes," N'tho said.

Richards still wasn't satisfied. "So I've presented my wishes in a sufficiently clear manner? In that, there can be no misunderstanding?"

"Yes, you have made yourself abundantly clear," N'tho assured her.

"Do you have anything to say in response?"

"I do indeed," N'tho said. He placed his hands on his armrests. "I would suggest you remain seated. Please hold on."

"Wh-what do you mean?" Richards brow furrowed in confusion. "I don't—"

It was at that moment that the engines of the vessel roared to life. The upward thrusters flared and *Mayhem* moved aggressively forward. The ship had been hovering stationary several kilometers above the Kenyan savannah, a good distance north of the portal site—but in a matter of seconds, all that began to change.

Instantly Richards was on her feet, as were Spartans Kodiak and Holt. Everyone else in the room had quickly understood N'tho's instructions and remained in their chairs. The only one who wasn't the least put out by the ship's unexpected movement was the Huragok, who simply hung there in the middle of the room. Even its tentacles weren't shaking.

"Stop this ship, immediately!" bellowed Richards.

"I do not believe that will be necessary," N'tho said with calm. "This has already been planned prior to your setting foot on this vessel. I decided to allow you to come along out of respect for our alliance. You could consider thanking me, although I will not view it as a breach of etiquette if you opt not to do so."

Richards started to turn toward the door into the room, but N'tho continued with his mild detachment: "I would be careful were I you, Captain. Yes, you do have troops in our hangar, but what will you have them do? Order them to fight their way through the corridors of my ship? *My* ship? Do you truly believe that to be the wisest course of action?"

"You're intending to go through the portal right now?" she said, and at the same time she reached for her communications link.

"I would not bother with that," said N'tho. "I have already instructed my communications officer to block any attempt you might make to speak with your vessel. Consider this a boon. If your vessel attempted to interfere with the *Mayhem*'s path, it would not end well for those aboard. I have no desire to destroy your ship or kill more humans."

"You," she said as stiffly as she could manage, "are kidnapping a line officer of the UNSC."

"In truth, I am abducting a significant number of humans against their will," N'tho said. "However, since I am undertaking the mutually beneficial endeavor of attempting to save the entirety of both our species, I am hoping that sooner or later, you will overlook this tactic as you contemplate the greater good, as well as the fact that you're still alive."

Without hesitation, Spartan Kodiak reached into his holster and extracted his pistol. He aimed it straight at N'tho and said, "Bring us back down right now or you die."

No one in the room moved to interfere. It was entirely possible they were too intimidated. Kodiak was fully decked out in his Spartan armor, except for his helmet. Slowly N'tho stood up as the room continued to shake around them, the corvette continuing its course toward the portal. "After sparing my life, this is how you wish to end matters between us?"

"I'm not doing anything," said Kodiak, the gun remaining level. "You're bringing this all on yourself."

Sparing his life . . . ? Luther thought. *What's he talking about?* Apparently, he wasn't the only one taken aback by the comment, as the captain seemed to do a double take as well.

"You will not fire upon me," N'tho assured him.

"And why is that?"

Out of nowhere, a tentacle whipped out and encircled Kodiak's hand before he could pull the trigger, yanking the weapon out of his hand and sending it hurtling across the room. Usze casually grabbed it midair, as though Drifts had intended for him to receive it. He did not aim it at Kodiak but simply held it loosely at his side.

The Huragok lowered its tentacle and returned to its detached floating. Kodiak snarled: "I thought those things didn't fight!"

"They are capable of responding to an immediate threat," N'tho said. "In this case, it perceived that threat as you. The rest of you likewise have weapons," he said, inclining his head toward the others in the room. "Are you also going to threaten me? Do you truly want all-out war here and now?"

There was no response.

N'tho turned to a Sangheili near him. "Navigator, are we ready?"

"Yes, Commander" came the brisk reply.

Most of the room was still trying to figure out what was happening. Kodiak, for his part, seemed fixed in his own world of frustration.

Richards took a step forward and leaned on the conference table. "Do you have the slightest idea what you're doing? Again, this is an act of war."

"Yes," said N'tho matter-of-factly. He came around to Richards, and it seemed to Luther that the Sangheili had grown several inches taller. "And when we manage to save the galaxy, you are welcome either to condemn me or else to claim credit for yourself. Whichever path you choose is of little interest to me. I was given a task, and I will complete it."

N'tho and the other Elites turned to face the viewport and various monitors, apparently entirely unconcerned and leaving the humans to stare at one another.

"So. I guess we're going to the Ark a little sooner than planned," said Luther Mann, quietly to himself. "Let's hope it's a smooth ride."

By all accounts, it wasn't.

The *Mayhem* continued forward, though cautiously. The portal's immense energy output had created a series of violent storms on the outskirts of the artifact, so *Mayhem* would have to carefully thread the needle. N'tho had taken residence on the bridge's outer platform and was now surrounded by several of his officers. There were very few of them here, though—the vessel was, for the most part, highly automated. A crew of ten or more at most was required for operations. Three Sangheili were at their stations as N'tho strode to the middle of the bridge and stared at the large holographic version of the artifact and the portal it was projecting, as well as the location of *Mayhem* and other nearby human vessels that seemed aloof to the Sangheili ship. Through the expansive viewport, the portal could be seen in its full glory, a dark, spherical cloud of blackness immediately before them. The Huragok was floating nearby, and N'tho noticed that Olympia Vale and Luther Mann had stepped over to communicate with it.

<<How did you do it?>> Luther asked Drifts Randomly. <<Open the portal?>>

<<*I tricked it,*>> the Huragok replied.

<<Yes, but how?>> He shook his head. <<I don't understand.>>

Usze, who was standing behind him, said: "The Huragok has been doing far more than simply repairing the equipment. It has been bonding with it, overriding its security systems and deceiving it into thinking that another ship, one to which the artifact is compliant, was requesting entry."

"The keyship?"

"Yes, but that is likely not all that was done," Usze guardedly replied. "The truth is that there are elements to it that even the Sangheili and the Covenant did not understand. Drifts Randomly does understand, but it is not truly capable, I believe, of properly explaining it."

<<*Are* you capable of explaining it?>> Luther asked the Huragok.

<<*Explaining what?*>> it asked.

Luther appeared to contemplate that response, but ultimately decided against it. <<Nothing. Never mind.>>

Now Captain Richards and Spartan Kodiak had stepped onto the bridge as well, having warily rendezvoused with their troops in the hangar bay. N'tho fired her a glance, and Richards, aware of the niceties of how one is to conduct oneself on someone else's ship, said formally, "Permission to come aboard."

"You are already here, but permission is granted," N'tho said indifferently. "You may go wherever you wish on this ship, as long as you do not cause any trouble."

"We're being kidnapped. Why should I wish to start trouble?"

"You realize that I could have undertaken this mission on my own initiative," N'tho reminded her. "The fact that you are here is not an abduction but a . . . courtesy."

"I think we'll have to disagree on the definition of courtesy," Richards continued. "Though I am surprised how quickly you discarded our species' mutual peace accords for control of this operation."

"Surprised? What good is peace between our kinds, Captain, if all those who would enjoy it have perished?"

One of the Elite officers spoke up. "The storms around the portal have abated—we now have a window."

"Excellent. Take us in."

The *Mayhem* angled toward the enormous spherical breach in the sky, when another Retriever exploded through the portal.

And unlike its predecessor, this one was heavily armed.

Massive weapons mounted on its front immediately sighted the *Mayhem* and opened fire. Energy blasts ripped across the shielding and the ship trembled under the impact.

"Target and return fire," ordered N'tho. The *Mayhem* canted hard to port, avoiding some of the attack, and its own weaponry opened a salvo of flanking plasma cannons on the Retriever. The Forerunner machine attempted to pull free of it, but it was not remotely as maneuverable as the *Mayhem*.

"I thought Retrievers were just for mining and gathering minerals!" Captain Richards shouted over the sounds of battle. "What is that one doing with ordnance?"

"I am unsure," N'tho replied. "Perhaps when we've gone through we will be able to determine an answer."

"You're still planning to go?!"

"Of course. Sangheili are not deterred so easily. But first we'll deal with this interdiction."

The Retriever shuddered under the *Mayhem*'s relentless barrage as the Sangheili ship let loose an avalanche of heat-seeking plasma torpedoes. Sparks flew from the Retriever's energy weapons and then the entire vessel exploded in midair, a fireball of destruction tearing through the atmosphere and enveloping the *Mayhem*. The ship trembled slightly from the impact, but otherwise showed no signs of damage. Moments later, the fireball dissipated. The vast gateway remained open.

"Take us through," ordered N'tho.

Mayhem hurtled forward, and Olympia Vale found herself holding her breath, caught up in the drama of the moment. She didn't know what to expect when they passed through the Excession's portal, because she had never experienced anything like it in her life. She was, of course, familiar with slipspace travel, but this was something quite different.

As the Sangheili ship entered the portal, Vale's stomach heaved. She got an acid taste in her mouth and was frightened that she would suddenly vomit. She clamped her teeth together and managed to force everything back down as time and space twisted around her. Energy swirled across the viewscreen, and all she knew for sure was that reality was bending. Quickly, she glanced about to see how everyone else on the bridge was reacting.

There was N'tho, staring ahead fixedly, as was Captain Richards. Spartan Kodiak looked mildly dyspeptic, but he always appeared that way. Otherwise no other person on the bridge seemed the least bit impacted by her own dizzying experience.

Vale took a deep breath and then let it out slowly to steady herself. Her surroundings continued to lengthen, and then suddenly snapped back, as if they were a vast rubber band.

According to the viewscreen, they were now tunneling ahead into the bright aureoles of energy, an effect that would subside after a while, drifting into the pure, black, emptiness of slipspace.

"Now what?" said Vale. "Based on what I've been told, it was going to take weeks, even with us using the portal and the most advanced slipspace drives at our disposal. How fast can your ship get us there?"

"Not much faster, I'm afraid," N'tho said. "We're limited by the sheer distance that separates your world from the Ark, which is immense—even in slipspace. Do not fret; we've made the necessary accommodations for your people. And we will fly quickly."

Then the Sangheili commander approached N'tho, taking him to the side where Drifts Randomly had been deftly manipulating a holographic interface. Vale tried to interpret the conversation, but it was nearly impossible, even with her extensive understanding of their language and culture. When N'tho returned, however, she could tell that his color had changed significantly and he seemed to totter in a way that Sangheili, even strong males, do when they are confronted with something that challenges them.

"What was that about?" Vale asked.

N'tho Sraom took his time to answer, his eyes fixed on the viewport and the blackness of slipspace that engulfed his ship. "Something has changed on the other end of this portal. Something significant. Evidently, it will not take us weeks, but rather hours."

This time it was Luther who spoke up, lifting his head from a cone-like machine in the corner that he'd been examining closely. "How is that even remotely possible?" He couldn't believe it. No one could.

"We . . . have no idea."

Hours later . . .

The news that the Huragok had conveyed to N'tho proved true, and the *Mayhem* shot out high above the ancient Forerunner installation, crossing an inordinately massive chasm of space in an impossibly short amount of time. Everyone on board was still reeling from the shock of that discovery, but being in the location of the Ark itself was enough to distract them all for a moment.

Luther gasped when he saw it. Though it wasn't the first time that he had actually seen the Ark, it might as well have been; he had certainly viewed plenty of images and studied detailed holo-videos retrieved from sensor-and-scan units aboard *Forward Unto Dawn*, the frigate the UNSC sent here at the close of the war.

When marines were engaging in combat, their helmets were auto-loading real-time footage and data, as were a number of drones. That information had been transmitted to the *Dawn,* and when it—most of it, at least—returned, ONI plundered every last bit. He'd always been stunned by the endless beauty that was buried in each detail of this enormous structure, even though only a fraction of it had even been explored. It had been nothing less than a living testimonial to the ingenuity of the Forerunners, and he had often imagined what it would be like to actively explore it. But that had always seemed a pipe dream, until right about now.

The entirety of the Ark's vastness was there before him, and it was a breathtaking sight to behold. There was no absolute certainty as to how long the Ark had been here, although data acquired from the Halo rings indicated that it was created not long before them, likely more than one hundred thousand years ago—and it had been used primarily as a foundry for the Array's installations. There was a seemingly perfect circular expanse in the middle of it, which was where the Halo installations were constructed, surrounded by a large surface area that fanned out into eight curved petals, or spires, of varying sizes, giving the entire installation the look of a gargantuan starfish or, perhaps, a flower. Within the circular core there was an expanse with a solitary moon that Luther knew was used as a mine for the fabrication of the rings, yet here it appeared noticeably smaller than before, heavily deformed on at least one side, with several smaller chunks orbiting it. It certainly seemed as though it had been aggressively relied upon as a mining resource in the short years that had passed since *Forward Unto Dawn*'s escape.

And almost out of view, fixed in the space high above the installation's surface, Luther could see the Ark's artificial sun, a large structure that resembled the classic human space stations of the twenty-second century, with huge fanning solar panels splayed in every direction—except, these panels were generating light rather than gathering it.

From one tip to the other, the Ark superstructure itself was nearly 130,000 kilometers in all, and its surface harkened not only to memories of the footage he'd studied, but to dramatic changes as well.

The Ark had endured extreme amounts of damage when the Master Chief and the Arbiter had activated an unfinished Halo installation to stop the threat of the Flood. When the ring fired, it literally rent itself apart, and between the intense energy released from the Halo and the debris after its destruction, the Ark had been ravaged. And now Luther could see this damage from the viewport of *Mayhem* high above. While some areas remained vibrant blues, greens, whites, and browns, covered with swaths of clouds, others were scorched black or gray, revealing a latticework of Forerunner materials below. On a few of the Ark's spires, large pieces had been completely torn free, and one of the smaller spires had been almost fully broken off, seemingly held in place by tensile-like materials and gravity fields.

There was even a large chunk of what was apparently the obliterated Halo ring that had impaled the Ark in its central hub; it now stood forth like a dead, arcing tree, climbing thousands of kilometers into space. Although it was a good ways off, Luther thought he could make out debris raining down even now from the various parts of what was left of the ring, hitting the atmosphere and blooming into flame before crashing into the ground. He had never seen anything like it before.

Luther could also tell that the surface temperature and climate varied wildly in some places, likely because of the damage that the Ark had sustained. Some of the trauma had evidently led to a failure on the habitability system's part, and although portions of the installation were clearly recovering, others remained in extreme flux. So before any of them dared set foot on the surface, they would have to make certain the intended entry point was at a hospitable temperature and maintained some level of sustainability. And that was just the beginning of their worries. Atmosphere balances, gravity fluctuations, habitable survivability, and structural fidelity—there were probably a couple dozen things that they needed to make certain were in place before exploring this strange world.

The *Mayhem* descended quickly toward the surface of the Ark. Luther wondered where the Retrievers had come from. He could not see any near them, and all of the former data had shown them hovering around the moon in the central hub . . . but that was now completely vacant, as far as he could tell at this distance. He glanced at N'tho, who was focused on the holographic projection of the Ark that the Sangheili ship had constructed—the Elite was clearly searching for the same thing he was. And almost as if eliciting it, Luther turned to see something happen off on the port viewport.

A section of one of the spires began to slide open on the *Mayhem*'s approach, but, as Luther examined it further, it seemed too incredible to be really happening.

An enormous, ocean-size body of water opened up like a gargantuan floor had suddenly dropped out, its waters pouring down on all sides into a huge hole. From this distance, the aperture appeared small, but it undoubtedly constituted several dozen kilometers of surface. There was a brief flare, and then three motes of light emerged from it. Luther turned to the holographic projection, and it validated what he was dreading: the trio of motes was, in fact, fully armed Retrievers. Although still far away, they had emerged from the body of water and were now rising toward them.

"Target the incoming Retrievers," N'tho ordered. "Fire at will."

Mayhem's gunners immediately found that these Retrievers were much faster than their predecessors. They cut left and right, darting around the *Mayhem*'s blasts, and they began shooting back heavy volleys of energy. The great ship shuddered as the Retrievers' firepower hit home.

"Evasive maneuvers!" shouted N'tho. "Sehar! Return fire!"

"Yes, Commander!" shouted Sehar, who was presumably the weapons officer.

The *Mayhem* angled around and its plasma cannons ripped out at the three Retrievers, seemingly firing everywhere at once. It was more of a feint than anything else, Luther could tell, trying to buy time rather than expose itself to a direct hit.

The Retrievers hammered the *Mayhem* from all sides. Luther was knocked off his feet, as was Vale near the holographic display. She hit the ground hard, and he wondered if she was all right. But before he could act, Luther saw Spartan Holt running over to Vale and crouching over her, effectively protecting her body from the ship's violent jostling, which continued with each hit.

Luther also had an instant to see that Captain Richards and Spartan Kodiak had managed to grab hold of something, but his own grip came up a few inches short, just missing a railing that would have provided support. He fell to the floor, the sound of explosions all around him.

N'tho was shouting additional orders, but he couldn't understand the Sangheili with his ears now violently ringing. Despite the carnage and naval maneuvering outside, Luther was surprised to find that the Sangheili in N'tho's crew were largely unaffected. They were used to the whirl and frenzy of space combat, whereas he was not at all. But then Luther came to the conclusion that the ship might very well be shot down and either explode in space or crash onto the Ark's surface. The thought twisted his stomach.

He started to clamber to his feet and suddenly saw Kodiak gesturing wildly at him and pointing upward.

Luther looked up. Something had broken off from overhead and was falling straight toward him.

He dodged quickly to one side, but wasn't able to get entirely clear. Part of the bridge's ceiling struck him on the side of the head, and he tumbled backward. The force from *Mayhem*'s aggressive movement slammed Luther against the deck, and blackness suddenly overwhelmed him.

N'tho 'Sraom noticed some of the humans falling but didn't have the time to intervene. He was too busy shouting instructions as the *Mayhem* continued its furious skirmish with the Retrievers. He had ordered the corvette closer to the surface of the Ark in an effort to shake it free of its pursuers, using a large mountain range in the central hub to split the difference. In space, the new Retrievers' numbers and speed gave them a distinct advantage. On the surface, however, the *Mayhem* might have a chance. Granted, it was no nimble fighter, but N'tho didn't have many options at his disposal.

He was having great difficulty believing that their attackers were entirely automated. It should have been a simple effort to outmaneuver or overwhelm them, and yet the Retrievers were engaged in a pitched battle that rivaled anything N'tho had experienced during the war on the humans. They attacked in a concentrated fashion, almost as though controlled by a single pilot.

And with a loud snapping sound, *Mayhem*'s energy shielding was abruptly compromised, exposing its hull to damage.

However, the end now seemed close in sight. Launching deeper into the steep range of mountains, N'tho continued to order his ship to fire a bevy of plasma back at the pursuing Sentinels, which forced them into a frantic dodging game. At his command, the *Mayhem*'s crew then deployed a collection of low-yield antimatter mines that cluttered the narrow wake of the corvette. With that, two of the Retrievers were disposed of in a twin bloom of white-hot energy. And now N'tho was facing off against the third, wheeling back around to deal with it head-on, confident that, in a one-on-one battle, it would take only moments to—

Suddenly the *Mayhem* was hit so viciously that the vessel spun 360 degrees several times.

This shot hadn't come from the third Retriever. And this time, almost everyone within the bridge was thrown around, trying to find something they could grab onto and failing miserably.

The Spartan called Holt had lost his balance and been thrown away from Olympia Vale. But the Huragok had, with its tentacles, somehow managed to lift both humans, who were either dead or unconscious, so that as the ship spiraled, they were kept hovering safely in midair. Were it not for the immediate peril, N'tho might have voiced his wonder at the Huragok's impressive ability to hold the Spartan aloft, given the armored human's size and weight.

"Another Retriever!" called out the weapons officer.

N'tho had figured out that much. *But where had it come from?*

"Return fire!" he shouted.

The *Mayhem* shuddered repeatedly as the corvette was hit over and over again. For a brief moment, it regained stability and rose up from the Ark's surface to get some space between it and its attackers. Fortunately enough, this short respite allowed the

Mayhem to return fire, evidently stalling out their pursuers—but then something remarkable happened.

As *Mayhem* banked hard right to center up on the remaining Retrievers, the two machines suddenly connected and quickly became one. Although somewhat similar in shape to the individual Retrievers, this new machine was even more problematic, dodging and twisting away from the *Mayhem*'s blasts. It seemed to take on the benefits of both Retrievers' speed and weaponry, with no noticeable drawbacks.

A detonation resounded from deep within the *Mayhem*, and the weapons officer shouted, "We have lost the main cannons!"

N'tho quickly ran through his mind all of the options available against this newly combined, augmented Retriever. And with that, he gave the only order he could think of: "Ram it."

"Sir?" The helmsman's head snapped around, confusion on his face.

"If we have anything left in our shields, put it at the fore. Otherwise, full speed ahead! I want this vessel on a collision course!"

Captain Richards called out: "Are you sure about this?"

N'tho did not respond, but instead silently considered her question: *Our success in killing this machine? Absolutely. Our survival? Not at all.*

The *Mayhem* bolted forward, straight toward the Retriever. The Forerunner construct held its position, firing away at the oncoming Sangheili vessel.

Sparks now flew from the bridge control boards, and the immediate area began to fill with smoke. What little remained of the ship's energy shielding pitched toward the front of the corvette, which would provide a formidable barge, even if it only served to protect those in the bridge.

"Stay on course!" shouted N'tho.

Seconds later, the *Mayhem* slammed headlong into the Retriever, and many of N'tho's own people were sent reeling into the bulkheads or across the deck, despite the ship's internal gravity systems attempting to hold them to the floor and dampen the jarring inertial effects. The ancient Forerunner machine, however, was smashed apart, gigantic chunks of debris bursting into flame and spiraling everywhere. The corvette's shielding had held, at least enough to save the bridge.

But that was when N'tho felt the *Mayhem*'s engines fail. It was not with a loud or pronounced sound, but with a subtle shudder, and for him, this was easily detected, as he knew every square meter of this vessel. So when the alert came in from engineering seconds later that the engines had ceased functioning, he was already strategizing. "Take us down," he ordered the helmsman.

"That is occurring whether we want to or not, Commander," came the reply.

The *Mayhem* hurtled downward toward the surface of the Ark, for the most part out of control. The helmsman was battling with the reverse thrusters, trying desperately to slow the ship's violent approach toward the installation. N'tho attempted to calculate just how fast they would be moving when they struck the Ark and, by extension, their slim chances of survival. His estimates were disconcerting.

Captain Richards staggered up to him and looked him in the face. "Nice work," she said quietly. He stared at her, trying to discern if the human was engaging in sarcasm, and decided that she was indeed sincere. He tilted his head in acknowledgment.

He braced himself, waiting for the impact.

And then he heard something new—the thrusters roaring

against their rapid descent, then choking, and then starting again. For a few moments, the ship was fighting the Ark's artificial gravity. The corvette's speed was dampened significantly, but not enough for a proper landing.

The *Mayhem* struck the installation hard, bouncing several times across the surface on impact while carving a swath deep into a vast forest. The large alien timbers helped deaden the ship's landing." N'tho heard the thrusters shut down again, this time unable to restart. He grabbed onto his command chair, barely managing to avoid being tossed about the bridge. The helmsman, to his credit, was still struggling with the controls, doing his best to control the damage the ship was sustaining.

The Sangheili vessel was now skidding across the ground, the sound of exploding trees and screeching metal filling the air. N'tho was holding his breath, wondering if the *Mayhem* would literally be torn apart around him. At least his death would be an honorable one.

Debris was falling everywhere within the bridge, and the smoke was so thick that it was impossible to see anything.

And then slowly, very slowly, the ship came to a halt.

Long seconds passed before there was any movement or sound . . . then all present were gasping for breath and surely wondering how they had managed to stay alive.

We live to fight another day, N'tho thought. He called out, "All hands, report."

"We have landed somewhat successfully," the helmsman said dryly.

"I am certainly aware of that—many thanks," said N'tho. "Where are we?"

"About thirty kilometers from the core," the helmsman told

him. "The current outside temperature is twenty units above freezing. The atmosphere and gravity appear to be regulated and viable for both us and the humans, but we're conducting scans with our passive sensors."

"How badly damaged are we?"

"The exterior held together, but barely. Inside, much of the materiel we had brought, including our recon vehicles and short-range fighters, sustained severe damage in the crash. We are running on emergency power while we labor to get the engines back online, although I am not sure that is even going to be possible."

"We have a Huragok on board. Therefore, anything is possible." Off to the side of the bridge, Luther Mann was emerging from a pile of debris, shaken but still in one piece. N'tho glanced down at Drifts Randomly, who had put down a recently awakened Spartan Holt, just now getting his bearings. The Huragok was still cradling the unconscious Olympia Vale in its tentacles. "Take her to the medlab. Fix her if you can."

<<I can.>> With that pronouncement, the Huragok and Vale headed out. Captain Richards and Spartans Kodiak and Holt watched them go with concern, recovering from their own evidently minor injuries sustained in the crash. It even looked like Holt's armor harness was damaged at some point.

And then N'tho clearly heard Kodiak say to Holt in a low voice, "Keep an eye on her, and get that fixed before we head out."

"Yes, sir," said Holt, and he exited the bridge.

"So, now what?" Richards asked N'tho.

"Now," N'tho said, his attention diverted, "we wait until the scans come back to validate our ability to leave this vessel, and then we head out onto the Ark, move out to the communications node, and attempt to do whatever we can to stop the countdown. If that plan meets with your approval."

"It does," said Richards, "although I suspect that if it didn't, you'd do it anyway."

"That is correct."

CHAPTER 8

Slowly, Olympia Vale opened her eyes, not expecting to see the Huragok hovering above her, but there it was.

She sat up, her head throbbing as she did so. As a lance of pain shot across her temple, she put a hand to her forehead and moaned softly. Then she glanced around and was surprised to realize that she was no longer on the bridge. She looked up at the Huragok. "Where am I?" she asked.

<<*The sick bay,*>> Drifts told her.

Vale's head snapped up and she gasped. "I understood you."

<<*Yes.*>> Drift's voice sounded jaunty, yet synthetic and detached.

"How is that possible?"

<<*The lack of communication was becoming inefficient. I just had the Sangheili affix me with a verbal translator. It scans my tentacle movements, then audibly projects a verbal translation in real time. The translation is into Sangheili, but humans can understand because of their own technology. And you understand Sangheili even without it.*>>

"Well . . . okay, then. Thank you for making it easier to understand you. Uhm . . . why am I in sick bay? Am I sick?"

<<*You were rendered unconscious. I fixed you.*>>

She realized that she was lying on some manner of bed

— 151 —

positioned at a forty-five-degree angle. "What do you mean, you fixed me? You can do that, like you can fix machines?"

<<*I fix things.*>>

"Yes, but I'm not a thing. I'm a human."

<<*I know. I am not a Lifeworker Engineer. Lifeworker Engineers can repair biological life. I have not seen one in many annual cycles. I used tools here to repair you. You suffered from a concussion. Now you are better.*>>

Vale was astounded. She put a hand to her head where the debris had struck her. But there was no injury, no blood, nothing. "That's amazing. How the hell did you do that?"

<<*Sangheili tools are primitive, but less so than humans'.*>>

That was when she remembered that the *Mayhem* had been under attack. "What happened? The Retrievers . . . ?"

<<*Destroyed.*>>

"Just that easily."

<<*We won the battle. Then we crashed.*>>

Vale was both relieved that they were still alive and somewhat regretful that she had missed what must have been a hell of a struggle. She climbed out of the bed and got to her feet.

"So now what?" she asked.

A powerful hand clamped down on her shoulder. Vale spun in surprise and aggressively shoved the newcomer.

An unarmored Spartan Holt stumbled and almost fell before he recovered himself. "What the hell—?" he managed to say.

"I'm sorry! I'm so sorry!" said Vale, even as she belatedly realized that she was likewise standing in a combat position. She was still a bit disoriented and recovering from the concussion, but now took a deep breath and then exhaled as she forced her body to relax. "I-I don't know why I did that."

"I don't know *how* you did that," said Holt. "That was surprisingly strong. There was nothing in your records about combat training."

"I studied martial arts for several years," she said. "It was required by ONI for anyone engaging in frontline diplomacy with the Sangheili. Attended the Green Cloud . . . wait. You went over my records? Why did you do that?"

Holt actually seemed slightly embarrassed by the revelation but did his best to act as casual as possible. "Standard UNSC operational procedure that Spartans study the records of anyone we're intended to have lengthy interaction with."

"Well, I work for ONI, so don't be too surprised that some things are missing."

"Point taken."

She wasn't entirely convinced of Holt's admitted motives, but decided not to press the matter. "It's been a few years since I've actively practiced combat, and I was never that good. . . ."

"Are you sure?" Her ability to defend herself had clearly taken Holt off guard.

"Yes, of course I'm sure." Vale cleared her throat in what she hoped sounded like a definitive manner in order to change the subject. "So what's happening now? Where are we?"

"We've landed on the surface of the Ark . . . well, *crashed* may be more accurate."

"Great. And are we going out onto it?"

"In . . ." He glanced at his chronometer. "An hour. The ship is conducting a passive scan of the immediate area to make sure it can facilitate both our species. The Sangheili seem pretty knowledgeable of the terrain, and determined on how to handle it, so for the moment, we're following their lead."

"Okay, then."

"Will you be joining us?" said Holt. "Captain Richards wasn't sure that you'd be up to it."

"Try and stop me," said Vale. She wondered if Richards was hoping for her to stay behind, given the tension just prior to them heading through the portal. The captain couldn't exactly be thrilled with what diplomacy and openhandedness with the Sangheili had gotten them so far.

"Considering you almost threw a Spartan across the room, I think I'll pass on the offer, if it's all the same to you."

Captain Annabelle Richards stared out at the surface of the Ark as she stood in front of the great viewport on the bridge. The *Mayhem* had set down on a large ravine, and its position allowed those in the front to look out across the vast central hub up toward the nearest spires. To the left was the circular expanse that lay at the center of the installation, with an oddly shaped moon-like structure looming in the middle. The core itself was only about thirty kilometers away, and somewhere down there was the communications array where they needed to travel. Their crash location had been extraordinarily fortunate.

This had been a rough last few hours, though. First, Richards needed to explain to her soldiers that the Sangheili effectively kidnapped them for the sake of the greater good. If they weren't so well trained, the entire business might have tipped over into full-blown insurrection. These were soldiers who had battled the Covenant in all-out war for years and who were not especially trustful of the Elites now, even under the best of conditions. She had managed to keep her people under control, but for a brief time there, it had seemed like a near disaster.

She had also privately conferred with N'tho over the best way to approach the current situation. On their surprisingly brief trip, she had finally given up on convincing or strong-arming the Sangheili, and acquiesced to N'tho's decision, act of war or not. Apart from not really having a choice, she also recognized that there was some validity to his stance. As a solider herself, administrative deliberations about action were a bane to her day-to-day work, and so while she defended ONI's right to assess the risk to Earth at the Excession, she had secretly nursed her own frustrations with the orders she'd been given.

Nevertheless, such a change of heart hadn't improved their luck. They had a single Condor, which had been severely damaged in the hangar along with many of the Sangheili's own vehicles and equipment. Weapons and gear, however, had been more resilient. As far as her component of this team was concerned, they'd be ready for boots-on-the-ground combat when the time came.

She was worried that the longer they sat here and did nothing, the more it would encourage additional attacks from the Retrievers, and N'tho shared the same concern. But none seemed to be forthcoming after the initial skirmish, and N'tho was convinced that the Huragok might be able to either repair *Mayhem*, at least enough to make it operable. Given what it had done at the Excession site, she was inclined to take the Sangheili commander at his word. She also suspected that, on the other side of the portal, ONI was now scrambling to dispatch additional teams. With the portal open, it was a game changer, and it no longer meant voyages to the Ark would take several months to accomplish, but only a few weeks . . . and perhaps, even shorter than that, given the trip they just experienced. She'd made a note to ask the specialists on board why it had taken only hours, when it should have taken much longer.

During her conversation with N'tho, she reviewed the current plan of action, which was largely adapted from the one she had developed with Luther Mann and the others designing this mission. Once they left the ship, a single detachment of them would proceed across the surface of the Ark, approximately thirty klicks, until they reached one of the installation's supraluminal communications arrays, which were nestled along the circular expanse at the center of the installation.

Based on data salvaged from *Forward Unto Dawn*, this fated place was a large, towering citadel hanging over the edge of the core, and also the site where the Master Chief and the Arbiter had stopped the Covenant from activating Halo. According to scans, it was still intact and largely unsecured, though they would have to approach from a different vector than their predecessors. And when she and N'tho finished their deliberations, they parted ways.

As Richards passed a small room—undoubtedly some sort of crew quarters—she saw Kodiak pacing back and forth, staring off into space. Apparently he and Holt had taken up residence in this place, which had a utility table off to its side. The Spartans had organized their weapons and field equipment across it, as well as some calibration and repair equipment for their armor. Both Spartans had brought their full GEN2 Mjolnir armor, along with a dozen or so other modular components for their suits. She'd ordered them to be prepared for extended combat before they boarded *Mayhem*, but, even then, she couldn't have anticipated that the Elites would pull the stunt they did.

"Spartan?" she said. "Is something wrong?"

"Is something right?" he asked.

"I know you're upset because of the current situation . . ."

"It's all my fault," said Kodiak.

That comment caught Richards off guard. "What are you talking about?"

"This. The fact that the Sangheili brought us here against our will. He was able to do this because of me."

"I'm not sure I understand."

He finally looked her square in the eyes. "I *had* him. N'tho. We . . ." He paused and cleared his throat, and she began to recall the brief transaction between N'tho and the Spartan moments before they'd left Earth.

After sparing my life, this is how you wish to end matters between us?

I'm not doing anything. You're bringing this all on yourself.

In the frenzy of the last few hours, she'd completely forgotten to ask Kodiak about it, but now it came rushing back to the front of her mind.

"We were sparring," said the Spartan. "Except we weren't really sparring, and both of us knew it."

"You were *fighting* him?" It was all she could do to keep her voice level. "How?"

"I have a sword, just like his." His eyes jerked over to the table, where she saw the Covenant weapon. Although it was against protocol, she knew that some soldiers kept souvenirs from the enemies they'd killed, so this didn't surprise her. But what Kodiak had since done with the sword completely caught her off guard. "I was dueling him with that. And then that Forerunner machine, that Retriever, showed up, and things were getting blown up right and left. And the next thing I knew, he was lying there with a tree pinning him down. And I could have killed him right there. I could have avenged myself on him for this"—he raised his mechanical arm—"and prevented any of this from happening. I was standing over him with the sword, and all I had to do was bring it down on him, cut that son of a bitch in half."

"And yet, you let him live."

Slowly Kodiak nodded. "Yes, ma'am. I cut him loose. If I hadn't done so, he could never have taken us off Earth."

"No, of course not," said Richards. "Instead we'd be involved in some sort of blood feud with the Sangheili, because that's exactly what we want to have happen right now."

"Captain, you don't understand . . ."

"No, Spartan, *you* don't understand. Fighting him was not only monumentally foolish and risky, but directly against my orders. You could have jeopardized the entire mission, and the peace treaty, for that matter. But you didn't, and when you chose to spare his life, that was your common sense dictating to you the proper way to behave." She raised her voice slightly. "We don't kill them anymore, Spartan. Do you understand that? We. Don't. Kill them. They are our allies now, and not for nothing, but at the moment they're working with us to try and save the life of pretty much everyone you know. So don't be sitting here blaming yourself for our current situation simply because you did the right thing and didn't kill the Elite out of revenge. And to be honest, if N'tho hadn't pressed the issue, we'd still be back at Voi, letting the bureaucrats and desk jockeys sort this out. As much as I hate to admit it . . . he was right."

"But if—"

"Spartan," she said sharply, "your commanding officer has not simply offered a suggestion. You have been given an order. Once again, might I add. There is only one acceptable response to that."

"Yes, Captain," said Kodiak without blinking an eye.

"Good," she said. "Now let's get prepared to go outside. We've got a galaxy to save."

When Luther Mann emerged from the *Mayhem*, it was his first opportunity to see the damage the Sangheili ship had sustained. He himself had suffered a mild concussion and had some pretty bad bruising along his right side, but his eyes widened when he saw just how bad *Mayhem* had it.

There were huge burn marks all over the hull from where the once-proud ship had been scored by the blasts from the Retriever or violently battered by the crash landing. Pieces of it had been blown off and were scattered around the entire area, as if a metal rainstorm had pummeled it out of the sky.

"Good Lord," muttered Luther. "How are we going to get back home?"

Usze 'Taham stepped up behind him. "My people have a saying: *The* velithra *can only walk the path one at a time.* It means that we should focus on the present problem first before worrying about what comes next."

Luther hadn't heard of them before. "What is a *velithra*?"

"A large beast of burden found in northern Yermo," Usze said. "We force them along the narrow paths up the mountains just before the rain season, so they can only move one by one. If they try to move too quickly ahead or pass another, they will fall off the side of the mountain. We have one task, Doctor: stopping Halo from firing. After that, we can worry about transportation."

They were standing in what appeared to be a forestlike environment. Just as on the Zeta Halo, the grass beneath their feet was greener than anything Luther had seen back on Earth, and what appeared to be fir trees of some sort were towering over them. He inhaled deeply and marveled at how clean and brisk the air seemed. Just as with all of the Forerunner creations that Luther had encountered, it was almost impossible for him to believe that everything around them had not been a part of some natural order and evolution. The Forerunners had built not only the Halo installations, but also this enormous Ark, either from whole cloth or through the actions of terraforming distant worlds. Incredible.

"So what's the current plan of record, then?" said Luther. "The briefings indicated that the *Endeavor* was going to be bringing a sufficient amount of vehicles to cover any terrain between us and the citadel that the communications node projects from. From a look at the hangar the last time I was inside the *Mayhem*, I'm guessing there aren't a lot of locomotive options. So . . . how are we planning on getting to the citadel?"

"We're going to walk."

Other members of the exploratory party were now emerging from the vessel. Luther had to admit that he was surprised when he saw Olympia Vale coming out. The last he'd seen of her, she'd been thrown to the floor on the bridge. Now she was striding forward, looking utterly confident. "Excuse me," he said to Usze and headed over to Vale. She saw him approaching and tossed off a wave as he drew nearer. "I see you're up and around."

"Yes, I'm fine."

"Are you sure?" he said, making no effort to hide his worry. "You took a pretty bad fall."

"I'm completely okay. Drifts fixed me up." He stared at the creature that was floating a few meters away. She clapped her hands together briskly. "We ready to go?"

"I suppose so."

Luther couldn't help but notice that Vale had a firearm fixed to her thigh, an M6 pistol from the looks of it—he hadn't noticed it before, so this must have been something she'd packed away on the Condor. It made sense, standing here on such an incredibly massive and largely unexplored world as the Ark, with potential dangers around any corner. Nevertheless, he hadn't touched a firearm in years, and he wasn't about to start now.

"You suppose?" She seemed amazed. "If you're not, you better be getting ready quick. We're all relying on you to figure this whole thing out, you know."

"If we fail here or if it all turns out to be a dead end, then that's it for everything. Forgive me if I'm having trouble mustering excitement on that prospect in particular."

"I'm sure you'll do fine. And if not, we've got Drifts."

Luther stared at her for a moment and then, to his surprise, laughed. This prompted Vale to grin broadly. The Huragok floated up from behind, its tentacles flowing in an easygoing fashion, despite the drama it had just endured.

At this point, everyone else who was going to be heading toward the citadel had emerged from the downed ship. The Sangheili were conferring with Richards. Apart from N'tho 'Sraom and Usze 'Taham, there were two others who would be involved in the expedition: the helmsman who had introduced himself as Zon 'Vadum and a Sangheili ranger named Kola 'Baoth. The rest of the Sangheili crew would remain behind, apparently assigned to help determine the extent of *Mayhem*'s damage and possibly initiate whatever repairs could be made without aid from the Huragok.

The two Spartans were standing off to the side, fully decked out with their cobalt-blue combat armor, not far off from Henry Lamb. They weren't talking with each other, but simply standing there, with their battle rifles at the ready, waiting for the order to start walking. They certainly looked more intimidating with their helmets on, and Luther noted that Kodiak had a deactivated Covenant energy sword magnetically latched to his thigh armor. He wondered where the hell it had come from.

Interestingly enough, Henry Lamb hadn't spent very much time on the bridge during the trip, but chose instead to explore the interior of the ship and was advised by Usze only to be careful and stay out of the way. When they were attacked by the Retrievers, he'd been locked down in a random corridor and managed to survive, completely oblivious of the attack and with only a few bumps and bruises. Right now, he was content fiddling with a long-range optics device, which allowed him to view extreme distances, as well as scan and record whatever he was seeing.

Several UNSC soldiers were milling about, too, getting their gear and weapons in order as they prepared to set off. They were obviously the ones that Captain Richards had brought with her when she first boarded the *Mayhem*. But not all of them would be making the journey to the citadel; the rest had been assigned to Lieutenant Radeen, in order to remain there and secure the vessel and, if possible, help the Sangheili with repairs. A handful were now gathering behind Richards as she approached the Sangheili and doing what soldiers were supposed to: waiting eagerly for their commanding officer to issue them orders.

"All of you, please listen to me," N'tho called out, his voice carrying above the low chatter all around. He pointed some distance away. "That is where we are heading." He then raised a palm-size device, which suddenly projected a hologram of the Ark at eye level. A beacon appeared on the hologram, and the projection zoomed in to show just the very narrow sliver of territory they were on at the innermost edge of the Ark's central hub, bordering the foundry that long ago manufactured the individual Halo rings.

The beacon clearly represented the communications array, one of several that existed on the Ark. This one was situated in the fortified citadel that happened to be the very same that the UNSC had encountered on their last visit here. *This place already had some history with us,* Luther thought, *even if it was only two years ago.*

"We will be going through some challenging terrain and some heavily damaged areas, so now is the time to prepare. Due to the damage that this structure has sustained, habitability and climate systems can and will fluctuate, but *Mayhem*'s scans reveal that we should be fine for the time needed to access the citadel and potentially deactivate Halo's firing mechanism. It is imperative that we remain together, so do not wander or fall behind. There were many perils on this installation the last time I was here, and no doubt, there are many more now."

Then, without another word, N'tho started walking, a procession of Sangheili and humans immediately following behind.

Luther noticed that the Elite seemed to be moving at about half his normal stride, and he quickly realized why: it was so the humans in the group would be able to keep up with him. Luther felt that to be rather considerate. Even though some kind of reconciliation had occurred, he still didn't think that Captain Richards, the Spartans, or any of the marines present would be remotely inclined to feel positive toward the towering Sangheili, considering the circumstances of how they had gotten there.

Luther had his equipment bag with him, filled with a number of sensors and networked communication instruments that he slung onto his shoulder. As he did so, Henry Lamb came up to him. "Need any help?"

"No, I'm fine. I have a handle on it. How about you?"

"Good to go." He breathed deeply. "Hard to believe we're here."

"It is. To be honest, having had some time to think about it, I'm glad we're not back at Voi, twiddling our thumbs while waiting for the ONI analysts to figure out what's most important. Although I'd appreciate it if you didn't mention that to the captain."

"Stays between us."

"Good."

They kept walking.

The line of individuals fell into step behind N'tho 'Sraom and the Sangheili ranger Kola. Usze 'Taham, Luther noticed, was walking alongside the other Elite, Zon 'Vadum, both taking up the rear. That made sense, as he was reminded that many species developed innate protection instincts when it came to their young, huddling them to the center of the pack. It was alarming on two levels, however: first, the Elites were protecting humans in this case, which was somewhat extraordinary given the last three decades of all-out war between their species, and second, the two Sangheili at the rear reminded him there was real danger in this place, because anything could come up behind them at any time.

And that stray thought began to cause him concern. Just what exactly *did* they have to worry about?

That's when the party stopped for a moment and collectively stared skyward as a series of large shadows passed above them. Luther's natural inclination was that it was simply a flock of birds, but then he looked up and gasped.

There was no real word for whatever the hell they were—a group of flying creatures moved slowly by, a few dozen meters above them. Luther had never seen anything quite like this species: they were leviathans, creatures as large as whales and bearing some similar features. Their large, somewhat-bulbous teardrop shapes appeared to be effortlessly cruising through the air. They had large toothy mouths that extended across their fronts and about a third of the way down their flanks. He couldn't see the tops of them at all, but their undersides were of the purest white, shimmering in the light that reflected off them.

But that was not the most striking thing about them. They were singing, sounding remarkably similar to the sorts of noises that Earth whales made when they moved through the oceans and conversed with each other.

One of the leviathans appeared to notice them. It drifted down toward the assemblage of travelers, all of whom stopped as it drew near. Luther noticed that several of the UNSC soldiers had elevated their rifles and firearms, aiming at it. He found this to be a ridiculous gesture. The creature wasn't attacking them, and even if so, chances were that their weaponry wouldn't do a damn thing against it. And up close, he began to ascertain its actual scale: this thing was the size of an ocean liner.

Still . . .

"No one shoot!" Luther called. "Don't provoke it!"

The soldiers barely afforded him a glance. That did not exactly fill Luther with confidence.

"They take their orders from me, Doctor Mann," Captain Richards said with just a hint of irritation. "Not from random civilians."

"Please have them lower their weapons, Captain."

Richards looked as if she were ready to start arguing; then, to his surprise, she gestured to her soldiers, who slowly and reluctantly lowered their ordnance. "Thank you, Captain," said Luther.

"If it makes the slightest aggressive move, we're going to blow it out of the sky," Richards warned him.

Luther nodded, but he was sure that that would not be an issue. It was a mammoth, gorgeous creature, and he felt there was no way that it was going to prove any sort of offensive threat.

Except . . .

The leviathan drew ever closer. Now it had definitely noticed the beings below and had apparently decided they were worth checking out. Even Richards was getting nervous, for she muttered to her soldiers, and they raised their weapons again.

But the closer the leviathan neared, the more evident it became just how useless their weaponry would be. Best-case scenario: they would land a lucky shot and somehow manage to scare the thing . . . at which point it might drop out of the sky and crush them all. So obviously that wasn't the best option.

The creature's shadow cast over all of them, its song becoming so loud that some were putting their hands over their ears.

And then, to the surprise of everyone, Luther sang in response.

He had his hands cupped around his mouth, making loud noises that sounded eerily identical to what the leviathan had just been bellowing. The creature stopped drawing closer. Instead it hovered above in silence, its entire focus astoundingly on Luther.

Then the leviathan replied. At least that was certainly what it sounded like. It sang to Luther, and he responded. For a moment, it seemed as though they were able to hold congress, yet Luther had only intended to mimic the creature's sound. After a while, it became clear that the jig was up. Luther wasn't a friendly fellow creature, but just a noisy speck next to this enormous beast.

At which point the leviathan then broke off. Its entire massive body tilted to the side, and what appeared to be its wings rippled before propelling it upward. Within moments, the great creature's shadow had diminished, rejoining the others and continuing on its way.

There were approving glances from Vale and Lamb, but most of the others were still on edge because of the proximity of the beast. Vale herself seemed astounded. "What in God's name did you say to it?"

"I haven't the faintest idea," he replied. "But I've heard its songs while studying some of the captured audio from the *Dawn*'s time here, and I was able to discern general intent. The songs don't seem to serve as a language in the same way that words do for us. It conveys feelings, sensations. I was just trying to mimic it to the best of my ability . . . and maybe in some way convince it that we intended no harm and were peaceful."

"Seems like you managed to convince it."

"More so than shooting at it," said Luther, giving an annoyed glance at the soldiers. His disapproval apparently didn't register, because they still kept their weapons in evidence until the leviathan was safely away. For a brief moment, Luther wondered if humans weren't, in fact, the most dangerous creatures on this installation.

The group then continued its march.

The temperature remained consistent for the first hour or so, but the closer they drew to the Ark's central core, the crisper the atmosphere became. This hadn't come as a surprise to anyone on the team, as Luther's previous research had accurately pegged the temperatures and conditions to expect from this part of the Ark. Fortunately, much of the gear and equipment needed for the expedition was already onboard the Condor, the dropship they'd originally intended to take to *Endeavor* when they left Voi. Despite the radical change of plans at the hands of the Sangheili, most of the team was properly kitted out in the appropriate thermal tech and gear.

The Ark was designed primarily for the manufacturing of the Halo ringworlds. This happened in the central core—effectively a foundry. The Forerunners designed this part of the installation so that the extremely hot temperatures generated by the materials forge, and the foundry itself, would be counteracted by an incredibly frigid atmosphere. This natural system seemed to be exacerbated by the trauma caused by the Halo activation and subsequent damage from years earlier. So cold weather wasn't unexpected at all.

He noticed that there were wisps of snow starting to appear beneath his feet. A wind was beginning to whip up as well.

Within another half an hour, there was no longer any hint of grass around them. Instead it was now all covered with snow. It wasn't thick, little more than a dusting. But before long, Luther was hearing a steady crunch of boots sinking into the thin layer of snow that had developed around them.

He looked skyward and was grateful to see that the artificial weather wasn't getting any worse. So that was a relief at le—

Then the snow started to fall.

And shortly after that, they were all under attack.

CHAPTER 9

old?" said a voice close to Olympia Vale. She had been so
focused on the trek and the surroundings that the sudden
address caused her to jump slightly. She turned and saw that
Spartan Holt was now striding next to her, his rifle latched to his
back. He was positioned a little closer to her than she found comfortable, but it might have been because he was fully armored and
he seemed much larger than before. She chose not to comment
on it.

"A little, yeah."

Vale wasn't sure what to make of Holt, or Kodiak for that
matter—especially when they were hidden behind their polar-
ized visors. She'd seen enough already to tell that one of the main
reasons she was involved in this operation was to try to keep the
peace between the Spartans and the Sangheili, and that wasn't a
sign of endearment. Their bedside manner as cooperative team
players left something to be desired.

She noticed that mist was drifting from her mouth. Had it gotten that chilly so quickly? "The weather around here is somewhat
unpredictable, isn't it?"

"A bit, yeah. Though I've been on enough alien worlds with
alien climates at this point to not take predictability for granted
anymore."

"Doesn't this make you consider the beings who created this place?" she said in wonderment. "What they might have been like?"

"I've haven't really given it any thought."

She looked surprised. "Really?"

"Really."

"But given its size, its power, its potential . . . I'd think that they would have crossed your mind at some point. We build spaceships, they build *worlds*."

"Frankly, Olympia—may I call you Olympia?"

"I don't see why not."

"I haven't really given much thought to anything but the task at hand. The Forerunners—or whatever they were—aren't really all that valuable if they're not practical or useful to our current situation. If there's value in hard facts about them, then I'm completely there, but if I'm to be really honest, I've never been much for imagining anything. And I've always considered that one of my strengths."

Vale prodded a bit more. "How is not having an imagination a strength?"

"Because a Spartan isn't trained to have an imagination. We exist for one thing only: to complete the objective. Everything else is secondary. It doesn't benefit me or anyone else to start contemplating about the architects of this site or their purposes or how they lived eons ago unless it's immediately relevant to the crisis we're trying to avert. We call it missional solvency—is it actionable or is it a distraction?"

"I'm not sure that's necessarily true," said Vale. "If you're in dangerous situations, don't you sometimes have to come up with some sort of creative strategy to get yourself out of it? Isn't that thinking out of the box?"

"Ideally, a creative strategy is the planned strategy, and that kind of thinking has happened long beforehand. The goal on the battlefield is to limit the variables and unknowns, so there's no need to be creative."

"That doesn't seem right to me. I think you're selling yourself short. Making decisions at the spur of the moment requires some level of creativity and imagination."

Holt actually laughed at that. It wasn't more than a chuckle, but a sense of humor was definitely there. "Miss Vale, don't get me wrong: I can fight better than most folks in the field, but I wasn't selected as a Spartan because I gave a lot of thought to nonfactors; I was selected because I'm good with a weapon, and because I can react quickly in a pinch. Maybe there is some fiber of creativity in me, but at the end of the day, I'd like to think that all of the unknowns have been accounted for. Especially in an op like this."

"Well, I'm glad that—"

"Hang on—quiet."

"What?"

"*Quiet,*" he said with greater intensity.

Vale quickly saw that Holt was reacting to something that everyone around him was also responding to. N'tho, still in the lead, put up a hand to signal that everyone should stop, the other hand resting on the hilt of the energy sword fixed to his thigh. Drifts Randomly huddled behind the Elite, clearly recognizing its relative safety there. Richards unholstered her pistol and gestured to her men, and they immediately brought their rifles to bear.

Dropping her voice to barely above a whisper, Vale said, "What's happening?"

"I hear something."

She struggled to listen. At first, all she heard was the steady blowing of the increasing wind. But then . . . a low rumbling. . . .

No. Growling.

She shielded her eyes, trying to pick up the origin of the noise. She wasn't seeing anything, however—nothing but a wide vista of endless snow, and with more falling from above. They had come down off a ravine and were traveling across a vast plain toward an outcropping of large boulders, when the storm moved in on them from out of nowhere, and it was now becoming angrier.

And here on the ground, there was now movement.

Everyone had their weapons up, and within seconds, Vale was able to discern exactly what was approaching.

Six creatures, appearing to be something like dinosaurs. They had no eyes or arms, but gargantuan fangs extended from the bottoms of their jaws, and nasty-looking teeth from the tops. They were bipedal, with a theropod-like anatomy, and slowly striding forward, their heads low and sweeping from side to side as if they were conning towers.

It was clear that they were moving toward the expedition with the intent of hunting them, like a pack of seasoned carnivores. This time, both the Sangheili and the UNSC soldiers leveled their weapons and were ready to open fire.

And then Vale whistled sharply. In unison, every head swiveled toward her.

"What the hell did you—?" Holt started to say.

She ignored him. Instead she shouted, "No one move! Don't say anything! Don't even breathe!"

The moment Vale shouted, the creatures bolted toward her, running across the white plain at high speed, bearing down on her.

Holt brought his weapon up to protect her but she shoved it down, putting a finger to her lips as she did so. Captain Richards, seeing what she was doing, did the same thing for her own soldiers, gesturing quickly that they should stay their weapons. Vale was pleased to see that Richards obviously trusted her, although she came to the bleak realization that if she was wrong, these creatures would likely tear them all apart before anyone could do anything to avert it.

Then she noticed that the Sangheili had their weapons fully at the ready. N'tho had removed his energy sword and was on the brink of activating it, while Usze was cradling an old, modified Covenant carbine with the intention of using it if necessary. The Elite had silently closed the gap between her and himself, his weapon now leveled at the incoming creatures. She supposed she should take some comfort in that.

The blind beasts still approached, but they were also now slowing. Moments earlier, their heads had been focused directly on where Vale had been standing, but now they appeared confused. One of them had taken the lead—the alpha. She had no idea how the things communicated with one another, but those behind the alpha fell back, making sure that they were able to follow its direction.

Vale remained rigid as the alpha drew within half a meter of her. Its head continued to sweep, but it was becoming visibly irritated. It snapped its great teeth in the air at random, and then let out a howling noise that sounded eerily like a wolf. Vale was holding her breath and was mildly surprised to realize that she wasn't having any trouble doing that.

The alpha went still, as well. It was checking the air, its nostrils flaring. That sent an alarmed jolt through Vale, because there was nothing she could do about her scent, and if this thing was capable of locating her through smell rather than, as she suspected, hearing, that would be the end.

Slowly the alpha turned its head so that, if it had eyes, it would have been looking directly at her.

And then it turned away.

It walked right past her and the group and came within centimeters of touching Vale. She remained silent and still as the other five creatures followed the alpha, ignoring human and Sangheili alike as if they weren't there. Within moments, the entire pack had moved on. Seconds later, they were back to their full speed and running off across the snowy ground, apparently on the hunt for some other hapless creature.

Vale let out a long sigh, realizing just how long she hadn't been breathing.

"That was a very good call," said Holt.

Richards gave her a thumbs-up and Vale returned it. She had to admit this was a major relief. She had guessed right: the strange animals zeroed in on their prey primarily by sound—

Wait a second.

There had been a low, guttural growling before the attack . . . but those creatures hadn't really made any sound like it.

So where had the growling been coming from?

That was when she saw the rocks move, a number of large, snow-covered boulders at the center of the plain that Vale had first not been paying attention to.

They were not, in fact, rocks at all.

"Oh, *crap*," whispered Vale.

The rocks now stood fully upon their thick-taloned paws, and they swung their heads into view. They were some manner of large, polar bear–like creatures, and these things most definitely had eyes. Not to mention large tusks extending from their mouths. Long, white fur rippled across their bodies, and they had horned protrusions sticking out of their backs. Abbreviated tails swept back and forth. These animals were the true source of the growling noises heard earlier. They had silenced themselves because of the other smaller animals on the hunt, but with the pack having moved on, these white-furred creatures were now running the show.

And there were many of them. They were approaching from the middle of the snowfield, a deep snarling in their throats. The snow crunched under their heavy paws as they advanced. Their faces were particularly fierce, now coming into view: between their two huge tusks and a pair of smaller horns, their mammalian snouts ended in three white-mandible pairs, one atop the other. The closest creature splayed its mouth wide open, revealing row after row of razor sharp teeth.

And then it roared.

"Fire!" Captain Richards shouted.

The soldiers opened up, blasts hurtling in all directions. Kodiak had immediately moved into action, strafing off to the right, while the sole Elite guarding the rear of their group spun off to the left, following suit. Usze had moved between Vale and the front of the group, coming alongside N'tho and Kola, as they protected the Huragok.

Holt had his weapon poised, and without a thought, aggressively pulled Vale behind his own body and stood in a defensive posture in front of her. Any hint of the pleasantness he displayed earlier was gone. Now he was in full battle mode, as the white-furred creatures charged at their group.

They were fast, horribly fast. The first few were struck dead-on, doubling over because of their size and momentum and flipping end over end. But the others seemed to adjust quickly to the barrage and darted rapidly left and right, managing to avoid the opening salvo.

Despite Holt's intention, Vale didn't appreciate being considered defenseless on her own. She removed her own sidearm and began laying down fire at one of the creatures that had tracked off to their left.

Holt had moved to the right and was firing at one of the creatures that was coming straight at him. His blasts trailed it as it dodged and then lunged at him, slamming into the Spartan front-paws first. Holt went down and lost his rifle but managed to grab the animal's forelegs and shove up with his knees, causing its large frame to spiral over his head. The Spartan scrambled to his feet, glancing around, trying to see where the gun had fallen to, but the weapon was buried somewhere in the snow. The white-furred creature charged again. Quickly Holt sidestepped, and as the creature tried to halt its forward movement, Holt grabbed it around its neck. He lifted it off its front feet, squeezing as hard as he could, trying to choke the life out of it.

It didn't work—the creature managed to gain purchase with its hind feet, and it threw its body forward. In doing so, it broke the Spartan's hold and with one swing of its heavy tusks, knocked him back.

Holt fell to the ground, and before he could get up again, the creature had scrambled forward and slammed its paws into his chest. Its weight was too great even for the Spartan to battle, and at that instant Holt must have realized he was looking straight into the mouth of death. It roared victoriously, its foul breath fogging his helmet's visor.

A concentrated explosion sounded out, and the creature shook violently in response. It spun around to face Olympia Vale, who was standing several feet away, her own pistol in hand, aimed squarely at the beast.

It charged at Vale, bounding across the distance that separated them, but it was moving slower, because she had already struck it broadside. Her hands were trembling, and she fought to steady them as she squeezed the trigger several more times. The last time she'd used this weapon was years ago, during a training exercise, so she strained to regain command of it. Each blast hammered through the creature, shaking it with every impact, and still it kept coming. With a final roar, it bounded the remaining space, its mouth opened wide in front of Vale. As it rocked her backward, she fired point-blank into the creature's mouth.

Then she fell to the ground, striking the back of her head on something hard. The creature lurched forward in death, its full weight nearly crushing down on her. She grunted from the impact, and then something lifted the creature off her. It was Holt, looking down at her with his helmet now removed. "Vale!" he called to her. "Olympia! Are you okay?!"

She heard continued firing from all around her. Everyone was fighting for their lives. *This is where it ends . . . my God, after all I've been through so far,* this *is where it ends. Me on my back, in the snow.*

Holt called to her again, and then his attention was elsewhere. He had found his rifle in the snow and started blasting away once more.

The world was turning black around her.

Again? I'm going unconscious again?

No . . . no, I'm not going to be unconscious this time. This time I'm going to die.

I'm going to die.

How depressing.

The world was spinning out around Vale, the blackness reaching out to embrace her . . .

You are interesting.

The words sounded in her head. She had no idea where they came from or who was speaking to her, but it was like someone had spoken directly into her mind.

Who are you?

You are interesting.

So you say.

I want you to come to me.

I don't know where you are.

You do not have to. I will bring you to me.

At that point, Vale's eyes snapped open.

She saw Holt a short distance away, firing at another charging creature. The humans and Sangheili appeared to be winning, but just barely.

The ground suddenly rumbled once more.

Now the eyeless biped animals were running back into the fray. Even from a distance, apparently they were able to perceive the sounds of the pitched battle.

The entire area was alive with carnage on all sides. The bipeds plowed into the white-furred creatures, clamping their wide jaws upon them. Human and Sangheili were desperately trying to stay out of the way, firing defensive shots as they attempted to back out of the area. Usze had now ignited his own energy sword and was wielding it deftly, hewing the attacking bipeds into pieces with remarkable speed and power.

Vale observed all this, but she did so as if she were far away, as if she were having an out-of-body experience. Very slowly she began to stride forward. Her mind was becoming hazy, and she felt strangely drawn to a specific location, a dense cluster of trees well off to the left of the battle. For reasons she could not account for, she had already begun heading in that direction.

With the onslaught all around them, no one apparently noticed her walking away.

Vale began to wonder, though, if there was something else going on. If whoever or whatever it was that was guiding her was somehow influencing the attention of everybody else. That didn't make any sense, and yet very little did at that moment.

She came to a halt in the middle of the tree cluster. One of the white-furred creatures had leapt directly in front of her. It stood there for a long moment, its breath misting in front of its heavily mandibled mouth, poised to attack like a rabid dog. It lowered its head, continuing to watch her for a long moment.

And then it stepped aside.

Vale couldn't believe it. The creature was actually getting out of her way.

Suspecting that this might be some kind of trick and that the beast would suddenly turn on her, she nevertheless strode on, never taking her eyes off it. It returned her gaze levelly, but made no effort to assault her. Vale felt like she should be afraid of it, but for some reason, she wasn't. Somehow, she knew it wouldn't harm her. She felt safe. Almost too safe.

As she walked past, she reached out and ran her fingers across its head. She didn't know why, but she just felt like she could. Like she *should*. It made a strange noise that almost sounded as if it was purring. Then it backed away and lowered itself to the ground, staring up at her. She kept walking, the creature now falling into step next to her.

At one point, a biped creature came toward them with

murderous intent. The creature next to Vale growled in its throat, but rather than serving as an incentive to cause the biped to attack, instead it backed away. On a certain level, Vale thought it made perfect sense, although she didn't understand why.

She continued to walk, her new companion accompanying her. She wasn't even paying attention to the battle that was transpiring behind her. She began to feel that was someone else's problem.

Her problems lay ahead of her.

We are going to have company. Won't that be lovely? It's a human female. I find her cerebral activity to be interesting and believe that she might be intriguing to talk to for a while.

(Let me die.)

Now why would you say that? I have given you a new life. You are far more than you once were. Why would you wish to leave it behind?

(Look what you've done to me.)

What I have done is make you far greater than you were. All of your human weaknesses have been left behind. I could have let you die, but instead you have been transformed into what you are now. And all you wish from me is that I allow you to die? Does that remotely sound like gratitude to you? I ask you.

(I don't want gratitude. I don't want to live like this. I just want it to be over.)

Not for a good long while yet. My sincerest condolences. Now . . . let us prepare to receive our guest.

CHAPTER 10

L uther Mann had never quite felt as frustratingly useless as he did during the pitched battle with these creatures that seemed determined to devour everyone around him.

Luther was crouched behind a large boulder, keeping his head low, watching in helplessness as he saw the others in his group fighting the beasts. He was pleased and relieved to see that, for the most part, things seemed to be going in the way that the humans and Sangheili would have preferred. He actually let out a sigh of relief.

That was his mistake.

One of the blind, bipedal creatures that resembled a carnivorous dinosaur, who apparently reacted solely to sound, snapped its head around and fixed directly on him. It was standing ten meters away, but somehow Luther's lone sigh had helped it home in precisely on his location.

His heart was pounding. He tried desperately to hold his fear in, but instead he wound up gasping again and making a vague whimpering noise, and that was all the biped needed.

It sped toward him, its jaws clacking together. Luther let out an alarmed scream—which was the absolute worst thing he could have done—and threw his arms up in front of his face, as if that would somehow ward off the beast.

It leaped at him, and then something flashed over Luther's shoulder, catching the creature broadside and slamming it backward. It tumbled to the ground, and then lay still.

Luther turned and saw that one of Richards's marines had come in behind him. The barrel of his weapon was still smoking as he put out a hand. Luther took it, and the man helped him to his feet.

"You okay?" he asked Luther.

Luther managed a nod.

"Try to stay low," said the marine, "and avoid the—"

"Look out!" Luther screamed.

The marine whirled, but it was too late. The bipedal monster had since clambered to its feet and lunged through the air. Before the marine could bring his rifle around, its jaws clamped onto the man's upper torso. He tried to shriek but was unable to do so, and he dropped his gun as the creature snapped its jaws left and right and tore the poor man's head off.

Without hesitation, Luther scooped the fallen weapon up and aimed it at the beast, just as it swung its head toward him, its jaws wide and prepared to rip into him.

"Eat this!" Luther screamed, firing at point-blank range.

The blasts ripped into the creature's mouth and out the back of its head. The beast fell backward, and this time there was no doubt that the thing was dead.

That was not remotely enough for Luther. His guilt over the abrupt death of the marine was so overwhelming that the thought of trying to hide now became anathema to him.

I never even knew his name.

Howling an indecipherable cry of both mourning and fury, Luther charged into combat.

It was as if his mind was splitting in two. Half of Luther was screaming to run and hide, to not throw himself into a fight. He was no warrior. The Spartans had been training to wield their weapons for who knew how long. And here was Luther, leaping into the fray as if he had any reason to expect that he could survive even seconds in a battle like this.

But the other side of his brain reminded him of what his father had done.

Because his father had never forgotten having to run from Verent, or the attacking Covenant, and he had sworn that he would do whatever he could so that Luther would never have to run from anyone, ever.

Which was why, when Luther had reached his teenage years, his father had taken him with regularity to a nearby shooting range. Luther had received gun training and instruction in marksmanship. He'd hated every moment of it and involuntarily winced each time he'd aimed and fired at the targets. Once his father died, he ceased all visits to gun ranges, resolving never to pick up a weapon again in his life.

Until now.

And, as it turned out, the lessons from his youth were about to serve him well. Because even though he had not practiced in years, everything that he'd learned now came roaring back to him, and he was able to sight the creatures with a calm and expertise that astounded even him.

In studying the monsters on the fly, he was able to discern right away where their weak spots were, and he made every shot count. Each one that he hit immediately fell, after a round or two from the marksman rifle: both the bipeds and the white-furred beasts.

Out of the corner of his eye, he saw Henry secured behind a boulder as he had just been. Henry was watching him with eyes wide. He clearly couldn't believe what he was seeing as Luther continued to fire upon the creatures. Henry wasn't about to join him, but tossed Luther a thumbs-up instead.

Part of Luther was appalled. He was a scientist, after all. He should've been interested in studying these creatures and their relationship to the Forerunners, not blowing them apart. And yet the fact was that, in this moment at least, Luther's instinct was to completely destroy them. One of them had killed a man whose only sin had been rescuing a stranger from being killed himself. All of Luther's scientific drive and inquiry had briefly vanished— he just wanted to annihilate these hellish things before they could take anyone else's life.

And in doing so, much to his genuine surprise, Luther Mann had never felt more alive.

He spotted another fallen soldier, a mangled mess of flesh and bones. Part of his mind had shut down by that point, so the grisly scene had little effect—he grabbed the dead man's handgun and threw it to Henry. His partner caught it, staring at it as if he had never seen a pistol before.

"Make yourself useful!" shouted Luther.

Spartan Holt had no idea how long it was before he realized that Olympia Vale was gone.

He was far too busy fighting the white-furred creatures and the blind bipeds that were alternately attacking one another and the humans and Sangheili.

Fortunately, it seemed as if the beasts they were battling had had enough. The furred creatures were heading in one direction, while the bipeds were still scrambling about, trying to track down targets and not appreciating being fired at. Holt didn't know how long the bloody fight had carried on, but the remaining creatures were all now scattering.

What was more surprising was the sight of Luther Mann actually running in pursuit of the beasts, blasting away at them with a rifle. Whereas Henry Lamb, following behind, seemed predictably tentative, Luther was chasing them with wild eyes and guns blazing, and it was becoming evident that the fleeing creatures didn't want any part of him.

That was when he looked toward Vale to make certain that she was okay, and he was astounded to realize that she simply wasn't there. His first instinct was to look around for a mass of blood and bone, because surely she'd been torn apart by one of the attacking beasts, but he didn't see anything. So that much was a relief, at least.

"What's wrong?"

The voice next to him was momentarily startling. He turned and saw that Usze 'Taham and Henry Lamb were standing next to him.

"Olympia Vale's gone," said Holt.

"Gone?" Lamb said. "Gone where? Where is she?"

"How would I know?"

"You weren't watching her?"

"No," said Holt. "I was shooting at creatures that were trying to kill me. As I assume that you were."

"Have you scanned the area?" asked Usze. "She couldn't depart from here without leaving tracks in the snow."

At first Holt didn't see anything. But there was something strange about the terrain twenty meters to the group's left. The collection of large evergreen-like trees that were currently there seemed, to him at least, to have shrunken dramatically. *How was that possible?* He looked down at the snow at his feet and immediately saw the footprints from some of the creatures, but he couldn't perceive any from—

"There." Usze was pointing. "Right there."

He didn't see what Usze was indicating at first. The Sangheili started across the snowy ground toward the cluster of trees, validating that the Elite's natural eyesight was a thing to be reckoned with. Upon reaching the tree line, Holt followed Usze's line of sight at the ground right inside the cluster. He saw a white-furred creature's tracks leading away from the battle scene, but . . .

Then his eyes narrowed and he saw exactly what Usze was seeing.

There were human tracks next to the ones of the white-furred creature, all evenly paced. There was no hint of struggle.

"That's her," Holt said definitively. "That's definitely her."

"She walked away alongside one of those beasts?" said Usze.

"So it would appear."

"Where the hell did she get to?" said Lamb, having quickly found his way over. "We need to follow her."

"Yes, we do," agreed Usze.

Now Captain Richards and Spartan Kodiak approached, curious as to what the three of them were talking about. "Where's Vale?" said Richards.

"Gone," Holt said.

"Gone where?" said Kodiak.

Holt let out a slow breath. "I don't know," he said, obviously restraining himself. "But apparently she departed the area in the company of one of those white, shaggy creatures."

"That can't be right," said Richards.

"I don't know about right or wrong; I just know what my eyes are telling me. How the hell do you explain those tracks? And something else: When we first approached this location, the trees off to the left seemed to be much larger. Now they're . . . well, not anything like they were before."

"He's right," Kodiak said. "The tree line has changed since we arrived."

"Doctor Lamb," Richards said, turning to Henry. "Is this explainable?"

"I didn't notice the trees, but there are records of illusion-generating systems used by the Forerunners: bafflers, concealers, and dazzlers. Never encountered one before, and I don't know why it'd be used here."

"Maybe to hide what happened to Vale?" Holt suggested. "Either way, we need to find her."

Richards stared at the tracks, seeming to assess the situation. "All right," she said slowly. "You three try and track her down. Once you find her, bring her to the citadel. We'll mark it on your nav; just keep us on the comm. Kodiak, you stick with me."

"Uh, Captain," Lamb interjected, "do you think it's a good idea for me to be separated from Luther here? I mean, the whole reason I'm here is to help him stop the Halo activation. What if you guys need me?"

"Do you really want to know, Doctor Lamb? Because I have to operate as though one of you is not going to make it. If you stay with us and this team gets wiped out, how the hell will we stop the activation sequence? By splitting you up, I'm increasing the chances that at least one of you will survive. And, to be honest, given what we've encountered so far, I don't want anyone on this op moving around without a specialist at hand. There's no telling what they might run into that'll require your expertise. Understood?"

Slowly Henry nodded. "Yes, Captain."

She turned to Holt with a serious look in her eye. "We've got radios; use them. And make it quick."

"Yes, Captain," said Holt.

Richards nodded and then, with Kodiak in tow, headed off toward N'tho.

"All right," said Holt. "Let's go."

Captain Richards and Kodiak strode up to N'tho. "Olympia Vale is gone," she said briskly. "Holt, Usze, and Lamb are going to find her."

"Was it possible she was killed?" asked N'tho.

Richards couldn't help but notice that N'tho sounded rather indifferent to the concept. "No body here, unless she was dragged off during the fighting. I doubt it. Those creatures weren't particularly discreet, but I think we would have seen some signs of a kill."

"A valid point. All right, then." N'tho nodded toward their distant destination. "We had best get moving."

"Hold it," said Richards. She was studying the area. Her face was visibly saddened for a moment as she looked at the bodies scattered about the landscape. Of the ten marines whom she had brought with her, she had lost three to the claws or teeth of the creatures that had assaulted them. "Gonzalez, Turot, Kapalos," she said to those behind her, "we don't leave soldiers behind. Even dead soldiers. Gather the bodies and return them to the Sangheili vessel and wait there for further instructions." That would leave her with four marines; it would have to be enough. She turned to the remaining soldiers, glancing at their IDs: TANGREDI, O'SHEA, STEIN, and CALDER. In some respects, they seemed interchangeable; yet she knew that each of them had their own story, their own reason for joining the Corps. She would have liked to know them, but was aware that she simply could not afford to think of these men as individuals. Then she turned back to N'tho. "All right. Let's go."

N'tho once again took the lead, which made sense since he had the longest stride. Spartan Kodiak fell in right behind him, and the rest of the crew followed, with the two Elites at the rear.

Richards was keeping a wary eye on Kodiak. She didn't believe for a moment that he would suddenly launch another attack on N'tho. There was far too much at stake, and besides, it was one thing to give in to temptation during sparring.

Not sparring. A duel to the death.

She couldn't get that reality out of her head, and so she continued to regard the Spartan with suspicion, even though she kept trying to tell herself that it wasn't necessary. She wondered for a moment if any of the earlier Spartan classes had similar issues, but couldn't recall a single time any had ever broken rank to settle a personal vendetta, or even took anything in combat personally to begin with. These new Spartans were certainly different.

They continued walking across the snowy expanse. The wind was becoming stiffer, the snow blowing briskly into their faces. "The climate is changing faster than your estimates indicated, Doctor Mann," N'tho muttered.

It was not a statement that provided her with any sort of positive feeling.

Her soldiers were closing in behind her and around her, and she quickly realized they were surrounding her, shielding her from the buffeting of the snow with their own bodies. She wanted to tell them that wasn't necessary—that she was capable of enduring the Ark's surface with the same determination. But they were doing exactly what they were supposed to do, and she had no business overriding their instinct to protect her.

What she also noticed was the obvious damage to the Ark's surface. The closer they drew to the core, the more pronounced the destruction seemed. Rather than snow-covered trees, she saw burned husks, areas with large black gashes across the ground, and exposed struts and beams composed of a strange alien alloy.

Richards's breath was becoming more pronounced, and she was starting to feel a numbness in her lungs. She glanced around and saw that the four UNSC soldiers appeared to be slowing down as well. Walking was becoming more of an effort, the snow getting thicker around them. It was rising a few centimeters every fifteen minutes—not blizzard levels yet, but it certainly seemed to be on its way.

Richards felt her legs starting to shake, which annoyed the living hell out of her, and she despised her body for threatening to give out. So instead she ignored it, forcing herself forward as the snow hammered down.

"Are you all right?" said N'tho, glancing back.

"I'm fine," Richards managed to say. "I'm totally—"

The world went sideways.

She hadn't been expecting any manner of abrupt depression in the snow ahead of her, but the crater was concealed. The damn thing seemed to be about two meters deep and perhaps three meters in diameter. The others had managed to wander past it, but not her. She stumbled forward and both heard and felt her knee snap. She cried out loudly and a profanity escaped her lips. Even though it was against her better judgment, she tried to stand, and instantly pain shot up and down her leg and she collapsed once more.

Spartan Kodiak was immediately next to her, down in the crater with her. "Back-up!" he shouted at the nearest soldier. He reached under Richards's arms and lifted her out of the hole with no problem. She let out another grunt of pain and the four UNSC soldiers were around her, hauling her upright. Richards tried to put weight on her foot and would have instantly collapsed had

Kodiak not been holding her elevated. The soldiers then took over, and Kodiak stepped away.

Richards gritted her teeth. "I'm fine. . . . I'll be fine. . . ."

"Don't be ridiculous," Kodiak said. "You've injured yourself. You need to get back to the ship. And you're going to need numbers to bring you there."

"I don't need—"

"He is correct," said N'tho. "Clearly you have injured yourself in a manner that precludes your continuing. Furthermore," and he glanced around, "the snowfall is becoming rather severe. Too much for your soldiers to endure."

"We can endure anything you can," Calder said, but Richards saw that he was shivering. The other three were, too. Not that any of them would have admitted to any sort of discomfort. Even the thermal protective gear that they had brought wasn't cutting it in this section of the Ark, at least not in its current state.

To her surprise, Richards noticed that the only one who didn't seem to be reacting to the cold was Luther Mann. He must have been cold, but he didn't appear to be at all bothered by it. In fact, he was blowing "smoke rings" with his breath, as if idly trying to keep himself occupied. And he had slung the marksman rifle from one of the fallen marines over his shoulders as well. Evidently, he wasn't as helpless as she had first surmised.

"Captain—" Kodiak began.

She put a hand up to cut him off. "I know," she said in irritation. "Believe me, I know." She turned to the men who were supporting her upright and growled tightly, "We're going back to the ship. We're not accomplishing anything out here, and we don't need to freeze to death. And not you, Spartan. You go with Luther and the others and keep me apprised of everything that happens."

"Yes, Captain," said Kodiak.

Just for a heartbeat, she wondered if she was doing the right thing, keeping Kodiak and N'tho together, and in a situation where if either one looked at the other the wrong way, another duel to the death could erupt. Granted, the other Sangheili would certainly step in if things went awry, but still . . .

Kodiak didn't kill N'tho, even though he easily could have. He knew it was wrong and he stopped himself. He can be trusted.

I know *he can be trusted.*

She wondered if she knew it for sure or if she was just telling herself that.

"Get me out of here," she said to her men. "And keep it quiet. We don't need those things coming back."

They nodded and started hauling her in the opposite direction, falling in, circling Richards just as earlier, working harder to shield her from the increasing heaviness of the snow.

The last thing she saw was N'tho and Kodiak watching her for a moment before turning away, vanishing behind a steadily growing sheaf of white.

"Let us proceed carefully," said N'tho. "We cannot afford any more losses."

"By my calculations, we should be about fifteen kilometers away," Luther said, checking a device he wore on his wrist. "Halfway there. It won't be easy, though." He looked up at N'tho. "Does any of this look familiar?"

N'tho briefly surveyed the surrounding terrain. "Not at all," he said flatly. "We approached from a different angle and by way of dropship the last time we were here. As we get closer to the citadel, no doubt more will become familiar."

"Let us walk," Kola said. "My legs sicken of our complacency."

It was a figure of speech that showed the Elite wasn't accustomed to waiting around for weaker humans and the problems that attended them. It made Luther uneasy. Kola's tone suggested that they were simply strolling along some riverside. This was definitely not a stroll, nor was it a riverside. But then he realized that he had no idea what sort of weather Kola and the other Sangheili were accustomed to back on their own worlds. For all he knew, this was genuinely equivalent to a walk in the park for them.

Luther kept a wary eye in front of him, wanting to avoid stepping into a snow-covered hole like Richards had. Anyplace where the snow appeared oddly thick was passed over as well. The last thing this splinter group needed was for another one of them to injure himself. If that happened, the other two would probably have to haul whoever back to the ship . . . and if it was any of the giant Sangheili that went down, then God help them all.

They continued to make their way across the snowy plain. Luther shielded his eyes as best he could, focusing on the Ark's core, which was still pretty far away. It was hard to judge just how much longer it would take, given the variability of the terrain. He felt as if they had been walking for ages and still weren't getting anywhere fast. Especially with the significant temperature drop since they first set out.

Something bounded around his feet. "What the hell?" he murmured.

The Spartan heard him and turned to see what had caught Luther's attention. He muttered, "What . . . ?" and now the Sangheili, who had been walking ahead of them and maintaining their steady stride, stopped as well to see what they were looking at.

It was a small, white creature that bore a resemblance to a rabbit, except for the leathery alabaster wings extending from either side of its body. It was sniffing around Luther's feet and, apparently, upon Luther staring bug-eyed at it, began to flap those wings. Within seconds it had risen to Luther's eye level and was studying him with open curiosity.

"I'll be damned," Luther said in a low voice. Then he reached toward the creature.

"Don't touch it," Kodiak warned him. "We have no idea what that thing might do."

"I'll take the chance," said Luther. He saw Kodiak then, out of the corner of his eye, raise his rifle and take aim. Clearly if the thing made the slightest aggressive move, Kodiak was prepared to blow it to hell.

Luther slowly brought his hand up to indicate that he meant no harm, then gently moved it onto the creature's head and slid his palm over it. The flittering thing made a low sound that seemed akin to a purr. Taking that as a good sign, Luther continued to pet the creature. Its wings sped up and it bobbed up and down for long seconds.

Then it pivoted and hurtled away, back into the snow.

"That was . . . intriguing," said Luther.

Kodiak had already lost interest. "At least it didn't try to kill us. I consider that a plus. Beyond that, it really doesn't matter."

They started walking again.

Luther was certain that the snow was coming down even harder now. Despite his tendency to resist the environment, he was nevertheless starting to lose feeling in his feet, and wondered if he was possibly in danger of having some of his extremities freeze out.

Then the ground under him shook. The unexpected movement startled him as he fell to the ground, throwing his arms out to either side to try to catch himself. The Sangheili didn't appear the least put out, but Kodiak had to stop in order to prevent himself from tumbling. "What was that?" said the Spartan.

There was another rumble then, and another. It was slow and steady, getting progressively louder.

"I think . . . I think something's coming toward us," said Luther as he stumbled to his feet, brushing snow off his legs. "Something *really* big."

"Of course. Perhaps we should push forward to meet it head-on," said Zon.

That was not a suggestion Luther was especially interested in hearing. "Maybe we should hide," he said.

"Hide?" Kola asked, genuinely taken aback by the suggestion. "Where would *you* hide exactly, human?"

It was a perfectly valid question. They were in the middle of a vast, frozen plain, with nothing around to secure themselves behind, and the Elites didn't seem very keen on the idea of favoring flight over fight. Their only real hope was the steady snow drifting down, which could possibly blind any approaching foe, but it wasn't something that they could count on for perfect camouflage.

The ground continued to quake underneath them, and then the cause separated itself from the snow ahead of them.

It bore a passing resemblance to an elephant, but it too was covered with white fur, much like the other creatures had been. It stood at least five meters tall as it walked slowly toward them on its four massive legs. It had a lengthy trunk that dangled from the front of its face, swaying slowly with each stride it took. Four alarmingly large tusks slung upward from its jaw, jutting out on both sides of its trunk and proving that it could easily gore the entire group if it was capable of charging. It made no vocalization as it approached, but it didn't have to: the sound of the ground rumbling from the impact tremors of each step was more than enough.

"Don't move," N'tho said in a low voice.

"I honestly wasn't even thinking about it," replied Luther.

Spartan Kodiak had his battle rifle out, but held it at the ready, in a distinctly defensive position. While Luther appreciated the thought, he wasn't sure if it would accomplish anything against the massive beast that was steadily approaching. If Kodiak actually succeeded in making a perfect shot to the creature's cranium, and all that managed to do was annoy it, the newcomer would reduce them to large red streaks in the snow.

"Did you come across this many animals in your previous trip?" Luther asked N'tho, genuinely curious about the seemingly endless menagerie they'd encountered.

"No. Not even one."

Despite the hostile climate and degrading conditions, this part of the Ark seemed to be teeming with all manner of life. *Why?* The answer eluded Luther, but there had to be a reason.

The creature came thundering within twenty meters of them and stopped. That was when Luther noticed something, and he tapped Kodiak on the shoulder and pointed. Kodiak nodded the moment he spotted it.

It was the rabbitlike life-form, fluttering around the white mammoth creature's head and making loud squeaking noises. It seemed for all the world like it was actually talking to the giant.

The beast huffed and then, very slowly, sank to its knees. The two humans and the Sangheili watched in confusion as it extended its trunk toward them. They continued to stand there, staring at it, unsure of what they were supposed to do.

Then, slowly and cautiously, Luther started toward the creature.

"Where are you going?" demanded Kodiak.

He made a move to pull Luther back but was waved off. As Luther's feet sank into the snow, he told himself that he was doing the right thing. That the creature wouldn't go berserk or bludgeon him with its tusks and fling him to his death across the snowy plain. Oddly enough, the aspect that bothered Luther the most was the thought of looking stupid in front of his companions.

Luther was impressed by the warmth radiating from this creature, and it seemed genuinely harmless, like the flying whales they'd encountered earlier. He kept walking until he was right next to it, and as he did with the floating rabbit, slowly extended his hand and touched its head. He stroked it a few times, although he did it so delicately that he wasn't sure the beast was even feeling anything.

Then he gasped as something suddenly wound around his waist. It was the beast's elephantine trunk, and for a moment, his entire nightmare scenario came to the fore.

Slowly Luther was raised into the air. "Go loose!" shouted Kodiak, bringing his weapon up.

"No!" shouted Luther. "Don't do anything! I think . . . just wait! Don't *do* anything!"

Kodiak froze, but kept a bead on the mammoth, aiming squarely at its head. Luther didn't like the odds of what might happen if Kodiak actually fired off a shot. Even if the Spartan managed to kill it, the beast's death spasms might well be enough to crush Luther.

The creature was continuing to raise him up and then, very delicately, it lowered him onto its back. Luther straddled it in surprise, finding the beast's back fur somewhat comfortable.

Slowly Kodiak lowered his weapon, staring in astonishment.

The creature then shifted its gaze to rest on the Spartan and the Sangheili.

"Come on!" Luther shouted, gesturing to them. "I think it wants you to get on too!"

"You cannot be serious," said Zon.

"I'm completely serious! Don't you get it? It came for *us*! Something sent it!"

"Maybe something hostile," said Kodiak.

"No, because if it were hostile, this thing would have already obliterated us. Don't you see? Not everything here has to signal an attack. Maybe we need to take this one on faith."

"You want us to place our faith in some unseen force that has command over small-brained animals?" asked N'tho.

"That's exactly right, unless you have a better idea. If this thing wanted to kill us, we'd already be dead. Plus the temperature is dropping out here faster than we expected, and I'm becoming less thrilled with our odds," said Luther. "There's a reason we've run into so many creatures here. It can't be coincidence. Something is directing them, and that something might be able to help us. So I say you get on this damn monster, would you, please?"

The Sangheili and Kodiak exchanged looks. Then N'tho shrugged and strode toward the beast. Kola and Zon quickly followed, with Kodiak bringing up the rear, obviously having no desire to be the only one left behind.

N'tho came up to the side of the mammoth, grabbed a handful of its fur, and pulled himself upward. The creature did not appear to react in pain. Instead it simply looked at him with a hint of indifference. The other Sangheili then followed suit.

Kodiak was right behind the Elite. He likewise scrambled on top, pulling on the creature's furry coat for support as he hauled himself upward. Moments later, he was sitting between Luther and N'tho, with the other three Sangheili behind him.

Meanwhile, the Huragok floated toward them. The cold air

did not appear to be impacting Drifts Randomly at all. The wind was blowing its tentacles around and snow was crusting on the Engineer's upper body, but it didn't seem the least bit perturbed. Luther felt envious of it. Apparently a Huragok didn't have to worry about hypothermia.

He wondered what would happen if the alien mammoth just remained exactly where it was, unmoving. How long would they stay perched upon it before acknowledging that he had been completely wrong and it was just settling down for a rest?

But then, much to Luther's relief, the creature slowly became mobile once more, the sudden vibrations rattling him to his core. He held on for dear life and would have slid off were it not for Kodiak grabbing Luther from behind, steadying him so that he remained safely atop.

There was a low growling from nearby and Luther felt his blood go cold. It was the blind bipeds from earlier . . . or at least a couple of them. They were now approaching the mammoth.

The giant beast stretched its trunk and produced an ear-splitting bellow so loud that even the Sangheili covered their earholes. Luther felt the creature's lungs resonate between his legs.

Their attackers promptly backed off. For a moment, Luther thought they would converge on the mammoth and try to take it down, but he was relieved to see that fear overrode the pack mentality; they were retreating and slinking away into the blowing snow.

Something is definitely going on here, Luther thought. *There's more here than just blind randomness at play. The animal behavior, the strange illusion with the trees, Vale's disappearance—something else* has *to be at work.*

The mammoth was now walking with slow strides, the ground rumbling beneath them. Luther had to admit it was rather impressive. He far preferred being on this end of the noise-making machine. For the time being, it was headed in the direction they had been, which added to the general oddity of this event.

"Where do you think it's taking us?" said Kodiak.

Luther turned his head and said: "I'm not entirely sure."

"Such a strange thing," N'tho said. "It obviously has a sense of destination. I suppose it's possible that it is being guided by the Oracle of the Ark."

"The what?" said Kodiak.

It was Luther who replied, shouting back: "The Ark may have an active AI on it. The Covenant called it an Oracle. The Forerunners referred to it as an ancilla, or, in this case, a monitor. It's like a caretaker or custodian, helping maintain the installation for extremely long spans of time. Most Forerunner installations such as this have a monitor, though all of our previous records indicate that there was no sign of one when humans came here in '52. It isn't impossible, however, that one does exist and that the artificial intelligence is somehow communicating with the creatures that reside on the surface."

"So you're suggesting that the AI is *telling* the local wildlife what to do?"

"Exactly."

"You do realize they *attacked* us at first."

"Yes," Luther said slowly. "That fact did occur to me."

"So you're asking us to possibly trust the actions of something that tried to kill us outright."

"I suppose I am," said Luther.

"Perfect," said Kodiak. "I'm sure it'll work out just fine."

CHAPTER 11

Henry Lamb, Spartan Holt, and Usze 'Taham were having much difficulty getting across the snowy vista. Lamb, in particular, found his breath coming heavily, large white puffs of mist drifting raggedly from his mouth.

The greater issue, however, was that it was becoming increasingly difficult to track Olympia Vale's path. As the snow continued to whirl around them, it was harder to discern the tracks now being filled in by the storm.

"This is getting problematic," Usze said. "What do we do if we cannot continue to track her?"

"Technically, if we keep heading in this direction," Lamb said firmly, "it will take us where we want to go: toward the communications array at the edge of the foundry, the citadel. So even if she deviates from this path, we want to maintain it. At least we'd reconnect with the other team." He hated saying it, because he had come to feel rather fond of Vale, but priorities remained priorities.

"What's the foundry again?" said Holt.

Lamb turned to him, speaking with confidence. If there was one thing he was comfortable discussing, it was the technology of the Forerunners. "It's a facility used to construct Halo installations, the same ones that are currently counting down—ironically, whatever drew Vale off seems to be headed in that direction."

"Wonderful," said Holt. "Didn't think this op could get any stranger."

They continued walking.

Vale's tracks eventually vanished completely. If she'd changed her approach now, they would never be able to find her. Nevertheless they kept moving forward, hoping that they would be able to pick up her trail again.

They had long lost sight of the other travelers on their range-finder as well and were now completely on their own. The last report they had received from the captain was that her leg had been seriously injured and she was headed back to the ship, but their close-band comm unit had performed poorly since, presumably due to the weather. The last two times Holt attempted to contact Kodiak, he hadn't be able to reach him, which is exactly what Lamb had feared would happen.

The snow was now coming down harder, and Lamb did everything he could to shield his eyes from it. Despite the thermal gear that had protected him earlier, he now felt his body temperature dropping, and his muscles were aching horribly. The environment was getting thicker, claustrophobic, and he was starting to think that this had all been a horrible mistake.

Then he noticed that the ground was starting to angle upward. That struck him as rather odd. Not only that, but it seemed as if the snow was tapering off here. Lamb stomped down several times and discovered that the consistency of the ground was changing; it felt harder. He knelt down and brushed away the crust of the snow and discovered that there was something gray and perfectly flat beneath it.

"This is manufactured, it's not natural stone," he said. "Technically, everything is artificial out here, but this is different. It's some kind of floor."

HALO: HUNTERS IN THE DARK

"You are correct," said Usze, running his big four-fingered hand across it.

"That's good, isn't it?" Holt asked.

"It means we are getting closer. Unfortunately," the Elite added grimly, "we seem to have completely lost track of Olympia Vale. Yet it may well be that she's being brought to the core, perhaps even the very citadel we seek."

"Let's hope," Lamb said.

As they moved forward, the gray, metallic floor became more and more prominent and the snow started to recede, both in the air and on the ground. It was a strange phenomenon, almost like passing through a curtain or veil. And as the flurried obfuscation suddenly lessened, it revealed that they had made their way to the height of a large wall, one that looked out onto the Ark's foundry and the distant mining moon at the very center. Off to the right, Lamb could just barely make out the citadel's center spire in the distance, an angular tower that hung over the lip of the foundry. Most of the citadel was hidden well behind a large mountainous ridge that protected it, but the sight made his throat clench up in suppressed satisfaction—they were actually getting closer.

They finally stepped completely out of the snow, and the first thing that Lamb noticed was that the ground actually felt warmer. That was certainly an interesting sensation—amazingly, the temperature was starting to change, and it seemed to be coming from beneath him.

Lamb pulled out his optics device and took a closer look around them. He could now see the citadel's single spire clearly, at least its highest point. It was surrounded by a large ridgeline that rose from an even larger body of water, with a trio of impressively sized pylons climbing out of the rock walls and forming three prongs. According to data acquired from *Forward Unto Dawn*, the pylons were capable of projecting a powerfully resistive energy barrier that could prevent any and all access to the citadel, even against the firepower of a Covenant capital ship. Lamb wondered if that'd be a problem this time, and then he started to take notice of his immediate surroundings. Just below the top of the wall they found themselves on, the land slung out toward the very lip of the foundry, about ten kilometers away. It looked temperate, maybe even warm, a complete shift from the conditions just twenty meters behind them.

"Were you expecting it to get this warm?" he asked Usze.

"No," said Usze, nodding in the citadel's direction. "Two years ago, we traveled across that large sea," he said, pointing to an enormous body of water that skirted the ridge that surrounded the citadel. Lamb could see that large sections of that sea were now frozen over, covered in thick sheets of ice and buried in dense snowfall. The other team would likely come very near this body of water, if not directly across it. "We and the humans took dropships and were deployed along the beach there," he pointed. "After we deactivated the shield-distributing towers, the Demon—your Master Chief—led us into the interior hub that surrounded the citadel. It was there that we made the final stand against the Covenant, seized the citadel, and stopped Halo from firing."

Lamb took in a long breath. It was hard to believe that he was nearing the same place that the final battle between humans and the Covenant occurred, where the Master Chief prevented the Array from firing. History was repeating itself, and the weight of the fact that he was playing a role in it made him shudder.

"Is that what I think it is?" Lamb asked, pointing to a huge mass of debris, even more alien than the Ark's surface, about fifty kilometers around the circular foundry. It looked like a mountain of blacks and grays, though clearly not part of the installation.

"High Charity," Usze said, "the Covenant Holy City. When the Flood had taken full control of it, the parasite used it to get here. That's why your Master Chief fired the unfinished Halo at this place. To stop the Flood from dominating the Ark, and thereby cutting off any chance of its spreading across the galaxy."

Lamb spent a full minute taking in the incredible scale of the debris, imagining what it might have been like to see High Charity in its prime. The group then pressed on along the wall to a place where it appeared to connect to a ridge leading back to the ground.

Around their feet, the snow had melted away completely, but as they moved further, it slowly became impossible for Lamb to see the material that composed the massive wall. Instead large patches of dirt were now becoming visible, and Lamb noticed that bright-green moss was beginning to appear around rocks and across the stony ground. He considered that to be a positive sign. It meant, to some degree, that the climate had been temperate here for a significant period of time.

"This isn't just weather change," said Lamb. "It's environmental, and not passive. We're going from one climatic zone to another. That makes me think that the weather conditions are entirely artificial and being actively controlled by a system or some distributed intelligence. The strange thing is that there was no record of a localized AI on this installation, at least from what was recovered from *Forward Unto Dawn*. I don't think it's something we were really anticipating."

"Anticipate anything," said Usze. He was kneeling, studying the ground. Then slowly he nodded. "Yes, she came through here."

"Are you sure?"

"I can see traces of not only her, but pieces of ground that were chipped by the claws of the creature accompanying her."

"Looks like she headed down the ridge there," Holt said, pointing down a narrow ridgeline that descended into a heavy cluster of foliage largely comprised of incredibly tall evergreen-like trees. It gradually grew in density, and farther down became a large forest that hemmed in this particular section of the circular foundry and a steep mountain ridge off to the right. Just beyond that wooded area lay a short mountain hike to the citadel.

"So that's good," said Lamb. "It means we're on the right track."

"So far. But I am . . ."

Usze's voice trailed off. Slowly the Sangheili rose to his feet, and when Lamb started to ask him what was wrong, Usze promptly silenced him.

"We are not alone," Usze finally whispered, smoothly removing his plasma sword from against his thigh and immediately activating it. Power rippled up and down the blade. Holt lifted his battle rifle in response, scanning the immediate surroundings through its sight.

"Who else is here?" asked Lamb quietly.

"I am uncertain. But there is—"

Suddenly Holt shouted, "There!" and pointed toward a row of trees that was a short distance away. Directly in front of them, the air distorted and pinched together, before four pockets of light snapped into existence. To Lamb, it was immediately clear that it was some sort of localized phasing or teleportation portal.

Something was emerging from each portal, and although it had the general shape of a biped, even a human, it was clearly not anything of the sort. Composed almost entirely of a metallic alloy-like substance, these robotic-looking constructs had the same posture and frame as a human, even down to the orientation of their plated musculature. Nevertheless, they clearly displayed the Forerunner design aesthetics, with eccentric bevels, angular apertures, and floating accoutrements; their bodies were lithe yet still formidably armored, standing upright at nearly a meter taller than Spartan Holt. Though difficult to discern at this range, their faces appeared to be symmetrical plates of the same kind of alloy, with two discernible glowing eyes that matched a number of slight breaches in and around the armor. Lamb suspected some kind of hard-light composition beneath, rigidly holding the components together.

And they had weapons. Stave-like devices with a geometrical blade of hard light at the end. They did not look friendly.

Does every goddamn thing around here have to be hostile? Lamb thought.

There were at least four of them that could be seen, all now charging in the direction of Lamb, Holt, and Usze.

"It's always something," said Lamb.

"Get behind me!" said Holt, and he began firing in the direction of the enemies. Lamb, however, did not retreat. He still had his weapon from their earlier battle against the creatures, and instead of hiding behind the Spartan, he stood next to him and opened fire. The handgun he used was surprisingly powerful, exploding with every round as he struggled to maintain its concussive jostling. Holt glanced briefly at him and, although Lamb couldn't be certain, he thought he glimpsed silent approval in the Spartan's helmet visor.

The blasts from their weapons collided with the oncoming combatants.

Lamb was worried that they would absorb the impact and continue forward with no problem. Instead the two closest spun their staves with lightning speed, remarkably blocking the incoming fire. But then the air around them seemed to bend again, and with a sudden snap of light they disappeared. The other two, however, persisted.

Usze had already burst forward, his energy sword extended to the side as he ran. It was extremely impressive to see a Sangheili run at full speed. Even with full armor on, he quickly closed the gap between him and their enemies. Holt followed at a slower pace, trying to get a bead on them, while Lamb trailed just behind, occasionally releasing a shot or two.

Usze slammed into the nearest being shoulder first, bringing up his sword to block the parry from the second. The Sangheili was suddenly in the heat of battle with the Forerunner machines, fending and attacking with his blade as they used their staves in surprisingly efficient coordination. The combat was a blur of light and armor, with the occasional spark and sizzle of blades coming into contact with each other. Usze was too close to the enemies for Holt to get a viable shot off, but the Spartan kept his rifle up, staring carefully down its sight and methodically strafing like a seasoned hunter. Lamb, meanwhile, wondered if the other two had disappeared for good, or if they were just waiting for their chance to strike.

With a sudden show of force, Usze severed the arm of one of the Forerunner machines, and then raked the blade up along the thing's neck, popping the robotic head off with a sudden, cracking burst of hard light. The other machine, however, managed to kick Usze hard in the side, sending the Elite into the air and across the ground, his energy sword skittering to a stop several meters out of reach.

The Forerunner machine lifted its stave high in the air, preparing to bring the weapon down hard on the Elite. Before it could exact its hit, it was prevented by a three-round burst of bullets slamming into its robotic head with a loud impact sound, bringing the machine down to its knees, before falling over onto its side.

Holt reloaded his rifle and slapped it onto his armored back, moving steadily toward Usze with Lamb right behind. "What are those things?" he asked, helping the Sangheili up onto his feet.

"Looks like some kind of Forerunner defensive machine, but I've never encountered anything like it before in my work," Lamb said, still looking around for a sign of the other two.

"Keep moving," Usze said in a low voice, retrieving and deactivating his sword.

The three of them made their way quickly along the ground, heading into the wooded area, in the direction that Vale seemed to have gone. As they moved through the forest, which quickly grew denser the farther they went, they noticed a ridge of mountains climbing up behind the landscape off to their far right, but it was impossible to see it clearly from their position. It looked steep and incredibly rocky, but it was likely the same ridge that connected to the mountainous territory surrounding the citadel. They chose to ignore it, however, continuing through the heavily wooded area, which was less steep, and heading toward where they perceived the foundry to be, although the incline to their right came closer and closer, until they were running along the very foot of the mountain.

A sudden and loud snap could be heard from above, and then a tree at least thirty meters high sagged and slowly tumbled down toward them. This was immediately problematic, as they were now at the bottom of a sharp incline, hedged in by boulders and large chunks of stony detritus. On the incline of the mountain, the two remaining Forerunner machines stood, now bearing what appeared to be long marksman-like energy rifles—though they seemed in no hurry to use them, despite holding the higher ground. It was clear, however, that they were responsible for the tree that now threatened the group.

"Run!" shouted Holt, though he didn't really have to; Lamb

and Usze were already racing ahead. The damaged tree hit the ground and started to roll downward, branches shattering beneath the massive trunk as it kept on coming, gaining speed with each passing moment.

Lamb tripped over an upturned root and fell forward. Panic and thoughts of certain death slammed through his mind. Then something hauled him up and off his feet—the Spartan had grabbed him from behind and propelled Lamb on his way to safety without even slowing down.

The tree flew past the group, missing them by only centimeters. But they kept up the fast pace as one of the machines let out a loud roar from upon the hill, presumably in frustration at their failure to crush their intended prey. The most chilling thing to Lamb was that, despite a strange robotic tinge in the vocalization, it sounded almost human, even though the beings' clearly artificial physiology belied any claim to humanity they might have.

"Just keep moving!" Holt shouted. "As long as we stay in the trees—"

There was a rumbling beneath their feet, getting louder by the second.

Avalanche . . . ?!

Something—the pursuing Forerunner machines, no doubt—had set a rockslide in motion, and now a dozen human-size rocks and grit were tumbling down the incline and heading right toward them.

Lamb was confused. *Why hadn't they fired their weapons? Were they just toying with them?*

The three of them turned and ran like hell.

Holt and Usze were both considerably more physically adept at running than Lamb and were quickly outpacing him. He had no intention of asking for help, though, and so continued sprinting after the others.

He vaulted over a hole, then a second one, his arms pumping, his breath rasping in his chest. He glanced to his right and saw with terror that the rolling boulders were getting closer, starting to catch up, and there were a hell of a lot more descending. Lamb dodged frantically as the first boulder nearly clipped his shoulder, and then suddenly his legs collapsed as something broadsided him across his knees.

He stumbled and fell once more, and now the rocks were raining down and bouncing all around him. He threw his arms over his head in a desperate attempt to try and protect himself.

"Get up" came the commanding voice of Usze 'Taham, hauling him to his feet. Were it not for the immediate fear of being dashed to pieces, Lamb would have hated the fact that he was proving to be so weak. Evidently, he always had to depend on others to save him.

Lamb's feet were no longer touching the ground. Usze was raising him through the air. Lamb felt completely disoriented as larger boulders threatened to crush them both, but Usze kept moving, catching up with Holt, who was just ahead.

"There!" shouted the Spartan. A sizable rock lay in their path, seemingly capable of protecting them from the avalanche. The three of them ducked behind it, taking advantage of the natural shelter as the rocks hailed down around them.

At least they had found refuge from the assault.

"Heads up!" shouted Holt.

The Forerunner machines were suddenly there, right on top of them. Apparently they had once again teleported down the hillside as their improvised avalanche had come to an end. Now they began firing, with pulses of bright yellow energy—which seemed to be pockets of hard light–like material—bursting from their very alien-looking rifles.

Usze was immediately up and swinging his sword around, deflecting the incoming fire away from the group while edging toward the approaching enemies. Holt ran alongside him, launching himself at the nearest one and planting his fist in its chest. The machine biped flew backward with the impact, rolling into the dirt before sliding to a stop on its knee, its rifle still raised and firing as though it was unfazed. Holt took the brunt of the fire on his Mjolnir armor's energy shielding before ducking behind one of the nearby boulders and retrieving his rifle.

The other Forerunner machine fired at Usze, who managed to again protect himself with his sword as he charged forward, quickly spinning around and delivering a hard kick at the enemy's midsection. The blow connected, knocking the rifle from the biped's hands, the robotic machine reeling back as it hissed at Usze. It held out its hand to the side and the stave suddenly appeared, seemingly forming from various bits and pieces of the machine's robotic arm. With a quick bob of the stave, the large blade of energy ignited and the Forerunner machine swung it deftly, entering a combat stance. Usze bounded toward the enemy and engaged it head to head. Despite the machine's speed and dexterity, it was no match for the Elite one on one. Usze's energy sword blazed as the blade sliced across the front of the Forerunner biped. The machine let out an earsplitting sound and stumbled back, falling to the ground in pieces.

Holt had now emerged from the rock, rifle in hand and his shielding recharged. He fired without mercy at the first biped. Although it was a steady and quick exchange of firepower, the

Forerunner machine couldn't withstand the ballistic rounds and took one too many in the chest, before collapsing.

"That was close," Lamb said, leaning near one of the fallen rocks.

"Looks like it's not over," Holt said, reloading his rifle.

Lamb peeked over the top of the boulder, and his eyes widened.

There were now a dozen of the Forerunner machines, armed to the teeth and each coming in through their portals, dropping to the ground from all directions.

"Run!" Lamb bellowed.

"The hell we will," the Spartan shot back. He was now peeking over the top of his boulder, firing at anything that came near him.

But they were advancing too fast for Holt to be able to adjust his strategy. One of them got close enough to pounce atop the boulder. *Man, could they really move!* Holt swung his rifle upward to fire off a shot, but the attack on him came too quickly and he was thrown backward. He lost his grip on the rifle and it fell from his hands. The Spartan swung his fists and connected with the side of the machine's head, knocking it to the ground as the others began to converge on their general position.

An explosion from behind Holt, and the advancing Forerunner machine's head was blown clean off its shoulders. Holt managed to break free, grab his rifle, and leap back over the boulder where Lamb and Usze were taking cover. Some of the encroaching machines had rifles and were unloading a fusillade of firepower at the boulder.

Lamb was lying there, looking stunned, still gripping his gun.

Holt quickly checked his own rifle for damage. "You saved my life."

"We're not out of the woods yet," Lamb gasped out.

The Sangheili, meanwhile, having swapped his sword with the Covenant carbine he had used earlier, was methodically firing away at the attackers. Both Holt and Lamb joined him. Despite being outnumbered, both the Elite and the Spartan were simply too skilled with their weapons, and they slowly chipped down at their enemies' numbers. Within a minute, only a handful of them remained, and the threat slowly abated. The Forerunner machines were now falling back quickly, snarling an eerie vocalization as they retreated, but at least they were leaving.

Holt fired off a few more shots just to underscore their desire to be left alone. "They're going," he said, as one by one the machines flashed out of existence into their strange portals.

"Thank God," Lamb sighed with relief. "That was not fun."

"You saved me," Holt said again.

"It's no big deal. Although I didn't do myself any good." He was sitting up and trying to flex his right hand, with little success.

"What's the matter?" said Holt.

"I hurt my arm. Or my shoulder. Something."

"Hold on," said Holt as he crouched behind him. His fingers probed, and when Lamb let out a pained grunt, he nodded. "You dislocated your shoulder."

"Must have been when I fell," he said, wincing.

Holt gripped Lamb's arm and shoulder firmly. "I want you to relax."

"Yeah, that's not happening."

"On the count of three? Ready?"

"You're going to do it on one, aren't you."

"No," said Holt. "On three. Start counting."

"You sure?"

"Yes, I'm sure."

"Okay," said Lamb, taking a deep breath and letting it out. "One—"

Holt pushed and pulled at the same time and Lamb let out a high, piercing scream. Usze's head snapped around in surprise.

Lamb rubbed his throbbing shoulder. "You said you weren't going to—"

"I lied. Get over it."

Lamb raised his arm and then rotated it slowly. He was able to waggle his fingers once more. "You did it."

"I know," said Holt. "Now we're even."

"How's that?"

"You saved my life, and I just fixed your shoulder."

"Let us go," Usze said. "This respite will not last forever." He gestured. "We must continue before they return."

Lamb kept a wary eye out as they moved—he was pretty sure that there were still some watching them, but fortunately enough they were keeping their distance. So that was something to be grateful for. The trio continued to press on through the trees, heading along the foot of the mountain in the general direction of the foundry core.

"We have an obvious problem," Holt announced. "Between the avalanche and everything else that just happened, we've lost track of Vale again. And this time there's not going to be any way of picking her up."

"Then we do what I said," said Lamb. "We keep heading in the direction we were going. It'll take us where we need to be anyway, and perhaps with some luck we'll manage to pick up her trail again."

"It's not likely," said Holt.

"I know. But it's all we've got." Lamb saw that Usze appeared to be tapping his wrist. "What's wrong?"

"I am attempting to communicate with N'tho," said Usze, "to inform him of our progress. But the transmission is not going through."

"I haven't been able to get through to Kodiak, either," said Holt.

"Are . . ." Lamb found it hard to say. "Are they dead?"

"No . . . well, not so far as we know," amended Holt. "Something is likely jamming us. I've no idea what or why, but we're cut off from the others. Given what's just gone down, I can't say I like this at all."

The snow was still savagely beating down upon Luther Mann, Spartan Kodiak, and the Sangheili, but the alien mammoth moved along with the same steady resolve. It certainly did appear as if it had some particular destination in mind; its riders didn't know where that might be, but they continued to hold on with determination.

"I am wary of trusting your judgment here, Doctor," N'tho voiced above the snow and wind. "Were it not for the untenable position of crossing the snow, we'd still be on the ground, heading to the citadel on foot."

"You do know what you're doing, right, Doc?" Kodiak asked.

Luther turned to address them, shielding his face from the blankets of snow now coming down. "We have very little to go on here, but I have a theory."

"Let's hear it," the Spartan prodded.

"The Ark isn't just a manufacturing plant for Halo rings. It was used as a sanctuary for life found across the galaxy, not just sentient life but species that depended on sentient creatures for their survival, whether for care or food or whatever."

"You are saying," N'tho attempted to clarify, "that the Fore-runners kept the natural predators of sentient species on the Ark so they wouldn't go extinct when the sentient beings on their own world suddenly died off?"

"Yes, they were trying to save entire ecosystems, not just sentient beings, whenever the Halo was activated. If they save a sentient being but return it to a world that is in the throes of eco-logical collapse, then no one wins."

"So that's why a lot of these critters have been trying to kill us," the Spartan asked with a bit of a growl.

"Mostly, yes. After the Halo rings fired a hundred thousand years ago, the Ark's automated systems reseeded the planets these species once lived on, including Earth and humans. Some of the specimens from other worlds clearly remained behind; we've en-countered other kinds on the Halo installations as well. When the Ark was damaged by the replacement Halo about two years ago, things clearly went a little haywire here. The various walled sec-tions of the Ark are called refugia. They're like wildlife paddocks the size of a moon—we're talking, enormous cages for different species. It's extremely likely that some of the walls were breached, allowing different specimens into one another's territory and de-stabilizing normal predation circles."

"That explains why we've seen so many species, Doctor," N'tho spoke up. "It does not explain why this one was so compli-ant, or why it appears that Vale was mysteriously appropriated by another."

"I'm getting to that. One of the things we've discovered is that the Forerunners could biologically program data into the animals.

I'm not talking about making food taste better; I'm talking about seeding behaviors and dispositions. Some have theorized that Forerunners could even communicate with and control creatures." Luther took a deep breath before he continued. "I think what we're being brought to is a Forerunner intelligence. Maybe even the one that was tasked with the care of this installation. I think it's telling some of these creatures to bring us to it. "

The group remained silent for at least a minute before someone spoke up.

"That is not particularly comforting, Doctor," N'tho said flatly. "If such an intelligence exists, is it not likely that it activated Halo? It may not have a high view of biological sentience."

"If it wanted us dead, we'd be dead. There's something more at work here. Think about the Retrievers. Why did they come through the portal back on Earth? Why haven't we been taken out by one yet during this expedition? And how did we even get to the Ark in a matter of hours, not weeks?" Luther caught his breath, and then continued: "Ultimately, if this AI somehow managed to activate Halo, it's not going to be as easy as simply flipping a switch. This is its home and has been for a hundred thousand years. If we want to shut off Halo, we need to find out what this thing wants from us."

For a long while, no one spoke, except for a few brief crooning sounds from Drifts Randomly. Then came a completely new sound.

A distant cawing. Luther looked up in confusion, unsure of what he was hearing. It appeared to be birds of some sort, but he couldn't be certain; the falling snow made it impossible to see clearly past more than a few dozen meters. As he shielded his eyes, Luther thought he saw some sort of forms pirouetting about high in the air above them. He nudged Kodiak. "What is that?" he said, pointing skyward. "Do you see it?"

Kodiak stared up, also trying to make it out. "Birds, I think? Impossible to tell for sure, at least at this distance."

Now N'tho was looking toward the skies as well. "Stay low," he uttered. "And hope they do not see us."

Everyone heeded N'tho's advice and lowered themselves on the back of the alien mammoth, the large beast still maintaining its steady pace.

Then Luther heard the birdlike creatures screeching once more. And he was convinced that whatever they were, they were getting closer. Given his theories on the Ark's current wildlife situation, Luther doubted the amicability of whatever it was.

He started to turn to Kodiak and express his concerns, when a scream exploded from overhead. He looked up in horror.

It appeared to be something akin to a pterodactyl, but it was covered with a combination of black and white feathers. The wingspan was massive, about twelve meters wide, as far as Luther could determine. Its beak was long and snapping, and it had claws extending from its feet. Unlike the dinosaur bipeds from earlier, this thing definitely had eyes. They were soulless, black things on either side of its head. The creature also had some manner of crest on the back of its head that curved back about a meter behind it.

Luther fell back against Kodiak, who was now yanking his rifle up. The creature was screeching so loudly that Luther was sure he would be rendered deaf.

And suddenly its claws snagged around his arm.

Its wings furiously beat the air as Luther cried out, but there was nothing he could do to stop from being lifted off the mammoth's back. Kodiak grabbed at Luther, trying to drag him back

PETER DAVID

down as the winged monstrosity attempted to hold on. Zon and
Kola reached up as well, grabbing his legs to try to prevent him
being lifted skyward.

Kodiak fired off his rifle once, twice, but it had no measurable
effect on the creature. It shook from the impact and let out caws of
protest but otherwise didn't appear to be bothered.

The creature screamed loudly once more and its wings beat
the air ever harder. *"Let me go!"* Luther shouted. *"It's going to rip
me in half! Let go now! Now!"* He kicked out desperately at the
Sangheili and Spartan who were attempting to keep him seated.
He did so with a strength born of sheer desperation, and because
of the odd angle that they were seated in, none of them could hold
on. With a cry of triumph, the creature angled upward, hauling
Luther with him.

This is it, Luther thought bleakly. *This is how I go out. Hauled
back to some alien nest somewhere and devoured by infants. Torn
to pieces, and I'll never even know whether the rest of the galaxy is
saved.*

For some reason, Luther suddenly realized that his greatest regret was never seeing his daughter. She could never know what
happened to him. *It's probably much better that way.*

The creature shuddered and let out a wrenching howl that was
completely different from anything it had uttered thus far.

N'tho's plasma blade was quivering in the creature's thorax
and then dropped free, falling within Kodiak's reach. The Spartan
snatched it out of the air before it could fall past him.

The beast pitched about wildly, screaming in protest, but it
was already too late. Black, viscous blood was seeping out from
where the blade had struck home, dampening the feathers as it
covered the creature's chest. Its wings were still beating the air,
but the monster was sinking rapidly.

HALO: HUNTERS IN THE DARK

Its claws lost their grip on Luther, and he started to fall. But then Kodiak's hand grabbed him as he tumbled past the mammoth, and a moment later Luther was atop its back again. He was breathing heavily but was relieved to still be alive.

"Are you all right, human?" asked Kola.

"I'm fine, I'm fine," Luther managed to gasp out, though he wasn't fully convinced himself. "Thank you, all of you, for trying to save me."

"It is our understanding that you are required for the mission," Kola said dispassionately. "It made sense to endeavor to rescue you."

Luther had no reply to that. Instead he shifted his attention to N'tho. "That was amazing. Thank you for saving my life."

"Here," said Kodiak, tossing N'tho his energy sword.

N'tho grabbed the weapon and examined it for a moment, then looked up at Kodiak's visor: "Thank you, human."

Kodiak said nothing in return.

N'tho locked the sword to his thigh and retrieved the cartographic device he used earlier to locate the direction to the citadel.

"Interesting," N'tho said.

"What is it?" Luther asked, still rubbing his shoulders.

"This beast is now headed in a straight line toward the citadel. And it has been headed there for some time. We're only a few kilometers away."

"Just how did it know to do that?" said Kodiak incredulously.

"I have only one guess, and it's the same as earlier," said Luther. "There is some sort of guiding intelligence that is governing this creature's abilities. It's telling it what to do."

"But if that is so," said Zon, "why did it not somehow prevent that bird creature from trying to make off with you?"

"It's clear that whatever is guiding this creature doesn't have

— 221 —

an effect on all of them, so don't mistake me: We're not completely safe here. We don't even know what the AI—if that's what it is— actually wants. The bird thing that came after me may simply have been a mother scavenging for its young."

"So you're suggesting that somewhere there's a nest of its babies who are going to starve to death," said Kodiak.

"Yes, I guess I am."

"Good," said Kodiak.

CHAPTER 12

Olympia Vale was trying to remember where she was. And who. And when.

She was starting to piece matters together, albeit with difficulty. She had the vague recollection of once being completely focused on a mission. But now those details had slipped away from her.

Something happened. Something got into your mind.

But what? Who? How?

She had no answers. Not only that, but she wasn't actively seeking any. Which she also found odd, but only in a very distant, detached way.

She was now riding a growling, white-furred creature with large tusks and strange twin horns protruding from its back. Some time ago, it had gently nudged against Vale's legs and more or less insisted that she climb onto its back, and she had obediently done so. This apparently enabled them to move much faster, especially when they got to open areas and the creature picked up speed. Somewhere way back in the distance, she became aware of voices and tremors and the sound of fighting. The sources were unknown, and Vale realized that she didn't especially care anyway.

She lowered the front half of her body, in order to cut down on wind shear, gripping tightly onto the horned extensions that rose out from the middle of the creature. It didn't seem especially stressed from the labor, nor was it breathing particularly hard.

Vale had no sense of space or time. Her mind had simply spun away into a dull, disconnected yet subtle awareness of the ground moving rapidly past her.

The creature was now slowing down.

The snow had long fallen away, and for a time there were simply acres upon acres of extremely tall trees heavily crowding the foot of a steep mountain that rose to her right. But the flora slowly dissipated, and the creature had eventually taken her into a large stretch of arid land. The trees there looked scorched, dead husks that seemed to have endured a violent conflagration of some sort. Everything was dirty and blackened, as if a blazing fire had ripped through at some point. The entire area was barren.

She tried to make out the details of what looked like a looming, sphere-like structure in the distance, but she couldn't see any from her vantage point. She supposed it didn't matter. Nothing mattered.

The horned creature came to a halt. Clearly it was waiting for her to dismount, but she didn't precisely understand why. They didn't seem to be in any notable location, at least as far as she could remember. Which wasn't much. But for some reason, the animal had just stopped suddenly.

Vale remained astride it for a long moment, trying to get her bearings. Eventually the creature started growling and moving its head about, which was obviously its way of letting her know that it was time to get off it. She quickly obeyed, swinging her leg over and standing next to it, scratching her chin thoughtfully as she looked around. The creature stared up at her for a moment more and then, surprisingly, it sprinted away. Moments later, she was left utterly alone.

Vale stood there for some time in the barren area, trying to figure out what to do.

Why here, though? Why did it bring me here?

Vale knelt down, put her hands in the dirt, and immediately felt the hard metallic surface. *This wasn't real ground.* She stood up and took a deep breath, and then she felt something like a mist lift from her. A murkiness departed and she began to remember things.

The mission. She was on something called the Ark. There were other people with her. They were doing something of incredible importance. She strained her memory, but it felt just out of reach. The background started to come into focus, a large sphere sitting in the gaseous expanse, and then beyond, an alien horizon. Things started to become clearer. She recognized something in the far distance: a series of pronged petals resembling the curved shape of a flower that seemed to wrap around on all sides. Then she turned to face in her original direction, and at its center was a huge spherical structure hanging in the mist—some kind of strange moon.

And then, in the middle of her thoughts, she felt a sudden tremor below her feet. The metallic flooring shuddered for a moment and seams appeared around her, forming a perfect hexagon about ten meters across. Then it dropped.

It dropped so unexpectedly that Vale lost her footing and fell backward. She raised her head as she fell so that she didn't bang it on the floor, but then she lay there gaping in astonishment as the platform descended rapidly. Above her, the sky closed, dust and ash gentling drifting down as the flooring above moved back over where the platform had been before, almost as though it was covering the evidence. She was on an elevator of some sort and was now quickly dropping down far below the surface of this place, the only light coming from dim rows lining the walls. Suddenly

PETER DAVID

the elevator stopped and before her was a closed door, composed from the same material as the elevator. It shot open unnervingly quickly, revealing a hallway beyond.

Slowly she sat up and then stood, continuing to gaze at it. "What the hell?" she muttered under her breath.

Vale was there for a long moment, indecisive of her next move. Then, slowly, she walked toward the open door. She stared down into the corridor, trying to make out something in the darkness, but she couldn't discern anything. She took a breath and then stepped inside. The hall was dark but relatively short, ending in a small room with angularly plated ivory walls and muted lights running along the floor.

The room was completely empty except for one thing on the center of the floor: a hatch made from the same metallic substance as the rest of the room. The top of the hatch suddenly opened as she approached it, startling her.

The hatch was about two meters across, more than large enough for her to enter. She eased herself down onto the floor and edged toward the hatch's opening, trying to locate some sort of footing or grips.

Nothing. There's nothing.

She was not about to jump into a hole without the slightest idea of what was waiting for her, that much was certain.

And so it was that she was caught completely off guard when the room seemed to abruptly snap forward—or perhaps the gravity in the room shifted—knocking her into the hole. She reached out desperately, and for half a second her fingers caught on the edge. But then Vale saw the lid of the hatch rushing down and realized that if she tried to hold on, her hand would be broken or even severed.

She let go, spiraling down into darkness as the hatch slammed shut above her.

Vale was skidding out of control.

She realized that she was in some sort of angled metal tube, but she was unable to find any purchase. She thrashed her arms as she fell, trying to find a way of slowing herself, but to no effect.

Suddenly her back struck something. She barely had time to register that it was either a stairway or ladder, and then she bounced off it, tumbling forward and landing heavily on the floor, the impact knocking the wind out of her. She lay there, gasping for several moments, trying to get her breath back.

All this time, Vale had been in total darkness. Slowly she got to her feet and squinted again, trying to see something, anything, around her, but she couldn't make out a thing.

"Is anyone here?" she called out. No response. "Can anyone hear me? Maybe turn the lights on, please?"

To her astonishment, lights flared to life over her head, causing her eyes to dilate sharply. She could see.

She just wasn't certain what she was looking at.

She found herself in a corridor that seemed to stretch on forever. There was white tubing extending around the right side, and she had no idea what it was or what its function could possibly be. Even more puzzling to her was what appeared to be a series of holograms that were floating over her. As far as she could tell, she was staring at starfields. Stars were shining above her; they were not flickering, because their light wasn't being filtered through a planetary atmosphere. Instead the stars were steadily gleaming.

She reached up toward one, and her hands passed through them, touching nothing. More holograms ran the length of the hallway. She started making her way down it, trying to take it all in, to understand everything that was before her, yet hearing only the echoes of her footsteps.

"Hello?" she called cautiously. "Hello? Is anyone here?"

Nothing.

She didn't know how long she kept on; she just knew that the corridor seemed endless. She stared up at the stars as she walked past and became fascinated by their constant changes. It was almost mesmerizing, as if she were on some sort of interstellar voyage in this place.

"It's amazing," she whispered.

Thank you.

She jumped and cried out, grasping her chest as her heartbeat doubled. She leaned against the white tubing, trying to gather her wits about her.

It was the same male voice that had spoken to her earlier, during the battle, though she had a hard time remembering exactly what the battle was about.

"Who are you?"

She felt as if her mind was starting to come back on track again. The fog in her head was now rapidly starting to dissipate, but it didn't serve to calm her mood. "Where are you?" she said, managing to control herself somewhat.

She was turning in a slow circle, wondering if whoever had spoken to her would present himself. She stopped turning when she noticed something at the far end of the corridor.

Something was floating toward her at eye level. It was moving from a great distance, but rapidly getting closer.

She was unable to discern any detail of it. That was because the shape of the . . . the whatever it was . . . kept changing. There was a golden glow emanating from it, and she had to shield her eyes as it grew brighter by drawing nearer.

It was first generally triangular, then a square, then a rectangle. Then it started changing into other shapes, shorter, then longer, constantly moving. It was as if it was attempting to determine its final appearance and thus far had not come to a decision. Vale stared at it, captivated. There were a hundred questions she wanted to ask.

When it finally came within a few meters of her, it stopped and just floated there. She waited for it to speak, operating on the assumption that this had been the thing communicating within her head.

It continued to twist and turn and suddenly it lengthened. It remained at her level, but grew longer until its base touched the floor. Its gold shimmering continued as she realized that it was assuming something similar to a human body.

It's me.

It was contorting into an exact replica of Olympia Vale. She had never seen anything like it, and she stood there with her mouth hanging open. "Wow," she said softly. She was facing an exact duplicate of herself, except instead of being flesh-colored, the replica was still glittering gold. It smiled at her and nodded as if it were an old friend.

Then it spoke.

"My name is Tragic Solitude 000. I am the Keeper of the Ark."

"The monitor?" Vale asked slowly. "So you're an artificial intelligence that was created by the Forerunners."

"You are familiar with me?"

"I'm familiar with the concept of you. Someone . . . *Luther*," she remembered, "he told me that some Forerunner installations have custodians that protect them."

"That is correct."

"You were speaking in my head earlier."

"That is correct."

"But you're not anymore."

"That is correct."

This is getting repetitive. "How did you do it? How did I hear you before?"

"The animal that brought you here. Humans once called it *neldoruut*; the Forerunners called it *chaefka*. It is a predatory species, but some of those on this facility have been made servile through my work."

"You didn't answer my question—"

"This creature releases a pheromone that your species is susceptible to. Within it is an agent that generates a psychotropic effect."

"—you drugged me, then?"

"I utilized your communication earpiece and the effect of the agent to lull you out from the peril you faced when you encountered the *chaefka* and the *morolaath*, two very dangerous specimens. The concealer hid you well while you escaped."

"*Morolaath*?" she slowly pronounced. "Those strange dinosaur-looking creatures?"

"In your tongue, it means 'blind wolf,' though it has been some time since humans have encountered them."

She walked slowly around her duplicate, which was calling itself . . . "Tragic Solitude?"

"Yes."

"That seems to be a very sad designation."

"However, one that is accurate. I can assure you. I will not dwell on it any further."

"Why are you communicating with me?" said Vale. "And why aren't you spherical, like the others Luther described?"

"I'm sorry?"

"Why don't you look like the other monitors? From the Halo rings?"

"I was created just like the others by my maker, yet, over the great passage of time, I found such a form unaccommodating. I needed to merge with this facility in order to keep it. I have become one with it: I am the Ark. But I have created this shape in order to interact with you. To put you more at ease."

She didn't find this response the least bit satisfactory. Truthfully, it was even more unnerving to her.

"Why did you want to bring me here? There have been other visitors to the Ark over the years. I was told that a monitor has never, to my knowledge, presented itself to anyone . . . until now."

"That is correct. Partially."

"Then why me—?"

"Do you need a reason for such a choice? Is it not enough that you have been chosen?"

For some reason, Vale considered that amusing. The monitor didn't seem to share the sentiment. "Should I call you Tragic Solitude? Or Zero Zero Zero . . . ? Or just Solitude?"

"Zero would be the more accurate. However, 'Solitude' seems apt. Yes, I will allow it."

"Okay . . . Solitude. Look . . ." She was walking forward, trying not to make any grand gestures. It was strange enough talking to something that looked eerily like herself, but given what this machine really was, it made it even more bizarre. "What I'm more concerned about is the situation that brought us here . . . 'us' meaning myself and those who came with me."

"I know that a number of you are here. I am dealing with the others, though. They have now split into two groups. One group is being taken to the place they seek, though they will not find what they have hoped for. The others came to find you and are presently under assault, but are surviving handily. All of them are being tested. Some have already failed and perished. The rest will likely follow."

"What? You can't do that!"

"I am doing that."

She had to rein herself in, to remember that she was dealing with incredibly ancient machinery, not a simple, recalcitrant child. "You should not be," she said. "It's wrong. It's wrong to be dealing with people in this manner when they simply want to reach out and communicate with you."

"They have taken it upon themselves to tread upon me, and I will deal with them as I see fit."

"They are here, as am I, because we have no choice," said Vale. "We are here because the Halo Array—the weapon your makers built—is counting down, and we are concerned that—"

"They will activate? And upon doing so, destroy all sentient life in your galaxy?"

"Yes, that's exactly right."

"You are correct. That is exactly what they will do."

Her concerns about the others in her party were immediately shredded by what the monitor had just told her. "I'm sorry," she said slowly, "did you just confirm that the Halo rings are going to be triggered and destroy all sentient life in the galaxy?"

"That is correct."

"So . . . wait. Are you saying that you are aware of it, or are you saying that you set it?" *Please be the former. Please confirm that you were simply aware of it and that's all. Please don't tell me that—*

"I am aware because I caused it to happen."

Vale gasped, unable to wrap her mind around what she had just been told. It was all she could do not to panic. The notion that this intelligence was the cause behind the activation of Halo, and now it had lured and trapped her down here, was absolutely horrific, but she needed to remain calm, remain aware that she was dealing with an alien creation that was . . .

She cleared her throat, just to give herself a moment, adjust to what she had been told. "May I ask," she said, "why you would do that?"

"Yes."

It didn't reply beyond that, and she realized her error. "All right. Why would you do that? The galaxy is filled with sentient species. My people, humans, and others like—"

"Why would you assume that I care in the least about humankind?"

She tried to determine if the monitor was being sarcastic before she realized that was not in its toolbox. Instead it seemed genuinely confused as to the proposition that it should, in fact, have any manner of care for humanity in the slightest. She recalled a conversation with Luther and Henry earlier, about how humans could interact with some of the ancient machines because they held some kind of kindred bond with the Forerunners who made them. "Because you were designed by the Forerunners. Did they not provide humans with certain privileges when it came to these places?"

"Not all of them. Many Forerunners opposed humans and sought to eradicate your people from the galaxy. Others showed

mercy, but even they could not have known how utterly destructive humanity would become."

"What do you mean? What are you referring to when you say we are destructive?"

"The data is not lacking. Installation 04 . . . destroyed. Installation 05 . . . suffering from catastrophic damage in major containment systems. The replacement for Installation 04 . . . destroyed. In the process, Installation 00—my installation—was severely damaged. Your people presently occupy Installation 03 and Installation 07. It is only a matter of time, I am sure, before your kind's impudence manifests in more destruction. Even the Forerunners could be mistaken. I, however, am not. Would it not be better for the galaxy to perish that it might be reborn, free from your kind and those others who share in your hostility?"

"Everything has the potential to become hostile and destructive. Didn't the Forerunners activate the Halo rings in the first—"

"You may consider yourselves very important, but I do not. Besides, I needed the portal opened and I could not do it from my end. So I reasoned that if you were threatened with the imminent activation of Halo, you would find a way to come here in order to stop that."

"Wait, wait. You *wanted* us to come here?"

"Yes. That meant repairing the gateway placed on your world, which you accomplished. That is why I sent through a Retriever: to test your work. And you accomplished it admirably. You see, I am still in dire need of repair because of the sins your people have committed. I need raw materials: the types that are particularly prominent in your sector. My Retrievers will mine the worlds in your system and obtain for me that which I need to effect repairs."

"Your Retrievers?"

"Indeed. I have thousands at my disposal. And I will send them through the portal to do what must be done in order to repair me. I am the Ark, and I must be repaired."

"But that's our home system! There are billions of people who occupy it. My people!"

"And yet, I have found no reason to spare you. Shall you not pay for the evils of your people? Is there not a cost for what you've done to me?" he paused for a moment. "Human, I very much regret to inform you that there is absolutely nothing that you will be able to do about this."

CHAPTER 13

The team comprising Holt, Lamb, and Usze had been making their way along the ridge, having completely lost any sign of Vale, and were now progressing purely on the notion of continuing in the same direction. It was hardly a solid basis upon which to stake their pursuit, but they really didn't see much choice in the matter. In addition, they were getting closer to the citadel.

Meanwhile, in their travels, it appeared as if there had been an increase in the number of trees surrounding them. But the trees were bereft of foliage; instead they were tall, the bark of their trunks so dark they were nearly black. They didn't seem to have been burned, though; apparently they had simply developed that way.

There was a cliffside surrounding a basin-like environment off to the left, some distance away from the ridge, dotted with entrances to what appeared to be caves. Holt stopped and stared at them. His abrupt cessation of forward motion caused Lamb to bump into him. Lamb then almost fell backward, but Holt reached out and caught his arm, righting him.

"What's wrong?" said Lamb.

Holt pointed toward the cliff ledge. "Could Vale be there, maybe? Could she have climbed up into one of those caves?"

"Why would she do that?"

"I haven't the faintest idea," said Holt. "Shelter, maybe? We don't really have a lot to go on at this point."

"Anything is possible," said Usze. "But I am not certain that it would be wise to head over there and give up our current trail—"

"What current trail?" asked Holt. "We lost her anyway."

"Yes, some distance back."

"So don't you think she could have diverted her path and went off in that direction?"

"Perhaps, yes."

"So why don't we—?"

That was when they heard the growling. Their heads snapped around as one.

They were gazing at the trees, where the noise seemed to originate, but that was ridiculous. There was no way that the trees could be alive.

Suddenly the bark started to shift. It should have been impossible, but it was happening.

"Oh, what the hell is this now?" whispered Lamb.

It wasn't his imagination. The trees were moving. They were not budging from their roots, thankfully enough, but they were unquestionably pulsing with life.

"Is it possible," Lamb said in a low voice, "that the animals aren't the biggest threat on this installation?"

"What do you mean?" replied Usze.

That was when the ground beneath their feet erupted.

Roots were bursting up from below, whipping around. For half a heartbeat, Lamb thought that it was some sort of ground quake, but he quickly understood that the roots were actually moving on their own, alive and reaching for them.

"Fall back!" shouted Holt.

The Spartan moved away, his gun leveled, the problem being

that there was no discernible target. The ground was literally starting to undulate as the roots continued to tear up and lash out
at them.

Something roared in the near distance. It was one of the trees,
and its branches were moving as well, thrashing around in fury,
one of them coming so near to Lamb that it almost grabbed him.
Lamb stumbled backward, as much by accident as design, and
then barely flipped to the left in time to avoid another root. "What
the hell is happening?!" he cried out.

Usze pulled Lamb up, and the two of them stumbled backward, almost falling as the ground continued to be torn up.

The trio continued to retreat, bumping up against the incline
of the cliffsides, which prevented them from running. The one
thing in their favor was that the cliffs were not insurmountable.
They were at a steep angle, but could be scaled.

Wasting no time, Usze and Lamb immediately started to climb
the rocky slope. The Spartan came last, climbing backward.

The roots were stretching after them, clambering up the cliff,
trying to reach them, enwrap them, and yank them back down.
It was uncertain just how high the damn things could travel, and
their only choice was to keep climbing.

"Up here!" Lamb was shouting.

The Spartan took an instant to glance up and over his shoulder. Usze and Lamb had taken refuge in one of the upper caves.
Holt hoped that it wasn't occupied by something; that would be
just their luck. It seemed beyond the range of the roots, although
that was more or less guesswork on Holt's part.

Deciding to trade out defensive capabilities for speed, Holt
locked his rifle onto his back, turned around, and scrambled up
the cliffside.

Just as he was reaching for the lower lip of the cave wall, the

Spartan was suddenly pulled away from it as something took hold of his left leg. It was one of the roots. Automatically he kicked down with his right foot, trying to drive it away. He reached for his rifle, but it was positioned badly and inaccessible.

Usze threw himself out of the cave, swinging his sword around and down. Holt's leg came free as the blade sliced through the root, and he heard something scream; it was the tree. The cutting of the root caused it injury.

Injury, how? It's a damn tree!

Holt climbed upward with strength born of desperation. He fell into the cave and then immediately pulled his rifle clear and brought it around. "What was that thing? How can a tree do that?"

"Maybe it wasn't a tree," Lamb said. "Maybe it was a plantlike animal? Or just a really pissed off plant? Whatever it was, apparently it doesn't like us."

"It can join the club," said Holt. "Everything on this rock seems to be after us."

"Now what?" said Lamb. He was obviously doing whatever he could to keep his fear buried deep, but only partly succeeding. "I mean, it's not like we can wait it out. The damn thing isn't going anywhere."

"I wish we could call for help," said Holt, tapping his comm unit. "If we could, that would be . . ."

His voice trailed off.

"What?" said Lamb.

Holt looked up, sounding confused. "My . . . comm unit is working again. I've just got a clear signal. Whatever was scrambling it before has stopped."

"So, great!" said Lamb, clearly not questioning good fortune when it came their way. "Call for help!"

"Let's just hope they can hear us," said Holt.

Spartan Kodiak tapped the communications device. "Say again!" he said.

Holt's voice crackled back at him. *"We're pinned down! Some kind of . . . there's no good way to put it. There's some kind of creature here; it looks like a gigantic tree, but it's not—it ambushed us and is trying to tear us apart. We've taken refuge in a cave, but we have no way out of here. We could use some reinforcements!"*

"Tracking you now," said Kodiak as he ran figures through his comm unit and HUD. "We'll try to get there as quickly as possible."

"We'll be waiting. Holt out."

The Huragok continued to float nearby. It had been relatively silent for the entirety of the trip. That figured, as there wasn't much it was interested in communicating at the moment, given its limited functions out here on the vast ice fields of the Ark. They had been traveling across a frozen body of water for a while, and their objective was coming into sight.

Kodiak finished running the triangulations as Luther leaned toward him and asked: "What have you got?"

"They're about an hour's walk north-northwest of our current position." There was no true north on the Ark, only directions that coordinated their position and their objective. It was somewhat surprising to learn that the other group had actually moved closer to the Ark's center, where the foundry existed, as did the citadel they were all headed to. Holt's team must have had much easier passage than them.

Luther wasn't in love with the idea of walking that distance. It wasn't impossible. The snowstorm that had been pounding down on them had lightened to some degree, but it was still coming down. So he was reasonably sure he could manage it, but it wouldn't be easy going. "I'm pretty confident that we won't be able to get the mammoth to go in that direction. Like I mentioned earlier, something else is controlling it," he reminded Kodiak. "Any other ideas?"

"No," said Kodiak. "It's got to be on foot. N'tho!"

N'tho glanced up at him. "Yes?"

"I'm getting off here. Holt and the others need help."

"That might not be wise. It is obvious that the doctor is correct: whatever is overseeing this place wants us to go this way. It's leading us where we need to go."

"We don't know that for sure. It doesn't matter, though. Holt needs me now, and he's in that direction." He turned to Luther, "Stay close to these guys, I'll make this as quick as I can." Then Kodiak swung his leg over and vaulted to the ground.

Puffs of snow billowed up where he had landed. The mammoth did not appear to notice that he had disembarked; instead it kept trudging forward, one huge leg in front of the next.

Without wasting time, Kodiak started running. It would not have been the easiest endeavor for anyone else, but his enhanced physiology propelled him forward, the weight of his armor not even registering, since he was so accustomed to wearing it. It wasn't long before he recognized that the others, at least Mann for certain, wouldn't have survived long on the ground in these conditions. The snow was simply too dense for normal travel on foot.

Nevertheless, he removed any awareness of his surroundings from his consciousness. He did not dwell on the fact that he was sprinting across a vast, frigid body of water, and he had no clue how thick the ice actually was. Instead he focused on a singular purpose: another Spartan needed his help. If Holt couldn't handle this on his own, he knew it was serious.

Every ten minutes, he would check in with Holt via comm, confirming that the group's condition remained stationary. "So what are you dealing with?" he asked in their first communication. "A tree . . . ?" He had a vague recollection of a centuries-old fantasy story that had living trees, but he couldn't remember much beyond that about it. "Is that right?"

"Not exactly. Lamb's current theory is that it's some sort of carnivorous plant that blends in with the trees and apparently eats people-size things. Whatever the hell it is, it's not playing around."

"And it's got you pinned down?"

"Its roots, which it's able to project above ground, are thrusting around below the cave entrance. They're either not rigid enough to penetrate the rock, or not long enough to get up here, but if we try to go anywhere, the thing's going to drag us down before we're five meters out."

"Can you climb up any higher?"

"No go. The angle's too steep. We're pretty much stuck here for the moment."

"Okay. Sit tight; I'm en route."

"You and the others?"

"No, just me."

There was a pause on the other end that Kodiak couldn't help but be amused with. Holt obviously was not thrilled by the fact that their rescue party consisted of just one Spartan and not the Elites as well, but he wasn't about to risk insulting Kodiak by commenting. *"Copy that,"* Holt finally said.

The further Kodiak went, the more he noticed that the snow was beginning to thin out. Glancing back, he could barely make out the mammoth in the distance behind him. He stayed steady, his legs scissoring, his arms pumping back and forth, keeping his attention on the area, making sure that nothing else was encroaching on his position. For a second, he remembered the whales, and a brief spurt of fear shot through his veins: he was, after all, sprinting across a frozen sea.

His HUD readout also began to report the escalating temperature, which attested to the approaching shallow, stone ridgeline. Soon he found his feet on frozen ground, with dirt and muck being carved up at every footfall. Within ten minutes, the temperature had climbed several degrees, and with any luck, it would continue to do so.

With any luck. Because I've had an abundance of that.

Soon, he'd managed to get clear of the snow entirely, but it caught him off guard. The transition was almost instantaneous. He hadn't been aware that dramatic shifts in temperature were so close, but that didn't seem to be a positive omen. It cast a shadow over what exactly was going on. If there was some sort of intelligence controlling the mammoth, what exactly was it after? Was it involved in Holt's current situation? Or Vale's disappearance?

Even though he was drawing much closer to Holt's location, his instincts advised him to slow down, because he was immediately aware that there was something nearby. He could hear distant growling, and he assumed it was coming from whatever had Holt and the others pinned down. He slowed considerably as he reached the top of the ridge and clambered about a hundred meters across a barren plateau to the other side, looking down into a ravine below. For a moment, his concern was piqued: the steep decline into the ravine was covered by large evergreen-like trees. *Could they be the same thing Holt was talking about?* He decided they were not and chanced careful forward progression.

There were some small boulders scattered around that would serve to prevent anything from spotting Kodiak. He moved from one to the next, checking the area with caution the entire time. He kept his weapon at the ready.

"There," he whispered to himself.

The cliff on the opposite side was still some distance away, and he could make out a few of the caves. But there was no movement in them. The ground below seemed a bit unsettled, but none of the trees or roots were moving at all. For a fleeting instant, he wondered if it had all been some sort of twisted exaggeration on Holt's part, or maybe some sort of Forerunner illusion, but he discarded the notion just as quickly. That was simply a nonstarter; no Spartan—hell, no *soldier*—would ever do something like that.

He carefully scanned the area and tried to get a sense of what was out there manipulating the roots. His eyes were drawn to one tree in particular, which was larger than any of the others in view, and the branches were swaying gently. It *could* have been from the wind . . . except no other tree branches in the vicinity were moving.

Kodiak wasn't sure how long they were going to be on the Ark, but the last thing he wanted was to run low on ammunition. He'd prefer to save it for when he was sure that it would be put to optimum use. Instead he pulled out his Covenant plasma blade, but kept it deactivated for the time being. Very slowly he started moving toward the suspicious tree.

Damn, that thing is big.

And the closer he neared, the larger it seemed. In its fundamental shape, it resembled an oak tree. But here was a much vaster array of branches than he'd ever seen in a tree—ten people joining hands would barely be able to circle its trunk. Most curious, its bark, if it could be called that, was interlaced with streaks of purple.

Fortunately it didn't seem to be reacting to Kodiak's approach. Maybe it was dormant? Or perhaps focused entirely on the cave that Holt and the others were in . . . ?

His booted foot stepped on a fallen branch, and the snap reverberated through the still air.

And the tree trunk actually turned 180 degrees, revealing an eerie cluster of black and red eyelike protrusions.

All around the Spartan, the ground came alive. Roots ripped up from the dirt, sending it flying, and reached for him.

Kodiak activated his sword and sprinted toward it, plowing through the roots with his strength and sudden speed, using the superheated energy sword as a charging barge.

One of the roots pulled his feet out from under him, and Kodiak hit the ground hard, as another came up in an attempt to encircle his arm. Before it could do so, he swung the blade and sliced through it. The tree, if it could still be called that, released a deep guttural bellow, and then it lost its grip on his legs. Kodiak scrambled loose and got up, continuing to run toward his attacker.

He got within a meter of the tree and brought his blade around, sinking it deep into the trunk, and this time the resonant, heavy shrieking noise threatened to blow out Kodiak's ear drums, but his armor automatically compensated, rapidly reducing the volume of his in-helmet audio function.

Branches and vines descended from overhead. Had Kodiak not been in his armor, he would have been in deep trouble, because the tree-thing could have easily strangled him without much effort. And suddenly, to Kodiak's shock, he was being lifted into the air . . . and then he felt something. Within the Mjolnir armor.

That was when Kodiak realized: as solid a piece of construction as his armor was, there was still space in between the individual plates and his undersuit. Generally, this space was so tight that nothing could possibly penetrate, save for, perhaps, something as thin as vines from a tree.

They snaked in between these pieces, quickly going taut and wrapping around various plates in extremely rigid ways. Kodiak struggled furiously as he felt them making their way around his undersuit, which provided very little in the way of protection. He twisted around, tried to swing the blade, but he no longer had control over his arms; the vines had locked his armor in place. He put all his strength into it, trying to break free, but this creature was keeping him completely immobilized. The branches were now reaching down toward him, and even more vines were slithering into his armor. He heard the Mjolnir components start to moan under the duress of the vines, almost as though it were about to rip him from his armor like food out of a tin can.

Then the tree boomed again with a fierce roar.

The vines lost their strength and immediately receded as Kodiak crashed to the ground. Klaxons in his heads-up display were going off because of the strain the armor had endured, but those quickly died away. He lay there for a moment, unmoving, not understanding what was happening. Then he clambered to his feet and turned toward the tree.

Usze 'Taham was driving his plasma sword through the trunk, plunging deeply into it. Black ooze, very likely its lifeblood, was seeping out of the huge slice that the Sangheili had carved into the thing. Usze had used the tree's focus on Kodiak to sneak down and assault it before it noticed.

Kodiak charged forward and began carving it from the other side with his own sword. The tree writhed and shook and roots shot up, flailing at Kodiak, but with quickly fading strength.

Seconds later, the entire tree started to topple. Kodiak and Usze cleared themselves from its arc as it tumbled. It crashed to the ground, branches snapping on impact, the roots flailing for long moments afterward before finally sagging.

The two of them stood there for a time, completely silent and staring down at the bizarre creature they had just slain.

Moments later, Spartan Holt and Henry Lamb descended from the cave above. "Thanks for coming," said Holt.

"Spartans don't leave Spartans behind. So am I correct that you did not manage to locate Olympia Vale?"

"That is correct," said Usze, sounding somewhat annoyed. "We were waylaid by that life-form . . . as well as other strange things in this place. And now we have lost more or less all sign of her trail. So we were heading for the citadel in the hopes that we could possibly locate her there."

"Seems like a reasonable plan—the others are on their way now," said Kodiak. "Have you encountered anything out of the ordinary? Aside from this thing, I mean."

"There were these machines, these biped Forerunner creations," said Lamb. "They were armed with weapons and moving around like . . . well, like humans. Or perhaps Forerunners." He sounded almost fascinated by it, which Kodiak found strange. "What about you?"

"We were picked up by a mammoth."

The others exchanged confused looks. "I'm sorry, what?" said Holt.

"A mammoth. Or something like that. It picked us up in the middle of the snow and was transporting us."

"I am confused by this. Explain," said Usze. "One of the creatures on this place was helping you?"

"Doctor Mann has some theories. His belief is that this animal, and possibly the one Vale was with, was doing so at the behest of whatever AI is running this place."

"That is a strange theory," Usze said. "What of the beasts that are not particularly kind? Like this one?" he said, looking down at the gigantic, gnarled tree creature.

"Honestly, I'm not sure."

Lamb was looking thoughtful. "Well . . . consider this. Whenever anyone does anything, it's always for the same reason. They want something in return. That's just common sense. Nothing is done for nothing—if this AI, or whatever it is, was providing us a means of travel in order to bring us to the citadel, then it must want something from us."

"What could that possibly be?" said Kodiak.

"Nothing that I can think of," Lamb's voice trailed off. "At least, nothing good."

"We should try to make it to the citadel, then," Kodiak said, "before the other group gets there. They might be walking right into a trap."

◎

Luther Mann was relieved that the trip so far hadn't veered once again into chaos. He was worried about Kodiak, of course. He hoped that the Spartan was able to reach the others and aid them with whatever it was that had pinned them down. Still, he wasn't exactly enamored by the notion that Kodiak was making his way back across the snowy terrain, even if the snow had now ceased to be falling.

That's the damnedest thing. The way the weather seems to go on and off here. It isn't following any sort of weather pattern that I've ever encountered, even on the Halo installations. Could it be that whatever is causing the mammoth to transport us to it is also actually controlling the weather somehow?

He wished he could shut his brain off about the strange things that were happening here, but he couldn't help it. His thoughts kept carrying him deeper and deeper into the nature of things they'd encountered on the Ark. What they meant, not only now, but as it pertained to the Forerunners. It was a daunting possibility. Was this an AI causing these things, or was this the results of the Ark's damaged systems? Or was it both? Some things seemed absurdly counterintuitive, and it made him stop for a moment and consider what he was doing. He was attempting to second-guess the greatest known minds in the history of the galaxy, and who was he to do so?

There were no further violent incidents following Kodiak's departure. As a matter of fact, the journey had become extremely scenic. They had had to cross a huge body of water that separated them from the citadel, but there had been an ice bridge that the mammoth was able to cross with no difficulty. There was a large ridge ahead of them with distinct Forerunner pylons atop it, but the ice bridge brought them through a cavernous passageway carved right into the rock.

"Look familiar?" Luther asked, turning to N'tho.

"Very," he responded, his eyes fixed on the majestic Forerunner structures high above them as they began to move into the passage. "Those pylons each activated a portion of a shield that guarded the citadel from damage. When the High Prophet of Truth came here, he barricaded himself beyond the barrier and attempted to activate the Array from the citadel. It did not fare well for him, however."

"They say that the Arbiter killed him," Luther remarked.

"Yes, once we deactivated the barrier, both humans and Elites infiltrated the citadel side by side. We stopped the Covenant, and Halo," N'tho said, deep in thought. "Together."

"Well, then," Luther smiled, "This must be just like old times for you."

When they passed deeper into the cave passageway, they came upon a huge alloy gate, easily six meters tall. It was shut against them, and Luther was concerned that the mammoth had, for some reason, taken them to a dead end. But then he heard something like the sound of massive gears shifting, and slowly the doors began to slide apart. The mammoth never slowed, as if the beast knew that the great gate would automatically open itself to them. It prompted Luther to wonder just how intelligent the creature was. Was it knowingly doing any of this, or was its will entirely subdued by whatever force had brought it to him? As a scientist, Luther seriously disliked having so many questions and no answers for any of them.

The mammoth emerged through the gate and climbed into the basin that held the citadel. Luther let out a low whistle. The citadel itself was resplendent, even with the damage it had sustained from the Halo two years ago. None of the footage captured from the *Dawn*'s sensors did it justice. The scope of the building was gargantuan, sitting against the backdrop of the Ark's foundry, hundreds of kilometers wide, an immense gaseous redness of space and a silent moon brooding at its center.

Finally, they reached the citadel. Luther could hardly believe that it was true.

The citadel was a series of angular shapes that climbed up from the basin floor at what appeared to be a forty-five-degree angle before shooting out horizontally over the foundry lip. It had many struts and cowling-like structures that comprised its complex shape, with a single tower at its peak that climbed high into the air. Overall, its appearance was that of a single, massive buttress, holding an elongated corridor-like structure well over the edge of the foundry. Ivory and gray materials made up its composition, though there was light charring and damage across the structure and its exterior.

The basin was impressive as well, at least in terms of size, though clearly less remarkable in shape and design. There were traces of snow and ice, but it was mostly composed of gravel and dun ash, blankets of stone and slush. There were the remains of what appeared to be both human and Covenant vehicles scattered all over the place, including the empty husks of two huge Scarab platforms, extremely large and powerful Covenant occupation vehicles. Luther could see that they were covered with scorch marks. Clearly there had been a massive firefight here.

N'tho glanced behind him. "It was exciting to be here," he said, as if reading Luther's mind. "One of the most remarkable experiences of my life."

"I'm certain it was." Luther was looking ahead, trying to discern the mammoth's path. The citadel was dead ahead of them, and the mammoth seemed to be winding its way through the debris toward the very front of the structure. He wasn't sure how they were going to access it, though. Their path was bringing them to some manner of ramp that led up toward the front entrance, but then it came to an end. There was a sizeable gap, perhaps hundreds of meters, between the edge of the ramp and the citadel itself. "Guessing that's some sort of moat system . . . though without a moat. How did you manage to get inside? Over this gap, I mean?"

"There was an energy bridge between that ramp and the citadel itself," said N'tho. "But it appears to be no longer functional. Perhaps the Huragok can activate it. . . ."

And then, as if in response to N'tho's words, there was the sound of something slowly whining to life. Seconds later, a shimmering bridge of energy projected from the ramp to the citadel, covering the gap between the two. The mammoth's riders exchanged looks.

"Well, that was awfully easy," said Luther.

"Too easy," said Zon. "It is as if they want us to come in."

"So first they try to kill us," said Kola, "and then they bring us to this place and issue an invitation. Does this make sense to any of you?"

"Not particularly," said Luther. "But my earlier theory may still hold weight. The Ark's monitor—perhaps its control is limited only to some animals."

"Or perhaps it is a trap," Kola said.

"That's a possibility," Luther said. "Certainly."

"So are you suggesting we do not venture any further?" said N'tho.

"Far from it. I just suggest that we be ready for anything."

"We are Sangheili, human," said N'tho. "You should already know that we are always prepared for such things."

The mammoth was standing at the bottom of the ramp. It did not seem inclined to go farther. Instead it knelt down. Luther and the Sangheili disembarked, quickly dropping to the ground. The creature slowly stood up, and then turned and walked back the way they had traveled.

"Yes, this might very well be a trap," N'tho remarked, turning around to face the citadel. "The last time we needed the Oracle to activate the bridge for us. It was not done simply for our convenience. Whatever awaits us there in the citadel *wants* us to enter, and I have great difficulty believing that it is for our mutual benefit."

"I am not loving this situation, either," said Luther. "But I'm not really sure we have any choice."

"Then by my blood," said N'tho, "let us proceed."

Slowly they walked across the light bridge. Luther felt his muscles knot up with tension, as he somewhat expected the bridge to suddenly vanish beneath their feet when they were halfway across, sending them plummeting to certain death. Fortunately, it remained intact as they crossed.

Voices shouted at them.

The group stopped at the midway point and turned to look at the slope of the mountain circling the basin, to the far left of the citadel's position. To Luther's complete shock, several familiar forms were approaching.

"It's them!" he shouted. "They made it!"

Henry Lamb, Spartans Kodiak and Holt, and Usze 'Taham were moving quickly down the near side of the ridge. Luther waved to them in acknowledgment, and then they all hastened back to the ramp, remaining there until the rest of the group caught up.

They quickly brought each other up to speed. Luther was, remarkably, a bit jealous that the others had been attacked by some kind of a carnivorous tree, which, despite all they had experienced, was the most exotic creature they'd encountered. That was certainly something that he would have loved to see firsthand. But based on Henry's animated description of the encounter, it sounded as if he was quite lucky to have avoided it.

"So we're all in agreement that we're most likely walking into a trap?" said Kodiak.

"Yes," said N'tho. "But there are no alternatives to this. The controls for Halo lie within the citadel. It is our only hope at stopping the activation process."

"Do you think it wants the Huragok?" Lamb said. "Whatever it is that has brought us here, that is?"

Luther took a heavy cold breath, his mind deep in thought: "That does make sense."

"What do you mean?" said Kola.

"Well," Luther said, "let's say hypothetically that the Ark's AI is the cause of all the strange things we've encountered—the Retrievers, the animals, Vale's disappearance, the visual illusions, and even those defensive machines. There's definitely been an indication that this thing, whatever it is, has been harboring some level of hostility toward us. Well, if that's the case, our friend here—Drifts Randomly—may be the target. The Huragok's abilities may present a threat to it; it's easily more of a threat than anyone else in this group because of what it is capable of. So the simplest way to deal with a threat is to bring it to you . . . and then dispose of it." He turned to the Huragok. "Perhaps you should stay here with one of the Elites. Wait for us."

<<*I am needed,*>> it replied, its voice calm and entirely unaffected by the foreboding dialogue.

Before anyone could respond, the Huragok spun around and floated off toward the citadel.

"I imagine that is our answer," said N'tho, and they fell into step behind it.

They walked across the light bridge, and moments later entered the main foyer of the citadel.

It was a long, glimmering alloyed hallway, diamond shaped, with walls slanting on either side and coming to a raised point above them. There wasn't much lighting—just barely enough to make out the general surroundings. Most of the illumination was coming from the far end, from what appeared to be some sort of elevator. Luther nodded toward it and said, "Is that where we go?"

"It is," said N'tho. "It rides an energy beam up and down, like other Forerunner sites . . . and it appears to still be functional."

They reached the elevator pad—a tight fit, considering their number, but they managed, and slowly the lift descended.

"I recall much that transpired here," said N'tho.

"Good memories?" asked Luther.

N'tho didn't respond. He didn't really have to.

The elevator eventually glided to a halt and opened up onto the main hallway of the citadel.

Luther's breath caught in his throat. It was vast and long, an elevated platform or bridge with various small rooms at specific intervals. But that wasn't what caught his attention. Along the main hall was a set of holograms representing the Halo installations. The circles hovered before them, projected on individual stands that ran down the length of the chamber and ordered in such a way that each one encircled the bridge they followed from one end of the hall to the other. Luther noticed that one of the Halo rings—the fourth one—was red with various damage readouts, and he surmised that it depicted the Alpha Halo that had been destroyed by the Master Chief: Installation 04, the first Halo discovered by humans.

"Can you believe this?" he whispered.

"Yes, but last time it wasn't empty. We had to fight our way across," N'tho said indifferently. "The control console we are seeking is at the far end."

They made their way through the elongated Forerunner chamber, and at one point, Luther stumbled slightly because something had pushed him from behind. He realized that it was Spartan Kodiak and further understood that, as a scientist, he'd become so entranced with his surroundings that he'd slowed down almost to a halt. "Sorry," he muttered. The Spartan didn't bother to respond.

As they traveled down the hallway and through each of the

rooms that divided the long bridge, Luther soaked in his surroundings. This room held holographic representations and data readouts of every one of the Halo installations—he could hardly imagine the trove of information that someone like himself might indulge in if they were allowed an opportunity to explore and research this place. It was unprecedented. He could spend his whole life here. Hell, he could spend a dozen lives here and only scratch the surface.

At the far end, there was another energy bridge that led out to a round platform: the primary control console for the communications array. There was also a long, broken viewing window that looked out onto the Ark's mining moon, set in the mist like a stoic orb the size of a world. Luther thought he'd ask N'tho about the damage to the window, but at that moment, the Elite turned and gestured toward the console. "Human, you must take this great honor upon yourself."

Luther felt as if his mind was going to shut down as he stepped onto the energy bridge. His legs were shaking as he walked; he was having difficulty processing the implications of the moment.

This is it. This is where the Forerunners put the wheels in motion a hundred thousand years ago. The beings that I've been obsessed with my entire life trod these halls, stood in this place. It's like a devout believer being invited to step into the Garden of Eden.

He reached the platform and studied it. The floor was generally flat, but it appeared as though the console had risen up in a series of circles, much like elegant stairs, placing emphasis on the main purpose of this room. And really, the main purpose of this entire facility. Despite the advanced technology on the console itself, Luther found it incredibly easy to comprehend once he reached it. Upon its face was a series of glowing, pulsing lights that he understood to represent all of the Halo installations, wherever they were in the galaxy. And in the middle there was a holographic key that would halt the process, according to the cartouches and the angular schema.

This is it, he thought. *What we came here to do.*

Without any further hesitation, Luther reached his arm up and pressed down upon the holo-key.

A second later, the lights on the console panel went out.

"I did it," he whispered, and then shouted: *"I did it!"*

A ragged *"Yeah!"* came from Henry Lamb as Luther turned to face them. The group had taken position behind the console. Grinning, he strode down the circles to the floor, and they shifted in response, flattening once more.

And then the machines converged upon them all.

Two dozen mechanical constructs—evidently the same ones that Lamb and the others had encountered on their trip—armed with energy staves and what appeared to be rifles of some kind, appeared out of nowhere, and Luther didn't think they were any sort of Forerunner welcome wagon.

"Those you're friends?" Kodiak growled to Holt, reaching for his energy sword.

"Those are them," Holt said, prying his rifle off his back.

Luther turned to Drifts Randomly as Zon and Kola flanked the Huragok.

<<*Armigers,*>> Drifts said, in a neutral apathetic Sangheili.

"What did he say?" Kodiak asked.

"They're armigers, apparently," Luther said, taking a second to process it. He turned back toward Drifts: "Do you mean armor bearers? Like for knights?"

Seemingly content with his previous answer, Drifts made no response.

"I think he's saying that these Forerunner machines are

defensive drones that supported Forerunner warriors. Now they guard this place."

"If you say so, human," said N'tho. He activated his plasma sword.

For a long moment, the Forerunner armigers simply stood there.

Then they charged.

The Spartans and Sangheili, with a roar of fury, ran to meet them.

Two armigers came at Kodiak from either side, swinging their energy staves. Determined to conserve his ammo, Kodiak had already activated his Covenant plasma blade and now closed in battle. He blocked right, left, right again, doing everything he could to prevent the staves from striking him. He was only partly successful, as the constructs landed blow after blow, but his Mjolnir armor was able to withstand it. The armigers, by contrast, were not quite as durable. Kodiak slammed the blade forward, lunging under one of the armiger's strokes, and sliced the thing in half. He whirled and swung his blade at the one behind him, cutting off the arm that was wielding the stave.

Something exploded behind Kodiak, knocking him forward. A blast from one of the armiger's rifles had struck him in the back. He lost his grip on the plasma sword and it skidded across the floor.

A second later, an armiger had picked it up. Kodiak was still on the floor, trying to shake off the impact of the blast that had taken him down. When he looked up, he saw the armiger swinging the blade straight at his head.

This is how I die? With my own weapon—?

And the armiger was suddenly airborne, yanked off the floor, as a similar blade emerged from the front of its chest. N'tho was behind it, lifting the armiger into the air. It hung there for a moment, Kodiak's blade dropping out of its hand, and then N'tho slung the machine away casually.

N'tho shoved the hilt of Kodiak's blade with his foot. It slid across the floor and Kodiak retrieved it.

He saved my life. Damn him, thought Kodiak.

Luther's rifle was empty and there were no magazines left. Since he had no further offensive capabilities, he did the only thing he could think of: stay in tight behind someone who could handle himself. In this case, that was Usze 'Taham, who was firing intently upon the armigers with his carbine, blowing them back as they continued their efforts to advance. He saw that Henry Lamb had adopted a similar tactic, keeping close in behind Kola. "The elevator!" Luther was shouting. "Get us back to the elevator!"

"I am making my best effort," said Usze as he pressed his attack on the armigers.

The Huragok, meanwhile, was floating high above all of it, drifting toward the elevator. Luther couldn't help but notice that the armigers were making no effort to assault the Huragok, even though it was an easy target. *Henry was right. Whatever sent these things at us wants the damn Huragok, and it wants the Huragok alive. Incredible.*

The two Sangheili fought their way through the Forerunner constructs, pressing on across the bridge. The entire group managed to punch through the initial line of armigers by the time they reached the first of two sectional rooms that divided up the hall. They exited it on the opposite side and then continued quickly across the bridge, taking advantage of this moment of respite.

"Was that all of them?" Holt questioned, reloading his rifle.

"Unlikely," N'tho said, his head darting back and forth, looking for movement.

They reached the second room without trouble and began to pass through it. Beyond lay the final bridge and then the elevator. As they moved swiftly through the room, the internal lights flickered briefly, and then half a dozen bright portals snapped into existence, revealing five more armigers.

Luther and Lamb launched forward, sprinting alongside Kola and Usze, just barely passing through the door, and then seconds later they were running for the lift. Luther glanced behind him, and to his horror saw that the other half of the group hadn't made it out of the room yet. He wanted to go back and help them, but he was hardly in a position to do so.

"Should we go back?" Luther asked, but just then his question was answered. Ten more armigers appeared, facing them with their backs to the room.

"They're cutting us off," Usze sounded, his voice gravelly with rage. "Let us get you two and the Engineer to safety, then Kola and I will deal with these cursed machines."

When they reached the elevator the Huragok was already there. <<The elevator is nonfunctional,>> it informed them. <<I will fix it. It will take time.>>

"We don't have time!" Lamb shouted.

The newly arrived armigers were moving in, and more were appearing behind them. Both Sangheili fired down onto the bridge from their elevated position, attempting to stem the ever-increasing population of enemies. But they couldn't do it forever.

Luther looked around the room and spotted a small chute to the back, its rear-lit lamp flashing, which seemed to indicate that one could drop down it. There was no telling where it would lead, but it appeared to be the only reasonable option.

"You're not serious," Lamb said, his face pale.

"Do we have a choice?!" Luther shouted back, and then, entirely on impulse, he said the only thing he could think of: *"Jump in!"* He leaped into the elevator shaft, and seconds later the others followed suit.

Fortunately, it wasn't that far of a fall. Luther landed in a crouch and then bounded off to the side, and the others thudded to the ground behind him. The Huragok came last, still drifting in a leisurely fashion.

"Brother," Kola said, turning to Usze. "Should we attempt to head back for the others?"

<<*No need. The others are no longer there,*>> Drifts offered.

"Are they dead?!" Lamb demanded, still trying to catch his breath.

<<*No.*>>

"Then let's get out of here," said Luther, "and pray those damn things don't decide to follow us."

Kodiak was growing concerned. It seemed to him that the armigers were focusing most of their attention on the Spartans, and he wasn't happy with the way the battle was turning.

He continued to wield his plasma sword, striking at anything that came near. The blasts from the armigers' rifles were bouncing off his armor, but the sustained fire was wreaking havoc on his energy shielding, and now its strength indicator was hovering dangerously close to red on his in-helmet HUD.

N'tho was to his left, and Spartan Holt to his right. His intention had been to return to the elevator with Luther and the others ahead, but the sudden ambush had cut them off, and now the battle was driving them back through the door they'd just come through.

But the strangest thing happened next. As he took one step back, the entire world turned sideways around him. Then it seemed to violently compress and expand at the exact same time.

"What the—?!" Kodiak cried out as he stumbled forward and looked around.

He was standing in a completely different location, some sort of narrow hallway, devoid of natural light. An instant later, N'tho, Zon, and Holt fell to the floor right behind him. Kodiak looked around in confusion. "What just happened here?"

"A portal," N'tho said. "You fell in, and we followed. It must be how those machines travel so quickly across the Ark. We entered before the breach closed."

"Then we need to find out where we are and try to find the others before those things figure out what happened."

"And Vale," said Holt. "Let's not forget her."

"We can't help her if we're dead," said Kodiak. "Come on."

CHAPTER 14

Olympia Vale wanted to panic.

It was a gut reaction. She was standing there, staring at a holographic image of herself—created by Tragic Solitude, the Keeper of the Ark—that was informing her it was planning to strip-mine every planet in Earth's solar system, and likely any number of other worlds, in order to administer repairs to the Ark. Its plan to activate Halo was apparently a duplicitous one, in order to reactivate the Forerunner portal on Earth so that the monitor could accomplish its goal.

How very clever, she grimly thought.

Just as quickly as the desire to panic surfaced, she managed to shut it down. That would accomplish nothing. It was incumbent upon her to remain calm and handle this in as thorough and professional a manner as she could. She slowed her breathing and imagined that she could actually feel her heart beat.

"You will be pleased to know," the monitor said, **"that I have now enabled your companions to communicate with each other. You seemed upset over the prospect of their inability to converse. I changed my mind to accommodate you."**

"Thank you," she said in a formal tone. "That was very generous of you. Let me ask you this," she added slowly. "Why do you have to destroy the planets in my system? Certainly there are plenty of other worlds throughout the galaxy that the Ark is connected to."

"Yes. Several of them."

"And there must be other star systems that are uninhabited. Mineable worlds that could not possibly support life."

"Yes. There certainly are."

"Okay, then. So why us? Why was it necessary for you to repair the portal on Earth?"

"When the portal was disabled by the interlopers, it severed my ability to control it from this end. Although I could repair it, which I did, it required activation from your end in order to return to its previous state. I am impressed, however, with the way that it was activated. One of the Forerunners' servant-tools, was it?"

"You mean Drifts?" she asked. "The Huragok?"

"They are remarkable machines, are they not? Yours in particular is extraordinary. And to think I had planned to obliterate your vessel when you first arrived, and I very well could have. But when I discovered that you carried with you one of the most remarkable servant-tools in the lineage of those who labored over the keyships long ago, I was enamored. It will be quite useful in my service."

"What do you want him for?" Vale asked, wondering if anything had happened to Drifts Randomly since she'd been taken from the group.

"*Him*? It is but a machine, human. Nothing more than that. And my reasons I will not discuss."

"All right," said Vale, "so now that the entire portal system is functioning, why can't you go and strip-mine uninhabited worlds? Why Earth?"

"There are reasons for my choice of your world, human. But they would not improve your disposition."

Vale was listening very carefully to the monitor's voice: not to just the things that it was saying, but the manner in which it was saying them. There was something to it that sounded . . . wrong. It was difficult for Vale to place it at first, but he sounded . . .

Pleased.

Self-obsessed.

Capricious.

Some kind of emotion seemed to be wending its way through the monitor's voice, its words, its actions. Such a strange thing for an AI.

The entire Ark has sustained massive damage. Is it possible that this same damage somehow affected the monitor as well?

It was hard for Vale to believe at first. This was, after all, technology that had been developed by the Forerunners, and given all that she had experienced in the past few days, it was difficult to process the concept that anything they had created, like an artificial intelligence, was actually breaking down.

What made it even more problematic was that its presumed breakdown presented a very real threat to all sentient life in the galaxy.

But first things first.

We came here to deactivate the Halo Array. If it wants to strip-mine our worlds, that's a different topic, and one that I will have to deal with eventually.

"Okay," she said slowly, choosing her words carefully. "Then may I suggest that you at least disable Halo's current activation while you try to find the Engineer?"

"Why ever would I do that?" It tilted its "head," looking at her with what appeared to be genuine curiosity.

"Obviously, because you achieved your goal. You needed the portal fixed, and the Huragok accomplished that. Now that we're here, there's no need to activate the Halo rings."

"Why would I not want them to activate?"

"Because they will destroy all sentient life in the galaxy."

"Why should that concern me?"

It took her a moment to recover from that. "You're talking about billions, trillions of lives being ended. Now that the portal is active, there's no reason for Halo to be fired."

"Why do you believe there to be no reason?"

"Why do you believe that there *is* a reason?"

Solitude slowly paced around Vale, with its hands behind its back. It didn't reply at first, and she remained quiet, wanting to give it the time to say whatever was on its mind. No telling how it would react now.

"I have had the ability to observe what sentient life has been doing with the opportunities presented it. The war, the destruction. There seems to be no regard for life's sanctity among your kind, or others. It matters not the species, or the place, or the age—it always ends the same."

"You are not being reasonable."

"I believe I am."

"No, you're not. You're failing to take into account the progress we've made in just the few short years since the end of the war. The humans and the Sangheili, for example. We fought with each other for thirty years before finding peace, but now that we have it, you would take it from us? We are learning from our mistakes, learning together no doubt, and other species along with us, but we have only had a blink of an eye in the corridor of history. Do we not have a right to amend our sins? To repair the wrongs that have been committed by our ancestors? Why would you take away our opportunity to do this?"

"There is no guarantee that you would make any amends."

"Yes, but there is evidence that we *can*, especially when you look at what we've managed to accomplish when humans have come together. Just a few hundred years ago, we launched a spacecraft called *Voyager*." She smiled at the thought. "It was a clear testimony to human cooperation. It had greetings in over fifty languages and instructions as to how someone who found it could locate Earth. And songs. It was filled with works by some of the greatest musicians of that age. Its power systems ran out in the first half of the twenty-first century. By now, it's just a floating hunk of metal drifting through the galaxy. Yet it remains a symbol of what humanity can accomplish when we work together."

"And yet, within years you were again at each other's throats. And that is just humans. It is a problem prevalent not only with humans, truth be told. All species suffer from a tendency toward mindless destruction and an endless compulsion for battle. It is only a matter of time before your current peace turns again to war."

"It could, but it won't," she said firmly. "We came here together, did we not? The humans and the Sangheili. We are, despite the odds, creating a solid working relationship."

"One born of suspicion."

"It doesn't matter from what it was born. What matters is where we *are*. We are united, we are here, and both our species share the mutual desire to live, to survive, and to thrive in this galaxy. If you are the reason Halo is active, then we have come to plead with you not to do this thing. Please: cease Halo's activation. Do not bring it all to an end."

"You do not understand. I will not destroy the galaxy."

"You won't?" Vale cocked her head and took a step back.

"All will continue as it has been. The planets will orbit their stars. The stars will burn. The galaxy will thrive. It will simply be devoid of sentient beings."

Vale knew that it was too good to be true. She tried to think of another way to approach the AI. Something didn't seem right about its argument, but she couldn't place it.

"The galaxy will remain unperturbed. You have revealed the mistake that all of your kind makes: you set far too much store in yourselves. The galaxy does not require your existence. Rather, you require the galaxy's. Yet, you remain brazen. Even now."

Vale let out a sharp breath of exasperation, and her mind bent toward earlier conversations between her and Luther about the Ark. "But you can't think that you would be honoring the Forerunners, your creators, by erasing all that they had tried to preserve by building this place?"

"Perhaps not. Or perhaps so. As I said before, not all Forerunners agreed with the construction of this place. Some preserved your lives, but for what? To what end? So that you might mar the very things they created to save you? To destroy their rings, and this Ark?"

Vale was becoming increasingly frustrated, but something about this statement began to shed light on its motivation. This monitor was genuinely insane. It had to be. But from her perspective, an angle from which to approach it was starting to emerge.

Suddenly the monitor turned away from her and started to walk. Immediately she fell into step behind it. "Where are we going?" asked Vale.

"Elsewhere," Solitude replied.

She realized that the monitor wasn't going to be forthcoming.

"How about this," she said. "Why don't you meet with other representatives of the various species that we've brought here? Human and Sangheili. Speak to them about our motivations, ask them and see for yourself."

"The Sangheili? How would I possibly believe whatever motivations they might have for their future when their present is steeped in an internecine battle on their own cradle world?"

She hated to admit it, but that was a good point, and one she had even made earlier to the Elites. She was hardly about to admit that to the monitor, though. "They may be engaged in civil war right now, but that is being caused by some who are resisting the cessation of fighting with humans. The battle is being waged to protect us, to protect the peace our two species have."

"Do you now see? Even your argument stands in contradiction. The very peace you commend to me as evidence is already threatened. How much longer will it stand? Despite the paucity of biological sentience in the great span of this galaxy, its hubris is unnerving."

Vale wasn't quite sure how to respond to that, so she took a shot in the dark: "Well . . . you do know that the very reason the Sangheili had fought us for those decades was because they believed your makers were gods and that they were doing a service to them."

"Do you believe they were gods?"

Vale scratched her chin, her mind racing to come up with the safest answer. "Why don't you tell me?"

"You must have an opinion."

Yes. Of course they weren't gods. They were a brilliant race, and they built incredible things, but no, they were not divine.

"No, I really don't." She prayed that the monitor did not have some manner of onboard scanning devices that would inform it she was lying through her teeth. "I've never met a Forerunner, and so I've never had the opportunity to form any sort of opinion as to their status. I'd appreciate it if you could enlighten me."

The monitor completely stopped and stared at her for so long that she felt as if its gaze was burrowing deep into her skull.

Then it turned and started walking again. As before, Vale fell into step behind it.

"I do not know," Solitude told her. **"It is not information that they ever chose to share with me. So I am constrained to do only what I was made to do: to safeguard all that they left behind."**

"Is that what this is all about? What happened at the Halo installations? What happened here, at the Ark? Is this your revenge?"

The simplicity of it surprised even her, but Solitude did not seem fazed, continuing forward down the corridor that they were moving through. For a long moment, the monitor remained silent. Then it spoke up again.

"What kind of dialogue might we have had, human, were it not for the evidence against you? Upon your arrival at the first ring, Alpha Halo was blighted with the Flood, then obliterated by one of your own. Then later, Delta Halo too was allowed to be contaminated by the parasite, only to be scorched to char and ash by Sangheili warships. And finally, this place—the Ark. Here you came to put an end to your war, but in the process led the Flood to my sanctuary. One hundred thousand years of safety ended in a moment by the impudence of children who know not the deeds they wrought. Could they add to their sins? *Yes*. And they did. The ring I created here was meant to replace the one your people destroyed, yet you activated it before it was finished, obliterating it and mutilating the Ark in the process, in an attempt to cover your many crimes."

"You know that other species were involved in those events. It wasn't just us, or the Sangheili. We didn't have a choice. We had to deal with the Flood!"

"Nevertheless, it has been decided, human. No, this is not vengeance. This is justice. The only reason I have entertained our conversation this long is because you are trying to save the lives of those who came with you. Which is, I suppose, laudable. But everything about your history, about all your histories, is only compounded by the atrocities committed on my masters' creations. If you are allowed to live, what further cost will your kind accrue? I shudder to think."

"And how many thousands of centuries did it take for the Forerunners to reach the lofty place you hold them? Are we to believe that they came into existence fully formed as perfect and peace-embracing creatures? Of course not! I'm sure they had to struggle through their own problems for millennia until they reached the status that you recall. What if they had had someone who was sitting in judgment on them, who decided that they were never going to amount to anything? What if there had been some great, all-powerful race that decided the *Forerunners* did not deserve to live? Then there would have been no humans, no Sangheili, no Ark, no *you*. Did you ever consider *that* possibility?"

The monitor didn't immediately respond.

"I said, did you ever—?"

"I heard you."

"Well, then?"

"You know not what you speak of, human" said the monitor heavily. **"There *was* a judgment of my makers, and they were found wanting. The Flood was their judgment. Though they resisted for a time, in the end they recognized and submitted to punishment. The penalty: self-actuated immolation. Sacrificed in order to save you and those you protect."**

"And now you're going to undo all that they had hoped for?" Vale pressed. "You would bring death to trillions for the sake of your peace."

"There is no peace left."

The hall opened wide in front of them. They entered an area that was huge and round, akin to a gigantic fishbowl. It wasn't surrounded by glass, though. Instead it was solid metal, heavily reflective. Vale saw her image reflected in mirrors all around her.

She looked up and was surprised to see that there was no ceiling. The vast room appeared to be topless, although she knew that couldn't be the case. She also spotted floating holograms of various star systems hovering high above her. It seemed to be the entire galaxy.

"Are you hungry?"

The question caught her off guard, and the fog had still not fully cleared from her mind. "Yes, I suppose so. Hungry and a little tired. It's been a while since I've eaten or rested. But that doesn't matter."

"Yes, it does."

There was a subtle whirring, and a small platform rose up from directly in front of her. There were pieces of fruit sitting on it, small spheres that looked similar to apples. She picked up the nearest one, which was green, and bit into it. She didn't know why she had picked it up or why she ate it, but she had, and it tasted wonderful, possibly one of the best pieces of fruit she had ever had.

"You see what we are capable of growing here," said Solitude.

"Yes, absolutely." The juice of the fruit was running down the side of her face, and she wiped it away. She was trying to focus, but things were becoming hazy. *Was it this room? Was it the heavenly bodies spread out in every direction above? Was it the fruit?* "It's very good. But we need to talk about Halo . . ."

"Actually, we do not."

She heard an energized buzzing and saw to her surprise that there was now an energy field surrounding her, trapping her. The holographic personage of Solitude, a perfect replica of herself stood outside, its arms behind its back.

"For all your fury, there is little fight," the monitor droned to her, as if it were still speaking inside her head. **"There is nowhere for you to go. I suggest you sleep now."**

"Not until we . . ."

"Now. You will need your strength."

Despite her determination, Vale felt her eyes starting to shut. She tried to force them open, not quite understanding what was happening, but she couldn't do it. She felt her knees go weak, and then she sank to the floor. Darkness was filling her mind, and she strove to fight it off, but her exhaustion overwhelmed her, and the next thing she knew, she had tumbled to the side. The last thing she saw was her own face smiling down at her from above. And then she was unconscious.

CHAPTER 15

L uther was beginning to feel extremely confident that he would
not make it off this installation alive.

"We could have died back there," he said. "Now that
Halo's countdown's been effectively stopped, I'd like to get the
hell off this thing."

"I am open to suggestions," said Usze.

During the fracas with the armigers in the citadel's main hall,
Luther, Lamb, Usze, Kola, and Drifts had become separated from
the others. The chute they had taken had apparently brought them
several levels below the hall. They had been exploring what appeared to be the undercarriage of the citadel, where it connected
to the foundry wall. Thus far, it had only been a collection of corridors, with the Forerunners' typically elaborate cartouches and
angular designs along the walls, girded by a selvage of precisely
identical buttresses and support implements—though Luther
knew that the walls didn't actually need it. Forerunner architecture was generally eccentric, and this hall was no different.

They had found a small room at the end of one of the corridors.
There were displays and interfaces all along its walls, but none of
them seemed active. Despite the damage that the citadel's main
hall had endured, there was no rubble here, which was a welcome

change; at least they didn't have to pick their way through fallen detritus.

"Were these shut down?" asked Luther, pointing to the screens. "Or is there just no power going to them and so they're nonfunctional?"

"If I had to guess," said Lamb, "I would say the latter. Perhaps when the replacement Halo fired, the damage caused to the citadel destabilized something—maybe the power source was struck and shorted out. That makes far more sense than it just being shut down for no reason. Then again, with the AI out there, anything is possible." Lamb was looking closer at one of the screens. He frowned and then said, "Can you read this writing? Right here?"

He was pointing at something that Luther hadn't noticed before. It was indeed a string of script, and he stared at it, trying to make out exactly what it said. He preferred not to drag Drifts Randomly over just to translate simple Forerunner text. That was one of the main reasons why Luther was here in the first place.

"Okay, I think I've got it," he said after a long moment. "I think this is the citadel's primary control station. Whereas the hall above was dedicated to the Array, this controls the systems in the building itself. This particular interface is used for the map."

"Great, but the map isn't working," Lamb pointed out. "So how . . . ?"

"That shouldn't be an issue, thanks to our friend here," said Luther, and he turned to the Huragok. "Can you get power running to this thing?"

<<Yes.>>

"Okay, then. Please do."

The Huragok floated past him, and its tentacles opened up a panel next to the display.

Lamb was watching it work, intrigued. Every so often he would nod and mutter, "Yes, exactly," or something like it, as the Huragok pursued its repairs. Luther wondered about all that Henry had observed and learned on this expedition. If they survived it and made it home, he could probably fill multiple volumes with just what he had picked up on Forerunner engineering over the past day.

Luther stood next to Lamb. "What's it doing?" he whispered.

"Opening the junctions. Searching for energy flow and trying to determine the most efficient way to reroute it into the room." He shook his head. "Quite remarkable."

"I'd say so," said Luther. It certainly made sense. He knew there still had to be power available in the citadel somewhere. After all, the power systems were functional in the structure's main hall. And even in this room, there was light shining from overhead. It was very pale and seemed to flicker, but there was definitely still something, and he reasoned that it was up to the Huragok to find a way to get this station back online.

In the back of his mind, however, he was still thinking about the Forerunner machines they'd encountered in the main hall. The armigers, as Drifts had called them. They seemed to simply phase in and out of the room, which was extremely unsettling. If they suddenly decided to phase into this much tighter room, what could stop them?

Then Luther noticed that Henry was no longer standing near them. Something had caught his attention off to the side. He had moved a few meters away, his eyes on something in the shadows near the far corner of the room. "What's going on?" Luther asked.

"There's something over here. I think I found a Sentinel of some sort. One of the smaller kinds, but . . . it looks inert and non-functioning."

Luther wasn't sure he liked the sound of that. He took a couple of steps toward Lamb so that he could see clearer.

Whatever it was, it was seemingly locked in place, within an odd-looking hub-like console, almost like a model spaceship sitting on a plinth. It was positioned in such a way that its "eye" was staring up at Lamb, its arm-like booms slightly splayed and its claw manipulators extended. Luther had never seen one this small. Most of those they had recovered from the Halo installations were called Aggressors, and they were effectively an automated defensive weapon for the monitor. Aggressors were roughly three meters from front to back, but this one was only about one-third the size. Luther wondered if Henry had any idea what it was, but the fact that he was slowly getting closer to it seriously bothered him.

"Don't get too close, Henry. What the hell is it?" said Luther.

"I've no idea, but it's pretty remarkable," said Lamb. He reached down to touch its "head," and that's when it happened.

It leaped straight up into the air, letting out an earsplitting sound that Luther would remember to his dying day.

Its razor-sharp manipulators opened wide, and it snapped them down on Lamb's throat. He let out a strangled scream and tried to pull the machine loose, stumbling and falling backward onto the floor.

"Oh my God! Henry!" shouted Luther, running toward his partner. The machine was burrowing its two booms into Lamb's neck, and Luther grabbed at it from behind and pulled. At first he couldn't pry it loose, but then the Sentinel let its grip on Lamb go, twisting furiously around in his hands, blood spraying everywhere, trying now to get at Luther's throat.

Luther threw it a few meters away, where it landed in a mass of metal and blood in the corner. The thing spun around and launched back straight at Luther. Luther threw his hands up defensively as the little machine flew through the air for the kill.

Usze's blade suddenly swept in front of Luther's face, mere centimeters away from him, cutting the frantic machine in half. Emitting a final high-pitched tone of protest, it fell in two pieces and continued to skitter and shake about on the floor before it finally stopped moving a few moments later.

Luther ignored it and dropped down next to Lamb, staring at him in dismay. Blood was pouring out of the ragged, gaping wounds in his throat, so much and so fast that Luther didn't know what to do. He yanked off his jacket and, wrapping it around his hands, shoved down on Lamb's neck, trying to stop the flow. "Henry . . . Henry, just stay with me. We'll get this under control."

"I can't feel anything," he managed to say. There was gurgling in his throat as he spoke. "I can't . . ."

"You'll be fine," Luther assured him. "I have it under control."

Henry managed to focus on him, although his eyes were misting over. "I don't want to die here," he whispered. "Not like this . . . no . . ."

"You're not going to die. Don't be ridiculous." His jacket sleeve was soaked with red. "You're going to pull through this. The bleeding is slowing down."

" 'Cause . . . I'm running . . . out of blood."

"Don't say that."

Kola stepped in and stared down at both of them. "He is lost, human. You might as well—"

"*Shut up!*" shouted Luther. "He's going to be fine! You hear me, Lamb?! Ignore him. You're going to pull through. I swear, you—"

"Luther," Usze said, and he sounded regretful. "It's too late."

PETER DAVID

He looked down and saw that the Sangheili was correct. Lamb had ceased moving, his eyes staring at nothing.

He could have tried to apply some rudimentary first aid, attempt to force his heart back to life, despite the blood loss, but he knew that it would do no good. He growled in frustration and sat back, staring straight ahead. "Damn it. Goddammit. He was a good man."

"He was a fool," said Kola. "He should not have trifled with that machine."

Luther was immediately on his feet, and he shouted into Kola's face, speaking Sangheili, *"He was a good man! And just because he lacked your instincts for survival does not give you the right to insult him in death! He died with honor trying to stop Halo from wiping out our galaxy! Do you understand what I'm saying?!"*

"Yes," Kola said coolly. *"I do. I . . . apologize if I gave offense."*

"Of course you gave offense! You . . . !" Luther closed his eyes, steadied himself. There was no point in continuing to bellow at the Sangheili. He took a deep breath and then opened his eyes again, trying to regain focus.

He knelt down next to Lamb, pulling his jacket free from the man's neck. Luther couldn't bring himself to take it back; it was covered with blood. Instead he slowly drew it up so that it was covering Lamb's face. "I'm sorry," he whispered. "I should have been watching out for you better." Then he rose and stepped back.

At that moment, Luther suddenly became aware of something glowing behind him. He turned and gaped in surprise.

The displays along the walls were lit up with a detailed map of the entire underground assembly of the citadel and the local sections of the foundry wall. The Huragok was floating nearby, and though the creature was incapable of appearing proud of itself, Luther couldn't help but feel that its pride would have been warranted.

"Thank you, Henry," he said, "you found us a way out." Everything was clearly and cogently labeled on the display. Every detail of the entire citadel complex was spelled out, including the basin-like interior and the three energy pylons that guarded the entire site. It was quite impressive. His finger ran across it as he searched for something that would direct him to an exit. Some way out of this damn place.

It took a few minutes until he finally said, "Here. Right here. This is the Forerunner term associated with 'exit,' or 'exodus.' I think this is where we need to go to get out."

Usze moved in behind him and studied the map. "Where are the others, I wonder? If they even survived."

"It's difficult to tell," said Luther as he tapped the lower right of the panel. "If I were to guess, some kind of portal system took them well away from the citadel. There's no record of them here at all."

"And the exit is up here?" He pointed to the place that Luther had indicated seconds earlier.

"As near as I can tell, yes."

"All right, then. We should proceed. If there is anything else you need to do for the human . . ."

"And what would you suggest I do? We can't carry his body. So really . . . what do you think I should do for him?" Luther was unable to keep the mounting bitterness from his voice.

To his surprise, Usze put a comforting hand on his shoulder. "You should take a moment to mourn him. Resign yourself to both letting him go . . . and carrying his memory forever. Because he was a comrade and he was a warrior and he is owed that much."

Luther nodded. The words rang true to him. He knelt down beside Henry and did something he never thought he would do.

He prayed.

"Treat him well," Luther whispered. "He'll have a lot of questions, and I think you owe it to him to answer them. And if you don't . . . I swear, I'll kick your ass when I get there, which hopefully won't be too soon anyway."

Luther then stood and cast one last glance at the body of his trusted associate. "I'm so sorry, Henry," he said. Then he stood, turned, and walked away from Lamb's body, following Usze and Kola, who were marching forward with certainty.

At some points, the citadel wall's network of interior passageways was so cramped that Luther felt claustrophobic. The walls were tight around them. Then they would pass through an opening and be stunned by how large the new area was. Some parts of it actually seemed like hangars, capable of storing very large space vessels, but were nevertheless empty. He wondered if whatever had been contained in them had ever been built, or if they had been built but were then launched somehow. *Where would they have been launched to?* Luther wondered.

Might this be where the Retrievers remain when they are not active? The thought made him nervous.

They also found areas where rubble was still piled up, presumably from the damage caused by Halo years ago, and it was an effort to push their way past or climb over those obstructions. But they managed it briskly enough and kept going. At certain other points they passed by open parapets that looked out into the foundry, across a dense red haze where the moon that the Ark mined still hung—a silent, hollow visage that gave Luther goose bumps. From this close, it was a breathtaking sight, yet they still kept their pace.

At one point, though, as they were passing through another of the larger areas, Usze suddenly held his hand up and beckoned for silence.

"Why should—?" Luther started to ask.

Usze shoved Luther against the wall and clamped a large saurian hand over his mouth. Luther stopped struggling to get free, not that he could have done so anyway; Usze was far too strong.

There was some sort of loud clacking, accompanied by the heavy flapping of wings.

The lighting was especially dim in this chamber, which had a network of crosswalks high above that cast deep shadows on the floor below. Usze was keeping himself and Luther buried in the shadows, and Kola was hiding as well. The Huragok drifted over near them without having to be told. They were now covered in shadows, making it difficult for anyone in the upper regions to potentially spot them.

Seconds later, the area above them was alive with pteranodon-like monstrosities, with not one large wingspan but two—Luther had seen these four-winged creatures before, on Gamma Halo. These animals were certainly not safe up close, so their large numbers here made his stomach turn.

They barreled squealing through the upper reaches of the room. At this point, Luther wasn't even trying to breathe, as he was petrified that the things would spot them and descend immediately. There was little they could do from this particular position, if they got the creatures' attention. The memory of the thing that had tried to grab him while he was on the mammoth was still fresh in his mind.

Fortunately, these creatures seemed to be leaving the immediate vicinity. *Had something spooked them?* Usze kept Luther pressed against the wall until the heavy beating of their wings had

PETER DAVID

faded away; only then did he release him. "Why do you think they left?" Luther asked, his voice still a whisper.

"It matters little at present, as long as they are not concentrating on us," Usze replied. "Come." He started moving again and Luther fell in behind him.

Within minutes, they reached a narrow ramp that led upward. "Here," said Usze, and the three of them quickly ran up it, with the Huragok close behind. Luther was keeping his eyes on the shadows around them. It just seemed too convenient that the threat of the birds had just vanished, especially given all that had already happened on the Ark.

At the top of the ramp was a pair of large, closed doors, which did not automatically open upon approach, and there was no control panel near them. From the map, Luther knew that beyond the doors was one last corridor before the exit—a control suite for this section of the foundry. Now they just had to find a way through.

"How do we get through?" said Luther.

"Sometimes pure strength is the best way," said Usze, and he turned to Kola. "Help me force this open. . . . Luther Mann, get up against the door. Take the Huragok with you."

Luther did as instructed. Usze looked the door up and down. It was about two meters in height and from this close appeared to be solidly sealed.

Usze activated his energy blade, shoved it into the door seam, and then started prying back with all his might, Kola stepping in next to him, yanking in the opposite direction.

At first, the doors showed no sign of budging. Usze and Kola did not stop, though, applying every bit of their strength to the task. And then, very slowly, the doors began to part.

Luther pressed up against the open area that Usze and Kola had provided thus far, but it still wasn't enough for him to slide

— 286 —

through. He started to wonder why the doors weren't opening easily. *Was it possible that something—or someone—didn't want them to leave the citadel? Very possible,* he decided, *given the scene they'd just escaped in the main hall.*

The Huragok, on the other hand, was another matter entirely. Its body was astoundingly elastic as it shoved into the small space that the Sangheili had created and navigated itself through it. Luther couldn't believe what he was seeing. Within seconds, the Huragok had adapted its body to such a degree that it was able to pass through the very narrow space between the doors.

Luther was determined to follow. After a few more seconds, Usze and Kola had managed to create enough of an opening for him to shove his shoulder through. This was followed by the upper portion of his chest, and then after that, he was passing completely sideways through the space, the Elites straining hard to keep it open.

It was at that moment that Luther realized he had placed an overabundance of faith in Usze's and Kola's strength. If the Sangheili's power failed, the doors would slam shut and Luther would be crushed between them.

With time not on his side, Luther pushed forward, the Sangheili grunting as they strained to keep the doors open.

It was then that one of the Huragok's tentacles wrapped around his wrist and pulled him with surprising strength. Luther was yanked off his feet and seconds later fell into the open space beyond the doors. "*I'm through!*" he shouted.

The doors banged shut even as he spoke, and he realized that the Sangheili had simply lost their grip. The echo bounced around inside the room for a time as Luther scrambled to his feet and looked about.

Consoles and holographic panels of all manner lined the walls, and at the far end, an open doorway led outside. Luther walked quickly to the door's threshold and peered through it, just to make sure it was real. Gravel and moss had crept their way inside, and the smell of fresh air filled the entire space. This was finally their exit. Now they had to get the door open for the Elites.

Walking back into the room, which he had previously determined was the foundry control suite, Luther looked around. Apart from one large wall that was divided into horizontal brackets, the others had numerous displays and interfaces of varying sizes and shapes, all of which were presently inactive. They were intricately devised, and Luther knew it would take him quite some time to discern what exactly they controlled. *If only Henry were still alive.* Almost intuitively, however, Drifts had already gone to work, fidgeting with the largest of the displays.

Overhead, there was what seemed to be a maze of thin white tubing that stretched everywhere, although Luther was clueless as to what might possibly flow through it. Perhaps some manner of liquid or pure energy. There was no way to be certain. There was definitely power running through the walls, though, since pale lights were shining down from overhead. He briefly examined the empty wall opposite the displays, running his hands along it. For some reason, the shape and design reminded him of a Forerunner shutter system. Then his attention turned to the ground.

There was plenty of rubble and debris in the room, just as they'd encountered in other parts of the citadel. Something had happened to seriously damage this building and the foundry wall; he could see signs of it everywhere. Cracks in the walls, buckled support structures, and chunks of debris—the replacement Halo's activation and subsequent disintegration must have been an incredibly violent event for materials as resilient as these to show any strain or damage at all. Nevertheless, Luther could immediately discern where they were from the writing etched upon the wall, and it shocked him.

<<I think this is it,>> Luther said to the Huragok in its language. <<This is, in fact, the foundry's control station.>>

<<*Yes. It is.*>>

The foundry itself was an automated machine, its forge refining raw materials that Retrievers had carried from the mined moon at the center of the Ark. The system processed and stabilized the substance before casting the Halo's mold and fabricating the immense ten-thousand-kilometer ringworld one section at a time. At first, Luther was somewhat surprised that this important room would be so close to the outside, but then he realized that much of the outside was highly secured already, with energy barriers and other systems. To the Forerunners, there was technically no "outside," since they had built everything Luther now saw, including the ground and the trees, and even the sunlight by which he could see them.

<<Can you fix it? Can you get these online and get our friends through the door?>>

The Huragok had always answered him immediately up to this point. But now the Engineer simply floated there, studying one display after another in what Luther assumed was great detail.

<<*I do not know. There is nothing here to see.*>>

Those were not exactly the words that Luther wanted to hear. <<What do you mean: *Nothing here to see?*>>

<<*I see nothing. Maybe it is broken. Destroyed here . . . or being controlled elsewhere.*>>

<<If that's the case, then can we try to find another way to get this door open? I'm not particularly keen on keeping our friends waiting on the other side, especially given what we've encountered.>>

<<*There is another here. Inside.*>>

<<Another what? An artificial intelligence? A monitor?>>

<<*I do not know.*>>

<<Perfect,>> said Luther with a low moan. He looked around at the room, his mind racing. <<All right,>> he said, thinking out loud. <<We're almost out of here, though. We know that there's something in the Ark's network not cooperating with us. This *has* to be the Ark's monitor. So I guess my question is this: Is there enough still working in this place that you could tap into the remaining functionality of the room and attempt to access the Ark's primary controls?>>

He was surprised by the unhesitating answer.

<<*Yes,*>> said the Huragok.

<<Well, let's get started, then,>> he said briskly. If they couldn't get the door open, maybe they could get this AI's attention and strike up a conversation, possibly expose some of its vulnerabilities. He'd seen Drifts Randomly in action enough to not doubt the little guy in the least.

⊚

Spartan Kodiak almost fell into oblivion.

He had his flashlight mounted on his helmet and was making his way through a darkened corridor not long after the portal had dropped them in what initially looked like a vast bank vault, but with walls that stretched so high above that he couldn't see the ceiling. There was no ambient light in this particular section and nothing that he could find to illuminate the area for him. So he clambered over debris, making sure of his footing before he advanced. A part of him was becoming seriously concerned with how the battle had just played out, and, in particular, with them getting separated from the others and forced into the portal. The transition was alarmingly swift and electric, leaving a copper taste in his mouth, but his armor still seemed perfectly operational.

He had said practically nothing to N'tho or Holt as they made their way through the darkness. They hadn't seemed much for chatting. Furthermore, Kodiak was concerned that whatever might be said could lead the conversation back to the fact that N'tho had definitely saved his life. He had no idea how he felt about owing his continued existence to a former enemy, especially one that he'd hated for so long. Was he supposed to be grateful now? Was that how it was going to be?

He was lost in thought, until suddenly N'tho's hand grabbed him from behind, clamping onto his shoulder.

"Hey!" Kodiak shouted.

"Stop," said N'tho with an urgent tone.

Kodiak's instinct was to pull away while informing the Elite that he had no business barking orders at him. But something in the Sangheili's voice prompted him to obey and look more carefully at what was in front of him. The hallway was heavily shadowed, yes, but there was nothing directly in his path that appeared to be . . .

Then, suspicious, he angled his helmet so that the light was playing across the floor directly in front of his feet. That was when he saw the problem—there was no more floor. He didn't know if the vast gap blocking their way was part of the architecture or if a chunk of it had simply collapsed, but its jagged shape hinted toward the latter. *Man, this place was beat to hell.* Within moments, he found the other side, but it looked remarkably far away. He wasn't sure that he could clear it.

Spartan Holt stepped in behind him. "What do you think?"

"Can you make it across in one leap?" said N'tho.

PETER DAVID

Kodiak didn't answer immediately. He was running some mental calculations.

"I think we can," said Holt, but he didn't sound terribly sure. "Use our jump-jets, right?"

The jump-jets were standard-issue thrusters found on their current iteration of Mjolnir armor. They were generally reserved for low-gravity contexts, but in this case, they'd be damn helpful. The main difference between the Spartans and the Elites here was a few hundred kilograms of armor. This was a pretty big deficit, and the Elites knew it.

"If you wish," N'tho continued, "We could try to find another way around."

But Kodiak cut him off before he could finish the sentence. "I don't need to find another way around," Kodiak said in irritation. "We can make it. What about you, though? Perhaps *you* need to look for another way."

N'tho made some sort of odd noise that Kodiak realized was distaste. "I assure you, we can easily make it."

"All right," said Kodiak. "Back up."

He began shoving debris into the pit, clearing a path so that he could get enough speed. He listened carefully as it fell, waiting to hear when it struck. Nothing. *That's not good.*

Once he'd finished clearing a lane for himself, he backed up a good six meters and then took a deep breath. N'tho stood to the side, looking utterly disengaged, as if he didn't care whether Kodiak made it across or not—but then again, that's how Elites always looked when they weren't killing things. Zon was also watching intently, however, perhaps toying with the idea that the Spartans might fail and they'd have to explain that to the others.

Then Kodiak launched like a MagLev freighter, picking up speed with every step. Faster and faster he moved, and then,

— 292 —

the instant he hit the edge of the pit, he vaulted—and punched his jump-jets to gain speed—soaring through the air, his arms stretched out in front of him, hoping that he reached the other side before simple gravity took over. As he hurled across the open space, he briefly mused about what bothered him more: the thought of dying or the prospect of coming up short with N'tho watching. If the galaxy somehow survived, Kodiak could just imagine N'tho recounting the story to his brood: *I was once on an adventure with an ally, a Spartan who preferred to die in dishonor rather than admitting his limitations.*

And suddenly the floor was under Kodiak. He stumbled forward, the weight of his armor thudding heavily into the ground. He almost fell before he caught himself, and then looked around. He had cleared the jump by more than a meter. *I'll be damned,* he thought before calling out, "Who's next?"

"Okay, then, coming over now. Step back," said Holt, who was obviously feeling a bit better about the jump. He matched Kodiak's starting point, and then broke into a run. Kodiak braced on the other side as Holt vaulted over the space and punched his thrusters at about the midpoint. Kodiak was pleased (and admittedly, somewhat annoyed) to see that Holt landed a full meter past where he himself had hit.

"Good job, Spartan," he said to Holt.

"Thanks."

"All right, then," N'tho called over. "Stand back and give me room."

N'tho moved back from the gap, just as Kodiak and Holt had, and started to run. His muscular saurian legs pumped with a fierceness that they had yet to see, accelerating at an astonishing rate. Even Kodiak had to admit that the Elite's speed would easily carry him across.

Just as N'tho neared the edge, Kodiak suddenly felt a rush of hot air blowing upward from the pit and saw from the darkness a sea of lights rushing up to meet them. And he heard something as well . . . like the heavy hum of a hundred machines all moving at once.

"Wait!" he shouted.

Either N'tho didn't hear him or he was moving too quickly to stop. Whatever the reason, he ignored Kodiak's warning and vaulted over the pit.

And right when the Sangheili was at the midpoint, a cloud of flying Forerunner machines poured out from the depths, enveloping him, cutting off his forward motion. These were Sentinels—Kodiak knew them from the mission briefing. They were automated drones that protected Forerunner installations, and now there were dozens of them converging on their group from the pit below. The Elite was immediately grasped at by a Sentinel's boom manipulators, and some even fired bright beams of super-heated energy at him, their primary weapon. Directly above the endless chasm, N'tho thrashed at the drones, trying to knock them aside, and hoping that his momentum would still carry him across.

Instead he started to angle downward, coming up short of the other side.

N'tho slammed into the edge, unable to land on his feet. His torso struck against it, and he reached out desperately, clawing to find a grip with his hands. Meanwhile, the Spartans and Zon, who was still on the other side, had opened fire on the Sentinels, blasting a number of them out of the sky almost immediately. But despite their initial salvo of firepower, there were drones everywhere, and now they were closing in around N'tho while the Elite commander slid backward into the pit.

At that moment, Kodiak grabbed the Sangheili's left arm while

Holt got his right. N'tho's feet scraped the edge as he tried to heave himself up, but the walls of the abyss provided no traction. The Spartans quickly jerked him up onto his feet, though their shields were getting pummeled by the Sentinels' energy weapons. The Elite recovered quickly and joined the others in the fight, giving them time to recuperate their armor's shielding.

Though separated by a large chasm, the group had found cover points and were working together to take down the swarm of drones. Fortunately, when one of the Sentinels was destroyed, they emitted a small but violent explosion that sometimes damaged others immediately nearby. Although there were many of them, they were not individually formidable and could be easily dispatched.

"Are you all right, Commander?" said Holt.

"I am fine," N'tho replied, dispensing with what appeared to be the last Sentinel. When the coast was clear, Zon safely made the jump, and the four of them were once again together. "We should keep walking," N'tho said, after a brief moment of respite.

"Yes, we should," said Kodiak.

"Thank you for saving my life."

"Now we're even."

N'tho didn't acknowledge the comment and just continued ahead. Kodiak didn't really know what to make of it. It could be that he didn't think they were actually even, or perhaps the Elites didn't even have a concept like "being even" or any real debtor's ethic to begin with.

They headed down the corridor, all of them now far more cautious. But they encountered only twists and turns as they made their way. There was nothing notable about their location, and it was starting to piss Kodiak off. It was clear they were underground, far below the surface, but where exactly? N'tho had tried

his wrist-mounted cartographer, but it wasn't working, likely due
to the lack of a clear signal from *Mayhem*.

And where were Luther and the others? It was hard to believe
that only moments ago they had all been in the citadel's main hall.
Now they were separated, yet again, and this time he didn't have a
clue where the others had gone. He didn't even have a clue where
he'd gone, for that matter.

N'tho suddenly stopped. At first Kodiak assumed that there
was another problem, but the Sangheili appeared to be listening.

"Do you hear that?" said N'tho.

"No," Kodiak said.

The Elite continued to listen to empty air. "I heard her voice.
I heard Olympia Vale. She is talking to someone."

"Are you sure?" Kodiak strained to pick it up, but he still
couldn't detect anything.

"It would appear my hearing is sharper than yours."

"Yeah, you're terrific," Kodiak said sarcastically.

"Thank you," said N'tho, either missing the barb entirely or
just allowing it to pass. There was a crossway ahead of them, and
N'tho pointed to the left. "That way."

The Elite walked forward with confidence, and the others followed.

The corridor in front of them was opening up. There were
well-lit holographic displays lining the sides, and Kodiak considered that a good sign. It at least meant that wherever they were,
they were in a section of the Ark with power flowing through it.
Lights glowing overhead provided them the ability to see, even
though he wasn't exactly sure of what they were looking at.

Above the holographic displays and panels, the walls stretched
high into the air, the ceiling veiled in thin mist, hundreds of meters
above them. Small pocks of light darted back and forth from wall

to wall in the upper reaches of the room. Kodiak enhanced his visor's magnification and could see that they were small, flying machines. Although they were composed of the same material as the earlier Sentinels, they didn't have anywhere near the same shape.

"Constructors," N'tho said, though he seemed unconcerned.

"What are they?" Holt asked.

"They are Sentinels, but they were built by the Forerunners to exact repair where needed," N'tho replied, dropping his attention to the displays.

"So they're not a threat, like the others?" Kodiak asked. He already had his weapon aimed and readied. He was not planning on seeing a repeat of the situation they'd just come from.

"No," said N'tho. "These are Constructors, the others were Aggressors. They have completely different purposes."

Kodiak slowly lowered his battle rifle, and his head followed shortly after. Now that he felt comfortable, he began to explore the room they were in. It was rather large and spread across a series of dogleg-like intersections, with a number of doors on the opposite end from where they had entered. Along the walls were countless displays and panels, many of which bristled with light and color. Kodiak noticed, however, that on the walls above the displays and stretching as high as he could see, hexagon shapes with various keys on their surfaces could be defined. Their shapes allowed them to slot in between each other, covering the wall in a perfectly honeycomb-like network. Each was identical and looked as though it represented an individual and separate artifact, and there were literally thousands upon thousands slotted in the walls.

N'tho was studying the area very carefully. "This is a data center," he said. "All of these? These are resource and operation files for a distributed intelligence of some sort. Perhaps the Oracle of the Ark, as the other human believes."

"How do you know it's even a data center?" Kodiak asked.

"These remote stacks," he said, pointing up the wall, "are identical to those on other installations."

N'tho was studying one of the consoles but refused to interact with it physically. Kodiak didn't know if that was because he couldn't or because he didn't want to risk anything. Instead he simply read and observed what appeared to be words. At least he assumed that it was words. It looked more like symbols, although Kodiak couldn't remotely decipher what they meant. "Can any of you read it?" he asked N'tho.

Slowly N'tho shook his head. "The Huragok would have been most helpful here."

"So if this is the Ark's monitor," Kodiak began, "like Doctor Mann said, then this activity here, above us, is an indication that he was right? That the AI's alive and active?"

"I would say it is a very good indication of that, yes," N'tho responded.

"Then where's the AI?"

"It could be anywhere. This data center, I presume, can remotely communicate with any other part of the installation. Just like the others."

"Damn it," Kodiak muttered, almost too low for the others to hear.

"What?" Holt asked. "What's the problem?"

"It's nothing. It was just an empty hope."

"And what would that be?" asked N'tho.

"Forget it. We should be moving," Kodiak said, heading toward the doors on the far side. "Especially if you really did hear Vale's voice."

"Let's walk and talk, sir," Holt said, not wanting to let go what his fellow Spartan was referring to.

Kodiak let out a heavy sigh as the group moved. "I had a younger brother. His name was Bobby. He served in the Fifteenth MFR. An Orbital Drop Shock Trooper. He was a tough kid, a real killer. He got linked up with ONI about three years back and apparently worked on some highly classified ops. I don't even know what the hell they were."

The group left the data center through its rear door and moved into another corridor beyond it, their weapons raised and trained ahead as Kodiak told his tale. "So he goes on an op in late '53. Said it was skunkworks stuff, ONI prototype testing in an Oort near Thales. But I checked up on him, and that wasn't it. He was doing something else for ONI. Something he couldn't talk about."

They entered an incredibly large area, though it was still distinctly underground. Walking across what appeared to be some kind of platform, Kodiak could see the cavernous "natural" rock walls climb high into the darkness above, and between this and the other side of the room was an immense chasm connected by a single bridge. On this side, the platform was populated with large, squat machines shaped like blocks and enormous piping that dropped down into the chasm and out of sight. Approaching the ledge warily, Kodiak could see that the bridge was made of some ivory-like alloy and what appeared to be glass. It was an elegant structure, intricately designed, but entirely exposed to the environment. And it appeared to be the only real way to cross the massive gap. So they set out across it, and Kodiak continued.

"For a few months, I thought it was just a standard ONI scenario. He'd pop up after a bit. But as time went by, it was clear something had happened. Their official report was something akin to 'lost with all hands,' and that the ship they were manning—the UNSC *Rubicon*—lost its gravitic control systems and took a dive into a moon.

"*Rubicon*?" Holt asked. "Never heard of it."

"Neither had I. It turned out that ONI had erased all formal records of it from the naval registry. From any registry, for that matter. So it's pretty clear they were up to something."

"And what, Spartan, does this have to do with the Ark's intelligence?" N'tho asked, checking the sight on his weapon as they continued across the bridge.

"I think my brother was sent on a mission to the Ark. The timelines match, the registry trail of the ship matches, the fact that Thales's system was entirely vacant during this time," Kodiak said, taking a breath. "And some things he said before he left, that he'd been doing something that really no one had done before, going somewhere incredible—they just point to this being a classified op that ONI spearheaded. An op that led here."

"That's a pretty big presumption, sir," Holt said.

"It was . . . until Henry Lamb told us that his buddy knew of other expeditions to this place, ones that had been stricken from the records. Ones that ended badly. Ones that ONI didn't want anyone to know about."

"Lost with all hands," Holt said sympathetically, clearly recognizing the connection.

"Everything matches too well," Kodiak said, as they finally reached the other side of the bridge. "I was hoping that if there was an intelligence here, it might know if that was the case. Did the *Rubicon* ever come here? Did Bobby? It could put that part of me to rest."

"Silence," N'tho said, cocking his head as though he were listening to something. He had apparently lost interest in the story. "This way."

The Sangheili were walking quite rapidly now, up an alloy ramp ahead of them and back into a tunnel, and both Kodiak and

Holt had to hurry in order to not fall behind. By this time, Kodiak was able to hear what N'tho and Zon already had. It was Olympia Vale's voice, all right. There was also a low humming of energy, but Kodiak didn't know what that signified.

They turned a corner and stopped.

The corridor in front of them had come to an abrupt end, opening up into a much wider area . . . but the entire way through was cut off by a glowing field of energy.

The three of them approached the field, and N'tho stretched out his hand carefully. For a moment, he merely kept his hand close, sensing if there was any output from it. To Kodiak it smelled like ozone, but there was no sign of heat. Then the Elite touched the energy barrier, which fortunately did not generate any sort of kickback. But he couldn't penetrate it, either. He pushed against it, tentatively at first, and then with greater force, but there was no reaction.

Kodiak came up behind him, his eyes widening behind his visor. "Oh my God," he whispered. "We found her."

Olympia Vale was inside the fielded area, fifty meters away, floating in the air, her arms at her sides. She was surrounded by some sort of golden, shimmering force field that was whirling around her, elevating her in the center of this large, cathedral-like room. Near the ceiling were slowly wheeling lights. They looked like star systems.

She was talking to someone as well, another golden image. Kodiak realized immediately what it was: an exact holographic re-creation of her. *What the hell?*

"Vale!" shouted Kodiak. "Vale, we're here!"

She didn't turn around. "Hello, Spartan Kodiak," she called back. "Is anyone else with you?"

"It's me, Holt, N'tho, and Zon. What's going on? What is that thing?"

"Stay where you are. Don't move," she said, completely engrossed with whatever the bizarre holographic replication of herself was.

"And what might you be doing?" asked N'tho.

She responded in a flat, almost detached tone. "I'm trying to stop him from killing everyone."

And then the hum of the energy field increased aggressively, and they couldn't make out anything else she said.

Vale was unaware of how long she'd slept. All she knew when she woke up was that she was still on the floor, in the same place where she had drifted off.

Then she saw Solitude.

"Do you feel rested?" it inquired, sounding remarkably solicitous. *Had it just been staring at her this entire time?* The thought made Vale uneasy.

"Yes, I'm fine," she said impatiently. "Why do you keep that shape? Cloaking yourself so that you look like me?"

"For your peace of mind."

"What would give me peace of mind is if you stopped the activation of Halo and let me go," she said, keeping her voice even.

"I would like to remind you that you and your friends were not exactly at peace when I brought you here. This installation is not a safe place for your kind. Not anymore."

"But it could be once—"

"And even that was your own people's doing."

"If you have no interest in keeping my species alive, why did you take me? What is this all for?"

"Come up here," it said.

"Up there?" She was craning her neck to stare up at the floating holographic version of herself as it rose from the ground. "How am I supposed to—?"

Suddenly energy was swirling like a small tornado in the air immediately surrounding her. She tried to move her arms but was unable to; the energy was keeping them pinned to her sides, facing her in the direction of Solitude. And then, very slowly, she began to lift off the floor. "Why are you doing this?" she called out.

"You are regarding matters from down there. If you see things from my perspective, perhaps you will better understand them."

That made no sense to her, but she supposed it didn't matter. She was dealing with an insane machine, not a person who could be reasoned with.

Moments later she was hovering in the air, facing the holographic representation of herself. Then another image appeared before her: the Ark. It was here, in its present damaged state. From this angle she could see the scorched surface, the mangled spires, and the pieces of debris from Halo strewn across its face. The damage had certainly been comprehensive and dramatic, but she doubted that the image had Solitude's desired effect on her.

"If it's of any use," she said, "I'm sorry this happened. I'm sorry that your home was destroyed by my people. But what I'm seeing is you taking extreme measures that are not necessary."

"And you, human, are in a position to determine what is necessary?"

"These are people you're talking about. Living beings with lives and hopes and dreams. There must be another way."

"This installation is the foundation for all thinking life in the galaxy. Without it, your kind would have perished like the others. It is the single most important vestige of those my makers

left behind, and they entrusted it to me. Without it, there is no life, no hope, and no dreams for anything. Yet, despite this, you still resist my will to restore and protect it."

"The one who activated the replacement ring and damaged the Ark—we call him the Master Chief. He's a hero where we come from, and he's been missing for years. From what I've been told, he did this to stop the Flood, not to harm this place. He was trying to prevent Halo's activation, but his hands were forced to do what was done. It was not his intention to harm you—"

That was when she heard a voice. She could not turn and look to see who it was, but she recognized it well enough. "Hello, Spartan Kodiak. Is anyone else with you?"

"It's me, Holt, N'tho, and Zon. What's going on? What is that thing?"

"Stay where you are. Don't move," she shouted.

"And what might you be doing?" asked N'tho.

She responded in as even keeled a tone as she could muster; the last thing she needed was the arrival of these friends to further complicate her situation: "I'm trying to stop him from killing everyone."

And sounding almost sad about it, the monitor said, **"It is already too late."**

Her attention snapped back to him. "What do you mean?"

"Your friends have meddled with the communications array and deactivated Halo, but it matters little. They will not survive what follows, and when their rebellion is brought to an end and you have submitted to me, it will be reactivated. But for now, I must restore what your people have ravaged. Your star system will be the first. The Retrievers have already been launched."

"Again, why our star system? Couldn't you go to other worlds? Uninhabited worlds?"

"I could. I choose not to."

"It will still take them weeks to get through the portal," Vale said defiantly, though she knew that it hadn't taken her team that long at all. "You're making a mistake. We'll have an entire fleet there waiting for them by the time they get there."

"Weeks? No. More like hours," the monitor said. "The same as it took you. And do not threaten me with talk of human fleets. They are but a trifle next to the force that I have prepared."

"I don't understand." She couldn't believe what Solitude was saying to her. "How is it possible, given our distance from Earth?"

"I made it possible," the monitor told her calmly. "I have, in the time since the Ark was injured, crafted legions of heavily armed Retrievers, preparing for this very moment. All of my time and resources have been allocated with this single purpose in mind, and they will be unleashed on your star system without clemency. I have also exponentially increased the portal's power and astrogation systems to send and receive objects across the vast space that separates your world from here. It is an extraordinary exertion of power and information, and it very well could compromise a number of my systems. But I believe that to be necessary, and will gladly take the risk to undo the error of your people. So you see, it is—as I said—already too late. The Retrievers are even now rising from their bays, where they have waited long for this order. If you can take any comfort, it may be in this: at least no humans there will remain alive to perish once the Halo is reactivated."

CHAPTER 16

aptain Richards flexed her leg and nodded in approval.
She was seated in the medical lab of the *Mayhem*, which
was still suffering from the extensive damage incurred by its
crash. However, they certainly appeared to have the tools necessary to repair her leg. Stretching it now, she felt like it was completely restored to normal, and it had not taken very long at all.
The Elite who had worked on her didn't bother to identify himself
as a doctor or any sort of medical officer. Perhaps he was simply the weapons officer or an engineer pulling double-duty. But it
didn't matter, because he had been perfectly proficient in working
on human anatomy.

And just how he'd become so conversant with it was a bit trou-
bling. She began to wonder bleakly how the Sangheili had actually
had the opportunity to work on one . . .

The thought made her vaguely ill, but she decided that there
was no point in pursuing it. She didn't want to ask the question,
and she sure as hell didn't want to hear the answer.

The Elite was watching as she slowly got to her feet. "Is there
any pain?" he asked.

"No. None."

"That is fortunate. Be careful where you step for the rest of the
time that we are here."

"I will." She hesitated, and then mentally shrugged. "What is your name?"

"Sehar," he replied.

"Sehar. And you are the doctor on this vessel?"

"No. I am the weapons officer."

I'll be damned. Right on the money. "Yes. I forgot. Are you the one who attended to Olympia Vale?"

"No, I was busy with duties on the bridge. Besides, we had the Huragok here, and it was far more capable of handling those matters than I was."

"Do you have a doctor here?"

"No medical personnel are necessary. Any injuries that we sustain are usually capable of being tended to by the tools we have here. And if they cannot be, then we accept our fate."

How wonderfully pragmatic.

"In truth," he continued, "the Sangheili disdain the medical lab for their own use, but not for those of weaker species that once accompanied us. We would rather suffer injury or perish than to be pitied by an instrument or medicine."

She didn't exactly know what to make of that, but couldn't help feeling there was something deeply noble about it, even if it felt in part like a veiled insult.

At that moment, her lieutenant, Radeen, sprinted into the room. "Captain, we have a problem. I suggest you come right now."

As she nodded and started after him, Richards turned to Sehar and said, "Thank you for fixing me up."

"You are welcome, human."

She was relieved that, as she put full pressure on it, her leg didn't bother her at all. Sehar had definitely gotten the job done, all right.

Richards followed Radeen quickly through the corridors of the ship, arriving moments later on the bridge. The large viewscreen was illuminated, and her eyes widened when she saw it. "Is this actually happening?" she said, barely able to find her breath.

"Yes, it is," said one of the Sangheili.

In the far distance, Retrievers were emerging from the central core of the Ark, where, with any luck, her teams had finally arrived. Dozens, hundreds, no . . . thousands of Retrievers were now rising into the air.

"If they attack us, we are finished," muttered one of the Elite. "We do not have the ship remotely repaired yet. And we have nothing to stop such a force."

They watched in grim silence, but Richards soon noted the angle of their departure was skyward and toward the dark orb of the portal hanging high above the Ark's surface. "They're not going to attack us," she said.

"Perhaps we are now insignificant to whatever is controlling this place," an Elite remarked. "It now cares about something else entirely."

That was when Richards knew. "Oh God. The portal. They're going for Earth, the same as the others did. The others must have been just some kind of feint or test. This is the invasion force."

"The others were destroyed. These could be as well."

"The others didn't exactly go down without a fight. It took enormous firepower to bring down one. Now whatever is sending them knows that we don't genuinely pose any sort of threat," she said with growing concern. "I'll tell you right now what's going to happen. Those things are going to make a beeline for my homeworld, and they're going to pour through by the thousands. And then they're going to strip-mine the Earth, for the sake of repairing this installation. And there isn't a damn thing we can do to stop it."

Kola watched as Usze paced back and forth in front of the huge doors. "Why are you doing that?" he asked.

"It is the walking-guard form. I am staying vigilant."

"No, you are not. You are pacing. It is becoming somewhat irritating."

"I cannot help it," Usze said, keeping his voice modulated but still allowing his frustration to show. "I have no way of communicating with Luther Mann and the Huragok within, nor any way to determine if they are threatened. So I have assumed sentry duty in order to keep my mind occupied."

"And pacing is a part of that?"

"Yes."

"As you wish," said Kola with a shrug. "I wonder what is taking the Huragok so long to open the door."

It was at that point that Usze heard a distant scraping on the floor. It was soft and almost indiscernible. His head snapped around, and immediately his plasma sword was activated. Kola followed suit, revealing his own sword, which he had refrained from using until now.

One of the Forerunner machine bipeds—*armigers*, as Luther had called them—that had assailed their group in the citadel hall was standing a short distance off, at the junction of the corridor that they had just passed through. It had an energy stave in its hand and was looking at the Sangheili steadily, but showed no sign of movement. Usze 'Taham had no intention of perishing this close to the end of their journey.

He swung his blade in a slow arc, right to left and back—the battle stance of Sumai. The armiger's gaze fell upon him but it remained still.

"Come any closer," said Usze quietly, "and you will share your friends' fate."

The armiger initially made no attempt to approach, and for what seemed like a long time, stood there with its gaze fixed on the Elites. When it did finally move, it was not to attack. Instead it leaned forward and let out a deafening noise, repeating it several times, its voice carrying through the area. It sounded like an eerie cross between the howl of a predatory animal and a booming warship klaxon.

More movement behind it could be heard.

Now dozens of the same machines were emerging from the junction and the recesses of nearby shadows. They came up and stood behind the first, as though precisely following its lead. Then, as a single group, they began to walk toward the Elites.

Usze backed up until his spine was pressed against the door, Kola right beside him. Their swords were at the ready as the armigers moved slowly toward them, some carrying staves, and others Forerunner rifles.

"This does not bode well," Kola muttered.

"That is quite obvious," said Usze. "However, if it is a fight they are looking for . . ."

The machines continued to edge slowly toward them, in no apparent hurry. They finally stopped about two meters away, making little noise save for the slight whir of what seemed to be pistons and servos in their armor and the sound of their metallic frames clinking against the hard floor.

And then suddenly, as one single unit, they all let out a loud, unnerving howl and charged.

Oblivious to what was happening on the other side of the thick doors, Luther Mann was thoroughly engrossed in the Huragok's effort to take control of the Ark's systems. If it could, they'd be able to stop the intelligence that had been causing them so much grief this trip.

The Huragok was buzzing around the area, taking care to work with specific panels and displays, and these began to come on one by one. Sometimes it took mere seconds, other times much longer, but after ten minutes the room was filled with lights and activity. "What are you doing?" he asked the Huragok for what seemed like the thousandth time.

<<*Working,*>> it replied in the same manner every time it was asked.

But this time was different. Something metallic-sounding shifted behind him and, startled, he turned suddenly around.

But there was nothing. The opposite wall, the one not covered in monitors, seemed completely empty, but he knew he had heard something. After nearly a minute, he was about to turn back around, when the noise could be heard again and this time the source was revealed. The far wall was moving, sliding up like a hangar door or shutters. The wall was large, at least four meters high and ten meters long, and the entire thing started to open up.

Natural light began to pour in from what was now revealed to be an observation window. Below it was a vast hangar bay area, much like the space they had come through before. Inside this one, however, were dozens upon dozens of Retrievers. The massive Strato-Sentinels were uniformly parked in a vast structure that seemed to go on for at least a kilometer before ending in an incredibly large opening, one that looked out into the Ark's core and at the moon beyond. The "sky," however, was not empty. It was filled with Retrievers soaring upward; these had been dispatched presumably from the very similar bays that lined the foundry walls. Luther's suspicions about the location they encountered before had been proven right, but what he now saw was disheartening. As he contemplated its meaning, even the Retrievers in the bay he was looking at began to rise from their mounts and launch out into the foundry, climbing up into the space above the Ark.

He had a bad feeling about this, but wasn't in the least certain what it might mean.

<<Human.>>

Luther was surprised when the Huragok addressed him; this was the first time that the Huragok had done so and not vice versa. "Yes?" He glanced quickly toward the Engineer.

<<I have infiltrated the system.>>

Luther blinked several times, unable to quite understand what the Huragok had just told him. "Ex . . . excuse me?"

<<I have control of the Ark.>>

"What?! How the hell did you manage that? Why didn't you take control earlier, if you could do it now?"

<<I wanted to for a time. I was unable to. The mind controlling this facility is very clever at rerouting functions. The Ark controlling device was blocking my attempts. For the entire time, I had been analyzing systems to bypass. Something was distracting—>>

"Never mind—explain it later! Can you open the door?"

<<Yes.>>

Luther ran toward the large double doors and shouted, even though he suspected that the Sangheili had no way of hearing him. "Usze! Kola! Can you hear me—?!"

The doors suddenly slid open, and Luther stopped in his tracks, gasping.

Usze fell backward, hitting the floor heavily. He was covered in blood. His eyes were open, but barely, and his arms and face were torn up. He was still gripping his plasma sword with fierce determination, although his breath was ragged. Kola was standing to the side, but looked just as exhausted and likewise severely wounded.

Luther looked beyond Usze in astonishment. The entire floor was covered with debris from armigers, the same kind they had encountered in the citadel's main hall. Most of them had been cut to pieces, and a few still writhed mechanically about in their death throes. "Oh my God," he whispered, and then shouted, "Usze!" He ran to the Elite and dropped to his knees beside him. "Are you all right?" He turned to Kola. "Are you—?"

Usze stared up at him with incredulity. "Ask yourself, human: Do I appear all right?" he demanded.

"He is fine," Kola managed to say. "So are we both. There is no . . ." Abruptly Kola let out a loud sigh and slid heavily to the floor inside the room.

Usze started to stand up, but he seemed disoriented, unable to pull himself together.

"Stay seated," said Luther, pushing down on Usze's shoulders as Drifts shut the door behind him. The Sangheili actually paid attention to him, allowing himself to be placed in a sitting position. "There's no need to stand up. We're not going anywhere for the moment."

Usze turned and stared at him through bleary eyes, but then turned his attention to the wall-size window where the Retrievers were still pouring out of the bay and into the Ark's core and launching upward. He turned to Luther with an expression that suggested he couldn't quite believe what he was seeing. "What is this? What is happening?"

"Drifts," and Luther turned to the Huragok frantically. "What is going on out there? Where are they headed?"

<<*Earth. It is sending them to Earth,*>> said the Huragok.

Luther wasn't sure he had understood the Engineer correctly. "What are you talking about? The Ark's monitor, the one that was stopping you before . . . it initiated this?"

<<*Correct.*>>

"How do you know?"

<<*It has given the command to take from your home what it needs.*>>

"But why would it do that?"

<<*Intends to rebuild this place using your worlds. Retrievers are not under the Ark's command anymore. They are outside my control. It controls them.*>>

"Can we stop it, Huragok?" asked Usze.

Luther's mind was already racing, putting together the pieces. "Activating Halo was just a means to an end," he said slowly. "It needed us to open the portal. That's what this has been about. That's what it's always been about. Earth is about to be invaded by one of the largest hostile forces in history right now, and we're down here, helpless to stop it."

The monitor laughed.

It was a very disagreeable sound to Olympia Vale. She hadn't heard it before, but now she found it positively disconcerting. It wasn't remotely human laughter. Instead it sounded . . .

Demented. The thought that something created by the

Forerunners could go this far off the rails was, to put it mildly, upsetting.

"What's so funny?" asked Vale.

"Just an unexpected development. The Ark's system has been subverted."

"What are you saying? That something's subverted the—?"

"A Huragok—one that came here with you—managed to bypass my security emplacements, tapped into the Ark's core, and then seized control. A rather brilliant tactic, if I may say so. I must also say, however, that I found it quite amusing. The irony of an entity created by the Forerunners being stymied by another Forerunner creation contains a certain symmetry, do you not think so? Would that I had taken this servant-tool for my own ends when afforded the opportunity in the communications array earlier."

"What do you mean?"

"It matters little, human. Your world is about to be rendered lifeless. Do you accept that your fate is now with me?"

"Yes, I . . . suppose." Her mind tried to find a way to buy time. If Halo had been deactivated and the Ark's systems were being controlled by Drifts, perhaps she might survive this after all. She just needed more time. "You could stop the Retrievers right now, couldn't you?"

"Of course."

"But you won't."

"No. I was impressed by your argumentation, nevertheless. You are much more skilled at that then the other members of your species. Nevertheless, you must accept that your destiny is here with me. You will be the last of your kind. Did you think such a thing was possible?"

"No. No, I hadn't, but let me ask you a question: If I do promise to remain here, would you stay your hand for a moment? Would you stop the Retrievers from their current task and talk with me further before sending them?" To Vale, it had been clear from the outset that this intelligence—Tragic Solitude—though clearly erratic, was not mainly this way because of what had happened to the Halo installations. It could repair and replace those using any world it chose. It was this way because it had been alone for a hundred millennia. It had been abandoned by its makers. And for a brief moment, Vale actually felt sorry for it. A hundred thousand years of complete and utter isolation, no matter the mental rigor or constitution, was a recipe for madness.

When the monitor didn't respond, she asked another question: "How did you get your name? Tragic Solitude?"

"I chose it during the dark times following reintroduction."

"When you were alone?"

The monitor did not respond. It merely stared at her, a nearly perfect reflection.

"If I remain with you. If I promise to stay here, can you send the Retrievers instead to other worlds, as I asked earlier? Will you do this for me?"

"I am, frankly, disappointed, human. Do you think me a fool? You have nothing to barter with. You *will* remain here, as long as I am pleased to allow it. And when I am finished putting an end to your world and the others in that wretched, backwater system, I will use your very hand to reactivate Halo and silence this galaxy once more."

No one on Earth is prepared for the first assault of the Retrievers. How could they be?

All of the scientists who had been exploring the Excession had been shunted aside, and Home Fleet was now in control. Without anyone monitoring the portal's internal systems, they were blind-sided by the enemy's approach. And although there were dozens of UNSC vessels that now filled the Kenyan sky, poised and surround-ing the portal at every angle, they were but a fraction of the number of Retrievers.

When word was first received by the UNSC that the Halo acti-vation has ceased, there is out-and-out rejoicing by everyone who knew of it. It was first felt on Zeta Halo, then the others followed. It had not been expected in the least. After the Mayhem *had de-parted unceremoniously days earlier, there was significant cause for alarm. What had caused the Elites to leave without permission? Were the humans aboard taken against their will? The very fabric of the human–Sangheili peace accord was now strained beyond belief, despite efforts on both sides to calm their own people.*

Home Fleet's various battlegroups had also been brought to the portal and their combat advisories raised to red alert. The portal had remained active and surging in dark skies for the time, yet ONI and the branch heads of the UNSC were wary about the proposition of sending more ships in immediately. Still in deliberation, they were now weighing the cost and searching desperately for another solution to the threat of Halo.

It appeared now, however, that the Ark team has succeeded.

It was an interesting and dramatic turnaround in local philosophies. UNSC and ONI officers had been furious when the Sangheili vessel Mayhem *had vanished into the portal. Heated communications with the Arbiter had spoken darkly of how this would be perceived as an act of war . . . a response that the Arbiter had scoffed at, pointing out that if all sentient life in the galaxy was about to end, certainly spending the last weeks reopening old wounds and engaging in armed conflict was hardly the best use of anyone's time. But, under the guidance of Admiral Hood, cool heads had prevailed.*

And now that the Halo countdown has been halted, all threats of hostility and drums of war were silenced. Both the humans and the Arbiter's Sangheili waited with bated breath, discussing what might be the best course of action to retrieve Mayhem *and their people.*

While the portal remained open and the UNSC's naval forces amassed around it, meetings were being held for after-action analyses, but they were mostly exercises in self-congratulations. Everyone was complimenting everyone else for this close call, curious how the operation had been a success only days later, when a trip to the Ark should have taken weeks, if not months. No word had been heard back from the team that had actually gone to the Ark.

It was at that point that they become aware that something was coming through the portal.

The first of thousands of Retrievers come pouring out. The portal flickers wildly at the amount of Forerunner machines passing through it, but it manages to continue functioning.

The Retrievers are everywhere. So many now that the sun is blotted out. Some are angling downward toward the Earth's surface

*while others are quickly peeling away, moving toward the surround-
ing UNSC warships at impossible speeds. No one yet understands
why the Retrievers are here.*

*It is only then that the Retrievers commence their primary func-
tion. Hundreds of them, flowing down toward the Kenyan surface
with incredible speed.*

*The UNSC quickly engaged their fleet to address the encroaching
threat. Dozens of ships launched their salvos at the alien machines
above the Excession, hammering at the Retrievers with every weapon
at their disposal. On the ground, those below look up in disbelief.
But that lasts only a moment. As the enormous UNSC ships launch
their attack against the ancient Forerunner machines, the booming
of explosions is heard and the descending debris, some of it the size of
buildings, begins to slam into the ground. With the first thundering
sound of a Retriever's hull plummeting like a meteor into the savannah, everyone in the vicinity begins to run screaming for shelter. But
there is none that can protect them. And on the ground, many of the
machines have already gone to work, prying up the Earth's surface
with the force of a tornado. These Retrievers, despite the violence
of their actions, are slowly but methodically stripping away chunks of
earth and depositing it into their bins for transport back to the Ark.*

*The commanders of the UNSC vessels weren't initially aware
of what exactly the Retrievers are doing here, but it was quickly confirmed in the hostile machines' first efforts. They remain unaware,
however, that once the Retrievers have finished here, they will spread
out all over the planet, and then beyond, to Luna, Mars, and humanity's other interplanetary colonies. The truth is that the Retrievers are
going to dismantle every world within the Sol system that can yield
what they need. All they know is what is before them: an enemy that
must be stopped. And that's all they need to know.*

As the mining Retrievers are fired upon, other heavily weaponized

Retrievers unleash their own hailstorm, and their sole task is to battle the humans. Bolts of energy and high-density slugs are flying everywhere, turning the sky to fire as UNSC ships and Retrievers both shudder from the impact. The Forerunner creations, though many in number, have little to no shielding and thus are far less capable of enduring direct hits. It seemed, however, that no matter how much damage was done to the Retrievers' forces, more still came through. There is simply no end to them, and now the UNSC vessels are quite outnumbered and outgunned.

The realization now hits the humans here. There simply won't be enough ships to counter them all. This invasion has caught everyone by surprise, and there is no way that the local vessels can sufficiently recover. It is now the UNSC craft that are struck down. First one, then two, and within seconds ten—these once-majestic human ships are either sundered apart by a critical explosion, blooming into a thousand pieces in the sky, or are sent reeling toward the ground, only to detonate on impact. The humans are losing.

The Retrievers operate surgically, conducting their actions without any hesitation: uncaring, unfeeling, relentless. There is only their primary function, currently being carried out with simple determination. They fill the sky like locusts, uncountable and without mercy.

The fall of Earth is under way, its fate decided by an ancient construct hidden in the vast blackness that lies between galaxies.

CHAPTER 17

L et me show you what is currently occurring on your homeworld," said the monitor, Solitude.

The energy that was suspending Vale in midair began to
spin even more intensely. She felt it probing her brain, and images
began to spill through. She gasped as she saw an image, presumably captured by one of the Retrievers. The portal was still open
over Voi, and she witnessed thousands of Retrievers spilling out.
Humanity's homeworld was under attack.

"No," she whispered. "Oh God, no."

"The humans are fighting back, as you can see," said Solitude.
It actually almost sounded sympathetic. **"It will not avail them, of
course. But their determination is, I suppose, commendable on
some level."**

"Stop it," she said, emotion now gripping her throat. "Pull
them back. Call the Retrievers off. There must be something other
than this that you can do to make your repairs."

**"Not entirely. However, I find your persistent support for
your fellow humans to be remarkable. If you would like . . . I am
prepared to offer you a compromise."**

She had no idea what that meant but was eager even to grasp at
straws right now. "Yes. Yes, absolutely. What compromise?"

"Tell the Huragok to return to me full control of the Ark, then order your people to deliver the Huragok to me."

For a long moment, Vale was silent. She stared at the holographic representation of herself, which was clearly expecting a response. This was certainly a trick, but time was running out. She didn't have any options, and the longer she waited the more people died back on Earth.

"How can this be done?"

"Some of your fellow humans are in one of the foundry's control stations, along with the Huragok. They can hear you now. Tell them to withdraw their efforts, and I will, in turn, extract my forces."

"Drifts, Luther . . ." she said, and her voice was rising in urgency. "Can you hear me?"

"Olympia?" It was Luther! The sound of his voice made her happy to know that he had survived. "Is that you?"

"Yes!"

"How are you talking to us? Where are you?!"

"I'm locked in a facility with the monitor of the Ark. It's released an army of Retrievers to Earth. It's going to use them to mine and destroy Earth, then the other worlds in our system . . ."

"We figured as much. Vale, how can we get to you?!"

"You can't! Just listen to me, Luther," she said, recognizing that she didn't have much time left. "The monitor says that he won't stop the attack unless Drifts Randomly hands over control back to him, and then we're to surrender Drifts as well."

"Did I hear you right, Olympia?" Luther was surprised by the request.

"Yes, but listen to me," she said, her attention now directly on Solitude's face—her own face—and spoke in a cold, detached voice: "Do not give any control to this sadistic, pathetic little machine! I don't care what happens to me, but promise me that once Drifts is able, he'll purge this Forerunner garbage out of the Ark's systems once and for all!"

For the first time, Solitude staggered back and began to flicker. The monitor tried to get composure, but must have been genuinely shocked by Vale's command. The communication link to Luther broke off, and Solitude now stared directly at Vale, its eyes filled with rage.

"I have no desire to terminate your life. You are reacting in a purely emotional manner and have not given due consideration to—"

"I have given plenty of consideration," she said, her voice rising. "And I am done with you. If you really believe that destroying my people is the right course of action, then do it! End it—starting with me! I have no desire to wind up being a prisoner here on the Ark—because that's what I'll be. And you will be my jailer. I am a human being, not one of the animals currently running around on your installation's surface. If you don't release me and recall the Retrievers, then we have nothing else to talk about. You should know that no matter what happens to me, you will be hunted down and expunged from the Ark's system permanently. The Huragok managed to force you out, and it is only a short matter of time before it terminates your operability and your control of the Retrievers. And I'll be damned if I am going to listen to any more nonsense from your mouth. So, if you are inclined, kill me. Now!"

The monitor stared at her for what seemed like an eternity, and then very softly, it said, **"As you wish."**

Vale drifted back down toward the floor. As her feet touched it, the energy that had been surrounding her dissipated and she was able to move her arms.

The monitor drifted over her and said, **"I very much regret that you wish to end your own life. But if that is your wish, then at the very least, I can give you the privilege of one final request on my part."**

"What are you talking about?"

The holograph of Vale began to shrink and disappear, and moments later a spherical machine composed of metallic armatures and bearing a single eye was hovering over her. She had become so accustomed to seeing it in its pseudo-human visage that it took her a moment to put together that this is what Solitude truly was.

And then a section of the floor in front of her began to rumble. A circle about two meters in diameter slid aside and something began to rise up from beneath it. She squinted, trying to make out what it was.

She gasped as it came into view. It had been a human male at one time, that much was certain. He was about six feet tall, and when he spotted her, his mouth twisted into a snarl. His face was horrific, an array of scars, burns, and grown-over skin, as if it had been stitched together into something that barely resembled a human being.

As for his body—there was hardly anything remotely resembling a human. Instead it was constructed mostly of metallic alloy parts that were clicking and whirring together as if he were a walking clock mechanism, with only bits and pieces of his former frame shown between. There was a human eye in his face on the right side, but his left side featured only a dark hollow, scarred and empty.

What the hell? she thought.

"Tell me," the monitor said in a conversational manner. **"Have you ever heard of a human vessel called *Rubicon*?"**

"No," she said carefully. She had no idea where this was going.

"It came here more than a year ago with the purpose of investigating the Ark," it said. "Its crew dispatched teams to this installation. Despite their remarkable efforts, they fared much worse than you and yours. All of the teams, save for one, were exterminated and brought to an end. This man was part of one of those teams, and he was nearly killed. He would have perished there, on the surface of this world. But I found in him an opportunity and chose to spare his life. Well, what little of his life I could salvage. The truth is that, despite the power of this installation to activate the Halo Array, I am not able to do so. I need a human being, a Reclaimer. The activation you came here to stop was initiated by him, and whichever of you survives will be the next to initiate its reactivation."

The transformed man turned toward Vale and took a step forward. His metal foot clanged loudly on the floor and echoed through the chamber.

I really wish I were a Spartan right now, she thought.

"Oh no," whispered Kodiak.

The Spartans and Sangheili were still trapped on the other side of the energy field, and as it lessened they began to see once more inside. They watched helplessly as the human aberration rose from the hole in the floor. They were unable to hear the details of what the monitor was saying; speech from the other side remained muffled. But one thing was very evident: this cyborg monstrosity had not been introduced into the situation for the purpose of accomplishing anything beneficial.

"We've got to get through," Kodiak told the others. "We have to get to her and stop this, fast."

N'tho swung his plasma sword with all his strength, but it did no good. His weapon glanced harmlessly off the energy field.

"We need to find a way," Kodiak was hitting the field with his fists. "We need to stop him!"

"I'm not even certain how we would do that," said N'tho. "I have no idea what that is."

Kodiak turned and said, in a voice that sounded as if it were coming from the other side of the grave, "That's my brother."

"*What?*"

"That's my brother, Bobby. The one I told you of before. I'm sure of it. I don't know what was done to him, and there may not be much of him left, but I swear that's him."

Holt walked up to the energy field and peered in close. Inside, the monitor's true form could now be seen, a spherical, hovering machine similar to the monitors covered in their briefing days ago.

"I have an idea," he said, turning to the others. "How much firepower do we have?"

Vale stared at the abominable construct in front of her, uncertain of her options. He was studying her as well, looking her up and down as if she were some sort of newly discovered alien life-form. She couldn't even be certain that the cyborg was viewing her as a kindred human being, or for that matter, that he knew that he himself was no longer human.

"That single team that survived," the monitor informed her, **"returned to the *Rubicon* with an artifact—another powerful intelligence—and something that proved unforgiving to its entire crew. It took that ship far away from here, abandoning this**

human to me. That is what your people do. They pledge loyalty and then they break it. And that is what they have done to you."

Behind Solitude, she could now see that Kodiak and the others had left the place where they were behind the energy barrier.

Was this what he was referring to? Had they abandoned her?

The mutilated construct advanced upon her, while Vale carefully backed up. "Is that what the Forerunners did with you?" she said to the monitor. "Is that why you're doing this now, Solitude? Because the Forerunners abandoned you and you've been here a hundred thousand years without anyone or anything?"

"I did not need the Forerunners then, and I do not need you now," said the monitor resolutely.

The cyborg was suddenly running at her, moving with remarkable speed, considering his general bulk. Vale leaped to the side as he ran past her. *He has trouble shifting speed and direction. That's one good thing, I guess.*

He spun and came at her again. She waited until he was almost upon her and then vaulted out of his path once again. This time she was concerned to see that he changed direction faster than he had before. He was adapting to her strategy.

"Listen to me," she called out him, hoping that he might understand. "You don't have to do what the machine wants you to do."

"Do you truly think you can appeal to the man he once was?"

This time when the construct charged her, she was ready to jump out of the way. But he picked up speed at the last moment and, just as she sidestepped him, he grabbed her ankle and whipped her around. He flung Vale across the room with apparent ease, and she crashed into the far wall. The jolt rattled her teeth and scrambled her vision as she sank to the floor. *Shake it off, shake it off,* she thought to herself.

She got to her feet, and the construct came at her once more. Vale waited until the last possible moment, then she dodged to the right and drove a punch into his gut.

That was a mistake, because all she did was hit something that felt a hell of a lot like metal. Pain exploded in her fist, and she instantly realized that she may have broken something in her hand. She backpedalled quickly as he spun to face her.

He extended both of his arms, only one of which remained human, and half-meter-long, gleaming, razor-sharp blades snapped out of his forearms.

"Excellent," she said.

The construct advanced on her as she backed up. As she did so, she was sure that she heard something shouting from behind her. It was Kodiak without his helmet. He was back. She could see him behind the energy field on the perimeter of the room, slamming his fist into the semitranslucent barrier. He was repeatedly shouting something over and over. It was a name of some sort. It wasn't hers, but she could tell it was a name. She strained to make it out through the energy field still blocking the way, but was unable to determine what it was.

The construct came in fast and swiped his blades at her. She dodged left and right, managing to stay out of his way as he kept on coming. Then he suddenly spun and brought his right-arm weapon sweeping in from the side.

Rather than try to avoid it, she caught it in a deft block. For a moment the two of them were shoving against each other, the monitor's Frankensteinian construct far stronger than she was.

But it's not just about strength. There's more to survival than sheer brute force.

She twisted, spun around, and extended her left foot under the construct's right foot, using his momentum against him. The move caught him off guard, crashing him heavily to the ground.

Quickly Vale bounded back as he swept out with his blades, trying to cut her legs out from under her. She vaulted over the razor-sharp weapons and drove a hard kick into the construct's face. His head snapped back, and she tried repeating the blow. Instead he struck quickly and a blade sliced across her right calf. She let out an agonized howl and stumbled back. She'd been lucky; centimeters closer and he would have severed her Achilles tendon, hamstringing her and bringing an end to any defense she might have.

The construct clambered to his feet and came right after her. Vale's eyes were tearing up from the pain in her leg, and she quickly wiped them as he advanced. She circled the room, and this time when he came at her, she was ready.

He thrust forward with the blades and she stepped in so that her chest was right up against his. She slammed her head forward, her forehead crashing against the construct's nose. There was a loud crack, and for the first time, he actually let out a startled cry of pain.

Vale thrust the base of her hand forward repeatedly, hammering the construct again and again where she had just struck him. He became too busy roaring in agony to continue his assault, and she continued to pummel him, despite the excruciating pain mounting in both her hands.

For half a second, Vale felt triumphant. But then she looked toward the monitor and was surprised to see it floating off-kilter, the light in its single eye flickering momentarily.

What was going on?

But even as the once-human construct staggered back under

her blows, he lashed out with his right knee and struck Vale squarely in the chest. He did it with such force that Vale was thrown into the air, hit the floor, and skidded all the way to the far side of the room. She crashed up against the energy field and lay there gasping. She felt a sharp pain in her chest and was certain that he had broken a rib or two. The pain was almost unbearable.

Spartan Kodiak was right on the other side, centimeters away, but she couldn't see the others he had said were with him. *Where were they?* And Kodiak was still shouting something.

She frowned, unable to hear him. But she studied his lips carefully, trying to perceive what he was saying.

It looked like . . .

Bobby?

What the hell . . . ?

"Bobby?" she repeated.

Kodiak's eyes widened and he started to nod in affirmation. He was saying something else as well. What . . . ?

My brother.

And he was pointing at the construct.

"Oh my God," she whispered. "That's your brother?"

Kodiak was continuing to nod with urgency. Then his eyes widened in warning and he started pointing.

She instinctively bounded to the right and rolled to her feet, feeling the fire in her chest as she did so. The construct charged once more, blades out, driving them straight at her.

"Bobby!" she shouted.

He came to a halt, frozen in his attack position, the blades still extended. Now he was staring at her with uncertainty. She cast a quick glance to the monitor, who still appeared to be struggling to stay afloat. It had been silent for some time. She wondered what was going on, since this was the longest it had gone without comment.

Slowly she approached the cybernetic construct, what was left of Kodiak's poor brother, warily choosing her steps. "Bobby," she continued, her hands out in what she hoped looked like peaceful intent. "My name is Olympia Vale. Your name is Bobby—"

She hesitated as she saw the lights in the room flicker. In fact, the energy barrier seemed to dim for a fraction of a second. Then she turned back to the construct.

"Your name is Bobby," she said again. "And standing behind you, right over there, is your brother. I don't know the last time you saw him, but look. Turn around. You can see him. He's right there."

Very slowly the construct turned his head. His gaze fell upon Kodiak, who was continuing to shout his name and gesture at him.

"His name is Frank Kodiak," Vale continued. "He's your brother. And that floating thing over there, the monitor, is telling you to kill me, but you don't have to. We're here to bring you back home." She was continuing to approach him, speaking as slowly and carefully as she could. "Do you hear me, Bobby? Do you hear what I'm saying? My name is Olympia Vale, Bobby, and you need to—"

He launched himself at her. She let out a quick scream and barely managed to dodge the blades as they slashed past her.

She did the only thing she could think of. She darted in behind him as he moved past her and slipped her arms under his, and then her hands up and around and onto the back of his neck. She grunted and pushed forward, just out of range of the blades on his forearms, and the construct's head creaked under the full nelson.

She was unable to get her feet on the ground, and so she clung onto his back, still pushing as hard as she could. The construct staggered backward, slamming Vale into the energy wall. She cried out, because the pain from her injured ribs was as vicious as if he had been stabbing one of his blades into her torso, but she still managed to hold on. He slammed backward again and again, and each time she was agonized from the impact, but she still maintained her grip. Then, after a few seconds, he stopped, tilted forward, and collapsed to the ground. Vale stood up, holding her ribs where the most pain was emanating from.

"Stop!"

She turned to see Solitude's spherical shape shooting erratically through the air, its light sputtering off and on. Suddenly the energy barrier was down and Kodiak immediately ran in.

"Stop them now!"

"Stop what?" she demanded. *What was it talking about?*

"They're firing into my data stores! Stop them and I'll recall the Retrievers!"

She turned to Kodiak, but he was already on his comm.

"Stop your firing!" he shouted. "It's over. Come back."

The monitor stopped canting to the right and regained some of its balance. Apparently the others were shooting at something critical for Solitude, and he was having a severely adverse reaction to it.

"Are you recalling the Retrievers?" Vale demanded, "Or should I have my friends keep doing what they're doing?"

"I'm sending the signal now. Please stand down."

The monitor's voice was strange and weak. This was new for Vale, as he had been formidable and domineering throughout most of their dialogue. Now, between what they had done to his data center and the previous activity of Drifts, Solitude had apparently been compromised.

The construct was on the ground, gasping for air, looking stunned. Kodiak knelt beside him, trying to get his attention, but he was too dazed to focus. Then he made eye contact with his brother, as if truly seeing him for the first time.

His mouth started to move, and he drew in breath as if wanting to speak.

"What is it, Bobby?" Kodiak said. "Talk to me."

"Kill me," he whispered.

"What?" Kodiak asked, leaning in closer.

"Kill me," he said again, and his eyes darted toward Kodiak's rifle. *"Kill me now."*

"No," he said softly and then louder, "No." He locked his rifle onto his back. "I'm not going to do it. We're going to get you outta here, Bobby. We're gonna fix you up."

The monitor continued to study them in silence. And within seconds, Holt and the two Sangheili arrived from wherever they had assailed the monitor. The Elites looked at the construct with what might have been contempt, or shame. She could not quite discern their take on it.

"You okay?" Holt asked Vale.

"I think so," she said, taken aback by the question. She hadn't really thought about her condition during this entire time, and it was now catching up to her just how dangerous the situation had been.

Holt looked over toward the monitor, which was simply hovering in a stationary position, completely silent. He pointed his rifle in its direction.

"You want to fill us in on what exactly is going on here?"

The Retrievers have effectively overwhelmed the human forces at the Excession. There is no victory in sight, and every second more cascade out from the portal. What the machines lack in strength and resiliency, they more than make up for in numbers and fire-power. Some of the Retrievers even combine to form larger machines. Despite the spectacle of power that is brought with the Home Fleet, it is not enough to stay the Forerunner machines' incursion. One by one, UNSC vessels are brought down, until only a dozen remain. At this point, some might have appealed to a change of course, afraid that all would be lost if they continued—but that was not the case, too much was at stake. The last remaining ships charged deep into the fray, preparing to sacrifice themselves for the defense of Earth.

In their mind, it was a certain sacrifice. There was no survival anymore.

Except, to everyone's astonishment, the Retrievers abruptly cease their functions. The machines that had begun churning up the Kenyan surface stop doing so. At first the humans think that it might somehow be related to their counterattacks, but they quickly come to the realization that the Retrievers are being withdrawn to the Ark. By the dozens, these machines flee back into the portal, until not a single one dots the sky.

Minutes later, the African plains around the Excession, which were previously echoing the loud and violent booms of in-atmosphere naval combat between high-tonnage craft, are now silent, save for the wind and a smoldering fire on the debris that remains.

CHAPTER 18

"It is done," the monitor said, at last breaking its silence. **"I have summoned the Retrievers back to the Ark."**

Vale let out a sigh of relief. She had become fairly certain that such a peaceable ending would not be possible. She turned and looked at Kodiak, who had propped the construct up and was completely focused on the misshapen figure before him.

Bobby tried to speak again. *"Kill me,"* he said, his voice barely above a whisper.

"No. No, you're going to be okay. Like I said: I'm going to bring you home and we're going to get you fixed up."

Bobby shook his head. *"Can't be fixed . . . can't live like this . . ."*

"It'll be okay. I swear to you, it will."

The monitor was now hovering near Vale, evidently looking over her shoulder at Spartan Kodiak and his long-lost brother. Holt remained with her, but N'tho and Zon had continued to make their way across the room and through the far doorway, backtracking the direction Vale had first come. Uncomfortable with waiting around, they were attempting to find an exit from this underground labyrinth.

It looked as if, by some incredible miracle, they were all going to live another day . . .

And that was when the monitor chose to attack. An incredibly powerful blast of concussive energy from its single eye hit Kodiak like a road-train freighter running at full tilt. Even in armor, his body was sent careening across the room and against the far wall from the blast.

Vale jumped, grasping at her chest, startled by the unexpected action. It wasn't done, however. As Holt leveled his rifle at the machine, another blast fired from its eye. This hit the young Spartan square in the chest, sending him end-for-end into the corner. He hit with a heavy thud that shook the entire room.

"Fools!" Solitude boomed. **"Did you think I would be so easily deterred? I made the mistake of trusting your kind before. Never again!"**

Before Solitude finished its diatribe, Vale had already launched herself at the monitor's sphere, grabbing onto the metallic bands that comprised its armature and shaking it back and forth. It would not budge, and with a lightning-fast spin, the monitor flung her to the ground as though it were discarding a flying pest.

"Betrayal! This place is mine! I am the Ark!" it bellowed, its voice a frenzied, robotic sound.

"Betrayal?! I . . . I don't understand!" said Vale, as Solitude centered up on her, preparing to fire again. This blast would certainly kill the unarmored Vale. "What betrayal? What are you talking about?!" she cried out.

The monitor did not reply. Nor did it notice the figure lunging at it from its left. Bobby, who was composed mostly of machine, threw himself at Solitude. With the sound of iron colliding against iron, the construct slammed into the monitor, knocking it back through the air. Solitude was about to fling the cybernetic construct to the ground, as it had Vale, but it was too late. Bobby's bladed forearms plunged deep into the monitor's housing.

There was no question—Solitude had been fatally injured, the blades penetrating its entire frame and its inner components. Its eye flickered, and it thrashed about in the air, screaming at an extremely high pitch. It rose up higher in the air, with Bobby still attached and unable to free himself, and then plummeted headlong into the ground at an incredible speed, slamming down with a violent explosion.

"*Bobby!*" Kodiak screamed, recovering from the blast as only a Spartan could. Remarkably, the construct had remained intact, though now he was badly damaged and completely scorched by the explosion. He looked one last time at his brother, who was running toward him, and Vale thought she noticed the hint of a smile on his lips.

Then Bobby's head slumped back, and his eyes closed. He did not even utter a final breath, but his death was a certainty, even though Kodiak shook him violently, as if trying to awaken him from a bad dream. No response. Every mechanism in his armored body had shut down the instant that the monitor had blown to pieces.

Vale stood there, stunned. "What just happened?" she said, although she didn't know whom she was addressing. No doubt having heard the disturbance and the explosion, N'tho and Zon ran back into the room and surveyed the debris.

Holt stood up and shook his head, getting his bearings. "What happened to the monitor?"

He received only shrugs and blank stares in return.

It was at that moment that N'tho suddenly said, "Hold on. I'm receiving a communication from Usze. I've told him our position and he's on his way with the Huragok, Kola, and Luther Mann."

"What about Henry Lamb?" asked Holt, walking over to the Elite.

N'tho was listening to his communications device a moment more. "The human is dead."

Vale was crestfallen to hear it. She knew as well as anyone else that there was danger all around in this hostile place, but she had hoped that their group would somehow remain unscathed. "How?" she managed to say.

"He was attacked," said N'tho. "By one of the monitor's machines."

Vale nodded. "I am . . . I'm sorry to hear that."

Minutes later Usze, Kola, Luther, and the Huragok entered the room. Vale was studying the shattered pieces of Solitude, shaking her head. She was still having trouble comprehending what the monitor was referring to: *What did it mean about betrayal?*

"I'm sorry about Henry," Vale said to Luther, grabbing his arm.

"So am I." Luther's eyes watered at the thought. "We did it, though, Olympia," he said, swallowing the grief in his throat over the loss of his friend. "Well, not us, technically. The Huragok did it."

"Did what, exactly?" asked Vale, holding her injured midsection.

"Our friend Drifts Randomly. It—no, he, dammit, I'm going to start calling him *he*—he not only managed to seize control of the Ark, but after you contacted us, he infiltrated the monitor's central processes. Then he severed the monitor from them completely, which proved terminal for the machine."

"That must have been what Solitude was referring to," Vale said slowly. She didn't know exactly how to feel about the loss of the monitor. For some strange reason, a hope had arisen in her about the possibility of redeeming the machine, who had really only been the victim of a hundred thousand years of abandonment. But then she realized that it was a frail hope and tried to banish the idea from her mind.

Sitting down for a moment, she winced, which attracted the

attention of Drifts; the Huragok could clearly tell she was in pain. He had procured a medical kit from one of the Elites and was now applying a thick salve to her ribs and hands, as well as a coagulant of some sort to the wound on her leg. The Huragok explained that this would numb her injuries and stabilize any damage to her bones until they reached *Mayhem*'s medical bay.

She took a shallow breath. It was going to be a long trip home.

The Elites had located the path for getting to the surface, and the group quickly made their way through. The two dead bodies were recovered and carefully wrapped in a tarp-like material, with Spartan Kodiak carrying his brother over his shoulder, and Usze 'Taham carrying Henry.

Spartan Kodiak was walking alongside Vale, staring straight ahead, his helmet visor concealing whatever was going on behind it. She drew near him as they walked through the corridor and said softly, "I'm sorry about your brother."

He hesitated. "I suppose I should thank you. I mean, he's going to receive a proper burial . . . and I'm going to make damn sure that the record of his passing is updated so he's not simply listed as MIA. The man's a hero, but . . ."

"But?"

"That thing back there was not my brother," said Kodiak. "Not really. My brother died in this place years ago, but even what was left of him was noble enough to know what it means to sacrifice."

"I suppose you're right," she said.

He turned and looked at her for the first time, though she could not see his face. "I watched you fight him, though . . ."

"Yes, well, I nearly died in there."

"But you didn't. You fought well. It was impressive. Perhaps you may want to consider exploring the concept of enlisting with a higher authority."

She let out a brief laugh at the notion. "What, like a Spartan?"

But Kodiak didn't make a sound in response. Apparently he was serious.

They were heading upward and out. The corridor that they were walking through was angled toward the surface. It took over an hour, but eventually they reached a doorway that, thankfully, opened for them, and with it a blast of warm air washed over the survivors.

But their relief died when they saw what was waiting for them just beyond the exit.

It was more of the white-furred, horned creatures that they had encountered in the snow, one of which had carried Vale off. Immediately everyone who was armed brought their weapons to bear, bracing themselves for yet another assault.

But it never came.

Instead the creatures stared blankly at them. They had been in the midst of plucking leaves from the trees and eating them with their toothy, three-mandibled mouths, and once they had registered the group's presence, they simply returned to what they had been doing.

"Perhaps I shouldn't press it," said Spartan Holt in a low voice, as if he thought speaking softly would prevent them from being noticed, "but why aren't they attacking?"

"There could be a number of reasons," Luther said. "But if I were to guess, I'd say that many of the species on this installation had been predisposed to attacking us because of their genetic disposition. When the monitor—this Tragic Solitude, as it called himself—bred these creatures, it must have done it with particular genetic triggers that it could control through some impulse or neural communication system. With the monitor gone, the triggers may well have followed."

"I like the sound of that," said Holt. "Is that how he controlled the animal that carried off Vale? And that mammoth creature you guys encountered?"

"Presumably, but don't get me wrong. The Ark was designed not just for sentient beings, but also for the creatures that ate them. The Forerunners were attempting to preserve entire biomes so that the removal of a single sentient species from a planet wouldn't send it into ecological collapse. The creatures most dependent on thinking beings are the ones that eat them. So please don't mistake me: there's definitely still a threat. Some of these species are pure-blooded, natural predators, and they are not safe."

"What about the fighting machines?" N'tho asked.

"The armigers?" Luther responded.

"I have never seen that kind before," N'tho said. He had spent much time on Forerunner installations during his career in the Covenant. If anyone would have seen one, it would have been him.

"Neither have I," Luther responded. "It's hard to say what purpose they were previously designed for, but it's clear that the monitor was controlling them as well, along with the Sentinels we encountered, and even the incredibly hostile weather conditions. All of it was a ploy by the monitor. It needed a human like Vale, and Kodiak's brother before her, if it wanted to have any control over the Halo Array. It also needed Drifts, because it recognized that the Huragok was the only real threat our group posed to him, something that proved fatal for the monitor in the end."

"So it kept throwing enemies and challenges at us," Holt voiced, "hoping to pick us apart and ultimately take Vale and the Huragok for its own uses?"

"Essentially," Luther said, looking over at Vale, who seemed somewhat detached from everything. "It had assumed that by triggering a countdown with the Halo Array, we'd give the monitor everything it needed, including direct access to Earth. Unfortunately for Solitude, it underestimated the ability of our two species to work together."

The weather remained relatively temperate for a good long while as they traversed the distance back to the ship. Ironically, it would take them longer on this trip, because the inclement weather conditions that Solitude had instituted had actually created icy paths across large bodies of water, paths that they no longer had since the monitor's destruction.

They were receiving a steady signal from N'tho's cartographic instrument, guiding them back to the Sangheili, but even at this range, they could see *Mayhem*'s position a long ways off. It still looked like it was in bad shape.

Luther stared up into the Ark's blue sky and could make out the portal high above, a pulsating, blue-black orb of energy. He wondered if it would shut down before they could get *Mayhem* serviceable enough to go back through it. He wasn't confident at all that ONI would be able to figure out how to get the thing back on, but then he remembered that they had Drifts Randomly with them. If anyone could figure it out, it would be the Huragok.

Usze 'Taham came up alongside him, noticing that he was staring up at the portal. Luther looked briefly at Henry's body, wrapped snuggly and slung over the Elite's shoulder, and he felt his heart sink.

"What are you thinking, Luther Mann?" Usze said, nodding up toward the portal.

"I'm still surprised that we traveled here so fast. Wondering how long that's gonna be sustainable."

"What do you mean?" Holt asked, coming along the other side. "Olympia said that the monitor had made changes to get the portal to transfer objects faster."

"Yes, and she's exactly right," he said, clearing his throat. "My concern is how long it can operate given the amount of energy exerted. The monitor wasn't concerned about the damage it might cause to the portal's drive systems, because it was more focused on getting the Retrievers into the Sol system and recovering resources to rebuild on this end."

He pointed to the prong-like pylons on the tips of the spires in the far distance on either side. The Ark's petals were the primary energy conduits for the long-range portal that connected to Earth and other worlds. Solitude had managed to repair most of them from this end and only needed the humans on the other end to open it at the Excession.

"Those pylons help channel the portal-generating energy, but they're likely under a great deal of stress right now, effectively compressing realspace into an almost unimaginably small frame of slipspace by way of crystal-mediation. This, alongside several huge astrogation shortcuts, made the effective travel distance between here and Earth extraordinarily short. Whatever Solitude did, it's something that not even the Forerunners were comfortable with. I suppose it was only conceived of being used in extreme circumstances."

Eventually their path took them into a green forest that was growing steadily. The area did not seem as damaged as the one they had passed through after landing. There were some lightly scorched regions, but most of it was quite navigable.

Their only stumbling block occurred when they came upon a small pack of the blind, dinosaur-like biped animals at the edge of a river.

The nearest of the creatures roared and, snapping its teeth, charged at Luther. Immediately N'tho was between them and swung his sword. The creature fell backward, wounded but still snarling, and the others began to advance. At that point, Kodiak and Holt opened fire, blasting them back. The animals retreated, but they were clearly not happy that the group was passing through their territory. "Let us keep moving," said N'tho briskly. "We're not clear yet."

Vale spoke up as they moved along. "The monitor called these blind wolves. It had names for all of these creatures."

"It is an incredible thing, this place. To explore everything around here," Luther said, staring out across the impossibly vast surface, at mountains and oceans that were literally thousands of kilometers away, raising up immense arms into the empty space. Above them hung the Milky Way, a swirling cluster unspeakably far away—the Ark was a true testament to the Forerunners' technological mastery. "It's the stuff dreams are made of," Luther said. "I'm going to go out on a limb and guess that the UNSC's going to need to have some presence out here to safeguard this place. A research colony of some sort."

"You volunteering, Doctor Mann?" Vale asked, looking up at him with a smile.

"I don't know about you," he grinned, "but I think it'll be a good little while before I come back to this place."

CHAPTER 19

The rest of the trip to the *Mayhem* was relatively peaceful, something about which Olympia Vale was extremely relieved. She wasn't entirely sure how much more excitement and stress she could take.

The exterior temperature dropped rapidly with the shifting of the artificial sun, and they managed to reach their destination shortly before it hit the freezing mark. Once inside the ship, Vale was immediately brought to the medical facility, her injuries thoroughly treated. Despite their renunciation of medical care, the Elites certainly had the tools, left over from the Covenant years, to repair her broken body. It took only a matter of minutes before she felt better, which came as a shock to her.

After she had recovered, they brought Captain Richards and the rest of the Sangheili crew up to speed. The others had been repairing the ship nonstop since the expedition began, but they had seen little progress due to the extent of the damage. The hope was that the Huragok would be able to work a miracle and at least get the ship intact and operational enough to get back to Earth.

Vale excused herself shortly after the briefing and went to a free quarters. There she sat, staring at the wall, glad that she was alone for a moment. Her mind kept going back to her abduction at the hands of Tragic Solitude. She recognized the need for the monitor's destruction: it was a dangerous, grievously demented machine that could have easily turned against them at any time, had it been allowed to survive. But there was something about it that made her regret what had taken place. She didn't know exactly why that was, and it really bothered her.

There was a heavy knock at the door. "Who is it?" called Vale.

The door slid open, and Usze 'Taham was standing there. "I'm sorry. I didn't mean to disturb you."

"It's okay," said Vale in perfect Sangheili. "I just needed a little time to be alone."

The Sangheili slowly strode into the room, the door sliding closed behind him. "I wanted to talk with you about your encounter with the monitor. It was very remarkable, how you handled yourself."

"Thank you."

"Then why are you upset? It is my understanding that you are angry with yourself, but the others do not know why." He moved across the small room and sat in a hovering chair at its corner.

"I thought you didn't sit down," she said with a smirk.

"I will make an exception here," he responded flatly. "Please explain what your reason is for concern." He was clearly trying to put her at ease.

"The monitor died thinking that I had betrayed it. Which I know shouldn't be a huge issue, considering what it was trying to do, but still . . ."

"And you know differently. Though it may not help."

"Not in the least," she said, taking a deep breath. "My life's work is cross-species confluence and communication, that's why I was on this mission to begin with. Working with your people to help eliminate decades of hatred and mistrust between our species. I've developed skills in this field over the years, skills that

I'm extremely proud of. But ultimately, they did little to help me against the monitor. I couldn't convince it to stop Halo, I couldn't convince it to recall the Retrievers, and when I finally did break through, we ended up killing it."

Usze stared at her for a long moment. "Olympia," he said finally, pronouncing the syllables in her native language as well as she could expect, "the entirety of the galaxy owes a debt to you for what you did. The monitor would have never been convinced of peace between it and our peoples. And I believe that you know that. It would have turned on us in time, and when it did, would we have you there to halt its attack? Or would we perish, with no one to stop it? That is what you should be focused on."

"Well, then, how come I feel like things could have ended up differently?" asked Vale. "I was so close to stopping it."

Usze seemed to shrug. "I do not know. Some things do not feel right, even when they are. We have a saying in my clan: *Those who always look to the sky never see what is right before them.* Do not spend your time looking at the sky, when our victory is right before us. You were sent only to keep the peace between our species, yet you achieved so much more. Do not miss that fact, Olympia Vale."

It would have taken at least a week to repair the ship, even with the Huragok, were it not for the fleet of UNSC vessels that came through the portal a day after the expedition returned to *Mayhem*. It had been decided that reinforcements needed to be sent through to investigate the source of the Retrievers' attack. It took only minutes for the UNSC *Witness* to locate *Mayhem*, and what was recovered of the comparatively diminutive Sangheili corvette was lifted into the much larger human carrier. The ship and crew were stabilized within the cargo hold for the journey, and *Witness* began its cross-checks in preparation for its return to Earth.

On the ground, the UNSC fleet was already deploying large-scale, forward-operating facilities and firebases in various parts of the installation. Like Onyx and the Halo installations before, the Ark would be colonized by the UNSC in an effort to prevent the threat of Halo from resurfacing again . . . at least as far as this installation was concerned. It even looked as if plans were under way to assist in the repair of the installation. The monitor would get its wish after all.

Spartan Kodiak was standing in the cargo bay of the *Witness*, his helmet tucked under his arm, staring out a nearby viewscreen as space opened up to it. From here, the Milky Way galaxy looked remarkably brilliant. It seemed so far away, but he knew that the portal would make that great distance miraculously disappear.

Funny. Outside of the Ark, in that little bright swirl of lights, was every single thing I will ever know or meet or fight. Humans and Elites. And they all live there together.

He suddenly became aware that N'tho was standing next to him. He said nothing.

"I am sorry about your brother."

"Thank you, but I'm fine."

"Were it someone from my bloodline—"

"No, really. I'm fine. I appreciate the sympathy. Thanks."

"I also want you to know," N'tho said unexpectedly, "that I am sorry that you were maimed at my hand. I can only imagine the anger you have been burdened with all this time . . . the need for vengeance. Sangheili wear their battle scars with pride but . . . I admit that I would have felt the same, were it me."

Kodiak shrugged. "As you said, it was war. Things happen in

war. And now it's over. Nothing to be gained by dwelling on it." He turned to look directly at N'tho. "Thank you again for saving my life."

"And you for me as well." N'tho paused. "If you would like, I can arrange for you to visit my homeworld sometime. I think you might find it interesting."

"Thank you," said Kodiak, with the slightest of grins. "But I think I'm going to take a break from traveling to places with aliens on it that want to kill me."

"Captain Richards. Welcome back."

Serin Osman stood when Richards entered the office, which was an immense surprise. It wasn't typical for Osman to acknowledge anyone coming before her, save in the most offhanded of ways. Standing up was a genuine show of respect. Richards wondered if Osman was feeling all right.

"Thank you," said Richards. Osman gestured for her to sit, and Richards did so.

"You're walking well, I see. Injury all healed?"

"Yes, ma'am."

Osman sat back down behind her desk. "I've read your debriefing and final report. I want you to know that I have recommended that you be awarded the Medal of Honor."

Richards's eyes widened. "What?"

"You and your team saved us all, Captain. I know there was a lot of tension early on between our people and the Sangheili, but your decisions and cool head ultimately saved UNSC lives. That certainly warrants some manner of reward. I am also recommending you for a promotion."

"Ma'am, please. There's no need for that."

Osman stared at her. There was no confusion in her eyes, merely interest. "And why would I not do that? Don't you think you deserve it?"

"No, I don't. You said you read my report. So you already know that I was effectively useless. I was kidnapped by the Sangheili. I was injured early on in the expedition. Everything that happened, up to and including our rescue, as you put it, was because of the actions of others."

Osman was silent for a moment. "Just out of curiosity, Captain, if the mission had failed, would you have passed that responsibility onto others?"

"No," Richards said immediately. "I would have taken the blame for my inability to control the situation."

"Then if you were willing to take the blame for failure, should you not also be awarded some credit for success? You had a bit of a powder keg on your hands with this team. Spartans and Elites and thirty years of dead bodies. That's not an easy thing to manage, no less command."

"Perhaps. But although the gesture is appreciated, I still don't want to be promoted. With all due respect, of course. I may even put in for a bit of shore leave. I think I've seen enough action for a while."

Osman pursed her lips. "All right, then. What about the medal?"

"Yes, I'll take that. My father loves medals."

And to Richards's surprise, Osman actually smiled.

My name is Luther Mann, and my most recent memory is a stagger-
ing thing.

We are approaching the Ark's portal, an immense gate held aloft
in space, watching from the viewports of a majestic UNSC carrier
called Witness. *But it is the sight on the journey to the portal that*
will always remain with me.

Retrievers. Thousands of Retrievers.

They are simply adrift here—not firing upon us or on their way
to assaulting our homeworld. They are doing nothing except floating
helplessly through the void, like iron jellyfish adrift in a sea of black-
ness. Without the monitor to guide them, they are lifeless, and yet
terrifying in scope as we navigate through them. There are so many
it is almost unbelievable. Once, long ago, I might have called them
"pretty" as well. Now, they are anything but that.

But I do respect them, and their power. And I respect this place
as well.

Perhaps someday I will return to the Ark.

Once everything has settled down, maybe I can make the journey
back here, work with the teams that have been deployed for research.
Maybe even work with Drifts Randomly once again.

Perhaps we can take control of all the dormant Retrievers, open
up a portal to another system to strip-mine lifeless planets for the

resources and minerals required to fix the Ark. Perhaps we can, in fact, fix the Ark—finish what the monitor began. And in doing so, we may atone for the mistakes of our past by securing this place and a future for those who come after. Perhaps we can assure the continued life of the creatures residing upon it, and even prepare it for what might come. Henry would have wanted it this way.

And until I return, I will dream about this place.

But in the meantime . . . I know what I must do, and I have waited too long to do it. No more wasted hours. I have searched this galaxy to unlock the mysteries of an ancient species and the artifacts they left behind. I have uncovered secret upon secret in places few men have even tread. I have pushed the boundaries and fought and survived, against all the odds.

But now I must do what I have yet to do.

I must find my daughter.

ACKNOWLEDGMENTS

PETER DAVID

My thanks to Jeremy Patenaude and all of the fine folks at 343 Industries for their incredible help in writing this novel.

343 INDUSTRIES

343 Industries would like to thank Peter David, Scott Dell'Osso, Kory Hubbell, Bonnie Ross-Ziegler, Ed Schlesinger, Rob Semsey, Matt Skelton, Phil Spencer, Kiki Wolfkill, Carla Woo, and Jennifer Yi.

None of this would have been possible without the amazing efforts of the Halo Franchise Team, the Halo Consumer Products Team, Jeff Easterling, Tiffany O'Brien, Kenneth Peters, and Sparth, with special thanks to Jeremy Patenaude.

ABOUT THE AUTHOR

PETER DAVID is a prolific author whose career, and continued popularity, spans more than two decades. He has worked in every conceivable media—television, film, books (fiction, nonfiction, and audio), short stories, and comic books—and acquired followings in all of them.

In the literary field, Peter has had more than a hundred novels published, with numerous appearances on the *New York Times* Best Sellers list. His novels include *Fearless* (with his daughter Caroline), *Tigerheart*, *The Hidden Earth Chronicles*, the *Sir Apropos of Nothing* trilogy, the *Knight Life* trilogy, *Howling Mad*, and the *Psi-Man* adventure series. He is the co-creator and author of the bestselling *Star Trek: New Frontier* series for Pocket Books, and has also written such Trek novels as *Q-Squared*, *The Siege*, *Q-in-Law*, *Vendetta*, *I, Q* (with John deLancie), *A Rock and a Hard Place*, and *Imzadi*. He produced the three *Babylon 5 Centauri Prime* novels and has also had his short fiction published in such collections as *Shock Rock*, *Shock Rock II*, and *Otherwere*, as well as *Asimov's Science Fiction* magazine and the *Magazine of Fantasy and Science Fiction*. He is also one of the participants in Crazy 8 Press (www .crazy8press.com), a self-publishing venture producing e-books and trade paperbacks available through Barnes & Noble and Amazon.

ABOUT THE AUTHOR

Peter's comic book résumé includes an award-winning twelve-year run on *The Incredible Hulk*, and he has also worked on such varied and popular titles as *Supergirl, Young Justice, Soulsearchers and Company, Aquaman, Spider-Man, Spider-Man 2099, X-Factor, Star Trek, Wolverine, The Phantom, Sachs & Violens, The Dark Tower, Halo: Helljumper*, and many others. He has written comic book–related novels, such as *The Incredible Hulk: What Savage Beast*, and co-edited *The Ultimate Hulk* short story collection. Furthermore, his opinion column, "But I Digress . . . ," has been running in the industry trade newspaper the *Comics Buyer's Guide* for nearly a decade, and in that time has consistently been the paper's most popular feature and was also collected into a trade paperback.

Peter is the writer for two popular video games: *Shadow Complex* and *Spider-Man: Edge of Time*. He has also authored the graphic novel edition of Disney's *Epic Mickey* and a series of tie-in digital comics titled *Tales of Wasteland*.

Peter is the co-creator, with popular science-fiction icon Bill Mumy (of *Lost in Space* and *Babylon 5* fame) of the CableACE Award–nominated science-fiction series *Space Cases*, which ran for two seasons on Nickelodeon. He has written several scripts for the Hugo Award–winning TV series *Babylon 5* and the sequel series *Crusade*. He has also written several films for Full Moon Entertainment and co-produced two of them, including two installments in the popular *Trancers* series, as well as the science-fiction western spoof *Oblivion*, which won the Gold Award at the 1994 Houston International Film Festival for best Theatrical Feature Film, Fantasy/Horror category. He is currently working with his wife on a new series titled *Headcases*.

Peter's awards and citations include: the Grandmaster Award from the International Association of Media Tie-in Writers, 2011;

the GLAAD Award, 2011; the Julie Award, 2009; the Haxtur Award (Spain), Best Comic script, 1996; the OZCon award (Australia), Favorite International Writer, 1995; the *Comics Buyer's Guide* Fan Awards, Favorite Writer, 1995; the Wizard Fan Award, 1993; the Golden Duck Award for Young Adult Series (*Starfleet Academy*), 1994; the UK Comic Art Award, 1993; and the Will Eisner Comic Industry Award, 1993. He lives in New York with his wife, Kathleen, and his four children, Shana, Gwen, Ariel, and Caroline.